Aftermath Horizon

A Romantic Adventure

James L. Hatch

Aftermath Horizon

James L. Hatch

Dedicated to the love of my life, my wife, and to finding true love when it is least expected.

Part 1: Rebirth

Chapter One
The Awakening

Antelope scatter as a distant helicopter draws near. With turbines screaming, it hovers for a moment and then settles to the ground. Two men in bright orange HAZMAT suits stumble out, dragging an unconscious man between them. Balancing the dead weight of his body between their bulky breathing packs, they struggle to a nearby tree. After placing the man and a backpack beneath its canopy, they pause while one makes the sign of the cross over the man's limp body. Then, as fast as their awkward suits allow, they rush back through the prop wash toward the waiting machine. The moment they re-board, the helicopter lifts off and heads due south.

* * * *

Aching spasms torment my back as if I've lain on the lumps beneath me for days. I will my body to move, but my muscles reject my mind's order. Reaching inward, I find enough strength to pry my eyelids open. It is difficult and painful, and the sun's glare is blinding. I squeeze my eyes shut. There is comfort in darkness, but confusion clouds my mind. My back feels bruised. My shoulder blades ache with dull, throbbing pain. My muddled mind drifts in and out of unwelcome oblivion as I fight to remain conscious. Nausea follows dizziness. With enormous effort, I roll onto my side, gasping for breath as acrid retching and dry heaves rake my body. Agonizing muscle cramps accompany every gag, and charley horse-like knots assault my legs as I curl into the fetal position. My arms shake with weakness, as if I haven't moved in weeks.

A singing bird catches my attention as I lie on my side, and I turn my head to see a small wren flitting from branch to branch in the tree above. I remain still, awestruck by its beauty. I watch the bird as I absorb the sun's warmth and adjust to the bright sunlight. My mind races, trying to sort things out, until pressure from small stones beneath my ribs force me to move. *Where am I? Why am I here?*

With great effort, I drag myself up against the tree's rough trunk. My head slumps to my chest as more dizziness overtakes me. A bead of drool slips down my chin onto my pale, uncalloused hands. I study them in detail as if seeing them for the first time. They are smooth and delicate, like they don't belong out here in the open. I force my head up to scan the area around me. I don't recognize a thing—everything seems wrong. A wide, pastoral valley flanked by steep mountains extends beyond my horizon, and I hear a small brook running nearby. I wipe sweat from my brow with a shaking hand before a queasy contraction doubles me over, and I clench my abdomen with my arms as the pain intensifies. When the contraction subsides, I rock back and forth against the tree trunk, breathing in short gasps. *How long have I been here? Am I hallucinating? Can any of this be real?*

Before answers come, my eyes focus on a dark blue backpack lying by my side. Though drained by sheer exhaustion, my curiosity keeps me from slipping into unconsciousness. I pull the backpack closer, untie the tent and sleeping bag from the top, and then empty its contents on the ground.

The backpack contains a light jacket, two butane lighters, a canteen, a hunting knife, an aluminum mess kit, a few medical supplies, and ten shiny plastic packages. The equipment indicates planning for an extended stay, but I don't see signs of a campsite. Being in this valley makes no sense. *How did I get here?*

Sun glinting from one of the lustrous packages catches my eye. I pick it up and turn it over in my hands, studying the writing on its aluminized wrapper while fighting to recall anything that might explain why I'm here. The small print on the label is faded and unreadable, but I can make out the larger words: "United States Army" and "Meals Ready to Eat." The expiration date on the package is redacted. I have no idea why. The blotted-out date only serves to add more questions to my general state of confusion. *What day is it? What month? What year?*

Try as I might, I can't force memories to the forefront of my mind, as if my past is a total blank. *How is that possible?* An image floats into my consciousness—the face of a young woman. The words "United States Army" also seem familiar, but I don't know if the girl and those words are connected or if I'm linked to either of them.

I stretch my arms and sit up straight against the tree, allowing the nausea I felt earlier to subside. My eyes water, tremors run up and down my torso, and my stomach rumbles as I focus on the package in my hand. Despite my hunger, I find the thought of eating repugnant. I take a deep breath, tear open the package with shaking hands, and force a bit of the dried material onto my tongue. Bile rises in my throat, and my stomach convulses with a violent dry heave. Keeping the morsel in my mouth is an act of sheer will. The packaged food doesn't have a bad flavor or smell, yet my body fights to reject it. I ignore my body's wishes, swallow hard, and grimace as the food grinds against my esophagus all the way down. Based on my body's reaction, I assume I haven't eaten solid food for a very long time.

Beads of sweat break out across my brow as I swallow another small portion while reasoning my way past my growing feeling of sickness. Each bite is a deliberate act of defiance and determination. After consuming the food in the package, I inch my way up to a standing position, using the tree trunk as a prop. My legs tingle as if asleep, and I flex one at a time to get the blood flowing.

Flashes of light and darkness that drift before my eyes gradually fade. I gasp for breath, trying to remember the last time I stood erect. I don't remember a thing. I flex my arms and shoulders. When steady enough to move forward, I weave toward the nearby stream. The sweet, cool water is almost as difficult to swallow as the food, but it settles the cramps rippling through my stomach.

I sit on the stream bank, overwhelmed by the feel of the soft grass beneath me and the panoramic expanse of the valley before me. Despite my weakness and confusion, I am mesmerized by the beauty of my surroundings. Unconstrained euphoria washes over me as I gaze spellbound at the azure sky, puffy white clouds, and birds flitting in the air. A wave of emotion precipitates an eruption of tears. There is something powerful about this place, something I don't understand. I take several deep breaths, shake off the ecstasy of the moment, and wipe my eyes with my sleeve.

Caution stirs within me as rational thought returns. This place is beautiful, but it might also be dangerous. I need to find other people. After stuffing the supplies into the backpack, I begin following the flow of water downstream. Walking along the bank isn't easy, and my movements are jerky and uncertain. I stop to rest often to calm my racing heart and slow my breathing while berating myself for being in such poor physical condition. *Why am I alone in this valley if I'm in such terrible shape?*

Off to my right, the frantic flapping of wings startles me. A covey of quail takes flight, rising almost vertically and then descending about fifty feet away. I drop into a protective crouch until I notice a herd of elk beyond the quail grazing without concern. I have spotted many deer and moose as I've followed the stream, and my initial fear ebbs as I focus on the elk. A fragmented memory tells me I am not part of their food chain, but I know I should not confront them. They watch with suspicion as I parallel their water source—unafraid, like they've never seen a human before. I find that puzzling. Stranger still, I know what they are, but I'm quite certain I have never seen a living one before.

I am exhausted by the time evening approaches. I need rest. I've consumed a variety of berries along the stream but haven't fully adjusted to eating, drinking, or swallowing. Whatever I eat causes dull queasiness and mild cramps. Exhaustion brings sleep to the top of my needs, and I use the last of my strength to set up the tent and crawl into the sleeping bag.

If I had dreams, I don't remember them the following morning. I sit by the stream in the warm sun while taking in the awesome beauty of the surrounding valley. Being here touches something deep in my soul, but I don't understand why it should. I am thankful the pre-packaged food and water are easier to swallow today. I flex my arms and stretch my legs. Nourishment, water, and rest have made me stronger, and I'm in far less pain today. Perhaps I can travel farther downstream now, maybe even far enough to find other people.

By late afternoon, the valley comes to an abrupt end where the stream cascades over a rock cliff that must be 1000 feet high. The plain below shows no signs of human life—only waves of grass and trees as far as I can see. Several streams join the one I've been following and flow into the plain as a small river. I decide to continue on my current course. I make my way down the least rugged adjacent slope and follow the water.

Walking on the plain is as difficult as it was in the valley above. Fewer stones and fallen trees impede my progress, but the tall grass is ever a hindrance. When the sun is almost overhead, I see a massive cloud of dust swirling above a rise toward the north, and I take leave of my trek along the rivulet to investigate. My head jerks back, and my eyes widen at what I see from my vantage point on the small hill. Thousands of bison mill around a huge buffalo wallow below—so many that it boggles my mind. They grunt and snort and ignore me as if I'm invisible, even with the wind at my back. Without understanding how I know, I believe they have poor eyesight; however, even if they can't see me, they must smell me. I survey the massive herd while wiping sweat from my neck. My mind fills with questions. *Why aren't they afraid of me? Why are they here at all? Weren't they hunted to near extinction? Is my perception of reality wrong, or do the few memories I have fail me completely?* God, I wish I could remember more.

Several days and nights pass as I walk deeper into the vast plain. I don't encounter a single road, human, or anything that smacks of civilization. By the seventh day, I am becoming concerned about my food supply. I only had ten packaged meals when I first woke up. I have limited my intake to grains, berries, and one prepared food pack a day. The combination has provided enough energy for me to move on and prevent constipation, but I only have two packages left. If I don't get off this plain soon, I'll need to hunt using the primitive tools I've got.

The thought of hunting, of killing, seems wrong. It jars me, yet my need to survive dominates everything I believe to be right. *Why should my survival matter? Who would care if I live or die?* As night settles in, I use a tent tie-down tether to attach my hunting knife to a straight, strong stick and hide in a stand of cattails at the edge of the stream where deer come to drink. I am surprised that stalking prey seems so natural, even though I'm quite certain I've never killed another living thing. I wait late into the night, but no deer show. The moon is high and full by the time I ignore my grumbling stomach and force myself to fall asleep hungry.

Even in fitful slumber, my mind continues to taunt me. The passing days have provided considerable time to think, time to review all I can remember. The image of the woman I saw when I first awoke occasionally enters my mind, but I have no idea who she is or why she should matter to me. I can't remember my family either, if they exist. I know for certain all that has happened to me since I awoke, but everything is blank before that—as if I woke from the dead.

At sunrise, I notice a nest containing duck eggs near my hiding spot and immediately seize them. Many quail and prairie chicken nests pock the ground around me, and I collect several more eggs before starting a fire. I note some of the eggs contain embryo birds as I crack them into the bottom pan of my mess kit, and I stir the small lumps of protein into a large omelet for breakfast. My mouth waters as I devour the meal. It is obvious to me now that my need for sustenance overrides my consideration for other creatures, but I am surprised I don't feel guilt. Following my first good meal since I began this journey, I fall asleep until early afternoon.

As I prepare to break camp, I decide to keep the remaining two food packets in reserve in case of emergency. I'll live off eggs, speared fish, and whatever I can catch for now. I have no idea how long I might be out here or where I am; however, I do feel a growing need to be more cautious.

I have recovered most of my strength over the past week and push hard to cover as much distance as possible. With nothing but time on my hands, I count my paces and estimate I can cover ten to twelve miles a day. Fed by tributaries along the way, the adjacent river has grown larger. It also has periodic rapids that are too rough for a raft, even if I could put one together. I continue on foot, fighting my way through the tall prairie grass and reeds along the river's edge.

As dusk approaches, I stumble into a small opening in the tall grass. A sleeping deer panics, leaps up, and thunders toward me, but my startled shout causes it to veer off. My heart hammers as the deer disappears into the reeds, and sweat breaks out along my forehead. It takes several minutes before my breathing returns to normal. "Fight or flight" must only apply to those who are prepared because I could only stand in rigid fear and scream. The deer is a clear reminder I might not be the top predator here. If it had been a bear or mountain lion, my scream might not have been much of a deterrent.

I am also disappointed my lack of preparedness allowed such a good source of food to escape. Had I been ready with my spear, I might have feasted on venison instead of eggs. As my heart rate slows, I weigh my alternatives. Should I be prepared to kill at any opportunity? Is it worth exposing myself to the danger of confronting a wild animal, even a deer? After due consideration, I begin beating my mess kit with its metal spoon to warn animals ahead of my impending arrival.

As I step out to leave the small clearing, a large mottled snake slithers from just inside the taller grass toward the river. The pattern on the snake's back warns of danger, but I can't remember why it should. It's a cottonmouth, and I believe it hates noise—all the more reason to continue beating my mess kit. To be safer, I move farther from the river's edge to avoid the snakes that lurk close to the water. I need to find a campsite. Traveling after sundown is far more dangerous than paralleling the river during the day.

On the eleventh night, I wake to rattling noises outside my tent. As I peer out through the tent flap into the flickering light of my campfire, I see the distinctive ringed tail of a raccoon disappear into the surrounding weeds. *Oh, damn!* I crawl out as fast as I can but am already too late. Raccoons have raided my campsite and made off with my backpack. My heart sinks as I take in a ragged breath through a hand cupped over my mouth. Some of the backpack contents might be scattered nearby, but in the tall grass and poor light, it'd be impossible to find anything. Raccoons are fast and intelligent. Even if I could locate some of my things, those thieves would have already opened my reserve food packets and eaten everything I had.

I stare at the ground with hunched shoulders and a drooped head. I want to curse, but that isn't my nature. Besides, who would notice? I haven't seen another human being, and the raccoons might enjoy my tirade. I won't give them the satisfaction; they have hurt me enough already. The only survival gear I have left is what I slept with—my spear, one lighter, the tent, and a sleeping bag.

I wring my hands as I contemplate what to do next. Dawn will break soon, so I roll the tent and sleeping bag into a tight bundle, tie them to my waist, and set out following the river. I don't get far before disaster strikes. An old beaver mound gives way as I cross a small tributary, and a sharp stick drives into the lower fleshy part of my right calf under the full force of my falling body. My agonizing scream disappears into the steady, howling wind as the clear water around me turns murky red. I flail about, trying to regain my footing and extricate my leg and then, through debilitating pain, slog to the opposite shore. I clean the dirty gouge the best I can and fashion a makeshift bandage from dried river moss and strips of material torn from the bottom of my shirt. I bind the wound as tight as I can, believing that keeping oxygen away from the wound will slow the growth of bacteria. Why should I believe that? I don't know. It just seems right. All I'm certain of is that I'm in serious trouble. The puncture is bad. I must find civilization soon or I'll die on this plain.

By the fifteenth day, infection has set in. Fever and weakness are my constant companions. My injured limb slows my progress, forcing me to stop and struggle for breath on several occasions. My spirit and stamina reach low points. All I want to do is sit down, close my eyes, and not wake up. Before I can prepare a bed of grass as my final resting place, I see a flash of light—a glint of sun far in the distance. Squinting and straining my eyes, the tops of grain elevators are barely visible on the horizon—an unmistakable mark of civilization. With renewed strength and delirious hope, I push hard toward the structures, hoping they aren't a mirage.

Chapter Two
Civilization

I reach the silos by early afternoon, and my heart drops at what I discover there. The entire area is deserted. The silos contain aged grain but no one to manage the facility. The small community surrounding the silos is crumbling with age and covered with vines and other vegetation. A rusting railroad track runs along one edge of the settlement but has not been used for a very long time. Everything is covered with layers of dust and dirt. Except for the wind itself, the town is quiet as death. *This town is dead, just as I'll likely be soon.*

I rummage through a half-collapsed drugstore until I find hydrogen peroxide, antibiotic ointment, amoxicillin pills, Tylenol, and bandages scattered around on the decaying floor. The medicine containers show age, but the expiration dates on them mean nothing to me. I don't know today's date, and even if I did, they're all I've got. They will help, or I'll die. There are no other options. After treating my wound, I lie down on the floor to rest. Either my deliriousness or the fact that I've slept outside for so long makes the hard floor feel as good as a cushioned couch. Whichever it is, I welcome sleep as it sweeps me away.

I'm weak and dehydrated when I come to, and my fever has broken. It's impossible to know how long I've been out—one day, two? I just don't know. I gather enough strength to redress my wound and limp to the neighboring general store. I am in desperate need of water and food. A brief search yields bottled water and a few jars of food that don't have bloated lids. The jars with flat lids are old and dusty, but could contain edible food. As with the medicine, the expiration dates don't mean a thing. I open a few jars and smell the contents. The peaches have a disgusting odor, but the applesauce smells like it should. I dip a finger into the jar and then dab it on my tongue. It tastes good, so it's probably not poisonous. Trying many jars, I devour what I consider safe.

Two days later, I feel strong enough to scout the remainder of the village. Almost everything has been ransacked but little taken. The people who lived here must have left in a hurry. That's fortunate for me. Enough food and first aid materials are scattered about to restock for the next leg of my trip, wherever that takes me. In an old home with a caved-in roof behind the silos, I find an elongated object wrapped in an oily cotton fabric. This is my lucky day. Inside the material are a well-preserved Henry 30-30 rifle and a box of ammunition. The gun barrel is rust-free, and the loading mechanism works well. I dry-fire the weapon a few times and then slip five shells into the receiver.

The rifle is heavy in my hand, but it feels like a natural extension of my arm—like it has always been a part of me. I seem to know a great deal about firearms, as if by instinct, yet I am repelled by the thought of killing for food. *Why?* My memories are like an onion. The outer layers must contain information I need to survive, while the inner layers, the real me, are still hidden. *Will I ever know my past? Who am I...and where are all the other people?* Without thinking, I crank a shell into the chamber and gently lower the hammer. Up to now, I haven't needed to protect myself, but the ability to hunt could save my life in the days ahead. I must be prepared.

I continue looking through the house until I push open the master bedroom door and then recoil back. Plastering myself against the hall wall, I listen for the faintest sound. I feel my heart beating near my temples and hear a slight pounding in my ears, but all else is quiet. With great caution, I peek around the doorframe until I can see the bed. The remains of two skeletons, still holding hands as if they just drifted off to sleep, lie next to each other. I relax a little as I ease into the room, trying to understand what might have happened here. Everything is covered with dust and cobwebs, there are no footprints, and I see no signs of violence. It's as if these people knew they were going to die and simply gave up living. This is frustrating; I don't understand. *Why would two people surrender their lives without a fight?* I shake my head and sigh aloud. The skeletons aren't something I can deal with now. I'll notify the authorities when I find them.

Resuming my search, I find an old bicycle in a rundown outbuilding near the outpost's crumbling water tower. The tires are flat but not rotted by sun exposure. I also find an oily hand pump lying nearby to air the tires up. With transportation now available, I forage through the remaining decaying buildings, looking for more ammunition, food, and anything useful I can take with me. I am amazed how native plants are consuming the village, as if anxious to erase every vestige of man-made creation. In some buildings, where the sun's rays stream through windows or collapsed roofs, large trees have grown through the floors and ceilings. Bushes and vines grow profusely on every conceivable surface.

I continue bicycling around the village. There isn't much to see. In addition to the drugstore, general mercantile, and a few houses, there is a small restaurant, a service station/vehicle repair shop, a simple church, a farm supply, and a health facility that provides medical, dental, and undertaker services on a rotating basis. According to the faded sign on the front of that building, doctors and dentists visit on various days of the month. The building could provide additional medical supplies, so I enter with caution, being careful to test the creaky old floor's strength with each step I take. There isn't much inside I don't already have— just some scissors, sealed suture materials, and stretchy tape.

Through a dirty window near the back of the building, I spot a small community graveyard. My eyes are drawn to an odd, whitish lump under a large tree near the back of the cemetery, but it is difficult to make out what it might be through the dust and dirt on the window. It looks out of place, so I decide to check it out. When I round the back corner of the building, my hand juts to my mouth, and my body tenses as I stare unblinking at the macabre find. The whitish lump is a pile of sun-bleached human bones, jumbled together as if bodies were stacked like cord wood and left to decay in the open.

I count skulls as I walk around the assortment of bones—twenty-two. That is far more than I would expect, even if everyone in this tiny village died at the same time. I shake my head as I try to comprehend what might have happened here. *This is a farming community. Some of these people must have come from surrounding areas. What killed them, and why would they come here to die? Why weren't they buried properly?* As it has been since I began my journey, everything I encounter elicits more questions than answers.

The next day, I redress my wound and head south with makeshift saddlebags slung over the bike's back fender. I'm anxious to leave the village behind. In about four miles, a faded green sign indicates I-90 just ahead, and another points toward Billings, Montana—150 miles east.

I stop to rest as I chuckle at the confused irony of my situation. Somehow, I know what the road sign means. I know Billings is a large city, but I don't know my own name. *Is Billings my home? Do I have family there?* A hawk screeches in the distance, covering my deep sigh. I might not know who I am or where I belong, but at least I know where I am.

* * * *

The Interstate is overgrown with grasses and trees and rife with large cracks and pavement splits. A few automobiles are scattered along the road, some wrecked and some not. As it was in the town I left behind, the only vehicle occupants are skeletons. This part of the country has been left for dead, abandoned, and allowed to return to nature. In seven miles, I enter the town of Bozeman. The city limit sign indicates the town has 30,720 residents. If they exist, I should be able to find other people here. If not, perhaps I can find something to explain what happened to them.

My general confusion turns to deep concern as I complete an initial assessment of Bozeman. The town is deserted. Nothing has been maintained. I don't find any operational utilities, running water, or any indication that people have been here for a very long time. *Where is everyone? Why would they leave this city?*

By the time I discover a crumbling Home Depot on 19th Avenue, I am breathing hard, light-headed, and my arms and legs are shaking. I need to get hold of myself, so I take several moments to settle down before entering the store. This store could be my salvation. It might contain equipment I can use to answer some of my questions. In addition to two skeletons—one on aisle four and one on aisle ten—I find a small propane generator, a full six-gallon propane tank, and an AM/FM radio. As in the village eleven miles back, the skeletons don't make sense. *They were apparently left to decay exactly where they fell. Why?*

After an hour working to service the generator and get it running, I begin scanning the airways. It is not what I find that surprises me but what I don't find. Something bad has happened, and it's not just the skeletons. Static fills every band. I can't find a single coherent signal or human voice.

I'm frustrated that I have no memory of what caused this desolation or even the faintest recall of recent history. It's clear everything around me has been deserted for many years. Nevertheless, whatever happened is recent enough that I should know something about it. So where have I been since then? I wish I could remember something, anything.

Maps of Bozeman at the back of the Home Depot Service Counter phonebook show the location of the Public Library on East Lamme Street.

I make my way there through the deserted streets, trying to imagine what kind of town this was before whatever happened took place. Would children be riding their bikes? Maybe jumping rope or running around in a game of Hide and Seek. Was this the kind of world where Mom bakes cookies while Dad cuts the grass? Or would both parents work long hours and the children be looked after by a sitter? It disturbs me that I don't know the answer to such simple questions, and from the emptiness of the town, I'm not sure if I ever will.

The library is built of stone and steel and is largely intact. To my relief, its interior hasn't been ransacked. Rows of dusty books are decaying on its shelves, emitting the comforting smell of old paper. The library reeks of civilization modulated by age. The library is a time capsule, untouched by destruction, and being here infuses me with hope. Something in this building might help fill gaps in my memory, so I begin searching.

A stack of yellowed newspapers to the left of the checkout counter grabs my attention. I shudder as I read the large, red headline on the top paper—*The End of Days*. The paper is dated September 8, 2021. Based on the growth of large trees inside the decaying buildings in the towns I've passed through, the condition of the Interstate, and the accumulated deterioration associated with everything I've seen, the paper must be at least fifty years old. I am relieved to know both where I am and the approximate date, but what do I do with that information?

The article in the first paper isn't too revealing— mostly saying goodbye to a readership that already knew what I am desperate to learn. Older newspapers take me back in time, and the further back I read, the more horrific the news.

Saudi terrorists created a virulent necrotizing fasciitis called beta-hemolytic streptococcus, BHS—a genetically engineered, flesh-eating bacterial infection of the protective covering of fibrous tissues beneath the skin. BHS proved to be a biological warfare superstar—an efficient killer that caused death within eighteen hours of exposure. An airborne infectious agent like smallpox, BHS spread like a raging fire among unprotected populations. Unlike smallpox, humans had no immunity to the man-made genetic creation. Without resistance, rapid and painful death came to everyone within an expanding ring of death dubbed the Kill Zone.

Two weeks after the first satellite photos showed rampant death in Mecca—the apparent site of the pathogen's accidental release—the Kill Zone approached Tabuk and Al Jawf in northern Saudi Arabia. Jordan, Turkey, and Israel braced for the worst. The lethal BHS pathogen cleared infected areas of all human life—no one survived. As a result, United Nations and NATO troops established quarantine corridors within cooperating countries and ordered anyone attempting to cross a corridor be shot on sight.

Iran, Iraq, and Syria remained defiant, with imams proclaiming that Allah would protect the faithful from the evil cast upon the innocent Muslim world by the unholy West. Multitudes believed, armed themselves for *jihad*, and died. The list of suicide killers also grew as the call to arms spread faster than the disease. Called Ambulatory Infected Agents, Muslims seeking martyrdom lined up to bring glory to Allah by carrying the highly contagious disease to the West.

The newspaper articles continue to astound me. Because of defiance, propaganda, and overt intent to bypass quarantine corridors, Iran, Iraq, and Syria were excluded from efforts to contain the Kill Zone. That forced quarantine corridors to extend into southern Russia and the mountainous regions bordering Iran. Nothing held, and desperate Western nations reacted with Project Sanitize—a last-ditch attempt to stop the expanding Kill Zone by saturation bombing its perimeter with nuclear weapons. Millions lost their lives, but the bacterium did not die in the nuclear fire as hoped. Instead, BHS dispersed on stratospheric air currents to every corner of the world.

A medical research team located inside Cheyenne Mountain, Colorado, developed a serum to kill BHS, and worldwide inoculations began. The serum worked as advertised, but the scientists who created it did not have time for rigorous testing. Several months after inoculating the population with the serum, serious problems emerged. The serum that killed BHS interfered with human reproduction and triggered rapid aging of internal organs. In the end, either BHS killed everyone in eighteen hours or the serum used to prevent it killed them in twelve months. Total annihilation of the human population over the entire globe must have followed.

By the time I finish the last newspaper, the horror of what happened to the planet begins to sink in. Tears stream down my face. Stunned and shaken, I weep with deep sobs as wave after wave of sadness rolls over me. It's hard to believe human life has been eradicated. It takes some time to regain my composure, to set aside my feelings of overwhelming loss, but when I do, I sit with folded hands in a hard-backed chair, staring across a deteriorating wooden library table at the dusty racks of books beyond.

In the silence of that abandoned building, a structure specifically constructed to propagate knowledge, I am struck by the irony of it all. Without places like this, without the accumulation of knowledge, we might still have a world. Without the knowledge to engineer a foreign life form, people would still exist. My body stiffens with rage as a surge of righteous indignation and anger flashes through it. For a moment, I am paralyzed by revulsion and hatred. Everything I've read is senseless and stupid. What gave the Islamists the right to play God? Did they *really* believe killing everyone would purify the world for Allah...or get them virgins in Heaven?

I'm tempted to rip up all of the newspapers I've read and scream at the top of my lungs. I could knock over the books and curse the bastards who did this to the world, but what good would that do? Anger can't help. That is futile now because there are no people to be angry at.

Or are there?

My brain tries to grapple with the enormity of what I've read, but my own existence counters every story in every newspaper. If everyone died, then how did I survive? If I am alive, then isn't it possible someone else might be as well?

I shuffle through the papers and reread some of the articles to confirm what I thought I saw earlier. *Yes!* Cheyenne Mountain is at the center of everything. The president ordered Doomsday teams sequestered there prior to Operation Sanitize. Could any of those people still exist? I need to know more.

Despite its small size, the library is a treasure trove of information. I continue reading until I've exhausted everything I can find on Ambulatory Infected Agents, biological weapons, and the Cheyenne Mountain Air Force Station complex just south of Colorado Springs. During the Cold War, the United States and Canadian military remotely scanned the skies over their borders from Cheyenne Mountain's Operation Center. Although designed to withstand a thirty-megaton blast within one nautical mile and constructed behind two twenty-five ton blast doors 2,000 feet underground, the government considered mothballing the entire operation. They deemed it "non-survivable" from a direct hit by a powerful, intercontinental ballistic missile.

They spared the Operation Center; however, because its metal-plate floors and walls were designed to bend rather than break. The entire complex sat on huge, shock-absorbing springs, and thousands of bolts drilled into the rock strengthened the granite ceilings. The government questioned the Operation Center's nuclear survivability, but the facility could withstand earthquakes and had many features that made it ideal for a critical new mission. Filtering outside air removed radioactive, chemical, and biological hazards, so the entire staff could be sequestered underground in complete physical isolation. The facility also housed enough food, water, and fuel to last for months, perhaps even years.

I also find information on the pathogen that killed everyone and how its development impacted the Cheyenne Mountain facility. The 33rd World Health Assembly declared global eradication of smallpox in 1980, but virus samples retained by the United States and Russia were still a threat. Following the Cold War, the threat materialized when some Soviet samples, purchased by wealthy Saudis, became the basis for biological weapons more lethal than anything previously imagined.

IL-4 smallpox, a predecessor to BHS, became the first bioweapon delivered by Ambulatory Infected Agents. Terrorist scientists created the pathogen by inserting the human IL-4 gene into the natural smallpox virus. Humans had little immunity to the artificial bug. Millions died. Far more effective than nuclear weapons, the self-replicating IL-4 spread quickly and killed only people—livestock and infrastructure remained undamaged.

After the IL-4 wave of death, extensive laboratory facilities and elite medical research teams were brought into Cheyenne Mountain, and the Operation Center's biological warfare mission began. Following massive supercomputer upgrades, the addition of living quarters, and installation of the most advanced biohazard containment equipment available, the Operation Center became ground zero for worldwide pathogen research, identification, and response.

By the time I finish reading, my path ahead is clear. If others survived BHS, they'll be in Cheyenne Mountain. I find maps to guide me to Colorado Springs in the library's map drawers before I dust off an old sofa and settle in for the night.

I don't sleep well. It's not just the information I've gathered today that bothers me, but my total lack of recall about past events in general. Everything I read today surprised me, but information like that shouldn't be a surprise to anyone. How could I not know things that horrific? How could I not know I might be the only living person on Earth? I can't remember my name, who my parents are, or how I got to the valley I woke up in three weeks ago. On the other hand, I seem to know other basics, like how to read and reason, ride a bike, survive in the open, and use a weapon.

I place both hands over my eyes and force myself to think back as far as I can, trying to recall anything about my parents and extended family. Try as I might, I can't recall a thing. *Did BHS kill them all? How did I survive?*

I sigh in frustration. I can't even remember how old I am. I tighten the muscles in my arms and legs, and then release the tension to relax. Closing my eyes, I let my mind drift to that pleasant moment on the bank of the stream when I first woke up, coaxing my body to give in to unsettling sleep. "None of this makes any sense," I whisper to myself, and I'm suddenly worried that my own voice might be the only voice I'll ever hear again.

Chapter Three
Cheyenne Mountain

The following morning, I locate a new four-wheel-drive truck in the mechanic's bay of a Ford dealership—a vehicle outfitted for ranch life in the rough Montana terrain. It has dual fuel tanks, two spare tires, and a blade and winch up front. Beneath its factory-installed camper shell—something I'll need if I encounter any of the powerful thunderstorms common during the Colorado summer—are a small generator and a bed-mounted fuel tank for remotely servicing farm equipment. I would question how I know about Colorado's thunderstorms, but the lack of answers would only frustrate me more.

The faded yellow sticker on the truck's windshield indicates it meets all standards for Liquid Petroleum (LP) vehicles mandated by Congress in 2020. Thank God. Without that, this truck would be gummed up with old gasoline residue and completely useless.

I stop to reflect a moment. How do I know about gasoline residue? I'm not sure I've ever seen a gasoline engine. I shake my head and sigh. I need to stay with what feels right in the here and now, like servicing this vehicle before trying to start it. I replace its old oil with fresh synthetic oil from sealed cans stocked by the dealership. Next, I check all the fluids, and after adding water to the truck's battery, I fire up the generator to charge it. It takes several hours for the battery to charge, and I'm elated when the truck kicks over.

My first stop is at a collapsed grocery store about two miles from the Ford dealership. I fill a shopping cart with a few large boxes of tea as well as canned and bottled food scattered about on the floor. Next, I grab antibiotics, bandages, and salves from the store's destroyed pharmacy.

As important as those things are, I find the real mother lode in an adjacent decaying hardware store.

The store's aisles are full of useful survival gear, making me feel like an excited kid at Christmas. I bring a shopping basket lying on the floor upright and start walking each aisle. It takes several trips to the truck to move LP adapter hoses and five full fifteen-gallon LP tanks. Sockets, screwdrivers, and other hand tools are next. I cannot remember ever repairing anything, but for some reason, I feel confident I could if I had to. The thought makes me shudder. Having to repair the truck before I reach my destination is not a task I'd relish. On still another trip to the truck, I take plastic water jugs, a coffee pot, cooking pots, and utensils. I've been living out of a simple mess kit for so long I'll feel pampered having these luxuries. It just gets better as I load a propane camp stove, lantern, and gas cartridges into the basket, and place an electric chainsaw and several extension cords in the rack below. As I stuff the equipment into the truck bed, I remind myself I need to leave room for my sleeping bag. Without question I'll be spending nights back there. After surveying the remaining space in the truck bed, I believe I have room for one more shopping basket full of supplies. On my final trip into the store, I take two first aid kits, a small animal trap, rabbit pellets, some nylon cord, heavy ropes, two chains, and some clothing and gloves that aren't completely rotted. On the way out, I spot a GLOCK 19, several boxes of 9mm ammunition, and a selection of hunting knives in the Sporting Goods section. Even if I have to sleep in the cab, I won't leave those items behind.

I pack everything into the truck for the long ride to Colorado Springs, and for the first time since I woke up in this nightmare, I feel prepared for what might lie ahead. I have only one more thing I must do before setting out again on I-90.

On my way out of town, I pull into the overgrown parking lot of a funeral home adjacent to the Bozeman cemetery. Even though I am quite sure what lies ahead as I walk beside the ruin of the old sanctuary building, I'm sickened by the utter hopelessness arrayed before me when I round the corner. Atop hundreds of graves in the heavily-treed cemetery, thousands upon thousands of sun-bleached human bones litter the ground in the stark afternoon sun. The bones are piled in the open and intermixed with a few mummifying bodies. It must have been hard to put loved ones here without proper funerals. I can scarcely imagine the heartache—and the stench—at the time. I suspect this is the situation in every town and city across the planet.

Emotions of horror from the night before overtake me, and I weep again in total despair, incredible loneliness, and the disturbing realization that I must get used to seeing piles of bones at every stop I make.

It will take at least two days to cover the 780 miles to Cheyenne Mountain, maybe more if the roads are bad. I would hate to get stranded in some desolate area between here and there, so I try to bring everything I might need for any emergency, even stopping to fill up my water jugs at the first free-flowing stream I cross. I'll follow I-90 into Wyoming, and then take I-25 south into Colorado. The remains of the interstate highways are probably my best hope of getting to Colorado Springs, but a lot can happen to a road that hasn't been maintained for fifty years.

The highway through Montana into Wyoming is hilly but drivable. I avoid derelict vehicles along the way and make it to Casper by the end of a very long day. As I found in Bozeman, and every town I passed through along the way, the city is deserted. I'm too tired to investigate anything, so I lay my bedroll in the space I left in the back of the pickup and sleep well into the next morning. After breakfast, I'll scout a few areas of the city, collect a little more food, find additional fuel, and then continue down I-25.

The next day, I am forced to clear a few rock falls off the highway before I reach Denver, but nothing the truck's blade can't handle. Beyond Colorado Springs, on NORAD Road off Colorado Highway 115, fallen trees from a windstorm in years past litter the road for about 200 yards. The chainsaw and winch are invaluable, but I'll never make it to Cheyenne Mountain Air Force Station tonight. By evening, I've cleared a path halfway through the fallen trees when I encounter something strange, something that shouldn't be here at all.

A tree lies at the side of the road. It has been cut with a chainsaw and the cut is aged, but how can that be? If the tree had been cut before road maintenance ceased, it would have been removed from the right of way entirely. It is still here, so it must have been cut after they stopped maintaining this road. Someone had to be alive to do that, but whom? In the fading light of day, I inspect the cut in great detail. If this tree was moved off the road in the past fifty years, then whoever did it must have made the same connection to Cheyenne Mountain I have.

The thought that another living soul could exist just ahead makes me giddy, and I work at a frantic pace, trying to complete a path through the fallen trees. It is a race with the setting sun I cannot win. My heart pounds from exertion, and sweat pours from my head by the time I set the chainsaw down, remove my gloves, and resign myself to finishing the task tomorrow. As much as I want to get through—as anxious as I am to see if other people exist ahead—tree trimming at night is far too dangerous to continue. I take a deep breath and shudder as I exhale. What lies ahead might not be positive. *That cut was made a long time ago. The person who cut that tree might have died by now.* I'll get through the remainder of the trees tomorrow. Then, I'll confront Cheyenne Mountain.

* * * *

The *clunk* of my small animal trap wakes me the next morning, and I am delighted to find a large rabbit inside. It is a beautiful creature with soft eyes and fluffy gray fur. I take a moment to thank the animal for its sacrifice before killing and skinning it. On the one hand, the act seems barbaric and cruel; on the other, it seems necessary. Preparing the animal for cooking seems natural, as if my hands know what to do without my brain explaining their movements, but I don't remember having dressed a rabbit before. The smell of the fat droplets that pop and sizzle as I turn the carcass on a makeshift spit over an open fire makes my mouth water. I don't remember the last time I had fresh meat, and I don't want to rush this.

It is a beautiful summer morning, and as I sit on a flat rock enjoying a cup of fresh-brewed tea while the rabbit cooks to perfection, I reflect on the peace and tranquility of my surroundings. As it was when I first woke up in the valley, something primitive stirs within me, something that makes me spread my arms, close my eyes, and breathe the scent of pine deep into my lungs as the sun warms my face. For that moment, I relish just being alive. When I reopen my eyes, gentle air currents blow a whiff of smoke into my face. As I wipe the sting from my teary eyes, I am reminded of how different my view of the world must be from those who suffered the end of it all. Those people died by the billions, at war with an enemy they could not see, but they did not die alone. On the other hand, the entire world is mine to share with the few animals that stare at me with curious caution. My only enemies are carelessness and lack of knowledge, but if those foes win, I will die alone. I wonder which is worse.

When the rabbit is golden brown and trimmed with a few black charcoal streaks, I remove it from the spit and let it cool a few minutes before enjoying every morsel. The meat is succulent and flavorful, almost beyond description. By the time I finish my second cup of tea and clean my utensils, I am mentally prepared for what lies ahead. I slip on work gloves, fire up the generator, and then reach for the chainsaw.

After many hours of hard labor, I complete a path large enough for the truck, but I don't see any additional older cuts like the one I noted yesterday. With the tree fall behind me, I soon reach Cheyenne Mountain Air Force Station's entry gate. Parking lots full of abandoned cars that are overgrown with vegetation surround the entrance, and the gate to the complex succumbed to its own weight many years ago. I begin to worry that this might not be the salvation I had hoped for as I push the gate out of the way with the truck's blade. I suspect I would've been shot if I had tried that back in 2021.

I leave the truck near the facility's main entrance doors and approach on foot. Disappointment rises within me. There are no signs of life—just dirt piled up by the wind on one side of the driveway and lots of small rocks scattered around, apparently fallen from the stone facing above. Two ominous-looking doors embedded in the granite face of the mountain stand before me. Judging from the vegetation growing around them, neither has been opened for a very long time. The larger door must be for vehicles. It doesn't have a knocker or anything that a person might use to announce his presence, but the smaller door does.

Not knowing what to expect, I place my index finger in the fingerprint reader adjacent to the small door. A light-green glow emanates from the device. Seconds later, a buzzing noise penetrates the silence, followed by a faint click. Something has unlocked the small door. My excitement spikes. There could be someone alive inside.

As I pry the door open, bright sun glints back from an immaculate stainless steel chamber about six feet square and nine feet tall. That makes sense. Cheyenne Mountain is a secure bio-facility, so I suspect the tiny room is a decontamination chamber. Although I can't remember ever being here, the chamber has a familiar feel, like I've seen it before. Hairs on the back of my neck bristle as a sudden tremor ripples across my skin. I step back, studying the beckoning entrance. My body's reaction could be a warning. Nagging inklings of forgotten memories aside, one thing is clear: if I want to enter the facility, this is the way in. I see a door with an associated keypad and thumbprint reader on the opposite side of the chamber. People could exist on the other side of the door…or they could all be dead. I'm torn. If I enter the gleaming chamber, and the large door closes behind me, that small space could become my final resting place.

After a few moments of indecision, I take a deep breath and step inside, scanning for anything that might stir my memory. The only thing I did not see from the outside is the dim red glow from a light several feet above my head. A low, whirring sound behind me draws my attention, and I turn just in time to see the thick steel door dovetail into its polished doorframe. I don't have time to react before the door's internal hydraulic deadbolts slide closed. I feared this might happen. This room has sensed my presence and sealed me inside. I tamp down my growing concern and place my thumb on the fingerprint reader. Nothing happens. This could be bad. I have no idea what the combination for the keypad might be or even how many numbers are required.

Beads of sweat break out across my forehead as I push hard on the large door to the outside. It's a waste of time and energy; the door doesn't budge. It's probably my imagination, but the air in this small space seems harder to breathe. Have I come all this way just to die in this stainless steel casket? Before I can work myself into a full-blown panic, a sharp hiss permeates the room, like a leak in a high-pressure hose. The gas is odorless and colorless. I can't tell where it's coming from, but I can feel its effects. I grow increasingly dizzy and soon can no longer stand. Everything goes dark as I slump to the floor.

Chapter Four
E12-B

When I come to, an excruciating pain stabs deep into my right side below my rib cage. I gasp through a contorted wince and immediately feel a cool rush enter my left arm and heart. The horrible pain across my lower back begins to subside, diminishing in intensity from that of a deep rip in my flesh to that of a dull bruise. I am comforted by both the diminishing pain and by the certain knowledge that someone must be watching me. Other people are alive in this place.

I struggle against straps that bind my feet and wrists but have no strength. Disorientation washes over me like a breaking wave. My awareness fades as darkness closes in from my peripheral vision. Before unconsciousness takes me, I see a blur of IVs in my arms. The bright lights in the ceiling cannot stop the enveloping blackness. I cease struggling as dizziness sweeps me away. Whatever I've been given, I welcome it. The pain is gone.

I have no idea how long I've lingered in unconsciousness when I wake in a much larger stainless steel room than the one where I passed out. IVs no longer puncture my arms, and I'm not strapped to the bed. My right side throbs as I force myself to sit up, and I reach back to comfort it while gritting my teeth and groaning. *My God, I am covered with gauze and tape.* As much as I am able, I fight the pain as I turn my head to the side to glance at my source of discomfort. Bandages cover a portion of my side and back. It's hard to breathe. It feels like someone sucker punched my kidney.

I grimace and shudder from head to toe. Before I can consider what I might do next, hidden speakers fill the room with a soft female voice. "Please, relax and watch the video. Everything will be clear to you soon."

Why is that woman's voice familiar? I squeeze my eyes shut and try to remember something…anything…but nothing comes to mind. I clench my fists, frustrated, and shout, "Who are you? What's going on?" My voice echoes in the room, but there is no response. I exhale a resigned sigh, allowing my frustration to ebb. I am only delaying the answers I've been so anxious to hear.

The woman's voice is more authoritative this time. "I said relax, please. You'll understand soon."

The room goes dark, and a video screen illuminates through the glass beyond the foot of my bed. My eyes widen as I stare at my own image on the screen. My image is casual and wearing the clothes I woke up with in the mountains. It also seems comfortable, and it's not going insane with confusion and unsettling fear as I am now. The video begins with a simple greeting as if nothing unusual has happened.

"Hi, buddy. Welcome back. If you're watching this, then you've made it back from Montana."

I continue to stare with mouth agape. *Why am I in this video…addressing myself?*

"You're probably pretty confused," the image says with a sheepish grin. "Sorry we put you so far out, but we knew there were reasonable roads near your drop site for your return home. We needed to know if we trained you well enough to survive in the open, even considering your memory loss."

Trained? I look down at my shaking hands, remembering all I had gone through to get here. Was prior training the reason I knew how to hunt, set traps for animals, use a rifle, and operate a chainsaw? Survival training?

"First of all," the voice continues, "congratulations. You are the second person to make it this far, and since you have, you've also discovered what's out there. Pretty frightening, isn't it? What you've seen is the reason I volunteered—*you* volunteered—for this mission. But in case you've missed some of the finer details, here's the short version of the story. A biological attack eliminated all human life on Earth's surface sixty-two years ago."

Sixty-two? That's worse than I thought. I had guessed only fifty.

"The survivors we know of live here in this mountain. Anyone who leaves this facility, for any reason, must live in isolation for the rest of his or her life. The brave volunteers who manage our farms, water supply, and maintain our fuel and external equipment have dedicated their lives to that service. They leave this mountain dressed in overpressure suits that provide processed air for breathing, and they must be fully decontaminated before they are allowed back in. Even then, they must occupy separate quarters. They live solitary lives, apart from those of us deep inside and separate from everyone who works outside as well. As it stands now, they will never again experience close contact with another human being. Even when they work alongside another who has volunteered for the same fate, they must be protected by a biohazard suit."

Without thinking, I reach back to scratch the bandages on my lower back, and a stern female voice rings out throughout the room, "Don't touch that!"

I jerk my hand away. Before I recover from the startle, the video version of me takes a deep breath and begins speaking again. "I tell you this because you are now one of them—a very special one. I volunteered for this experiment knowing I'd never again be allowed near another unprotected person. On the upside, I also knew my participation might provide information that could help our community. Collecting new data on the pathogens that contaminate our world outweighed any other potential contribution I could ever make."

I frown when I hear those words. Was I really the type of man who would sacrifice himself in such a way? After everything I have gone through outside, I feel like the answer should be a resounding *no.*

"Our medical staff believes the original biological killer was a genetically-modified bacteria called beta-hemolytic streptococcus, or BHS. The Islamic scientists who created the superbug died when the pathogen broke out in Mecca—probably the result of an accident. Along with its creators, we lost any cure they might have had. The science team sequestered in this mountain developed a serum to counter BHS using a genetically-altered prehistoric bacterium called V5 as a base. The bacteria had been resurrected to create renewable oil from organic waste—its apparent function in prehistoric times. It also had a unique primitive defense mechanism that worked against BHS. Everyone knew the risks of injecting the general population with something that ancient; nevertheless, after limited testing, the Army major in charge ordered worldwide distribution because people were dying by the billions."

"But then everything went to hell," I mutter, already knowing the rest of the story. My video counterpart feels the need to explain it all anyway.

"V5 worked but had unexpected side effects that became evident over time. People outside this mountain suffered a quick, agonizing death from BHS…or succumbed to a slow, painless passing due to V5. Either way, everyone died. V5 causes internal organ aging and interferes with human reproduction—problems our researchers have worked to counter from the beginning. After stopping BHS, the military ordered the people they had sequestered in this mountain to stay put. Those people did not get inoculated with V5, and their children have given us several generations of babies since the original catastrophe."

Now, the video has my interest. Nothing in my library research talked much about what happened after the tragedy.

"Children are trained in chemistry, biology, and other specialties, beginning their tutelage as laboratory assistants and trade helpers when they are very young.

Subsequent generations now man our laboratories. Despite our best efforts to overcome BHS and V5, the toxins still occupy the external environment and are as alive and deadly today as they were sixty-two years ago. That brings us to the bandages on your side and the reasons I volunteered. My mission was to test the latest experimental approaches for mitigating the negative effects of V5 and BHS. I am the twelfth person to do so, knowing full well the others didn't survive long. We don't have many people, so we run very few experiments. Occasional sacrifices are necessary in the hope that, someday, our community might leave this mountain."

I suddenly feel worried about where this is going and wonder what could've possessed me to take part in this experiment. Still, I sit and listen, hoping that something good will come of it.

"The experimental serum you received is called E384, and it has known side effects. Irregular memory loss and prolonged coma are two of them. Those side effects are the reason you probably felt disoriented when you woke up. Nevertheless, we believe the benefits of E384 could outweigh its side effects, but we aren't certain of its long-term consequences. Samples of exposed tissue are needed over time to baseline the serum's effectiveness. You contributed your right kidney to furthering our understanding. That's the reason your side hurts and you are bandaged up, but the experiment is just beginning. In case you don't remember, the functioning of your reproductive organs will be tested from time to time, assuming you survive, and additional organ samples will be required as you age."

"Terrific." I answer the video with sarcasm, as if it can understand me.

"Now, you understand. You...*we*...are the experiment. You have come home, and you're somewhat of a hero for making it this far. Completely unprotected in the outside world, you've survived BHS longer than anyone before you. In doing so, you have brought back important new data relative to the residuals of V5 within your tissues. Because I volunteered, our people are one step closer to beating this thing, one step closer to getting our planet back. I know you'll have lots of questions, but I wanted to talk to you first. You're not being held hostage. You are not an unwilling lab rat. You are where you are because I chose this path for you, and I'd make the same choice again. All I ask is that you honor my decision, our decision, even if you don't remember making it. Cooperate with your doctors fully, and do whatever they ask—even if it means your death." Then, he pauses and nods his head toward me. His soft eyes radiate compassion I haven't felt in weeks. "I hope you understand. God be with us all."

When my image disappears, the lights on the other side of the glass come on. A very pretty young woman in a white laboratory coat scoots her chair up to a microphone. She looks to be in her mid-twenties with flowing, sandy-blonde hair. She stares into my eyes and places the palm of her right hand on the glass, as if reaching out to me from another world. I probably imagine it, but for a moment, I believe I see the glint of tears in her eyes.

She also seems vaguely familiar. *The girl in my dreams?*

"Welcome back, B. It's really good to see you. We know your adjustment will be traumatic, so I've been assigned as your transition monitor. I'll be with you pretty much constantly for the duration of testing. Please direct your questions to me. If I can't answer them, I'll find someone who can. Can I help you with anything now?"

Ah...I recognize the voice. She's the one who ordered me to leave the bandages alone. Do I have questions? That's an understatement if I've ever heard one. I begin with something easy. "You called me 'B.' Is that my real name?"

A broad smile crosses her face before she answers, like she's known me for years. "Silly boy. E12-B is your given name, but we've always called you B."

"Seriously? Whatever happened to Brian or Brandon?"

She chuckles. "It's good to see that you still have your sense of humor."

Her familiarity is disturbing. A distant memory stirs out of reach deep within me. I can almost picture this woman, only a bit younger, without the lab coat, and with a smile on her face. I have to ask, "Do we know each other?"

Her face grows far more serious. This time, I'm sure I see tears. "Oh, I see. It's the E384 memory loss. You could say we know each other. I'm your sister."

I gasp as my mouth falls open—a door to my past just opened. With halting speech, I press for more information. "If you are my sister, can you tell me if…if our parents are still alive? Are they here in this mountain?"

"Yes, they live. We don't know them, but the computer does. Your question isn't relevant."

Her answer makes my head want to explode. It creates far more questions than satisfaction. It's clear to me that my memory is more screwed up that I thought. How could she not know our parents? For that matter, how could I forget a cute sister like her?

I sigh and press with a question that might have a rational answer. "Why am I called E12-B? Is it coincidence that I'm on the twelfth mission of this type, or is my name related to the mission number?"

Her face looks puzzled, as if she is having a hard time believing I've forgotten so much. She places her hand over her mouth as her head moves slowly back and forth. In a few moments, she responds in a measured, business-like voice, "I see you've completely lost most of your memories, so I'll start at the beginning. Stop me if I start to cover things you already know."

"No problem."

"In this mountain, we're all produced *in vitro*, and it's the duty of every able-bodied female to carry the children assigned to her. We keep the population in tight balance, providing a sufficient number of people to run the facility but not so many as to overpopulate our limited space. Our DNA is analyzed before and after birth, and the computer uses that information to select optimum genetic pairings. That way, known genetic diseases and the negative impacts of certain recessive genes are mitigated. Fetuses are also constantly monitored to ensure that offspring with genetic flaws don't go to term. We are too few to permit development of even one non-productive individual. The computer also determines our function within the community, the training we receive, and our names before birth."

The blank look on my face probably gives my thoughts away, but under the circumstances, her unusual view of procreation makes sense. I accept her comments for the moment, but I know I'll have more questions about that later. "Why am I called E12-B?"

She responds so quickly, I assume she must be a geneticist. "Not all DNA need be natural. Some gene sequences can be artificially altered, becoming components of an individual's genetic engineering. You have survived BHS. If your modification weren't successful, you wouldn't be alive. Once your modifications are verified effective over time, they will be incorporated into most branches of next-generation newborns."

"Most?"

"We strive to retain some original material, in case latent problems develop in the future, as in the case of V5."

I ignore the pain that stabs me in the kidney and shift my weight to alleviate it. "If I understand what you're telling me, your scientists modified me from birth to be the twelfth volunteer. They specifically prepared me for this mission.

Did I really volunteer, or did they condition me from birth to take this job?"

"Both. They modified two, but only one volunteered. They trained you on survival techniques, knowing you would lose most of your memory after receiving the E384 serum. They also conditioned you from birth to return to this mountain. That training must have been successful, since you are here."

"If my DNA has been modified to protect me, then what's the purpose of E384, besides screwing up my memory?"

She smirks. "And there's that sarcasm I remember."

"At least one of us does."

She wags her finger back and forth and bites her lower lip as she cocks her head in a silent, scolding motion. "Now, now. You volunteered for this. Let's assume your BHS immunity is real and that you don't die anytime soon. Then, E384 is the only remaining issue. The serum is an attempt to render V5's buckyballs ineffective inside the human body. It's a genetically-engineered leucocyte specifically designed to self-replicate and seek out and bind buckyballs. The engineered leucocyte is similar to a granulocyte—one of the two natural leucocytes—but its function is different than that of the other two. It creates powerful bipolar proteins that coat the exteriors of buckyballs, thus neutralizing the buckyball's capability to bond with human DNA."

It should be obvious I have no idea what she's talking about, but she doesn't respond to the blank expression on my face. "Buckyballs?"

"It's short for buckminsterfullerene, a carbon-60 molecule named after Richard Buckminster Fuller, the same man who popularized the geodesic dome. A research laboratory discovered them in 1985 as a byproduct of laser-vaporized graphite. After that, they joined diamond and graphite as the only known forms of pure carbon. They are so stable they can withstand a 15,000 mph impact against stainless steel without damage. They are also an essential component of V5."

"Ah, of course…buckyballs."

"Do you actually get it, or are you still confused?"

My silence confirms the answer to that question, so she continues. "Buckyballs look like molecular soccer balls. Because of their stability, scientists believed they could be nanoscience superstars, with potential uses as lubricants, drug delivery agents, and superconductors. Unfortunately, they were subsequently shown to damage fish brains, kill bacteria considered helpful to the environment, and bond with and disturb the functioning of human DNA. As a result, many considered them more dangerous than asbestos."

"I'm puzzled. If buckyballs are so dangerous, why did the military inoculate everyone with V5?"

"They didn't have anything else back then, just as the genetic modifications made to your genome might be all we have now. V5's buckyballs provided the delivery mechanism for the original agent that killed BHS, but the scientists took a calculated risk when they used them. In retrospect, even knowing what we know now, we would probably do the same thing. Dying from buckyball poisoning is far less painful than dying from BHS."

"And my coma and memory loss?"

The microphone magnifies her sigh, but she answers with blunt honesty. "That is caused by the same bipolar proteins that bind the buckyballs. We are working to overcome those problems. We believe there's a balance point, where the charge distribution on the bipolar molecule is sufficient to coat buckyballs yet not impact the electrochemical flow within and between neurons in the brain."

I shrug. "Is there a chance I could regain my memory?"

"We really don't know, but you *did* recover from your coma. Others before you did not. By the time of your death, we should have a better understanding."

Her forecast of my death jolts me from curiosity to reality. For some reason, I thought she'd be a bit more compassionate since she's my sister. The word *sister* is still foreign to me, especially with her being so nonchalant about my death.

It has been a short Q&A session, but I am exhausted and losing the ability to control my eyelids. I have the presence of mind for only two more questions. "How old are you? What's your name?"

I can barely hear her answer as I slip rapidly into much needed sleep. "I'm 23 years old, silly—the same as you. My name's E12-A. You can call me A, like all my friends do."

Chapter Five
The Final Experiment

My dreams are chaotic, as to be expected from someone waking from a nightmare into a brave new world. Yet I see the sense of what they're trying to do. It's a high-stakes game, where the players face oblivion if they make too many wrong moves.

The reality of my situation fades, and I soon walk in dreams along the beautiful Montana stream where I awoke in what now seems another life. The birds swooping in the air are breathtaking, and the sounds of the wind and water are hypnotic. The nightmare isn't what I encountered out there; the nightmare is living in this mountain and the religious insanity that precipitated this reality sixty-two years ago.

As night passes, I relive the freedom of my trek through the mountains, relishing the beauty of the world outside. I am at peace until daybreak. Lingering between sound sleep and wakefulness, I am overcome with grief when I realize my sister hasn't a clue what it's like to be free. She has never experienced the natural beauty of the outside world, has never seen a single wild animal or a bird in the air, and maybe she never will. Deep sadness grips me when her soft but distant voice enters my mind, "Wake up, sleepyhead. It's time for breakfast."

I'm groggy as I pry one eyelid open and see E12-A smiling through the glass beyond the foot of my bed. A motorized cart with a tray of hospital food stands nearby. I smile back. "Any chance I can get an order of rabbit and eggs?"

"Not a chance. Eat up. I need to move you to the inspection area. The doctors will be here soon."

The food isn't bad but not all that imaginative: Jell-O, some type of soupy gruel, reconstituted OJ, pills, and a few berries. It's nice to know that Jell-O survived the apocalypse. "What's the inspection area?"

"Something you will have to adjust to. You're a biohazard now. The doctors won't touch you, but their robotic arms will. They even removed your kidney robotically. Once a person leaves this facility, he can never reenter the inner sanctum."

I remember. I told myself the same thing in the video.

Like the cart holding breakfast, my bed is motorized. The panels covering the side of the room opposite E12-A move aside, and the bed positions me next to a glass wall bristling with an array of containment gloves and robotic arms. Five individuals in white coats on the other side of the glass nod as I grin at them and waggle my fingertips. Two are quite young, and three are considerably older. The oldest offers a gentle smile. "Good morning, E12-B. Please roll onto your left side with your back toward us."

Precision instruments strip the bandages from my side and back as remote-controlled swabs clean my wound. After replacing the bandages, one of the younger people tells me there'll be minor discomfort when he extracts some blood. He is right, and I let out a mild curse. All in all, everything seems routine, except I'm not touched by anyone.

The five confer just out of earshot and then return with their verdict. "You're doing quite well and should be up and about in no time. If you have any questions, please direct them to E12-A. Of course, we have questions too, so we've assembled a debriefing team behind the opposite glass wall."

I expect to be questioned by a military authority but am confronted by another team of curious people wearing lab coats. The older individual who led the medical team begins with a summary of my condition. His announcement that I am in stable condition and that my removed kidney does not show deterioration due to buckyball accumulation is met with applause. When he completes his rundown, he introduces me as E12-B and offers the excited group an opportunity to question me directly. I feel like a monkey in a cage.

A pale young man in a light blue lab coat steps up to the microphone. He squints through thick glasses at his clipboard before looking directly at me through the glass partition. "Before The Annihilation, there were thirty-two oil and gas production facilities in Casper, Wyoming. Did you have the opportunity to assess the current state of any of them?"

"The Annihilation" catches me by surprise. I suspect it's easier for them to label mankind's destruction of the world with such a term rather than discuss it in terms of stupidity. That aside, I believe the question itself is weird. Why would anyone care about oil production when there is no one on the outside to use it? Besides, these people have been in this mountain for sixty-two years. I would think they would want to know about the beauty of the world outside—the colors, smells, how it feels to move unconstrained in the open without fear, and the freedom of mind associated with not knowing the world is dead.

I shake my head while looking down at my feet and then respond by telling them what I did see—the decay, the rust, and the infusion of nature into everything created by man. I conclude with, "If the production facilities weren't made of heavy steal or stone, then they are likely no longer viable or repairable. Even the heavy steel components will be rusted together, like the train tracks I saw along the way."

A middle-aged woman with stringy brown hair, a long grayish face, and protruding upper teeth nudges the young man aside. She clears her throat before beginning. "Good morning, E12-B. In your opinion, can anything in the world outside be salvaged? If so, what?"

Her question makes more sense. I explain that items protected from the environment can still be restored or used as is, like the rifle and bicycle I found, and I end with,

"Everything depends on the amount of time things are exposed to the open environment. In time, even the strongest buildings will fall. The longer things remain without human care, the greater the probability they cannot be recycled."

Without a hint of emotion, the woman mutters as she moves away, "Yes, entropy tends toward zero."

A young man who appears to be around twelve years old scoots up next. His smile is infectious. "Hi, E12-B. Can you tell me what animals you saw?"

An older man to the child's right glares down at him, but the kid has asked a question I want to answer. I chuckle before beginning with, "Now a chicken can cross the road without anyone questioning its motivation."

The kid scrunches up his face and shrugs as he looks up at the older man. When he looks back at me, tears mist my eyes. I clasp my hands in front of me, take a deep breath, and then respond with trembling voice. "It's marvelous beyond belief out there—the green grass, the blue sky all the way to the horizon, and the clear water in the streams. Deer, elk, wolves, bison, coyotes—they all thrive in the wild." I try to relate the emotions I felt when I saw those things for the first time, and tell him of the deep connection I felt with the animals, even though they were all new to me. I suspect my words will fill his dreams for years.

A young woman with a bun of reddish hair tries to move the kid away from the microphone, but he gets in one last question, "Weren't you scared being outside alone?"

I smile. "I think I was more overwhelmed at the size and openness of it all than frightened. The natural world is at peace with itself; the only thing that threatened me was my own lack of memory. I believe if I could go outside again with what I know now, I would feel safe and secure. Even more, I would relish every moment."

The remaining questions are more focused on available resources and the state of disrepair of commercial facilities than on the breathtaking splendor of the world outside. I suppose that's natural. Life inside the mountain is about survival and little else. Only on the outside are there other considerations. These people have no idea what they're missing. None have ever seen what I've experienced, and they aren't likely to either, unless the community brings forth some significant breakthroughs.

After they've exhausted their curiosity, I have a nagging question for them. "I hope you'll excuse a rather naive question, but why did you drop me in Montana for this test? Why not just throw me out the back door?"

An older man moves to the microphone. "There were a number of reasons, E12-B. Most importantly, we needed you to remain outside long enough to be fully infected, to ensure the defenses we built into you had time to kick in. You are right. We could have placed you in the parking lot outside our gate and posted a sign on the fingerprint reader telling you to try entry in six to eight weeks, but we also wanted to collect information on the state of the outside environment." The scientists all nod in unison before the one at the microphone continues. "You are our scout. Your body contains information on BHS and V5's buckyballs, and your mind is filled with information on the status of the world we might repopulate someday, assuming we succeed with our experiments."

I understand. I'm an experiment within an experiment, sent forth to collect both biological and environmental data for future generations.

When the scientists leave the room beyond the glass, E12-A returns. "Nice job, B. Do you have additional questions for me?"

E12-A's demeanor is so crisp and professional it's hard to believe she's my sister…and she's so darn cute I wish she weren't. I just grin. "Any chance you can join me for dinner?"

She places one hand on the glass with her palm toward me, and her eyes soften before she winks. "I'd like that, but my food will be better than yours."

* * * *

By the end of the month, the cut to remove my kidney and the leg I impaled crossing the plain are healing without infection. The scientists' initial wave of curiosity about the outside world has also subsided. Now it's just me, E12-A, and an occasional biopsy or other tissue removal.

Over time, I give sperm, am prodded by instruments, and am cut so many times that I lose count. It is hard for me to be taken apart piece by piece, but the medical team remains upbeat. The E384 seems to be mitigating the negative effects of my buckyballs, and I haven't developed any BHS symptoms. Despite that good news, caution will prevail. The first negative effects from V5 took many months to materialize. These researchers aren't rushing to judgment.

Assuming E384 continues to work over the long haul, and my body doesn't reject its living leucocyte organisms, the medical team will engineer human genes that can create the leucocytes without need of the serum. If such modifications are incorporated into a generation of people— made part of their DNA so immunity can be passed from generation to generation—then humans can again inhabit the earth. Engineering to accomplish that has been going on for some time. In fact, some artificial genes live within me now, within the stem cells used to create the E384 leucocytes.

Genome modification is a long and laborious process. It takes years to complete, but they've done it before. My apparent BHS immunity is a permanent part of my genome. Those modifications should pass to my children, assuming I can find a like-modified female and the two of us are permitted to have offspring. I mentally scoff at the thought. I imagine that before all of this, the decision to have children was up to us, not a room full of scientists.

I wish I had been born many years in the future, at a time when everyone's genome included BHS and V5 immunity. Then I could have a real life instead of the hell I live now. I have experienced the exhilarating freedom of being outside. Existing inside this mountain is not living at all. I dream of being out in the world again, to be back at my campfire cooking a fresh rabbit.

My mind constantly fills with escape plans, although I'd never act on them. Still, I observe the routines of the people and robotic devices around me, looking for weakness in the protocols. Perhaps it's just a game I play to keep my mind occupied between medical tests and procedures, a way to hold on to my sanity in this insane existence. I'm quite certain the man who volunteered for this job would never consider leaving, but he had no idea what he was giving up— he couldn't have. It's much easier to agree to forfeit your life when you have no concept of how much you might enjoy it.

The months pass slowly. I am thankful the scientists monitoring me have extended the interval between painful internal tests and tissue removal. That's a good thing because each time they take more tissue, my body rejects the surgical intrusion with greater intensity, as if it knows I'm being murdered in incremental steps. Perhaps I am dying, but I remain steadfast. I'll see this experiment through until it kills me; I'll be faithful to the video message I left for myself. Duty and service to others is much more than a slogan for the society in this mountain. Those concepts are a way of life here or, as in my case, a way of death.

Despite my desire to meet my own expectations, it is becoming increasingly difficult to accept my status as a terminally ill patient when I believe there is nothing inherently wrong with me. My declining strength and worsening general health have more to do with being imprisoned in isolation and being poisoned by various anesthetics than anything to do with V5 or BHS. Each surgical operation and tissue extraction brings another round of sickness, as if I'm being subjected to chemotherapy.

My attitude sours. I'm tired and depressed most of the time. I'm sick of feeling sick. My sister is the only bright spot in my life. She parks the motorized food tray against the glass wall between us, and we sit across from each other at every meal. I look forward to those times. There are no doctors present while we eat, and my pain lessens when she is near. Even when my appetite fails me and I can't eat, her uplifting spirit buoys mine. At other times, we play games through the glass. Backgammon and chess are our favorites. We also share a love of classical music, but she has no way to relate to the love of life that must have inspired such beautiful scores. Oh, how I wish I could walk with her through the plains of Montana. What an incredible gift that would be.

My allergic reaction to anesthetics continues to deepen, and my keepers are running out of alternatives. No one is immune to a steady diet of that poison. I've lived in a fishbowl for months on end and spent more time retching in the toilet than most people will during their entire lives. Most of the time, I look and feel like walking death; only E12-A keeps me going. She accepts me as I am, regardless of my state of spirit and wretched appearance. I dream of her often now, even during chemical-induced sleep—dreams I should not entertain. My heart rate increases, and I perspire when she comes near the glass. I know I should not feel as I do because she is my sister, but I am also a man. Her lithe body flits around in the adjacent room like a butterfly sampling nectar. She is beautiful and kind. It would be a wonderful thing to hold her in my arms, but I know that can never be.

As the months pass, it becomes clear to me that the only purpose of my life is to die in agony, and I begin to entertain ways to end it all. I know escape is out of the question, just as E12-A is out of the question. Sick and frustrated, I want to pass from this life into the peace beyond. All that holds me back is a desire to not disappoint E12-A.

During a bout of anesthetic rejection, after I've puked blood for over an hour, my spirit reaches a new and desperate low. My will to live fades, and I give up trying to survive this ordeal. I glance at E12-A. She is plastered against the glass wall with tears streaming down her face, as if she can read my mind. My life is a torment for both of us. I cannot go on. Bent over the toilet with dry heaves so bad I can barely catch a breath, I project a final thought to E12-A, even though I know she cannot hear my silent plea, *Please forgive me for my weakness—for what I am about to do.*

Blood splashes into the toilet bowl one more time from an intense stomach contraction, and I shake with painful convulsions as I gather the strength to plunge my face into the water. One final flush and a deep breath is all that stands between my life of pain and the end to my torment. I exhale my last breath as the bowl refills and lower my face into the water, focusing only on the little wren that sang to me so long ago. The water is cool, caressing my face in a grip of peace known only by the terminally ill in the last seconds of their life. There is resignation in that peace. It is over.

As I prepare to take my last deep gasp, welcoming the cool water into my lungs, warm hands grasp my shoulders and jerk me back from the brink. I cannot remember being touched—they must be the hands of an angel. In that instant, I know without question things will never be the same.

I'm not a religious man, but the comfort of being touched fills my soul with hope. My despair vanishes. Without the strength to stand, I bow my head as deep sobs rake my body. *Is this what dying is like? Did I take that last gasp of water? Is God real? Have I been saved?* If anyone ever needed saving, it's me and it's now.

Nothing I've known in life could have prepared me for the shock I experience next. The hands that help me stand turn me and then E12-A pulls me tight to her body. Her tears flow with mine while she chokes out, "There, there, B. Everything will be okay. I'll never let you leave me again."

We've grown close over the months, I in HAZMAT isolation and she on the other side of the glass, but I didn't expect this. She entered this room of horror to comfort me in my time of greatest need. In that moment, cradled in her arms, I discover the true meaning of love. I surrender to her completely as I melt into her embrace. She buries her face into my damp shirt as I kiss her softly on the head. The sweet smell of her hair tugs at memories buried deep in my mind, but I cannot resurrect them fully. Holding her seems right, and I relish it. Entwined in each other's arms, we continue to sob together, ignoring the Klaxon horns and rotating red lights in the room beyond the glass.

The alarms seem to grow more intense, jolting me from the awe of the moment. I push her back to arm's length with one hand while the other juts to my mouth. A sickening reflex of regret penetrates my heart as the horror of revelation stuns my mind. E12-A entered this room without protection, knowing it would end her life—my act of cowardice is my sister's death sentence. A sorrowful moan emanates from the bottom of my soul. "Oh, no. Not you. You can't be here!" Tears stream down my face. No one has ever survived BHS.

As the scientists outside my chamber scramble to determine if the protocol breach can be contained, E12-A pats my hand on her shoulder and smiles through her tears. "It's okay. I entered through multiple overpressure chambers. The others aren't in danger."

A crowd gathers in the area from which E12-A normally observes my every move. Each new arrival looks through the glass in abject horror. It has been a long time since anyone has witnessed death from BHS, and I assume the only good that can come from the current situation is a lesson for those looking in on us now. The excruciating passing of E12-A will be an example, a reminder that isolation procedures *must* be followed, no matter what an individual might feel.

E12-A must know she will die, but she doesn't seem to care. She pulls me close again and holds me tight, weeping with me as if the world on the other side of the glass doesn't exist. When she releases me, she looks up through welling tears. "We were killing you, torturing you with every new test. I just couldn't let it go on. I need you to live."

The reality of her being here, of what she's sacrificed, moves me to the point of not being able to speak. I can barely breathe—the feeling of being touched is overwhelming. I believe nothing could affect me more profoundly than this, but in the next moment I am proven wrong. E12-A takes my face in her hands, looks me in the eyes, and then places her lips on mine. It is a long, passionate kiss—not a sister to a brother kiss, but like one lover to another. I am stunned and captivated by her outpouring of love and, without thinking, return her kiss with all the passion my sick body can muster. As she prolongs the kiss, a war erupts in my mind. Part of me is screaming, *This is wrong on so many levels,* but another part whispers in a voice I can barely hear, *This is as it was meant to be.*

Despite my weak condition, kissing her seems natural, like I've done it many times in the past. I breathe in the smell of her cheek and open my heart as her love fills voids in my soul with utter bliss. In that moment, another distant memory stabs my mind. I pull back and gasp. My eyes widen as I hold her shoulders and stare into her eyes.

My God, I remember! E12-A and I are lovers.

Before conception, she and I shared a common womb. We have the same birth mother, but before our donor DNA came together *in vitro*, the computer had genetically paired us. E12-A isn't my biological sister; she's my womb sister, my life mate. Understanding floods my mind as I caress her with overwhelming joy. I bring the side of her face against mine and whisper, "I remember now, darling. I remember you."

Her tears continue until what I've said registers. She breaks my hold and steps back as a puzzled look crosses her face. Over the din of alarms, she responds in raised voice, "You remember? Everything?"

I pull her close once again. "Maybe not everything, but I remember you. I remember we were once together. Why didn't you tell me?"

She cradles my face in her hands as she suppresses her sobs. "I've so much to tell you, B, so much to explain."

When she settles down, she leads me back to my bed and lays my shaking body on the crisp white sheet. She sits beside me and strokes my face while taking deep breaths to control her sporadic sobs. I can't begin to describe the look of love on her face. Before she speaks again, she looks into the room beyond, points to the Klaxon alarm, and then draws her index finger across her throat. The alarms fall silent as she returns her attention to me.

"You and I are 'Experimentals,' dear, part of a genetic modification project that began long before we were conceived. We have the same DNA modifications but different V5 serums. Your E384 put you in a coma for about a month and damaged your memories. Because of your convulsions, I received E385, a less polar version that didn't harm me like E384 did you. I'm your control group, a tissue comparison against yours during testing, as well as after your death."

I am bewildered. "But why not tell me about us?"

She strokes my face with the back of her index finger. "My darling, weren't you suffering enough? Would it have eased your agony to know you could never again touch the one you loved? You volunteered to leave this facility so I wouldn't have to, knowing we would never be together again. You returned unable to remember the love you left behind. I considered that a blessing. How could it help you to know how much I suffered watching you die? You sacrificed your life for me—I could do no less than remain silent for you."

The depth of her love overwhelms me, but my mind can't dwell there, not now. "When you say we both have the same DNA modifications, does that mean you have BHS immunity too, at least as much as me?"

She nods while holding my hand to her heart. "I think so, and V5 immunity as well. We've both been genetically engineered, identically prepared for this experiment. I'm Experimental 12-A. You are Experimental 12-B."

Oh, my God. We're two of a kind. The video said I *am* the experiment, but it did not say I had a partner. A glimmer of self-doubt slips into my mind, probably a leftover from the altruistic guy who volunteered for this experiment. "By coming together now, have we failed our people? Have we ruined the experiment?"

"The experiment isn't ruined, dear, but it will change. There is no choice now. We'll test the natural passing of BHS and V5 immunity to our children, something that has been hypothesized but never tried. Our children should receive E385 leucocytes through my placenta and amniotic fluid, so they'll be the only experiment that matters. The original experiment would've eventually gone there anyway, but using your sperm and my eggs in a controlled environment. That's the reason I've never been tasked to carry *in vitro* fertilized eggs, so my body would be completely natural—an unaltered landscape without antibody feedback from other children I might have produced."

She holds up her rectangular plastic access card. "Your descriptions of the outside world have stoked a fire in my imagination for months, dear, and I have planned for this moment. This is our pass to the outside if you're strong enough to use it."

It's amazing how little strength a person wields when he has everything to die for, and how much he can muster when he has everything to live for. I sit up, stand erect, and take E12-A's arm in my trembling hand. In the next moment, we enter the first overpressure chamber and exit away from the lab. I am weak, but she pulls me faster than my keepers can override the doors leading to the outside. She prepared our escape route well. She knows the maze of overpressure chambers by heart, and her card takes us through three more before I recognize the one I entered so many months ago. In a heartbeat, we step outside and walk toward my waiting truck.

I relish the sweet mountain air and welcome the sun's warmth on my ashen face. I take a deep breath and smile at my darling walking beside me. Being outside with the love of my life is an answer to a prayer—a dream come true. I walk with slow, measured paces in a euphoric state I have never known. The relief of having my death sentence commuted, the sheer joy of being free, and the warmth of my love's hand in mine makes me want to shout. I contain myself. There is no need to hurry. No one would dare come after us without a HAZMAT suit. It takes time to put one on, and no one would pursue us without one. No one would take that risk.

* * * *

As we leave the main gate and drive through the swath of fallen trees toward Colorado Springs, I glance over at my love. She has a death grip on my hand, and her arm is trembling. She slowly shakes her head. "It's one thing to dream about this; quite another to do it. I've never stared death in the face before, yet BHS is all around me."

I am certain she is experiencing an incredible mix of fear and unbridled awe. I feel it, too. The sky, the trees, the sun, and the smell of the outdoors—everything is new to her.

Tears slip down her cheeks. "In time, my research partners will understand. If you and I survive, they will come to see the logic of this. They will know the reasons we had to leave."

I'm frightened too, but we are free. I lift her hand and kiss the back of it. "We haven't left them, dear. We will give them time to settle down—time to adjust. Then, we'll come back to explain."

She smiles through her tears. "Those who came before us didn't consider their imprisonment in the mountain the end, my love, but the beginning. The environment could not survive the overpopulation it faced. In the long run, to save any of us, everyone had to die. The planet needed time to heal. The original people sequestered in the mountain were the survivors, planted in the womb of the earth, and we've been reborn from their sacrifice into the magnificent world all around us."

She looks out the window and takes everything in with wide eyes. I wonder what must be going through her head. The world outside is so different from the world in which we were created. Without looking away from the scenery she whispers, "Inside the mountain we had to live together without harming what little space we had. That's what we've been doing for the past sixty-two years. We've been in training, learning to live together in harmony with each other and Earth. Our people had to make a life and death choice. They chose life. You and I face the same choice now, although our domain is larger. We will start over, and we will take care of Earth as it takes care of us."

We will stay in Colorado Springs tonight and return to Cheyenne Mountain tomorrow. Our freedom only means we can live unprotected in the open. We've been given a great gift, and we'll use that gift to work the farms that provide food for our people. We'll fill two agricultural slots so two of our brethren won't have to live in isolation for the remainder of their lives, risking certain death from a tiny tear in a pressure suit.

My eyes mist as I glance at E12-A. "You'll have to adjust to hard labor now—as a farm worker. No one in our community is an individual. No one is alone."

She nods as she continues to absorb the vibrant beauty along the road. "I welcome it."

A decaying variety store provides shelter as the sunlight gives way to darkness. After searching the store's inventory for soft bedding material, we barricade a store room's entrance with metal shelving. Still, animal sounds penetrate the darkness. E12-A shudders as I pull her close. It's not just fear she's experiencing. Cheyenne Mountain provided years of security, but it did not provide intimacy. Here, alone in the dark, E12-A's breathing becomes ragged as she presses her body to mine and gives me passionate kisses over my chest and neck.

We have been lovers for years, but intimate contact was forbidden for fear of contaminating the experiment. Now, in incredible moments of tenderness, I discover for myself that fatigue and residual sickness can be overcome by other needs. The warmth of E12-A's body and the sensation of her touch propel us to a place of peace and serenity neither of us has ever known, and we soon drift off to sleep joined as tightly physically as we are emotionally. Once again we have broken the protocol of the experiment. We do not care.

We have taken the first step toward producing children the natural way, a process far more satisfying than *in vitro* fertilization. Nothing will ever be the same again. We have been exposed. We could not return to our former lives even if we wanted to. However, we know we cannot leave the mountain either. If we successfully produce offspring, their mates must come from inside just as we did—genetically-engineered to tolerate BHS and inoculated to survive V5.

The experiment that brought us life will now continue through us but with far greater consequences. Our children will be the final experiment. They will be the ultimate proof that genetically-engineered modifications to combat BHS and V5's buckyballs can pass naturally from parents to children. Our children will prove that reclaiming Earth is within our grasp.

We return to Cheyenne Mountain the following day knowing we must dedicate our lives to those inside or waste our lives completely. Our ancestors were the beginning of understanding. They taught us to live inside; they understood we all must work together or our species won't survive.

We are overjoyed to find our community has anticipated our return. A note attached to the door where we exited directs us to a dome structure near a soybean field. There we find instruction for the care and harvesting of that crop. We welcome the labor. We are also thankful there are no recriminations for our willful act of disobedience to achieve our freedom. I believe there will now be great pressure on our leaders to allow other engineered individuals to leave the mountain. In time a community will develop around us. After consulting with E12-A, I name our new habitat and the area around it "Salvation."

Although crop care and farming were not our fields of study while we were sequestered, we are thankful others worked these issues for years. The soybeans that surround us now are not like the originals. These beans are genetically modified to thwart crop destroyers like the bean leaf beetle, soybean aphid, soybean leafminer, green cloverworm, alfalfa caterpillar, cabbage looper, yellow woolybear, painted lady, and longhorned weevils. Once again we have reason to celebrate our geneticists. Our survival as genetically-modified humans is dependent on our genetically-modified crops.

Over time our labor in the fields becomes routine. E12-A and I enjoy minding the plants and watching the natural growth of everything surrounding us. Being in the sunshine and fresh mountain air revives us daily, and we look forward to whatever tasks our monitors inside assign to us. I have become proficient at rabbit trapping. Dead rabbits are both tasty and less of a threat to our crops.

In three months, it is clear E12-A is also growing a crop of her own, and our monitors are ecstatic to celebrate her pregnancy with us. After sonograms confirm the baby is female, we name her Beth. In the old world, the name was a shortened version of "Elizabeth," which has the ancient meaning of "pledged to God." Religion is frowned on in our society, but it is difficult to live in this bountiful world without acknowledging that a power greater than us might exist. Besides, E12-A likes the sound of the name. She also refuses to allow the programmers in the mountain to assign the number "1" to our baby.

Even without such a designation, I am certain they will find a way to track every detail of our baby's life, especially where her genetics are concerned. For many generations, the genetics of every individual outside the mountain will need to be tracked just as they are inside. Developing enough people with our immunities and sufficient genetic diversity to sustain the human race will be a slow process, but it will happen over time.

The subsequent birth of our baby was a time of great joy for our entire community—the first naturally conceived and birthed baby in nearly 65 years. To celebrate that event, two additional people were released from the mountain to serve beside us in planting, servicing, and harvesting crops. The slow repopulation of Earth has begun.

It is clear to me that many skills in addition to farming will soon be required in Salvation. As our children develop, they will need schooling. Interactive classrooms will be needed so the knowledge of the best and brightest within the mountain can be passed to those on the outside. Medical people will need to be trained, and facilities built where they can carry on their work. The tasks facing our society are enormous, but every soul knows whatever it takes will be worth it. One need only look around at the beauty of this place to understand any amount of effort is justified to be here. The curse of those who remain inside is to endure that enclosed space where our toxic environment cannot reach them.

As E12-A and I age, we watch many miracles come to pass—our first grandchild, the first hospital in Salvation, the first school, the first interactive library—all the firsts that lead to a functional society. Our family soon included five children, and each one became a contributing part of our developing society.

Life was good until E12-A passed. That was also a first of sorts. While we existed in the mountain, the elderly were encouraged to self-terminate when they could no longer serve the needs of the community—only productive people were allowed to exist in the limited space available. As E12-A grew infirm, that option was out of the question. The community revered her as did I, and her passing was a time of mourning for the entire village inside and outside the mountain.

I spoke on behalf of the community before we committed E12-A to the soil. "The life of E12-A will continue to teach those who come after us. Her example carries the fundamentals of our existence inside the mountain to our new life on the outside. She will be remembered forever among our people, not as the courageous Experimental who risked her life to prove we were ready to venture outside, but as the woman who ensured all future generations live in harmony outside as we lived inside. She lived what she taught—that we must be one with each other and Earth, or we won't survive."

I stepped from the podium knowing many generations would follow in my footsteps and those of E12-

A. My only wish is that I could look into the future to see what great things time has in store for our society.

Before she passed at age seventy-eight, E12-A and I enjoyed many pleasures. Our favorite was the graduation ceremonies when our children passed from childhood to adulthood. Our children accepted their computer-assigned tasks with dignity. The day they received their work assignments became known as The Day of Posting—the day the computers output what careers new graduates would pursue for the remainder of their lives. Our community also made that day part of our yearly Freedom Festival, commemorating the time E12-A and I made our escape from Cheyenne Mountain. Celebrations such as these would have been unthinkably frivolous inside the mountain, but they are natural outside. They are part of the difference between our society inside and our society outside the mountain.

I look back over my life with great satisfaction. Great grandchildren often visit and my children ensure I want for nothing. My memories are rich and vivid, and E12-A lives within them as the beautiful and loving wife she was when she saved my life. Neither of us could have foreseen what changes we would precipitate in our society. The town of Salvation is thriving. Most newcomers are natural births now, although some *in vitro* individuals still enrich our genetic pool. That will end soon. There is talk of opening the mountain to outsiders after all those with immune deficiencies have passed away. Our underground home for so many years will become a protected vault where the accumulated knowledge of our society will reside.

On my ninety-third birthday, I lie on my deathbed with my children, grandchildren, and great grandchildren at my side. Just as E12-A and I named one of our children "Beth," our family has continued that tradition. Three female children of that name comfort me now. Breathing is difficult, my vision is fading, and my last thought is of E12-A pulling me from the toilet basin so many years ago, and, as I take my last breath, I can feel her warm arms embrace me once again.

Part 2: The Perilous Journey

Chapter Six
The Day of Posting

My induction into adulthood is finally here—the Day of Posting, the most important day of my life. I've followed our community's strict rules for growing up. I've met my assigned responsibilities and studied hard, the main requirements to be posted with my peers. Basic training's rules and regulations are too regimented to permit much experimentation, so those of us who made it through have had precious little time to learn about life apart from the protective cocoon of our family and school.

That will all change now.

Today's posting marks the beginning of Salvation's 121st Freedom Festival. We celebrate the time when the first genetically-engineered people walked away from Cheyenne Mountain, and we give thanks for those who endured sixty-two years inside so we could be free. The first two Experimentals who overcame the biological toxins that killed our world and survived outside the mountain are our founding Mother and Father. They established the town of Salvation at the base of the mountain. Far more important than any of us being posted today, they are the real reason the whole town turns out for this spectacle.

Don't get me wrong. I love what the Freedom Festival stands for. I just wish the Day of Posting could be less public. As it is, our whole community watches as some of my classmates receive their assignments in tears, while others react with extreme joy, literally dancing off the stage. I fear I might be one of the former.

Only thirty-five students completed basic training this spring, and I now inch ahead with the others, waiting for what might be my greatest embarrassment ever. My eighteen years, two months, and five days haven't provided much opportunity for comparison, but I'm terrified of what might be posted on the freshly painted wall ahead, the packet that could change my life forever. I bite my nails and fan my face as I shuffle forward. As I spit a nail fragment to the ground, I catch a glimpse of my mother out of the corner of my eye. She isn't frowning at me for chewing my nails as she normally would. She's proud I'm here, even if I have ragged fingernails.

Not knowing how my classmates did on their performance exams, I can't tell if "You reap what you sow" applies to those who sob openly as they leave the stage. I'll have to wait my turn to find out. I studied hard to reach this day, this moment, but I don't know if my scores are good enough to allow me to stay in Salvation. I've lived here since I was born and don't want to leave, but class placement determines everything. I did my best. I never held back. That should weigh in my favor. Soon it will be my turn. I press my knees tightly together. Why do girls have such small bladders? I run nervous fingers through my hair. I need to pee.

Salvation is the capitol of the Federation of Colonies, the center of all efforts to repopulate Earth. More than anyplace else, it epitomizes our directive to live in harmony with nature. Crystal clear air surrounds the city, and the fragrance of spring flowers permeates its thoroughfares. Today is especially beautiful, belying the seriousness of this ceremony. It's as if nature itself is offering a new beginning, like it knows what's in the packets ahead.

Salvation swelled from just two to over ten thousand during the past 121 years. The fifty or so women of child-bearing age sequestered in Cheyenne Mountain were required to carry twins with the same genetic modifications as the original two survivors. Those women produced over two hundred babies in the first four years. Twenty years later, those two hundred begot nearly eight hundred, in addition to children born to women who couldn't leave the mountain.

It wasn't long before the geometrical expansion of our new population set in, but even with women inside and outside contributing to our growth, some of the outer colonies are still very small, with populations of less than a few hundred people. I can't imagine what life would be like in such places. I desperately hope I'm not about to find out. You hear things but never really know what's true. My best friend in year nine, Frankie Watley, was banished to one.

Frankie didn't study much and didn't follow the rules, so they sent him to an outer colony collective farm. I haven't heard from him since. Despite the seriousness of his situation, I still snicker at the memory of his antics. I suspect a colony populated by a few hundred like him would be chaos, but I know the authorities wouldn't allow that. If Frankie continued to screw up, he would've been sterilized and paired with a similar mate.

I count the heads in front of me again, perhaps for the hundredth time—ten, all with owners as nervous as me.

I take in the natural beauty surrounding the ceremony, inhale the sweet mountain air, and then exhale a deep sigh. It's so beautiful outside; I can't imagine what it must have been like for our forefathers to be locked inside Cheyenne Mountain for so long. With such a memory still fresh in our cultural, it's no wonder my training to reach this point has been so severe. Everyone must be productive. Foolishness isn't permitted.

New leaves are appearing on the aspens, and patches of snow still dot the northern foothills. I love the outdoors, especially in spring. I'd give almost anything to be on Mount Cole right now rather than standing in this line. I close my eyes and imagine myself sitting alone on a ledge overlooking the birds and valleys below. I want to linger in my imagination, but the student behind me nudges me forward.

For those who put in the physical and mental effort to survive twelve years of basic training, the packets posted ahead contain our life assignments. The directives inside those packets will define the remainder of our lives. Just six students precede me now, and then I will exchange the certainty of youth for the uncertainty of adulthood.

Mother and my local relatives are already clustered around the stage exit. They must be as apprehensive as I am. There is an element of history packed into this moment, as if I didn't have enough pressure without it. Generations ago my great-great-great-great-whatever grandmother approached this same wall for the same purpose I do now. She was my namesake, the first child of natural birth in Salvation. I wonder if she was as nervous then as I am now.

While I'd hate to screw up generations of successful people with a huge black mark, I doubt I could have done more to prepare for this moment. I put everything I had into it, but some things were out of my control, like heredity. Being far too important to be left to individuals, mate selection is rigidly controlled by the Federation's computers based on my own genealogy and that of my selected mate. The packet ahead will identify him—the male I'll be paired with. It's that simple. We are what our past has made us from a genetic perspective, and nothing can change that.

Proper mate assignments are vital to reestablishing humanity on Earth, but work assignment is more interesting to me. Other than laborers like Frankie, there are two basic work categories—technical and practical, each with hundreds of subcategories. I desperately hope for a technical appointment, but an assignment in either category will mark the beginning of my education, not the end. The only difference is where training will take place. A technical slot will almost guarantee I'll stay in Salvation, the center of all Federation knowledge, but who knows where I'll end up if I'm issued a practical badge.

I'm up next. I tell myself to remain cool and steady, but my breathing is quick and shallow. My legs tremble, and sweat breaks out along my brow as *Beth Gooding* flashes on the wall's prominent LED display. This is it. The wall beckons. My life will either unfold before me now or completely unravel.

I retrieve my packet from its posted location and walk toward my assigned counselor. She's dressed in black and has a very large nose, like a medieval witch. When I reach for the chair opposite the table from her, she smiles like an executioner who really enjoys her job. The wooden chair screeches as I pull it from beneath the table, causing her to grimace. I offer a sincere smile and greet her with a cordial bow as I take my seat. "Good morning, Mrs. Hathaway."

She responds in flat monotone, "Good morning, Beth. Some instructors believed this day would never come for you, so it's especially good to see you here. After you look over your assignments, I'll be happy to answer any questions you might have."

Mrs. Hathaway is an imposing woman in her early sixties. I'm quite certain her square jaw and bulky figure would have left her celibate in the Old World, but times have changed. It's no longer important what form genes take on the outside. She is strong and committed to our culture, as is her husband, and her children are like tanks.

I continue smiling like a proper young lady, trying not to expose my true inner thoughts. I didn't get in trouble all that often, but Mrs. Hathaway obviously hasn't forgotten the incident with the toilet paper. Despite my repeated assurances that it wasn't personal, she believed it was and has never forgiven me. She might be right. Maybe it *was* personal.

Sitting down doesn't ease my nervousness. My spastic hands shake uncontrollably as I attempt to open the package by sliding a finger along its glued edge. The stiff envelope resists, cutting into my skin with a vengeful paper cut. I jerk back with an awkward spasm and spill the envelope's contents onto the table. Mrs. Hathaway's scowl deepens. I shrug and grin before crunching the papers back into some semblance of order.

Mrs. Hathaway crosses her arms and raises one ragged eyebrow in a disapproving glare. "Why don't we begin with job placement, Beth—the crumpled yellow paper at mid-stack?"

"Yes, ma'am. A good place to start." I pull the rumpled paper from the stack and swallow hard as I read my assignment. Shock hits me with such force I can barely gasp, "Oh, crap—Cultural Anthropologist."

Mrs. Hathaway's face lights up, and she attempts to put a positive spin on my assignment with rising enthusiasm and an elevated, squeaky voice. "That's wonderful, Beth—a potential technical position. Training for most anthropological subcategories is conducted in the colonies, so you might get to see some wonderful new places."

Good grief, she's already excited I might be leaving town. Despite the name, a Cultural Anthropologist assignment could go either way—technical or practical. Everything depends on the subcategory. Unfortunately, most classifications in that category are practical. I wonder if she'd be so excited if I shoved my career assignment down her throat. Figuratively, of course.

I can't hide my disappointment and sigh aloud. "It's not what I expected. Don't Cultural Anthropologists mine garbage dumps while looking for restorable Old World technology?"

Through a forced smile, she answers, "Oh, no, dear. They do much more than that. Only a few actually work dump sites, although I'm sure you'll get that opportunity during your internship." She pauses to smirk, clearly pleased by my impending stint working in an ancient landfill at some remote location. She then adds in dry monotone, "But what's your subcategory?"

I look away from her evil grin and read further down the page, expecting to see some subcategory like "Diesel

Mechanic," "Welder," or "Body and Paint"—any of the skills needed to bring useful items from the ruins of the Old World into our world. When I locate the subcategory, I am stunned by what's printed there. "Linguist?"

Mrs. Hathaway's grin evaporates when she hears the word. She pulls her head back, and her mouth puckers. "Huh. That's a new one. Let me see that."

She takes the wrinkled job placement order and irons it with her hand before reading every word, even going through the fine print on the back. "In all my years, this is the first subcategory I've seen like that." Her executioner-like smile returns as she passes the paper back to me. "Your assignment is probably a good sign, an indication the colonies have finally reached a population level where frivolous studies are permitted. At least it's a technical position, although your training will take place in Hope."

I gasp, and my mouth drops open. *Hope!* I flip the paper over, wanting her to be wrong with every cell in my body, but she is right. Hope—the eastern-most colony in the Federation. The colony is so far away and so difficult to get to I might never get back. Mother will be devastated. To her, my assignment will be like losing another daughter, the same as when my sister died three years ago. Try as I might, I can't stop tears from slipping down my cheeks. I feel sick.

Mrs. Hathaway seems genuinely moved and tries to comfort me, or maybe she's just a good actor. "There, there, Beth. It's not the end of the world, and it could be an exciting opportunity. According to your paperwork, your mentor is a Cultural Archeologist with a Ph.D. and is already onsite doing field work. That sounds exciting, although there's no mention of his subcategory. Everything will be new for you. You'll be the trailblazer you've always wanted to be."

I glance at my parents out of the corner of my eye. Mother has covered her mouth with her hand, and Dad is embracing her, holding back his own tears. They can tell from my reaction the news isn't good. Even my rowdy cousins have fallen silent. Anger replaces deflation, and I fight to hold back the turmoil inside me. I turn my glare toward Mrs. Hathaway. "I wanted to be a trailblazer in the literal sense. I wanted something in the Forest Service, something in these mountains." I shuffle through the papers, looking for my next disappointment. "Let's see what else the Grim Reaper has in store for me."

I suspect Mrs. Hathaway is laughing on the inside, even though I didn't use *that* much toilet paper to fill her car. She pats me on the arm, still feigning sympathy like a good counselor. "It's the blue one, dear—your mate selection form."

I pull the blue sheet from the wad and smooth it with my hand, as much to mock Mrs. Hathaway as anything else. I'm not too surprised by what it says. "His name is James David Myle, a sixth generation like me, but there's no additional information. Not even a picture. I guess I'll meet him in Hope at the training center." I beseech Mrs. Hathaway's eyes with my own, although I know she can't explain my assignment and couldn't do anything about it even if she wanted to, which she probably doesn't. "Where did this assignment come from anyway? Why me?"

She looks truly sympathetic. Maybe I've misjudged her. "I don't know, Beth. Yours is the first assignment like that awarded in Salvation. I can only assume there must be a reason. There's a reason for everything. Survival is hard. Sometimes rebuilding requires sacrifice."

She's right. People wouldn't live like we do unless there was a damn good reason. I return to the blue form, reading my child-bearing assignments and expected delivery dates as Mrs. Hathaway scoots up to the edge of her chair, waiting for me to tell her the result. "Looks like I'll have four children—three female and one male. The outer colonies must be getting out of balance with too many males."

I feel a flash of heat on my cheeks, never having verbalized anything about having children. To be confronted with that requirement in black and white while an adult looks on is a bit of a shock. There is no societal stigma associated with being paired or anything like that—quite the opposite. The government now considers my mate and I married, or at least they will when we accept the assignment by consummating it…and it is our duty to accept. Like any teen girl, I have fantasized about the process for years, but not in terms of actual babies resulting from it. My internal curiosity is one thing, but the state's demand for actual consummation is quite another. The thought makes me shiver all over.

Mrs. Hathaway sighs and slowly shakes her head. If she notices my blush, she ignores it. "I've heard the distant colonies are pretty uncivilized. Not a good place for a young lady. Some of the girls in the last class chose local labor camps and farm cooperatives rather than accepting assignments there. That's an option for you too, Beth, until you get on the bus. After that, there's no turning back."

It's probably my imagination, but Mrs. Hathaway seems genuinely sorry about my assignments. Nevertheless, I don't like the alternative. I know farms and labor camps are honorable and vital to the survival of our culture, but I've worked too damn hard to get a technical assignment to throw it away now just to stay close to home.

The rest of my package is pretty bland—badges and authorizations needed for travel, lodging certificates along the way and in Hope, letters of introduction, and summaries of past achievement scores. I know what must be done. I understand my duty, but breaking the news to my family will be hard.

I politely thank Mrs. Hathaway for her time, although she hasn't helped all that much, and head for the stage exit where Mother is already gushing tears. As we cry together in a death hug, Dad softly whispers, "How bad is it, pumpkin?"

I can barely choke out a response. "As bad as it gets, Dad. I'm being sent to the frontier...to dig up the past in Hope."

Chapter Seven
Goodbye, Salvation

As my family and I walk in silence from the school to our house, I can hear a morbid funeral dirge playing in my mind. Dad and Mom alternately stare at my work assignment sheet and weep. Mother breaks out into a bawl as we round the final corner on the street leading to our house. My cousins trail behind, and I hear Tommy whisper, "Boy, she must have really screwed the pooch."

Before leaving for the Day of Posting ritual, Mother set out cakes and pies in anticipation of a graduation celebration. Now, the colorful paper decorations seem as out of place as the bright blue napkins. My relatives sit around in silent gloom, munching goodies like they would at a wake. I have no one to blame but myself. I tried hard to succeed in school. I thought I did well enough to stay in Salvation, but I guess I failed. Even so, I never considered I'd earn such a rotten assignment.

I scan the room full of sad faces. This is a lot like the gathering after my sister died, except only Mom provided food this time.

I pace near the stairs leading to my room, trying to be polite by staying at the gathering, but I am itchy to start preparing for the long trip to Hope. Two weeks. That's all I've got. Two weeks until the bus takes me away from my family, friends, and home—perhaps forever.

A tear slips from my eye as I catch a glimpse of Aunt Mary hugging Mom. Both are crying. I remember similar hugs when Jenna died. We are a close-knit family. When one suffers, we all suffer. Mom knows where Hope is—what my assignment means. She knows she probably will never see me again after I leave Salvation. I walk over and join the hug. "Come on now. I'm still here. Besides, I'll be able to talk with you guys by email."

Mother's voice catches twice as her reddened eyes beseech mine. "Will you? Do they even have email in Hope?"

I hang my head. "I don't know, Mom." We all hug again.

My family is hurting. I am hurting. I don't understand why the central computers assigned a subcategory of Linguist or why I must go to Hope. My assignment just doesn't make sense. I wonder if it's all just a typo. Maybe they meant "Linotypist." That would make more sense. Maybe I'll be restoring old newspaper equipment.

When our guests leave, I rush upstairs to my computer, anxious to read about the frontier. My initial search zeros in on the historical journal written by the first Experimentals. Their words speak to my soul:

> Surrounded by death, we begin our new life together. Our first night of freedom will last only twelve hours, but before we can enjoy each other, we must prepare for the night. Of utmost concern is security, so we gather materials to enclose ourselves in the back room of a decaying variety store. People don't exist here, but marauding wolf packs, pumas, and bears frequent these ruins. We'd be easy prey without precautions.

> I set out my small animal traps and bring in undamaged supplies from the truck. In retrospect, coming here may not have been such a good idea. Cheyenne Mountain's outbuildings are far better protected than anything in Colorado Springs, but we didn't think about that when we made our escape. We ran to save me from a life of painful medical experimentation and almost certain death. We're here now, and we'll make the best of it.

E12-A's agitation rises as the sun begins to set. She's never spent a night above ground, never been outside. The animal sounds piercing the darkness frighten her. She treats my wounds and gives me a vitamin shot, but what I really need is sleep.

Their journal describes incredible adversity but also deep love and commitment to each other and their community. That was all they needed to survive. Will my life be like that now? Will my husband-to-be love me like E12-A loved E12-B? Even more, will I be able to offer my life for his, if it comes to that, like E12-A did?

It takes several days for the cheerlessness of my graduation party to dissipate. I spend the time researching Hope, trying to find out what I can expect. There isn't much in the archives—just that the colony was established on the extreme East Coast as a fishing village. It is also the location from which salvage operations on Old World Boston are conducted. I grimace. I suspect that's what I'll be doing; that's what Cultural Anthropologists do. I can picture myself filthy from head to toe as I rummage through the old ruins like a sewer rat, trying to find anything that can be salvaged, restored, and used productively in the New World. Gag me with a screwdriver. I'm so excited I could barf.

Life on the frontier will be very different from what I've known in Salvation. Our colonies have spread over thousands of miles during the past 121 years, but the outer settlements are primitive. Hope will be like that—primitive. It lies at the edge of the great Atlantic Ocean—a vast expanse I can scarcely imagine. I tremble just thinking about it and delve again into my survival texts.

Survival training was mandatory throughout my twelve years of basic study—shelter building, fire starting, trapping, foraging, basic tool making, first aid, leather working—skills needed to survive in a primitive colony environment. Much of that teaching seemed a carry-over from a time when there were far fewer people than there are now. Living in Salvation, I didn't think that training important at the time, but I believe it might be vital now. I wish I had studied more and practiced my lessons while I had the opportunity. Now, it will be trial by fire—there are few people in Hope.

My job classification still troubles me. As far as I can tell, Cultural Anthropologists are assigned functions ranging from extending the knowledge base of our civilization to repairing and restoring refrigerators. Some of those functions, like resurrecting industrial processes that were not openly documented, are quite technical—things like implementing proprietary chip etching techniques and rediscovering secret military advancements. The people who get those assignments also develop experiments to recreate and improve on the technology used in the past.

Job classifications are determined by the needs of the community, things like plumbing, electrical, medical, oil creation and extraction, computer science, chemistry, and genetic research. The list is long, and the jobs are all necessary. Linguist, however, is a new classification with little definition and no job description at all. How can a linguist contribute to the community or the repopulation of Earth?

Maybe it's like Mrs. Hathaway said—frivolous.

There isn't much to pack for the long bus ride east. Books aren't necessary because I'll have wireless access to the online libraries in Cheyenne Mountain—the storehouse for all knowledge, including the digitized version of the Old World Library of Congress. Food is provided at stops along the way, and only two service uniforms, a hairbrush, and a toothbrush are allowed in my laptop bag along with one small optional item—a journal with pictures of my family inserted inside the front cover.

I remove the picture with Jenna near the center of our family, hold it close to my heart, and mumble, "I wish you were here, big sister." Tears fill my eyes. Three years is not much time to forget such a vibrant life and mourn the loss of such great potential. The picture was taken by a fellow hiker at a happier time. Mom, Dad, Jenna, and I were hiking in the mountains. Jenna loved being at high altitude, just as I do. We all held hands while pretending to jump together off a large bolder. I place the picture over my heart once again. *I miss you, Jenna.*

Mother was not the same after Jenna died. The depression lasted almost eighteen months before she began to act normal again. Dad was more resilient, and I grew quite close to him as Mom grew more distant. The past year has been much better. Mom has come out of her funk. She finally accepted the loss of Jenna as Dad and I did much earlier. I hope my departure doesn't send her back into her world of darkness again.

While I worry about a setback for Mother, I know I must accept the hand I've been dealt. My friends agree, even though we might never see each other again. I will especially miss Ruby—my partner in crime. She secured the toilet paper we put in Mrs. Hathaway's car, but she was on the opposite side when I was nabbed. We still laugh about how she hunkered down in the poison sumac while I got hauled off by my ear. I will miss my friends as much as I miss Jenna.

I will document my journey manually as well as electronically. Those who follow in my footsteps will have the benefit of my thoughts just as I've had the benefit of the thoughts and experiences of those who preceded me. The paper journal is a backup. I shouldn't be out of wireless range, at least I hope not. The expansion of our colonies always follows wireless access. That's a mandatory requirement, so we can all learn from the exploits of our settlers.

Every colony is carefully planned by advance crews who establish roads, communications, and essential infrastructure before settlers are allowed in. Older communities support new colonies with commodities and services until the new ones become self-sufficient. Everyone contributes to expansion, but how a linguist fits in at the outer edge of civilization remains a nagging question. Even more, what advanced training could they possibly have in Hope that I can't get in Salvation?

I have only one mandatory stop before leaving the only life I've ever known—the infirmary. A complete physical and a couple of tattoo barcodes are required for anyone going to the outer colonies—something to identify a dead body in the worst of circumstances. One barcode will be placed on the outside of my left foot and one on the wrist of my right hand. I'll forever be marked as a settler. I'm not happy about the tattoos but accept them as a basic requirement. There's a stigma associated with them in some rungs of our society, as if the "settler marks" make their bearers inferior to those lucky enough to live their lives surrounded by the comforts of civilization.

I check the contents of my computer bag one last time on the eve of my departure. My eyes feel swollen from all the goodbye tears downstairs. Even my male cousins broke down this time, except Tommy. What a dork.

I take a deep breath as I lie down on my bed, perhaps for the last time. Sobs shake my body as I bury my face in my soft and comforting pillow. I am so frustrated, I could scream. I don't even know if they have pillows in Hope.

* * * *

The bus to the outer eastern colonies waits patiently while I say a final goodbye to my extended family. Thunder peals against the mountains and reverberates through the pouring rain. Without question, the mood on the departure platform and the weather are in synch. My uncles, aunts, cousins, and father hug me. Mother continues to hold onto my hand until the last moment and then whimpers as I break her hold and step aboard. I don't have the strength to look back. The tears streaming down my face would just make my leaving worse for everyone. Reporting for my assignment is my duty to the community. We all know there is little choice, so I mentally force my feet up each step leading to the interior of the bus.

The bus driver looks only slightly older than I do. He ignores my tears and smiles as I reach the top step. "Access card, please."

I hand him the badge from my packet, and he places it on the scanner. As he waits for the approval light on the panel to flash green, he asks, "First time to the outer colonies?"

The name on his service badge is Edward Bole, but I'm still too choked up to address him directly and just nod. He nods back and points to a flat panel adjacent to his badge scanner. "Please place your hand on the palm reader, and we'll have you settled in no time."

I comply, and his console emits a soft beep. He winks like a much older man might, like a father, or maybe even a grandfather, trying to comfort me. He's probably seen hundreds like me pass through the door of this bus. "You're in seat 5B. I'll make sure you don't miss any meals."

I'm the last to board. Edward closes the door behind me. As I take my seat, the bus lurches forward into the downpour. Out of the corners of my eyes, I see Mother on the elevated platform, scooting alongside the bus with her hand outstretched as if trying to touch me one last time. I can't bear to watch her fade into the distance and break down in deep sobs with my face buried in my hands. I feel like a homesick fool and haven't even left Salvation.

By the time the bus passes the city limits sign, I gain control of my emotions. It helps to reflect back on the events of the last two weeks. My farewell party with friends was especially enjoyable. They brought gag gifts and gave me a roast. Even Frankie showed up, although I have no idea how Mother got hold of him or how he managed to get a break from his labor assignment. Of course, my friends brought lots of toilet paper. I deserved that. I will cherish every memory. I will never forget any of them.

The trip to Hope will take about two weeks, so I pull out my journal to make the first entry. "April 10, 121, my Day of Posting, the first day of my new life." I summarize my preparations for the trip to Hope and jot down a few of the best roast comments from my farewell party with my friends. I especially liked the William Shakespeare quote Frankie read, "There is flattery in friendship." Then, looking into my eyes, he said the sweetest thing: "I'm flattered that you count me among your friends." My breathing catches, and I conclude my entry with, "I have never felt so utterly alone." I return the journal to my backpack, my sobs hidden beneath the roar of driving rain pelting the sides of the bus. After taking a few deep breaths in an attempt to calm my outpouring of emotions, I curl into the empty seat beside me and cry myself to sleep.

Four hours later, the bus begins to slow for a fuel stop. The change in the whine of the motor during downshifting and the hiss of air brakes wakes me. The rain has passed. Other passengers rush out to use the bathroom facilities, but I stay behind to get my bearings. The rusted sign above the old fuel stop building reads "FS Limon." All fuel stops have wireless internet, so I bring up my computer and study the route from Salvation. The digitized map indicates the bus traveled northeast, following the remnant of Highway 24 to old I-70. The roads are official links between settlements and are for authorized travel only— never for pleasure. Labor crews work them relentlessly, but they're still rough and, in some places, single lane. Nothing exists between settlements except an occasional maintenance shack, inn, and fuel stop. We've only gone 85 miles. No wonder it takes several weeks to reach the eastern colonies.

I bring up my email program—my lifeline to home—but before I can open anything, an older man with an official-looking hat pokes his head into the bus. "Ed said I needed to check on you. You better take care of your bladder, lady. This rig isn't toilet-equipped."

I jump in startled surprise but manage to catch my laptop before it careens off my lap. "What happened to Ed? Are you a new driver?"

"We don't get far from home out here, lady. Ed takes Bus thirty-four back to Salvation while I take this one on to Fuel Stop Brewster, about four hours down the road. There's only one bus a day, but we'll keep you moving until you get to your final destination."

I take a moment to glance at the map before closing the screen. FS Brewster is exactly in the middle of a vast plain of nothingness, so far from everything that homesickness closes in again. The new driver's head is still there when I look up. "We leave in exactly twenty minutes," he says. "You'd better hurry, or be prepared to hold it for four more hours."

I sigh aloud, put my laptop away, and then step from the bus into the cool spring air. A chill slithers down my spine as I walk to the powder room, hoping the line has dwindled. It hasn't. Four girls are still queued up when I arrive, chatting amongst themselves. The youngest is several years older than I am and stares with faint familiarity as I approach the end of the line. Her face suddenly brightens, and she blurts excitedly, "I remember you. You're the toilet paper girl, aren't you?"

I feel my face flush as the other girls stop chattering and focus on me. The silence is uncomfortable. After clearing my throat, I respond in droning monotone, as if I've answered the question a million times before, "It wasn't personal."

They all break into a chorus of laughter, even though only one understands what we're talking about. There's no place to hide, so I just look down at the floor. The youngest extends her hand. "I'm Helen. I graduated three years before you and just finished intermediate Chemical Engineer training. I'll be mentored at the West Hackberry depository site in Old Louisiana during my advanced study and probably end up working in the energy development facility there. How about you?"

I glance up at Helen's face before returning my gaze to the floor. Her flowing red hair outlines a beautiful freckled face, and she exudes confidence. I hate this. I'm certain my demeanor radiates defeat. I can't even look her in the eye. "I'm Beth Gooding. I'll be raiding old garbage dumps."

Amid more snickers from the potty line, I glance up to see Helen's eyebrows dip and little ripples form across her brow. She places her fists on her hips. "Seriously? What's your assignment? Where's your intermediate tutelage?"

I sigh and add without looking up, "Cultural Anthropologist...in Hope."

A synchronized gasp replaces the girls' laughter. They all recognize the seriousness of my situation.

Helen removes the hand she'd inadvertently placed over her mouth and shakes her head. "How bad did you screw up your tests, girl? What'd you do?"

I shrug, now looking even more intently at my feet than moments earlier. "I don't know. I thought I did okay. Maybe it was the toilet paper."

Mild indignation replaces her disbelief. "If that was it, they sure didn't cut you much slack. Did you do anything else to call attention to yourself?"

I shake my head as the line shortens by one. "Not that I'm aware of. Maybe they just wanted to make an example of someone, or train a linguist—or both. I had high verbal skill scores. That's the only thing that makes sense to me."

A grin breaks out across Helen's face. "Reward the mediocre, send the good to the primitive East Coast. Maybe they just need an infusion of culture out there?"

I ignore her attempt at humor. "Something like that, I guess. Although, I don't understand why they'd need a linguist where everyone speaks English."

I glance up to see a wry smile replace her grin, like the answer should be obvious to any fool. "It's pretty clear to me, Beth. You're going overseas. We all speak English here, but any resurrection of foreign technology will require knowledge of the destination foreign language. You might even get to visit some Old World Russian garbage dumps."

Oh, God. She could be right. What's the Old World Russian word for vodka, anyway? Why else would they need linguists, except to interpret technical residue in foreign garbage? I fall sullen as Helen takes her turn in the toilet. It's clear to me now. There are many worse places on Earth than Hope. Questions still fill my mind. Has somebody found something important overseas? Do they even have internet there? Will I completely lose contact with my family?

I settle back into seat 5B and am both relieved and delighted when Helen plops down beside me. She grins. "A sweet smile from a pretty face can still get a girl a seat change."

I smile back and pat her lightly on the arm. "It's good to have the company. This is all new to me."

We chatter like magpies as the bus heads east into flat and desolate territory. The highway becomes straight and boring, and the afternoon sun burns dimly in a cloudy sky. Pronghorn antelope dot the horizon, interspersed with deer, buffalo, and elk. Other than the animals, there is no natural mountainous beauty like that surrounding Salvation. The animals make me think back to the original notes made by E12-B. He had never seen animals before and was awestruck by them. I, on the other hand, take them for granted because they are so plentiful around Salvation. It's a sad commentary that I might soon be awestruck by something as simple as a pillow.

Helen is a fount of information concerning apprenticeship and training. It's all she's known since leaving Salvation the first time. She's also pregnant and quite excited about it, having returned to Salvation for her mid-training break and insemination. I'm surprised by the insemination. If she returned to Salvation to get pregnant, then I might not meet my mate in Hope after all. In fact, I might never meet him in the flesh. My curiosity is killing me. "Have you ever met your assigned mate?"

Helen winks and offers a thin smile. "No, I haven't, but a girl can find satisfaction when she feels the need. Lovers can be a joy. Just stay on your pills, and don't get pregnant by the wrong guy."

Of course she's right, but I've never looked at it exactly like that. I've never considered having a lover. We all endured a great deal of sex education during basic training, and the message was crystal clear. The genetic makeup of children is a function rigidly controlled by the Federation regardless of anyone's personal preferences or desires. If individuals made random selections recessive genes could be paired, and our population could suffer as a result. Our community has too few people to permit that; therefore, birth control pills have always been freely available. Unfortunately, time to experiment with them hasn't.

When the Federation makes mate assignments that aren't consummated in the flesh, there's no societal stigma against a girl having a lover. In fact, that's part of what gives the outer colonies their wild reputation. The Federation can and does intervene in adulterous relationships—that's strictly forbidden. What the Federation physically joins, no man or woman shall separate...at risk of very nasty work camp assignments.

I look at Helen with new eyes. She literally radiates satisfaction over her pregnancy. "Is it a boy or a girl?"

"She's a girl. My assigned regiment is for two more boys, and then another girl. That'll change my life for a few years, but I look forward to it. My apartment has been far too empty for far too long."

"All by the same sperm donor?"

"Actually, two—one boy/girl combination from each. There's been a push to diversify the gene pool lately. I've heard the population might be reaching the point where enough genetic variation exists that Federation involvement in mate assignments won't be necessary. Wouldn't that be a hoot? Can you imagine having to find your own mate, as if training isn't hard enough already?"

Her comment causes me to think back over the boys I met during basic. None really moved me. "I see your point, both about finding your own mate and about having a baby, but I've never allowed myself the luxury of thinking about children. Deep down, I've always wanted them, and frankly, I envy you. Only a single mate has been selected for me, but I don't know if we'll be a family unit or if he'll be a remote donor. I guess I'll find out when I get to Hope."

Helen tilts her head to the side and gives me a sympathetic pat on my arm. "For your sake, I hope he's waiting when you get off the bus. Going through the hell of intermediate training with a partner would be far more fun than an occasional tryst with a stranger, especially if you actually like him. A permanent partner should also improve your focus, since your thoughts won't be disrupted by yearnings your body orders you to follow."

Helen continues to delve into different aspects of the regimented training she's endured and some of the yearnings she *did* follow. Clearly, when the Helen butterfly left the cocoon, it sampled a lot of pollen. She holds my rapt attention with her exploits, and more than once I slap my hand over my mouth and feel my face flush. She is not that much older, yet she's nothing like anyone I know in Salvation. My friends there would *never* do the things Helen has done, let alone talk about them. It's also clear to me, now that she's pregnant, motherhood is the assignment she wanted all along. About thirty minutes into a discourse on how she intends to raise her baby, she glances at her watch before looking at me with great seriousness. "You haven't mentioned your travel-time work assignments. Didn't your mentor give you any?"

On the Day of Posting, Mrs. Hathaway didn't mention there'd be work to complete during my trip to Hope, but I won't be surprised if there is some. Basic training was rigidly structured, and there's no reason to believe intermediate training will be any different. I open my laptop to scan the message subjects waiting unopened in my inbox. Mother has already written twice, and there are two messages from former classmates. The email at the bottom of the list, however, commands my attention: "Assignments for Beth Gooding."

The email contains a long list of articles—reading to complete during my trip to Hope. The assignment will take precedence over chitchat with Helen. I shrug and grimace in her direction. She understands. She has been through this herself. She smiles back. "I thought as much. I have one, too. With so few people and so much to do, idle time isn't permitted."

Helen settles into her assignments, but I'm completely blindsided by mine. The articles in my reading list all relate to language development, but in a language of ancient Persia called Old Persian. I've never heard of it. Why on Earth would anyone care?

I scan several summary documents to learn a few preliminaries. Old Persian was written from left to right like English but in syllabic cuneiform script, containing thirty-six signs representing vowels and consonants, eight logograms, and three signs that could be combined to represent any numeral. More surprising, the origin of the cuneiform script was never determined—it simply appeared during the reign of Cyrus the Great. How odd that a language sprang out of nowhere, but when I think about it, maybe English was that way too? Perhaps being a linguist won't be so bad after all.

As I delve deeper into articles on the list, I can see my assignments are not light reading. I've transitioned from basic to intermediate training, and any slack in the former will now be eliminated. In response to my deep sigh, Helen glances at the article currently on my screen. She must be surprised by the irrelevance she sees there because all she can say is, "Good God, girl. You must've really pissed someone off."

I shrug. "The articles are interesting, but I have no idea why I'm reading them."

Helen raises her shoulders and palms. "No one wastes time during intermediate training. I can't imagine why they assigned that to you, but you can be sure there is a reason."

I smile back while shaking my head. "I love history, but this information is not useful history at all. It's more like looking at the world through the wrong end of a telescope. I mean, really, what possible value can there be in ancient cuneiform script, or Sanskrit for that matter? Can anyone name a single technological advancement from that time in history that's needed in our world today?"

Helen offers a sympathy sigh and then returns to her studies, but I have difficulty focusing on mine. The text on the screen seems to blur, and I jerk my head side to side to snap myself alert. Perhaps it's the irrelevance of the assignments, the boring nature of the reading, or the gentle rocking of the bus, but my laptop and I soon enter rest mode as I nod off and collapse onto Helen's shoulder. It seems only minutes before she taps me on the head. "Hey, girl. Wake up. We're coming into Fuel Stop Brewster."

I stir, rub my eyes, and stretch. "Oh, God. At this rate, I won't impress my mentor much."

New messages greet me as I nudge my laptop to life. Two are from Mother. I still haven't responded to her earlier emails, but that will have to wait. There's one from my instructor in Hope that demands immediate attention.

His message is simple but with significant overtones.

Dear Miss Gooding:
Please comment on Old Persian. I anxiously await your reply.
Very Truly Yours,
Professor James

Crap. I chose a bad time to sleep. I quickly glance at our route of travel as the bus continues to slow. The next stop is FS Hog Back, and then we move on to FS Salina. I already dread reaching Salina because Helen will head south from there. Although I've only known her for a short time, I'll miss her a lot.

FS Brewster is configured much like FS Limon, except this fuel stop has food. Helen and I visit the grungy toilet facility before making dinner selections, not that there's all that much to choose from. I have the pot roast and peas. Helen has the pot roast and corn. My selections taste like cardboard. The FS proprietor provides water, but she seems inconvenienced. Her sneer as she places the water on the table with enough force to spill it is a sure sign she is far too busy to deal with her customers. There's no dessert. That's probably a blessing. The government provides food on sanctioned travel, but that doesn't mean it'll be good food.

It's getting dark by the time the new bus departs one hour and twenty minutes after our arrival. The bus we arrived on has already left on its return trip to FS Limon. Helen falls asleep the moment the drone of the engine reaches a constant pitch. The dim overhead lighting provides enough illumination to see the keyboard but not enough to disturb her, so I turn my attention to my emails. Answering Mother and my former classmates takes very little time. "Still on the bus. I'm suspicious about pot roast now." It amazes me that I can keep the email so short, considering how heartbroken I was to leave home. I believe I have Professor James to thank for that. His email is now my number one concern; it must be carefully considered. This will be my first contact with him, and I want it to be a good one.

One thing is certain. I can't possibly respond on an intellectual level because I don't have the background or time to delve into anything that might be of interest to a linguistic expert. I'd just look stupid trying to take that path. Professor James is probably only asking for my first impressions, to see if I've read any of my assignments, or maybe he's looking for an insight into how I feel about my assignment in general. I'll respond with as little information as possible—enough to let him know I've started on my assignments but not enough to reveal I've been sleeping for hours. I'll also add a question of my own.

Dear Professor James:
With ties to 1500 B.C. Pre-Classical Sanskrit, Old Persian is one of the more ancient members of the main Indo-European family of languages. Persian King Darius 1 ordered the Old Persian alphabet created around 520 B.C., mainly for royal inscriptions. I haven't found any reference that explains what inspired his order or why he didn't accept the alphabet prevalent at the time. Why was a new alphabet needed when the old one was sufficient?
Sincerely,
Beth Gooding

The smugness I feel when I transmit my message quickly changes to mild panic when a reply from Professor James arrives within minutes.

> *Dear Miss Gooding:*
> *Why indeed? Read. Read. Read.*
> *Very Truly Yours,*
> *Professor James*

What's this, some kind of game? He must know the answer to my question but isn't going to provide it. Now, I'll have to respond to his assignments and my own. *Crap.* That's not what I had in mind.

The ride to FS Hog Back is uneventful. Helen sleeps while I read, but despite the unrelenting dryness of the material, I find it oddly fascinating. I'm not sure if I'm motivated to answer my own question or simply impress my mentor, but I manage to stay alert and continue reading the entire trip.

Helen stirs, stretches, and then yawns wide as the bus comes to a gentle stop at FS Hog Back. Her yawn is contagious even though I'm not sleepy. The driver turns on the overhead lights and announces, "FS Hog Back. Bus change in thirty-five minutes. Take care of your personal needs while you can." Clearly, we're in for more bus checkers. That must be the reason we aren't allowed to bring much luggage on these trips.

The toilet facilities at this FS are immaculate—a welcome relief. After that important stop, we hurry to the food counter for a piece of pie and a flask of water. Helen is still groggy. "What time is it, anyway?"

"About midnight. By morning, you'll be heading south from FS Salina. I miss you already."

She gives me another of her knowing looks, but with tired, red eyes that almost match her hair. "You don't understand how this works, Beth. FS Salina isn't just another fuel stop. It's *the* major north-south, east-west exchange. We'll be there several days before all the routes are coordinated and the roads are certified travel-ready. The bus exchange system only works when all the equipment, roads, and people are ready at the same time."

It makes sense. Resources don't limit the expansion of humanity, as in the past, but birth rate does. With so few people, everything must be carefully coordinated before mass transit movement is allowed. The community can't take chances with the precious cargo the buses carry.

We soon board. Helen falls asleep before the bus leaves FS Hog Back, but I'm not tired. I pull out my journal to make a few entries and then read my assignments for about two hours before falling into a deep sleep.

* * * *

The rising sun penetrates the tinted windows of the bus as we enter FS Salina. This time, there are no announcements, but most of the travelers know what to do. I follow Helen to a large, barracks-like inn on the western perimeter of the compound. We are provided with small beeper devices and assigned bunks in a room with three other women and two men. I'm a little surprised by the sleeping arrangements, but Helen assures me no one is allowed to travel if they've ever demonstrated perversion of any kind or for any reason. The computerized badge and palm checks at every stop confirm both proper boarding and that each traveler's handprint matches the information recorded on their access card.

We walk slowly toward the mess hall for breakfast while Helen educates me about what I can expect over the next few years. First and foremost is the requirement to learn as much as possible about my subcategory. Mediocre performance is not permitted and will result in demotion to a practical category. There is also the requirement to have children. That usually happens during the third year of intermediate training...unless my performance is so outstanding that I am chosen for advanced training. Helen says only one out of twenty-five trainees are honored with advanced training. Those people are permitted to defer childbearing until the third advanced year. By the time we finish breakfast, it is clear that my life will never again be like it was in Salvation.

The FS Salina compound contains five major areas: bus maintenance and repair, mess hall, sleeping quarters, study hall, and living quarters for those permanently assigned to the facility. Helen and I spend most of our time in the study hall when we're not eating or sleeping. No one is allowed to leave the compound. Wild animals abound outside and are not monitored in any way. Although they would probably leave us alone, no one will take that chance. Too much has been invested in our breeding and training.

Helen and I are studying in the library on the afternoon of our fourth day in Salina when her beeper goes off. My heart sinks; her bus will be boarding in thirty minutes. We gather our materials and pack them in our computer bags. I walk with her toward the depot. I have dreaded this. Despite the short time I've known her, she has been like a big sister to me—like I've always pictured Jenna would have been if she had lived. Because she took the time with me, I now know more about what to expect during the next few years of my life than I could have imagined while I was in Salvation.

When we reach the departure platform, she turns to me and brushes the forming tears from the corners of my eyes. "You'll get used to this. New friends are waiting around every corner."

I throw my arms around her neck and hug her tight. Through suppressed sobs, I manage to choke out, "Thank you for everything. I'll miss you more than words can say."

She gently pushes me back to arm's length and smiles. Then, shaking her index finger at me, she adds, "Just remember to look me up in a few years when you have kiddos of your own. Maybe then you can tell me why you're studying Old Persian."

She pulls me close for another hug as the driver shouts, "All aboard!" She kisses me on the cheek, and I feel her tears on the side of my face. When she pulls away, she manages a stiff upper lip as she adds, "You take care of yourself. Email me." Helen then turns and boards the bus. As the bus pulls away, I am left to wonder if I'll ever see her again.

My heart is heavy as I trudge back to the library; homesickness strikes with a vengeance. When I settle in, I take the time to write a long letter to Mother, and then I send a short note to Helen, saying only, "I miss you terribly already."

Spring rains have damaged some of the roads to the east. Because all routes must be repaired and certified before travel will be allowed in that direction, my departure is delayed. Now that Helen is gone, I attack my assignments with renewed vigor. Constant study helps belay my boredom and mitigates the emptiness her departure has left in my heart. I miss her almost as much as I miss my family.

Chapter Eight
Hope

Two days later, the route east is declared open, and I board the bus heading in that direction. Over the next twelve days, the buses move slowly east, and the fuel stops and major exchanges blend together as one. The toilets, food, and sleeping quarters are the same wherever we stop. Only the level of hygiene varies from site to site. I read my assignments and keep Professor James updated on my progress. By the time I reach FS Boston, I thank God that Hope is just a short distance ahead. I'm completely exhausted and realize that's probably the reason people don't leave the colonies after they arrive. Not only are they assigned to specific jobs in specific locations, but travel is also extremely difficult.

By the time the bus pulls into FS Hope, I have concluded that living conditions in the towns we've passed through are inversely proportional to the town's distance from Salvation. Everything has just gotten worse, as if squalor is some sort of frontier virtue. I've also prepared myself mentally for the shacks and muddy roads that make up the colony. As our bus rolls to a stop, I see a few all-terrain vehicles moving cargo and goods from place to place, but most traffic is by horse or on foot.

There are few buildings. The nearby Old World city of Boston has decayed to almost nothing and is mostly overgrown with trees and shrubs, but it is still a source of building materials for Hope. The area surrounding the colony is beautiful, especially the view over the small harbor. A single ship is in port, and the wharf is abuzz with lading activity.

As I step from the bus with my backpack slung over my shoulder, a man holding a sign that reads "Miss Gooding" catches my attention. It must be Professor James.

He stands at a towering six feet with a ruddy complexion and sandy brown hair. He's not what I pictured. In fact, if he weren't twice my age, he'd be cute.

I size him up as I walk toward him. He has a slight build, piercing blue eyes, and muscular arms—probably from digging up trash. As I get closer, I note the rough hands characteristic of all settlers. Life is not easy on the frontier. He's dressed in blue jeans, a red plaid flannel shirt, and calf-high black rubber boots.

Mud squishes beneath my feet with each step I take. I'll probably need boots like that, too. I suck in a deep breath as I take the final few muddy steps into my new life. This is it. After leaving my home behind and sitting on a bus for weeks on end, this is it. I boldly step in front of him and extend my hand, "Hello, sir. I'm Beth Gooding."

A smile breaks out across his face, revealing off-white, straight teeth. He sets his sign down in the mud and shakes my hand with enthusiasm. His grip is firm, almost painful. "Good to meet you, Miss Gooding. Ready to get to work?"

Wait a minute—I *have* been working. I swallow the thought and nod. I'm here to learn, not to quibble. I wonder if the work he has in mind has anything to do with the large green garbage bag he's carrying. I try to deflect, ignoring the bag as if it's not there. "You bet! More reading assignments?"

He hands the bag to me and points to a nearby public toilet—a small building that looks like an outhouse. "Not now. We've got a little field work to do."

He hasn't said so, but I think I'm about to be tested—to see if I can stand the grime of hands-on garbage retrieval. Butterflies fill my stomach. I didn't expect this opportunity so soon.

The bag contains clothing similar to what everyone here wears, and the size-2 jeans, small shirt and jacket, and size-6 boots probably means he has access to my personnel records. The 34B bra confirms it. I'm not too surprised. The profile in my computer records leaves nothing to the imagination. Privacy be damned, everything fits, although the odor in the changing room is not suitable for human breathing. It smells like someone forgot to flush the toilet a week ago, except there's no flush handle—just a hole in a wooden board. The flies and foul odor make me put on my clothes as quickly as I can. When I emerge with my new duds, Professor James and a horse-drawn buggy await. I feel like I've stepped back in time to the Old World 1800s.

The first order of business is a familiarization trot around the colony. The highlights are the communications center, the power generator, the infirmary, and the general store. We don't stop at any of those places. Instead, we go to the Energy Reclamation Center and proceed immediately to a large green dumpster behind it. Professor James flashes an impish grin. "This is your stop."

I feel the blood drain from my face, and my stomach turns. I must turn pale as death. The dumpster is squalid. It stinks worse than the changing room. My hand flashes toward the gaping opening, and I blurt, "The dumpster? Are you kidding?" Frankly, I'd rather see the generators—fourth generation motors that use a mixture of reprocessed Strategic Reserve oil and man-made oil from recycled organic materials. I've read about V5 and V6 for years—the microbes responsible for oil production—but I didn't get to see any of that technology in Salvation.

"Yeah, the big green thing there. See if you can learn anything from what you find in it." He remains on the buggy seat. The horse doesn't move. The dumpster remains stinky and grimy.

I resist as much as my position as an understudy will allow. "Why would there be anything of value in there? This is a colony. No one in their right mind would throw anything of value away."

He smiles and waggles his eyebrows like the Old World Groucho Marx. "One would hope. Check it out. There will be a quiz."

The mud is four inches thick as I step off the buggy. I can feel the cool muck slither around my foot and over the top of my toes through my new rubber boots. Professor James watches with interest as I pull up a nearby wooden crate and push it against the side of the dumpster. I suppress the urge to vomit. It smells like dead animals inside.

I am not deft at this sort of thing. Even using the crate as a booster, it's all I can do to lift my foot to the edge, slip my leg over, and pull my body up and over the side. I might as well kiss my new, clean jeans goodbye because they'll never be the same. As I drop down into the gaping cavern, I hear Professor James and the buggy pull away. The thought that I might be here for some time is overcome by the stench surrounding me. My gag reflex kicks in, and I begin breathing through the sleeve of my shirt in attempt to tamp it down. The flannel fabric makes a lousy air filter, but it's better than nothing. I hope he moved the buggy because he was in a no parking zone and not because he's leaving me here alone for a long time.

I'm not sure what I'm looking for but find a sturdy stick and begin pushing stuff around with it. I need to find something—anything—that will buy my way out of this nightmare. After about five minutes, my need for fresh air overcomes my need to investigate the trash inside the dumpster. I poke my head out of the bin to suck in a gulp of fresh air at exactly the same moment an elderly lady tries to put more trash in. She jerks back. Her eyes narrow as she stares at me. "Why, who would throw a pretty young thing like you away? You look like you've got lots of kilometers left on you."

Not knowing how she can possibly know what I look like with half my face covered, I lower my arm and offer a sheepish grin. At the same time, I motion to the edge of the dumpster with a sideways flick of my head, and choke out a muffled greeting through the stench. "Just set your box there by the side, Ma'am. I'll go through it later."

The old woman winks. "My, you are a feisty one. Looks like Mule got a winner this time." She sets her box where I indicated and ambles off, leaving me to ponder what she meant by "this time" and "Mule." After a few priceless gasps of relatively fresh air, I dip back inside but still can't come up with much. For the most part, the bin contains organic recyclables—inputs for fuel pre-processing at the energy center. Based on its contents, I'm quite certain the foul odor isn't from the material in the bin but from the metal container itself. It must have been used recently for holding animal carcasses—another energy recyclable.

Professor James returns an hour later and helps me out of the bin. He seems upbeat when he asks, "I can hardly wait. What did you learn?"

I hold up my index finger and then pick up the box left by the old woman. "Hold that thought, sir. I'm not quite finished."

The contents of the old woman's box are typical of what I found in the dumpster: small wood chips and plant trimmings, a few crumpled pieces of paper, a few strips of tattered muslin, some spoiled berries, and several wads of horse hair. After inspection, I empty the box into the bin and climb onto the buggy with the recycle box in tow. I'll leave it at the front of the center with all the others.

Professor James waits patiently for me to get comfortable, but I can tell from his flinch I've brought the dumpster's aroma with me. I can't let the moment pass. "What? You don't like my perfume?"

He chuckles under his breath, moves the horse a small distance from the bin, and stops again, being careful to park so I am positioned downwind from him. His eyes seem to twinkle as he asks, "Now that you've begun dumpster diving 101, what've you learned?"

I assume there's more to this little quiz than a passing fancy, more than determining if I can get filthy with the best of them and still come out swinging. So, I give a serious answer. "I've learned people here still don't know how to segregate garbage correctly. Hair is an animal byproduct; it shouldn't be in that bin. There were also a few shards of broken glass—a recycling no-no. That's a clear indication more recycling education is needed. There were only a few edible organics, indicating most of that material is buried in gardens locally. It's also pretty clear they don't wash the dumpsters out after using them to collect animal by-products."

Professor James looks disappointed. "That's it, after an entire hour?"

I shrug. "There's more, but it's personal." He nods while his hand executes a "give me more" motion. I sigh. "Okay, then. From a scrawled note that was probably passed between two teenagers, I think Dianne McCarthy is pregnant. I don't think she has told her parents or Central Population Control. If she had, she would have passed that information to her friend electronically instead of on paper."

Professor James looks directly into my eyes. It gives me goose bumps to be stared at so intently, so personally. "That's better. Now, if you had to guess, what would you think some future Cultural Anthropologist might glean from that trash?"

A long silence follows. Without thinking, I bite off two fingernails as I study my feet and immediately regret it. My hands taste like the garbage smells. I simply *must* break that habit in this new line of work. I spit a few times, trying to rinse off my lips and teeth. It's clear I'm not making a good impression, but I didn't expect this line of questioning. The horse waits. Professor James waits. *Think, Beth, think.* I finally come up with something that seems reasonable. "Ah, probably nothing. None of that trash would last very long. It will all be converted to energy or reused in some way—even the plastics and toxics. A future anthropologist wouldn't know we existed at all, at least not from that trash."

A broad smile crosses his face. "Good, Beth. Excellent. Now, do you consider our current civilization more advanced or less advanced than the one we've replaced?"

Where is he going with this? Why should that matter? I sigh again. The question seems inane. "I guess more. The previous civilization might have had more fun, but they choked on the party."

The smile returns to his face. I guess he liked my answer. "So, a truly advanced civilization might not leave any clues to their existence, like the one we replaced did, right? And without a remnant of trash, an advanced civilization would be pretty hard to detect after they vanished into the annals of history."

My eyebrows dip, and I look at him with as much curiosity as I can muster. "I suppose so, unless they left things for future generations to find, either intentionally or accidentally. I'd consider the pyramids an accident because they were left for religious purposes rather than for the benefit of future generations. On the other hand, time capsules filled with relics are intentionally left to help future people understand past civilizations."

He taps the horse's butt with his long crop and commands, "Giddyup." The reluctant horse moves forward without the slightest hint of enthusiasm. Professor James asks, while continuing to gaze ahead, "What was the most significant thing you learned in there?"

It's good to be moving again. The light breeze seems to strip away the outer layer of stench. "If my interpretation from that single scrap of paper is correct, then probably the pregnancy. It's only speculation, though, because my conclusion required some inference. Our language isn't all that clear when people want to disguise the true meaning of their words. I mean, it's pretty easy to talk around something so completely that only inference remains."

We stop at the front of the recycling center, and I place the old woman's recycle box on the stack with all the others. "You're very astute, Beth, but what if you weren't familiar with our language or didn't know it at all? What conclusions could you draw about us then?"

Considering I only had an hour in the dumpster, he's asking some pretty deep questions. "I suppose, because there was so little paper, one might conclude we aren't a paper-based society. Also, because the paper *was* there, with writing on it, that the people in our culture are driven to communicate. That alone might spur me to look further...for something that might have been left on purpose, something like a time capsule."

His eyes twinkle, and his smile broadens. "My thinking, exactly, Beth. Now, let's get you to the office and cleaned up. When you've learned Old Persian more completely than anyone in history, then I'll show you something beyond your imagination. Something left behind intentionally that'll blow you away, something that might rewrite history as we know it forever."

Chapter Nine
Tutelage

As we drop the horse and buggy at the Hope Transportation Center, the attendant tips his hat toward Professor James and drawls, "Anytime, Mule. Just let me know what you need."

We leave the large wooden barn with my curiosity piqued. The old lady I met at the dumpster used that name, too. "Why do people call you 'Mule'? Are you stubborn, or is it just a local name for a professor?"

"A little of both, I suppose, but mostly it's baggage from my youth. Most of the people here have known me since my birth. I got that tag before basic training, and it stuck like mud on a clean carpet. I couldn't shake it off so I just accepted it."

My eyes widen as I look around at the primitive surroundings. "You've been here all your life…and *asked* to come back after your advanced training?"

"It's not that bad, Beth, when you get used to it. Sometimes it gets a little lonely, but you adjust to the solitude, even relish it. Frankly, I missed the quiet when I studied in Salvation and could hardly wait to get back." With a pleasant gleam in his eye, he quickly changes the subject, taunting, "My history isn't important, but getting you cleaned up is. You still smell terrible."

It's just a short walk to his office—a small structure made from recycled wood and brick. Narrow sidewalks of recycled pavers from the Old World city of Boston flank the gravel and mud streets. Few people mill about, so large sidewalks aren't needed.

The office is adjacent to the Hope Communications Center, probably because Professor James requires the high-speed internet to access the master library in Salvation. The office has two small windows that face the street, a small stoop, and an unfinished wooden door. Adjacent to the stoop at street level is a small pad made from street pavers. An elevated hose bib rises out of the pavers with a pole brush hanging from it. The reason for the pad is clear to me—our boots are filthy. After we clean our boots, Professor James opens the front door, which protests with a shrill squeak. He ushers me inside with a cross-body sweep of his arm. "Welcome home, Beth."

Home? I'm a little hesitant about that. I step inside with the caution of a stalking cat. It's not like any office I've ever seen. There are two desks, one on either side of the living room just inside the door, each placed directly in front of a window. A rudimentary kitchen lies straight ahead but without a dividing wall between the rooms. The three doors to the right are apparently bedrooms and a bathroom. It's clear Professor James lives and works here, and his office has all the earmarks of an austere life.

"You'll find fresh clothing in your room—the door on the left—and a shower in the bathroom. Be careful, though. It's a short-cycle, instant-heat shower. Be sure to turn the water off while you lather up, and be prepared to rinse quick when you finish. The hot water won't last long, and the cold water can be quite a shock if you spend too much time in there."

I'm stunned. Where's the dorm? "I'm staying here…with you?"

He raises his palms as he opens his arms wide, like Moses might have when he parted the Red Sea. "Bet you thought it'd be primitive here in Hope, right? But no, you've landed in the lap of luxury."

Oh, my God. He might even believe it. "Are there other…students? Will I have a roommate?" I can't help but wonder if my assigned mate will be joining me here. I've had a nagging curiosity about him that has been building inside me for years, long before I knew his name.

Professor James's expression becomes serious as he shakes his head. "We've had a little problem there, Beth. I requested two students, but the other one opted out. Apparently, she wasn't prepared to leave civilization as she knew it."

She? Oh, crap. If I follow Helen's path, that means I'll be fertilized *in vitro*, and my incessant curiosity about mating will have to wait. On the upside, since *in vitro* fertilization only takes place in Salvation, that could also mean I'll get to see my family when the time is right. I'm tempted to ask Professor James if he knows anything about my future mate but decide, since we just met, my focus must be on my work and not on things he might consider as peripheral distractions.

Following Professor James's lead, I kick off my boots on the slate entry area. I walk in my socks across the squeaky wooden floor toward the door on the left. My room is damp and chilly, has no windows, and is furnished with a single bed and a desk, chest, and end table. A straight-back chair, single electric lamp, and metal hamper for soiled clothing complete the décor. I've no idea how dirty clothes are washed here, or where, but I suspect there's probably a stream with a large, flat rock nearby. As promised, fresh clothes are arrayed on the bed: heavy flannel pajamas, a fuzzy robe, and house shoes. They are a welcome relief.

The bathroom is as stark as my bedroom. A small, walk-in shower stall without a curtain lies straight ahead. A small mirror is mounted above a metal pedestal sink on the left, and a metal toilet that was probably recycled from one of Old World Boston's prisons sits to the right. Two small cabinets flank the mirror—one labeled Beth and the other Mule. Each cabinet has a towel and washcloth hanging beneath it.

Touched by the amount of welcoming preparation evident in this house, and by my introduction to Hope in general, I smile as I step into the shower. Professor James doesn't have much, but he's done everything possible to make me feel welcome here. My feelings of warm welcome are short-lived. The shower's icy water hits me like a sledgehammer. Professor James must've heard my scream because I hear a muffled voice from the other side of the door, "Oh, I forgot to mention that the shower water takes a couple of seconds to warm up."

I shiver. His timing could've been better, but I don't quake long. The water turns from frigid to scalding, and I fight to not scream again. I swallow the unwelcome surprise and respond with, "Thanks for the warning" before adjusting the temperature to a point where I can lather up and shut it off. After scrubbing down, I face the snake-like showerhead again, but this time I know its tricks. No screams, just a refreshing flush of the residual smell from the dumpster.

I exit the bathroom refreshed and clean. I'm delighted to find that Professor James has prepared a simple lunch of a fresh garden salad, jerky, and a baked potato. Like one of Pavlov's dogs, my mouth salivates as I walk toward the table. Still towel-drying my hair, I flash a smile at my host and teacher. "You're a lifesaver, Professor James. It has been a long time since breakfast at FS Boston. I could eat a horse."

He snickers through a wide smile. "Maybe you will. I have no idea where this jerky came from."

I know it's more than a quip. Nothing goes to waste on the frontier. It makes perfect sense that old horses would be slaughtered and eaten, and sun-dried jerky would be a logical way to preserve the remains. Horse jerky wouldn't have been my first menu choice in Salvation, but I'm here now and will learn to adapt.

The table knife isn't sharp, but I manage to saw off a piece of the chewy meat while being as ladylike as I can. Professor James snickers. "If you think it's hard to cut with a knife, wait until you try to eat it."

He's right. It's like chewing rubber. I cover my mouth with one hand while reaching for my glass of water with the other. After washing it down in a lump, I look up with a grin and more than a little sarcasm. "That was tasty."

"The second bite is always better."

"I'll bet. While I'm chewing it, perhaps you can tell me why I've been reading material that, on the surface, seems pretty irrelevant to life on the frontier—or even life overseas, for that matter."

He wags his index finger back and forth without looking up from his plate. "Oh, no. Not so fast. I'm the teacher here, and I get to ask the questions." He adds a little salt to his baked potato and then looks into my eyes. "Tell me about your family."

I'm not sure if he wants the extended version or the abbreviated one, so I opt for the short version. He stops me when I mention Jenna.

"So, she must have been what, eighteen—the same as you are now? What took her?"

I set my fork down and take a deep breath. This isn't a memory I want to relive. After a short pause, I simply say, "She slipped and fell."

"At home? At school?"

"Mount Logan...rock climbing."

His eyebrows dip. "I didn't think that was permitted."

I take another deep breath, pick up my fork, and take another small bite of jerky. Without taking my eyes off my plate, I respond in a near whisper, "It isn't."

"I wondered how she died. Your records only indicate she had an accident. Nothing is included about what that might have been. She sounds as if she knew the value of adventure. Do you?"

What an odd question. "I thought you wanted to know about my family."

He nods. "I do, and you are a part of it. How do you feel about new things—taking a step into the unknown?"

I place my elbows on the table and rest the tip of my chin on my steepled index fingers. "I love being in the mountains and wanted nothing more than to be a Forest Ranger. Sometimes I think I belong outside more than inside. There is great freedom in sleeping under an open sky."

"Are you disappointed by your current assignment?"

I look around the cabin and sigh. "Well, this isn't Mount Logan, but I'll adjust. I'm adaptable."

He hooks one arm over the back of his chair while studying me. I feel like an ant under a microscope. "Your computer-generated profile indicated that, but I wanted to hear it from you. Tell me more about your family."

Before long, he knows the names of my extended family, my favorite colors and foods, and what I enjoy doing in my leisure time, but I know absolutely nothing about him. At the end of the interrogation, when lunch is officially over, he says, "Guess we should get on with our studies. The dishes are yours. Next time, you cook, and I'll clean."

Of course I can do that—everyone learns to cook in basic training—but the division of labor both surprises and delights me. It feels more like a partnership than an apprenticeship. I've heard of mentors like him but have never actually met one. Certainly, he's nothing like Mrs. Hathaway. I bet she'd let the dog lick the dishes clean before she'd wash one. He also tells me we'll work the garden every morning, feed the rabbits, turn the compost, and empty the composting toilet as needed. Gardens are mandatory in Hope, where every backyard is a small farm. With significant pride, he tells me Hope is almost self-sufficient and will soon be able to help support a new, extended outpost.

When I've stowed the last clean plate, he introduces me to his computer file systems and provides the passwords to access his library files in Salvation. Passwords are a surprise. I thought everything in the Salvation library was open to anyone who wanted to take the time to read, but for some reason, these files aren't.

"Why are your files protected?"

Professor James answers with reservation, his voice soft. "When you're ready, everything will be made clear to you."

After that vague response, I learn that my first assignment is to read all that Professor James has written over the years and any referenced documents needed to fully understand the conclusions in his papers. He has been a prolific writer. It will take months, perhaps years, to get through everything. Who would've guessed so much study had been done on ancient Persia and Old Persian? With human resources in such short supply, who would authorize such an activity? For that matter, who authorized my being here now? I remember his words this afternoon, that he would show me something to "blow my mind" when I have sufficient understanding of Old Persian. Despite his joyful exterior, Professor James seems to have a lot of secrets, and he's going to make me work to learn what they are. Considering all the reading now facing me, it could take a lifetime to have my mind blown.

I begin with the oldest documents first, reading papers and notes Professor James wrote when he first began his tutelage. If nothing else, I hope to find whatever caused him to enter such an unusual field of study. Doctor Peter Gene Noble mentored Professor James, and the initials PGN are interspersed throughout his early writings—insight from a man he apparently worshiped. I find it interesting that suggestions from PGN are more like directives than anything else, and I'm moved to look up Doctor Noble in the Salvation archives.

To my surprise, I find that Doctor Noble wasn't a linguist at all. He was a fifth-generation adventurer who bucked the system in every possible way by exploring dangerous areas on his own. In the early days, individual reconnaissance beyond Salvation's city limits was not allowed. Instead, exploration was always done in groups as a safety measure. There were far too few people to permit individuals to wander off on their own. Nevertheless, that's exactly what Doctor Noble did, and his journals are fascinating. He was a loner and a survivalist and quite proud of the statement most often attributed to him, "Give me a rock, and I can survive in the wild indefinitely."

Based on his journal entries, the statement credited to him appears to be true. He was one of the first to reach the East Coast, the first to set foot in Hope, and one of a handful of people who crossed the Atlantic alone...and returned. I follow his early exploits with rapt awe, knowing I could never summon the courage to attempt what he did. Making it across the ocean in his small sailboat, the Dorothy Elizabeth, was a remarkable feat—returning a miracle.

During my first week of study, I voraciously read everything I can find about him, following his life until his mid-thirties, where records concerning him terminate without explanation. There's nothing about his death. His story just ends. One moment he was there and the next he wasn't.

Reading about Doctor Noble is interesting, but I'm intrigued as to why Professor James has not weighed in to direct my study in any way. For the most part, he has worked at his computer, and I have worked at mine. We eat together, work the garden, and share chores, but we haven't engaged in extensive planning or direction relative to my becoming a linguist. I'm not too concerned. He can see everything I'm reading and every file I access from his computer. If he wants me to change direction, I assume he'll let me know. I also know what I've read is where he started his own studies, so it makes sense I should start there too. Still, I don't see Doctor Noble's connection to linguistics and certainly not to

Old Persian. This is a twisty road. It will be interesting to see where it ends.

Fascinating reading fills my first week in Hope, but my time with Professor James and learning about Hope are also enthralling. In a way, there is great satisfaction in sharing chores directly related to survival. The rabbits I feed in the morning could well be the stew I prepare for dinner, and the lettuce we carefully pick worms off each day will be our salad for lunch. Our extra vegetables and excess rabbits are taken to the local exchange and traded for beef and chicken, soap, cornmeal, and the like. Everyone produces something, everyone contributes, and we all have enough.

Skilled men and women populate the town, and each has something to offer to the community. It's not an accident. The people here received training for a specific role. That's the beauty of planned colonies. What we can't produce locally, we obtain from other communities in exchange for local food and raw materials. One of Hope's major exports is building materials recycled from the decaying Old World city of Boston—the primary reason new settlements are established near old ones. Our fishermen also provide an incredible harvest of seafood. As with every aspect of our lives, trade between settlements is managed by the central computers in Salvation. Inventories of available products are manages so that travel to exchange commodities is minimized.

After six days of study, I'm given a day off—something never allowed during basic training. Professor James prepares a picnic basket and takes us by carriage to a hill overlooking the sea. I stand on a gray granite outcropping and listen to the sound of the waves crashing below. I hold out my arms like I'm flying as I breathe in the sweet, salty air. It's easy to fantasize about what it must have been like for Doctor Noble to put to sea from this spot. The Dorothy Elizabeth was a small vessel. He must have known he might never return. I can't imagine the courage it took to do something like that.

Gulls circle above, calling endlessly, and I close my eyes as the warm sun bathes my face. I've only been here a week, and it's already becoming hard to imagine a better life than this. Except for family, I've almost forgotten the reasons I was afraid to leave Salvation. My first few days here, I emailed my mother three times a day—morning, noon, and night. Now I'm so lost in my reading assignments and life in Hope that I only write in the evening. Being here is nothing like being in Salvation. I'd never tend a garden there or use the resources of the land like we do here. People in Salvation don't realize how spoiled and dependent they are. I glance at the settler mark on my wrist. I now see that mark as a badge of honor rather than something to sneer at.

As I stand in the breeze in utter bliss, my long hair flailing in the wind, Professor James takes my hand. "You're getting a little close to the edge, young lady, and it's time for lunch."

I'm startled, but there's gentleness in his touch despite his rough hands. "Sorry, Professor. It's easy to get caught up in the beauty of this place. Is this really the spot where Doctor Noble set out to sea?"

He doesn't answer but leads me toward a large oak tree on the hill, upwind of the horse. We sit on a blanket held down by four corner rocks and the picnic basket in the middle. The jar of cherries adjacent to the basket immediately catches my attention. "Whoa. Where did you score those?"

His smile brings out the little laugh wrinkles around the corners of his eyes. "Canning season. You'll have your opportunity soon enough. We all harvest the fruit. We all can the crop. It's a ritual here. It's a lot of work but well worth the reward."

"I don't understand. I haven't seen any cherries in the cupboard or at the exchange."

"We have a root cellar, Beth. Everyone has one. We'll restock during harvest."

"To be honest, I didn't expect so much community interaction when I was assigned here. I thought everyone on the frontier was a loner."

"Quite the opposite. People here work together to survive. We depend on each other for almost everything. No one is alone. No one is a loner."

"What about Doctor Noble? Wasn't he a loner?"

Professor James reclines on the blanket with his hands behind his head and stares through the canopy above into the sky beyond. "He was different, all right, but taught me well—put me on a path I can never leave. He had an unrestricted vision of this world, as though anything was possible, but he didn't follow the rules. Many believed he put himself at unnecessary risk, and that's the reason they assigned him to labor service—an assignment he walked away from. He wasn't everybody's favorite puppy, and he refused to let others tell him how to live his life. To answer your earlier question, yes, he left from the sandy beach just south of the point."

I struggle to open the cherries and soon hand the jar to Professor James. "Would you mind?"

He rolls onto his side and props himself on one arm. "Not at all, fair lady."

Maybe it's the light or the warm wind blowing his hair, but I can't help thinking, *My God, he is cute.* My heart flutters just looking at him reclined on the blanket, and I force myself back to reality. Such inclinations are not taboo if proper birth control protocols are followed; however, inklings like those are not part of my upbringing. Such thoughts, however brief, must be a residual from my discussions with Helen. *Damn her anyway!* I need to nip feelings like that in the bud. I need to wait. Only the central computer can evaluate couples for the most optimum genetic parings. For now, I just need to study.

I smile as air hisses in to fill the vacuum beneath the lid. Canned cherries will be a delightful eating experience. I can almost feel those beauties sliding down my throat. "How many years did Doctor Noble mentor you?"

He strokes his chin, as if reliving memories. "Nineteen—some good, some bad, but all interesting."

My God. Is that what I have to look forward to—infinite study? Then I quickly do the math. "How's that possible? You're what, thirty-two?"

"Thirty-three."

"Then how? If mentoring begins at my age, as you're mentoring me now, how'd you put in nineteen years?"

He stares into my eyes and grins. "Things are not always what they seem. My tutelage began when I was twelve, not at your age, and continued to the time of his disappearance. Doctor Noble was my father."

It's clear this onion has many layers. I study Professor James with renewed interest. "If your father was Doctor Noble, then why is your name James?"

His grin widens as he resumes staring at the sky through the tree's canopy. "My father managed to piss off everyone important in Salvation. That's why he was sent here in the first place and the reason my lineage was subsequently linked through my mother, Doctor Dorothy Elizabeth James. When they sent him here as punishment, they never expected he would abandon his assignments, to throw his life away to seek adventure in the unexplored regions overseas, but he did. He was obsessed with knowing what happened there, after Project Sanitize."

I gasp, and my eyes open wide. "You mean he went to one of the sites, an actual detonation site at the edge of the Kill Zone?"

Professor James nods. "Probably the reason he disappeared at forty-two, but in the process, he discovered some interesting things—the reason I still follow him, and the reason the bureaucracy in Salvation supports us now."

I wonder what he found. Whatever it is, it could explain a lot. "Am I studying Old Persian because of something he found? Am I here now because of him?"

Professor James reaches over to take my hand again, causing a chill to shiver down my spine. It's a strange sensation, an odd feeling entirely new to me. Except for a few of my male relatives, I can't remember being touched like that by any other male. The sensation is unsettling...and itchy. "It's the reason *we're* studying Old Persian. We are in this together, and when you are ready, I'll show you his find. For now, I just need you to stay focused. The language may be awkward, even boring, but you need to stay with it."

He squeezes my hand to make the point and then releases it. The chill runs through me again. I close my eyes, suppressing a gasp. I'm not sure what to say. Clearly, there's more to this assignment than I ever could have guessed, but I'll have to perform to find out what it is. At that moment, I resolve to study harder than I would've believed possible, to force myself to continue reading regardless of how tired I might feel. No matter what lays ahead, I *will* overcome it. I'll do whatever it takes to master that damn language.

* * * *

It's good that we had a day off three months ago because there hasn't been another since. Nevertheless, time races by, and I've fallen into a routine that is both pleasant and arduous. The chores are many, and canning season is upon us. The work provides immediate rewards—delicious fruit and time away from study. Both are enjoyable beyond measure.

Professor James and I have become great friends. He is playful yet so full of knowledge that I can scarcely comprehend it. I enjoy my time around him immensely, which is, of course, all the time. We have become like one person, as if he is my left arm and I am his right. We work together so well he could be female. I am disturbed that I continue to entertain inappropriate thoughts about him, though—thoughts that would best be reserved for my intended mate. I wish he were here. More than anything, his presence would put an end to my tormented musing.

I have not heard a thing relative to James David Myle, my assigned mate. It's as if he has dropped off the face of the earth. I tell myself I mustn't be concerned. When the central computers notify me of my impregnation date, I will return to Salvation to do my duty, just as Helen did. I have only once broached the topic with Professor James, but he could not or would not offer anything, saying only that I will be told when the time is right.

Mostly, I continue to delve into Old Persian and especially King Darius 1, trying to answer my own question from what seems so long ago—why did King Darius create a new alphabet? By now, I understand the Behistun Inscription, located in the Kermanshah Province of Old World Iran. Left by Darius, it is the cuneiform equivalent of the Egyptian Rosetta Stone. The Behistun Inscription contains three versions of the same text written in three different cuneiform script languages: Old Persian, Elamite, and Babylonian, which itself is a later form of Akkadian and a Semitic language.

Early notes from Professor James indicate that the ruins of ancient Susa, the administrative capital of Darius 1, were uncovered by archaeologists around 1884. Also, in 1970, the Palace of Darius yielded a significant surprise when two stone tablets inscribed with cuneiform characters were found beneath its walls. They were apparently placed there at the end of the sixth century B.C.

The perfectly preserved tablets were made of gray marble and engraved on all six sides. The one placed under the east wall of a corridor was written in Akkadian. The second, from beneath the west wall, was inscribed in Elamite—the language of Elam, an ancient country to the east of Babylon. A third tablet was never found, but Old

World scholars speculated that if it existed, it would be inscribed in Old Persian, as was the Behistun Inscription.

Except from a historical perspective, religion is discouraged in our society. Basic training provides comparative religion courses, but always from the perspective of the havoc fanatical believers rained down on humanity over the ages. Cultural anthropologists in particular need to know about past religions to understand some of the resurrected artifacts. From that point of view, it is interesting these old tablets answered a question many Old World Christians once asked—how long is a cubit? The tablets clarify that measurement within a millimeter to 33.60 cm. According to the Old World Bible, Noah's ark was three hundred cubits long, fifty cubits wide, and thirty cubits high. I wonder if it was real. If so, could it have held two of each animal alive at that time?

I shake my head. What difference does a story about Noah's ark make when I'm supposed to be focusing on the reason King Darius ordered the creation of a new alphabet when it wasn't necessary? I am deep in thought when Professor James places his hand on my shoulder. "Hey, sunshine. Let's take a break."

My knees weaken at his touch. I feel a current of electricity pass through my body. The feeling isn't unpleasant, but there's something about it that makes me hungry for more. *Get ahold of yourself, Beth.* I breathe deep, exhale slow, and then rotate in my chair to face him. His face is only inches away. I gaze into his deep-blue eyes for only a moment and am totally stunned when he moves in close and brushes my lips with his. My heart races. I am both confused and delighted. Without thinking, I place my hands behind his head and return his kiss with all the passion that has been building inside me for months.

With all my heart, I don't believe either of us planned this. It just happened, and I am swept away with feelings I've never known. I want to prolong his kiss indefinitely, but he lifts me gently from the chair and embraces me, pressing his body against mine in a way that makes me want to throw away everything I've ever been taught. I squirm into him, welcoming his touch—trying to scratch an itch I've been suppressing for years. My body quivers so hard, vaginal fluid dampens my underwear.

In that moment, I know without question I am so totally in love with him that anything is possible. I want him, and I want him to want me—all of me. I move my legs slowly together, trying to stem the flow of oozing fluid, but that only drives him more. He lifts me from the floor during a prolonged kiss and carries me toward his bedroom. I melt into his arms and do nothing to resist. I want him. More than anything in my life, I want him now.

He lays me on his bed in a gentle, fluid motion; I am awash in a wave of passion. Kisses upon kisses follow as he lies beside me, slowly unbuttoning my clothing. I am lightheaded and breathe in short gasps as he removes my garments. It's like stepping into cold water, but instead of shock, I am pummeled with pleasure. When he removes his clothing and pulls my body to his, exquisite satisfaction fills my mind. I want more. I squirm against him and pull him atop me. It is an automatic response, not something I need think through. It just feels right. In the next instant, the passion of the moment erases the taboos of a lifetime, and we move together as one in a fog of utter bliss.

I give all of myself to him, holding nothing back. He is my first and only lover, but he is gentle and leads me down the path of love with great care, knowing I've never walked this path before. Tears of joy trickle from the corner of my eyes as a surreal pressure builds within me—a driving need—a hunger that urges me to squeeze him ever closer. I want to be inside his skin, to merge with him as a single person. An explosion of pleasure rips me from the tips of my toes to the top of my head, and I gasp for breath. I cannot stop the low moan that drives him to shudder with me. My climax cannot possibly be described in words. It is a transforming experience from girlhood to womanhood that will forever be our precious memory alone—a treasure of incomparable value.

I sleep more soundly that night, held in his arms, than at any time in my life.

Chapter Ten
The Shard

I wake alone the next morning. As I review the events of last night, guilt and recrimination set in. I have really screwed up this time and can hardly imagine the shit storm that will ensure if I turn up pregnant. No one cares about having lovers outside of assigned mates when children are produced by insemination; however, having a baby without Federation sanction is a *huge* problem that could even result in my reassignment to a work camp.

Before I can beat myself up in a big way, I hear rattling in the kitchen. I chew off another fingernail. *I hope I haven't crossed a line that cannot be uncrossed.* I pick up yesterday's clothes scattered about the floor, put them on, and step out to a table set with fruit, eggs, and hotcakes. *Odd...it's my day to cook, isn't it?* I decide to fake bravado. "Good morning, Professor," I coo. "You must know it's your day to do the dishes."

He is in an unusually good mood and smiles back. "A new tradition, Beth. On our anniversary, I'll do both." He pulls a chair out for me. "Come on over and sit down. We need to talk."

He holds my chair, tucks me into the table, serves my plate, and takes a seat directly across from me. It might be my imagination because I have so little experience, but his eyes seem to radiate love. As I begin eating, he places both elbows on the table, forms a teepee with his fingers, and looks me in the eyes. "You'll have to call me something besides Professor now, you know."

I smirk. "You mean like 'Mule'? That's not very romantic."

He grins. "No, anything but that. My real name is David. You can call me that."

A sudden revelation hits me so hard that I drop my fork. My hand darts to my mouth. "You're the one? You're David Myle? I thought 'Mule' was just a nasty nickname."

He raises his shoulders in a shrug and responds without hesitation. "David Myle at your service. I saw the error in your files but didn't want to correct it. I thought it best to let things develop between us naturally, the old fashioned way. The powers that be in Salvation omitted the comma after my last name. 'James David Myle' should have been, 'James, David Myle.'"

Still in shock, all I can babble is, "Myle? I...I didn't link that to Mule."

He nods. "Kids will be kids. It doesn't have to make sense."

I'm caught up in the irony of it all, having difficulty with words as I sort out the obvious. "So, you and I are paired—sanctioned by the Federation's central computer and already approved for offspring?"

He smiles wide and nods in agreement. "You are so beautiful, Beth, and I love you so much. I'm a very lucky man."

I glare back with a standoffish, impish expression while tapping my knife on the table. "So, last night you knew. While I believed I was violating every taboo I've ever been taught—even though I was doing nothing wrong—you knew."

He snickers through a broad smile as he places two hotcakes on his plate. "Don't get carried away with that knife. Yes, I knew, but not telling you made the experience all the more exciting for you, didn't it? Even if you weren't doing anything wrong."

He has a point. The exhilaration was incredible, the excitement breathtaking. "Makes filling the teacher's car with toilet paper seem tame. I'll give you that."

We settle into breakfast, discussing the previous evening and its meaning. There's no question that I love him, and I tell him so whenever there is a lull in the conversation. He's equally forthcoming with me, and he frequently leaves his chair to hug and kiss me. I'm ecstatic. He makes me feel warm all over. I feel secure with him. I belong with him. The computers are right. We are meant to be together.

After breakfast, David gathers the dishes and sets them by the kitchen sink. I don't want to move. I sit transfixed, adoring every move my lover makes. *How can there be such great pleasure in watching this mundane task?*

He slips behind my chair and kisses the back of my neck—a kiss that sends shivers up my back. His soft kisses work their way around to my face, and then he pulls back. He flicks his head toward the sink. "It'll be much more fun to do them together."

He runs his hands down my arms, and then pulls me out of my chair by my hands. "Come on, Princess. The sooner we get these done, the sooner you get dessert."

I can't help but giggle. "Are you dessert?"

He winks as he hands the dish towel to me. He shakes his head before gathering me in his arms and pulling me close. He nuzzles his face against mine and whispers, "I love you so very much, Beth. You are and always will be the love of my life."

I kiss his face, relishing the salty taste of the tear that has slipped down his cheek. We embrace each other for what seems like minutes until I feel him take a deep breath as he releases me. Holding hands, we stare into each other's eyes; love radiates between us. I am swept away with joy, drop one of his hands, and begin pulling him toward the bedroom. I look back and grin. "The dishes can wait. I want dessert now."

By mid-afternoon, we're both spent, lying next to each other and breathing hard. He runs his hands over my breasts, pulls me close for a gentle, full-body hug, and winks. "Think it's time for a little work break?"

We're both ready. Making love is fun, but at some point life must go on. After a light snack, we do the dishes and then settle in at our computers. I immerse myself in the Old Persian alphabet without delay, trying to understand all that's recorded about it and, even more, why it should exist at all. Engaged as I am in deep concentration, I don't notice David leave his desk and slip into his bedroom. I note his return, however, because he places a small object wrapped in felt by my mouse. I reach up, cradle his face in my right hand, and pull him down for a short kiss, "A gift for me? How sweet."

He answers with a sly smile. "I'm pretty sure you'll like it, but don't get too far ahead of yourself, dear. It just means more work. Be very careful with it."

What an odd response. I unfold the felt with great care, and my heart almost stops when I see what's inside—a wafer-thin shard of polished black material with writing on both sides, unlike anything I've ever seen. The shard is flat, about five inches wide on one end, three inches on the other, and weighs virtually nothing. I study the smooth edges. Whatever it is, it didn't break off something bigger. The piece seems complete as it is—exactly as it is.

The symbols on the shard, if they represent text, are *not* Old Persian. Old Persian is cuneiform—in the shape of wedges—but its individual symbols do not correspond to older systems with similar, phonetic values. The shard's inscription keeps the cuneiform appearance, but the shapes of the symbols are completely original. This text is not like anything I've studied.

After turning the shard over several times in total fascination, I look back at David. "What is this?"

"It's our project, Beth—the reason you're studying Old Persian."

I examine the object again, still confused. "But the imprints on this thing aren't Old Persian...and the substrate material looks modern."

He grins and nods. "So it does—and it is—but at the same time, it's not. In fact, it could be the oldest man-made artifact ever found. The small scratch near the edge was for testing. Carbon 14 dating places its age at three million years old."

I gasp as questions flood my mind, "Holy crap! How's that possible? Where did you get it?"

"My father found it in the Kill Zone, across the Atlantic. What do you make of it?"

I return my gaze to the shard. The symbols look a bit familiar, somewhat similar to Old Persian, but none show exact equivalency. The substrate material is also foreign. "I haven't the foggiest idea. What is it made of?"

He takes the piece and turns it over in his hands, gently rubbing his thumb on its smooth surface, as if loving it. "That's the surprising part, almost unbelievable. According to the Cheyenne Mountain electron micrograph scientists, it's a carbon composite called a buckysheet—an esoteric material with carbon atoms at each apex of an atomic hexagon. Its chicken wire-like matrix is extremely tough, almost indestructible, as might be expected from its age."

I'm puzzled. "Something like V5's buckyballs?"

David holds the shard to the light in deep admiration. He's had it for years, but I can tell he's still awestruck. "Very similar, except this material is flat. There are no pentagon carbon structures in it, so it can't form a sphere." He continues to turn the shard over in his hands and then adds, "This is our puzzle, and we'll probably spend the rest of our lives trying to solve it. Father didn't make much progress, but he made me promise I'd never give up."

I'm still amazed. How can anything but dirt be three million years old? "If it's as old as they say it is, wouldn't that mean everything we thought we knew about the Old World is wrong? Hell, even the people who were alive before BHS wouldn't have had a clue about something that old. So, is this the reason Sanctuary politicians tolerated Doctor Noble, even though he defied them at every turn?"

"It is. It's also the reason you were offered as my mate. They wanted to make sure someone far younger could pick up the project if something happened to me. Your testing proved you had excellent language skills. That satisfied them and is the reason they included you in the list of candidates submitted to me. You were also the cutest, and that satisfied me."

I give him a disgusted but playful look. "Chauvinist pig. What about the other female student you requested?"

He just snickers. "She was cute too but must have been afraid to get grimy. She opted out. The important thing is that you're here, and I've got you now."

I set the shard down, stand, and hug him with all my might. My heart is racing. "Researching this together could be fun, but is there anything else I should know, anything important you're keeping from me?"

He pulls back and flashes a sheepish grin. "There is one thing, and it's a big one. I hope you're up for the greatest adventure of your life."

Oh, my God. What could be more exciting than what I went through last night? "If you're there, sweetie, I'm there. What have you got?"

"A little trip…arranged two years ago. We leave this coming April. That should give us ample time to prepare."

I'm more than a little surprised. Nine months is a lot of time to prepare for a trip. "Someplace civilized, I presume? I hope?"

Holding up his finger, he adds, "Hold that thought." He then disappears into the bedroom. On return, he holds out a small bottle of pills. "It won't be civilized where we're going, Beth. Far from it, so you'll need to start taking these. They'll keep you from getting pregnant."

My mouth falls open. I feel stunned and deflated, like I've been hit hard. My eyes brim with tears. I step back without thinking, putting distance between the bottle and my womb. "But last night we talked about this. We both know my assignments—three girls and one boy—I thought you wanted that too. I want your children. I don't want those damn pills."

He steps forward and pulls me close again, rubbing his face on my hair. "I *do* want our children, sweetie, and we'll have them…just not now. If you get pregnant, I'll have to go alone. There'd be too much risk to take you. There are no doctors where we're going."

His statement hits me like a second blow. Even Hope has a doctor. Doctor Noble's notes flash through my mind. "You don't mean the Project Sanitize area, do you—the part of the Kill Zone where your father disappeared?"

He strokes my hair and kisses me on the forehead. "It has taken months to get you to this point, darling. I would never let anything bad happen to you. We have my father's notes and a pretty good idea where he might have found the shard. The nuclear blasts probably unearthed it, and there could be more like it."

Now I understand the reason for an April departure. The North Atlantic hurricane season runs from June through November, with peak activity from August to October. We are going by sea. As I begin to sort out the potential risks of such a trip, a blistering thought enters my mind. "Did radiation kill your father?"

He shrugs. "I don't think so, but I don't really know. He was overseas when he disappeared, so I'll never know for sure. Neither he nor his last notes were recovered, but he did return from his first trip, so I doubt radiation is a serious problem. Not all radioactive components decay with the 10,000-year half-life you studied in basic training. For example, Cesium-137 and Strontium-90 have half-lives of only about 30 years and 28 years, respectively. Even if some of the blast holes are slightly radioactive, they should be quite cool by now. Besides," he pauses to kiss my forehead, my cheeks, and my lips before he continues, "natural erosion over the past 183 years has certainly carried most of the really bad residue away. Overall, I expect radiation levels around the blast sites will be about the same as natural surface background levels."

I sit down and begin fondling the shard again, avoiding the pills in David's hand by picking up a magnifying glass to study the piece in greater detail. David seems impatient, but I know the longer I make him hold the pills, the more he'll realize how utterly disgusting the thought of taking them is to me. There's a standoff between him with the pills and me with the magnifying glass. I stare at the shard, concentrating hard while refusing to look up. That's when I notice something I had missed before, something that seems oddly…ordered. "Everything is so precise on this piece, it couldn't have been made by hand. A machine had to manufacture this."

I glance up to see David's eyes light up. He pumps his fist. All things shard are natural highs for him. "I agree, as did my father, but it's odd typing paper to say the least."

My brow furrows as I look closer. "Or not typed at all, unless by omission. Have you looked at the spaces between the symbols?"

He sets the pills directly in front of me, takes the shard and the magnifying glass, and moves to the light, studying the surface with extreme intensity. "What about the spaces?"

"The surfaces between the characters aren't smooth and level. There could be another layer below. That thing could have multiple levels."

I take a deep breath and exhale a loud sigh as I pick up the pills. David doesn't notice. He is so lost in studying the shard that he doesn't pay attention to my reaction at all. The damn thing is compelling beyond belief. Like him, I would really like to know what it means. If the pills are necessary to find out more, then I'll take them…whether I want to or not.

The next morning, we rise early, eat as fast as hungry dogs, pack a lunch, and head for the Hope Transportation Center. The trip to the outskirts of Old World Boston will take a couple of hours, and the weather is perfect for a day trip. We poke fun at each other and banter as the buggy bounces along, stabilized by oil shocks and air springs—the best of the old merged with the reality of the new. Although the birth control pills still nag at the back of my mind, it's nice to be able to smile and laugh with him, the life-changing decision of the previous day tucked underneath our laughter.

It's on days like this a person realizes how truly beautiful this country is. The trees are in full foliage, the breeze off the water is cool and refreshing, and animal life abounds along the narrow road. This isn't the main thoroughfare the bus followed when it brought me to Hope, but a back road that more or less parallels the coast. The road surface is made from recycled asphalt, finely ground so as not to harm the horse's hooves, and even the horse seems delighted to prance along in the warm summer air.

I can see the Old Boston Reclamation Center long before we reach it—the largest building for miles around. It is a hulking warehouse that must be a half-mile on each side and three stories high. Every large city has one—a place where Cultural Anthropologists generally end up. I'm fortunate to only be visiting. We pull up to the gate, and David hands his access badge to the gatekeeper. The man scans it into his computer, verifies access, and then asks, "What section?"

David takes his badge back and tips his hat to the guard. "We don't need much, just an item from Section M."

The man points south along the huge building, "About a quarter mile down on the right. There's a big sign. You can't miss it." We thank him, and the horse trots in the proper direction on its own, as if it understood the directions. Despite yesterday's disappointment over the birth control pills, I'm almost giddy with anticipation. As promised, an arrow with a large red "M" points the way to the interior of the building. We tether the horse by a small watering trough, grab a backpack out of the buggy, and strut in like we own the place.

The walk inside is spellbinding. The place is huge, even if one ignores its flanking outbuildings. Everything one can imagine from the Old World is reclaimed here: motors of all shapes and sizes, motorcycles, monocles, medical equipment, machinery of all descriptions, mess kits, metronomes—far too many things to mention. Each item is cataloged with multiple descriptors in the Salvation central database.

Among the treasures are a plethora of microscopes, each resurrected from the decaying old city, and every one meticulously restored. I am immediately drawn to a stereo version with digital attachment. I hold it up for David to see. "We can view the images on our computers, and it's even painted metallic blue. What more could you want?"

David looks it over but doesn't touch it. "Its maximum magnification is 500 power, and only one of us can use it at a time. We need something for serious study."

I'm a little deflated as I put the microscope back on the shelf. I love the color. I trail along behind David until I spot a large system in the back corner of one of the shelves. I call David's attention to it. "That's a big one. Would it do the job?"

He looks it over while shaking his head. "No, it wouldn't. It's a fluorescence microscope, capable of imaging the distribution of a single molecular species based solely on the properties of fluorescence emission. The shard is opaque, so that monstrosity wouldn't do us any good at all."

He seems to have something very specific in mind because he studies several before lifting one off the shelf to show me. "What do you think? It's dual view with1,000-power magnification. We can both view the shard at the same time through its dual stereo lenses."

"It's gray."

A serious scowl crosses his face. "The color doesn't matter, and you know it."

I shrug and then wink. "I guess it'll do. We can always paint it later."

With the microscope tucked inside David's backpack, we walk arm-in-arm with it to our buggy like proud parents. As we exit the facility, the gatekeeper carefully scans the bar codes on our prize and on David's badge. All restored items are extremely valuable to our society, so inventory control is rigidly enforced.

It has been a long morning, and nature is calling. I ask David to stop the carriage at a stand of trees about two miles from the exit to the compound. While I scout out a convenient bush, David sets out lunch. When I return from the edge of the small clearing, he is kneeling on our blanket in front of a large, flat rock. I approach from behind. "Do you always pray before lunch?"

He brushes me off with a wave of his hand. "Come on over. You've got to see this."

The microscope is in front of him. "Are we torturing some innocent insect with our new magnifying glass?"

He moves aside. "Take a look."

I have seen many ants in my life but none like this. Even the tiny, raised rim around the base of each of the ant's body hairs is visible. "Wow. No wonder you wanted this microscope. The clarity is amazing."

We are both hungry but more interested in looking at the 500-power ant than eating. As we study our captive under the lens, a horde of its relatives attack our food basket. We are enthralled until David slaps the back of his hand.

"Damn. It bit me." He scans the blanket. "Ants are everywhere. We need to move."

We shake out our basket and brush the ants off the salvageable items. The sandwiches are so infested that we leave them as spoils for the victors. After ensuring our clothes and blanket are ant free, we move to a new location where we take time for a few kisses. I'm open to far more than that, but David interrupts my growing passion and admonishes, "It's far more important to reach Hope before dark than to go to heaven now."

We pull into the Hope Transportation Center as the sun begins to set, drop off the horse and carriage, and hurry home. The moment we set the microscope on the kitchen table, David brings out the shard. We adjust our eyepieces at maximum magnification and focus on the blank spaces between the characters. Both of us see clear evidence of telltale lines beneath the black substrate. As thin as the shard is, it must be layered. David just shakes his head, "Astounding. For years, I've been so focused on the characters I overlooked the spaces between them. I wonder what they mean."

I continue staring into my eyepieces. "The slant of the faint lines is similar to that of the cuneiform-like characters we can see on the surface. Maybe there's another layer of symbols below. Old World masters reused canvases. Perhaps that's in play here as well."

He makes a fine adjustment to his binocular eyepieces. "I don't know, Beth. Why would they? If they had the technology to make this thing in the first place, would they bother to reuse part of it? Why not just remake the whole thing?" We study in silence until he adds, "Starting tomorrow, let's try to map the lines below, one space at a time, to see if we can find a pattern similar to the characters we see on the surface. If there are characters below the top layer, we might be able to make some out."

It seems a reasonable approach. We prepare for the task by moving our computers close to the microscope on the kitchen table, with David on one side and me on the other. It will be a monumental task that will take considerable time, but despite the repetitive nature of the work, I am delighted to be part of the team. Nothing in my life compares to the excitement of this investigation, except perhaps my first night of intimacy with David.

After a long evening of staring at the faint lines beneath the surface of the shard, I lean back in my chair and rub my eyes. I waggle my eyebrows at David and flick my head toward our bedroom door. "If this shard has survived three million years, then I suspect it will still be here tomorrow. Any chance we can go to bed?"

I see David's eyes shift to the clock on his computer desktop. "Good grief, it's almost midnight. I didn't realize it was getting so late."

He closes his notebook and winks. "You're right. There is at least one thing more exciting than this shard."

As we lie down, I feel quite itchy, and it's not just that I want David to make love to me. His soft kisses take my mind off my growing misery for a moment, but as our physical exertion increases to the point that it dampens the sheets, my itch goes berserk—the heat and sweat produced by the two of us make it impossible to go on. David is in the throes of ecstasy when I push him back to arm's length while squirming my butt into the sheets to relieve the incessant itch. "Sorry, dear. Something's wrong. We've got to get to the bottom of this."

David chuckles. "I thought I was."

"Damn you. It's not always about sex. There's something wrong. I need you to look at my ass."

His grin broadens. "That would be my extreme pleasure, ma'am. Is there anything else?"

"Just look down there, and tell me what's causing the problem. I itch like hell."

In a moment, I hear, "Oh, dear. That doesn't look good."

I tighten my buttocks to scratch the itch I don't want to touch. "Cut to the chase. What is it?"

He sweeps his eyes across my crotch, pauses, and eventually continues upward to make contact with my eyes. "Have you been sitting naked in something forbidden?"

"I don't sit naked anywhere except..." I stop mid-sentence. Oh, crap. I didn't think I'd need to fess up. I look down and to the side. "I didn't tell you at the time because I was embarrassed, but I fell on my butt when I squatted to pee this afternoon."

"Any chance your tumble was cushioned by Poison ivy? Or maybe an ant hill?"

"No. We have those in Salvation. I know what they are. All I saw were some pretty yellow flowers with darkish centers."

"Like daisies?"

"Sort of."

He shakes his head. "Probably Black-eyed Susan. If you're allergic, they can cause a rash. You could be out of commission for a few days." He gets out of bed and dresses. "I'll be back in a half hour. The infirmary is bound to have some Fluocinonide. That'll fix you up."

When he returns after what seems an eternity, the relief is almost immediate. The rash won't disappear for at least a week, but I've learned an important lesson. No matter how excited I might be, I will always stabilize myself when squatting to pee.

* * * *

Over the next three weeks we study the shard with renewed urgency, piecing together a rough map of the slightly raised edges we see beneath the surface. As we agree on the symbols we can discern within the layers, we bring them together on a shared electronic drawing space. Most of the infinitesimally raised edges can't be identified as anything we've seen before, but a few can. The partial outlines of those isolated symbols are clear enough that we can say, with almost complete certainty, they are the same as the symbols we see on the shard's visible surface.

There is no immediate reward for all our painstaking work. Any meaning to the characters, on the top layer or below, eludes us. Then, after a hard day of canning cherries, we have a breakthrough. While we rest at the table, staring into the glow of our computer screens, and still wondering what it all means, David suddenly interjects, "I'll be damned. Maybe they're not character symbols at all."

I'm caught off guard as I look up at his thoughtful face. "I'm sorry?"

"They might not be characters, honey. There could be an Old World primitive parallel to what we see in the shard. Before BHS, growing circuitry on a substrate, one layer at a time until the board performed the desired function, was revolutionizing layered circuit board construction. The major problem, the reason they never achieved a complete revolution, was heat dissipation. Resistance components generate heat and are hard to cool when layered. If heating hadn't been a problem, or if superconducting components could have been developed, supercomputers could have been grown in a laboratory and reduced to a tiny speck."

I'm stunned again. "You mean the shard might be an assemblage of electronic components, like resistors?"

He snickers, "Maybe, but it could be much more complex than printed circuit boards from the Old World. From the beginning, we've thought of the symbols on the shard as characters, but what if the symbols are a gold cooling coating over resistive and amplification material— logic elements? In that case, the spaces between the symbols could be the equivalent of printed wiring. What we're seeing might actually be a layer of circuit components, with another layer deposited below the surface. If true, the shard might represent technology far beyond anything we're aware of—far beyond the ability of modern humans to create it."

My mouth drops as I consider the possibilities. If David is right, the historical meaning of his comment would be overwhelming. When I can no longer contain my thoughts, I blurt, "If ancient man found something like that, they would have no concept of what it might be. I mean, what if one of King Darius's soldiers found something equivalent to the shard, and Darius took it to a seer? What message would a seer give to a king? The material is unlike anything in the Old World. It is lighter than wood and stronger than bronze or any other weapon they had at the time—and the characters written on it would have defied logic then. For that matter, they defy logic now."

I can't stop talking. Thoughts pour out of my mouth as fast as my mind can generate them. "Can't you picture it? What if the seer tells the king the object is a message from God? The seer would earn the favor of the king by revealing God's message, and the king would believe he was empowered by God to do whatever the seer told him. Don't you see, David? The king *is* Darius, and the message from the seer must have been simple: 'Set out a new alphabet in accordance with these symbols, and spread the language over all the earth.'"

I can't stop now. I'm too excited, too eager to put all of the pieces together. "That could be the reason Old Persian departs dramatically from other scripts at the time. It could also explain why Darius conquered the entire known world. With a directive from God, he would've been motivated to go forth in strength. Perhaps that's also the reason Darius was such a benevolent king, why he was so good to the people he overcame. He allowed religions of all types to flourish, never restricting the worship of God in any form. A shard like this could have been the example for crafting a new alphabet, and the impetus for spreading the new alphabet around the world."

David's eyes are wide open by the time I take an excited gasp, and all he can say is, "Wow. What if?"

We look at the shard with renewed respect and then at each other with incredible excitement. We could be on to something never discovered by Old World scholars. It will be difficult to sleep tonight. The shard is three million years old but might be more advanced than our own technology. The concept defies logical rectification. We have several months before our scheduled departure for the Old World Middle East, and we'll need every minute to put together a consistent theory that might explain some of this.

Chapter Eleven
The Long Journey

Over the next several months, we prepare for the 8,800-kilometer trip between Hope and the most distant point in the Mediterranean. We must plan with great care. For many months, we will explore an area devoid of other people—an area with no hope of assistance from any quarter. Very few people make such trips, and I can't help but feel a mix of excitement and dread. The hardships will be great, but we have the opportunity to make incredible discoveries.

We have secured passage on the Marco Polo—a 752-foot oil recovery ship that makes one or two trips a year to the old Suez Canal with a crew of men specially trained to scavenge whatever residual oil they can from existing tanks and wells.

After they drop us at their destination, we'll be on our own. Therefore, our preparation must take us far beyond my basic survival training and David's years of accumulated knowledge. There will be no opportunity for resupply. We will have what we can carry with us and nothing more. That means it won't be enough to know how to operate a firearm. Since bullets are heavy, and we can only carry a few, I must hit everything I shoot at—every time I pull the trigger. Creature comforts will also be limited due to space and weight concerns. Instead of recyclable, absorbent paper feminine hygiene products, I'll need to take cloth squares that can be rinsed out and reused. We must also become experts on desert and mountain survival techniques, shelter building, and potential safe water sources.

I grimace when I think of the physical conditioning I will have to endure. The trip will be like going back in time to the beginning of the Old World. Life will be primitive.

Mother's emails continue arriving on a daily basis, but her level of concern has spiked. Internet does not exist where we are going. She is worried because she will not be able to communicate with me after we leave Hope. A passage from one of her emails is especially poignant: "As you know, your father and I are delighted David is your assigned mate. We believe children between the two of you would have great potential. We beg you to consider, from the bottom of our hearts, that you produce children before undertaking your journey. Your father and I would consider it an honor to care for them in Salvation while you are overseas."

Tears slip from my eyes and run down my cheeks. She's right. Having children now would be a good idea. I pull the birth control pills from the desk drawer and glare at them as a prickly shudder slithers down my back. *What if I just stop taking them? What would David do if I became pregnant? Would he reschedule the trip or just go without me?* Thoughts of David going alone jar me as strongly as not being able to be with my own children while they are young. I exhale deeply. There might not be another opportunity to have children—we might never return—but there is no way I'd let him go alone. We will survive together, or we will die together. Besides, an assigned berth on an oil ship is a rare commodity. If we pass it up, there won't be another chance for many years. The only response I can think of for now is to ignore her comment completely.

As the months pass, we read everything we can about Middle East plant and animal life, dangerous snakes and insects, and study maps with oasis locations and nuclear detonation sites. Doctor Noble's notes are invaluable, but he didn't return from his second trip. David knows his father prepared for the second trip at least as thoroughly as we are. That's a concern for both of us. Something not written in his notes might have taken his life—and whatever it was might take ours as well.

On the morning of our departure, we retrieve our most precious item—the shard. We have fashioned a small leather scabbard for it that I belt securely to David's chest under his shirt. Because we understand so little about the shard, we can't rule out that it could provide additional revelations when we get to our destination. On the other hand, if we never return, Salvation's support for research into the shard's origin will end. There is no downside to taking it.

I snuggle next to David in the cool air as a small tender craft pulls up to the Hope pier. We are allowed only three trunks and two suitcases. One of the trunks is packed with jerky. Another is stuffed with dried fruits. Both are waterproof and insect-proof. A third has exploration equipment, firearms and ammunition, a small tent, survival gear, and our microscope. The suitcases contain our clothes and personal supplies. We intend to establish a base camp for the trunks when we reach the Kill Zone. From our base camp, we will venture into the wilderness, taking only what is necessary for austere survival.

The ride to the ship on the tender boat is choppy, and my heart sinks as I watch Hope disappear into the salt mist. David reaches over and holds my hand, rubbing the back of it with his thumb. I try to focus on his comforting gesture, but all I can think about is the last email I sent to my mother, telling her I would miss her and explaining my decision to hold off on children in favor of exploration. I think David knows the thoughts running through my head, but he doesn't say anything. He just holds my hand, not letting it go.

By the time we reach the ship, seasickness is already having a negative impact on me. I feel queasy, so I keep my eyes focused on the horizon in hopes that will prevent the nausea from taking me completely. As much as anything, motion sickness is a state of mind. It can be overcome with sheer will—a fundamental fact taught during any beginning pilot training course. I know that, so I keep telling my mind

I'm not sick. Unfortunately, my body isn't getting the message.

As soon as we board the ship, two members of the ship's crew haul off our trunks and secure them beneath a tarp on deck. We are told our assigned quarters are too small to accommodate them. As a result, the trunks won't be available until we reach our destination.

They are right about the cubbyhole they take us to. The closet-like room is only large enough for us to edge in next to two bunks situated one atop the other. There is little room to move. The smell of diesel fuel permeates the mattresses and every corner of our tiny space, pushing my urge to vomit even nearer the edge. Even though there is one small porthole opposite the door to the room, it is clear to me we'll spend the majority of this trip above deck.

After sliding our two suitcases beneath the bottom bunk, we take a slow tour of the ship as it begins its long journey. There is no rush. At twenty-seven kilometers per hour, the ship won't arrive at its destination for at least two weeks. I'm relieved to reach the open-air deck two floors up from our tiny cabin. The air is fresh and sweet above deck. It calms my seasickness but stokes my homesickness-even now we can no longer see land. The first officer corrals us almost the moment we step into the sunshine. "You've got to go through safety procedures before you can be out here alone."

He proceeds with his standard spiel, shows us the location of fire and rescue equipment, and issues life vests to each of us. "If you're above deck, put 'em on or the crew will send you below. No exceptions." I'm not sure why, but most of his comments seem to be directed at me.

The deck is loaded with heavy machinery and smelly oil recovery equipment. The mechanical things show considerable wear, like they were heavily used in the past and not well cared for since then. Everything is grimy with sludge. The clear walking path that snakes among and around the rusting piles generally follows the outer perimeter of the hull. At the bow, we are able to peer over the edge into the deep blue water below. Dolphins arch up alongside the minimal bow wave. They are a delight to watch. The sun sparkles off the gentle swells, and the wind feels warm on my face as it tosses my hair about. The beauty of the moment completely takes my seasickness away.

Four days out, we run into a small squall. Despite its size, the ship rolls like a cork in the angry seas. My seasickness returns with a vengeance, and I retch until I pass out from exhaustion. David holds me as I sleep on the deck, covered by a small tarp. The sea settles by morning, but we are drenched and freezing cold.

We make arrangements for private use of the ship's shower facilities—an area designed to accommodate men only. David holds me as I shake uncontrollably under a stream of hot water—the only luxury I've experienced since we left Hope. I have missed my daily shower, and I relish it now. The warmth eases into my skin. My incessant shivering slows and then comes to a stop. A change of clothes and breakfast bring me fully around. I now appreciate the value of a calm day more than ever.

Time passes slowly at sea. Each day blends with the day before. One week out, and our small stateroom seems to be getting smaller. I have not adjusted to the stench of diesel and doubt I ever will. Sea sickness comes and goes, so we spend as much time on deck as possible. I have come to dread meals. Being the only woman on board, I believe the men wistfully watch every move I make as I move through the chow line. I try to steer David away from as many men as I can after we fill our plates, but David usually opts for the first available table. That the men seem to leer at me could be my imagination. David says they are just being friendly. I'm not at all sure I want those friends.

Late afternoon one beautiful day, David leaves me alone on the deck while he seeks out the captain for an update on the progress of our trip. Standing by the rail, I look back to see the arrow-straight wake disappear into the distance in the direction of Hope, now so very far away. It is ironic that what I once considered primitive, I now consider luxurious. With all my soul, I wish I were home.

My sheer isolation in the middle of the ocean hits me hard. I have left everything I have ever known, even my family, to be here on this deck at this moment. I shudder as tears fall from my eyes. David has only been out of sight for a very short time, and I am awash with homesickness the likes of which I have never known. I place my hands over my face and bawl like a child.

By the time David puts his arm around my waist, my nose is running and tears streak my face. I am a mess. I bury my face in his shirt as I turn toward him and sob while he pats my back. He seems to know what's wrong without asking, and he whispers, "We'll see them again, Beth. We will come home. I promise."

I look up as I wipe my tears. My voice trembles. "You shouldn't make promises you might not be able to keep."

He gently lifts my chin with his curled index finger. "I promise—we will get back. My father made the round trip in a tiny boat, and our boat is much bigger."

He holds me until my emotional outburst ebbs along with the setting sun. As the ship's lights flicker on, he smiles at me. "How about we eat out tonight?" He points to a crate resting against the bow beneath the green glow of the large starboard running light. "The concierge has an open table."

After receiving our nightly ration, we pull up two small spools for chairs. The only breeze is that produced by the ship cutting through dead calm air. It's my kind of evening—peaceful. David takes my hand. "Feeling better now?"

I nod as I take a bite of the greasy gravy over pasta. I believe it's supposed to be some sort of Stroganoff, but the beef tips are chunks of gristly, reconstituted meat-like product. God only knows what it is. I sigh. "The fish might appreciate this more than me."

David chuckles. "When we get where we're going, you might wish you had food that good."

Even though I can do without that kind of encouragement, I smile back. David is my constant companion and cheerleader, and I am his solace. We have made a pact that I will never break: no matter what the obstacles, no matter what challenges lie ahead, we will do this together. I lift my water glass in a toast. He does the same. When the edges touch, I commit once again, "To our love."

The days drag on. Our hearts are uplifted when the coast of Old World Gibraltar passes to our port side, and we enter the crystal clear waters of the Mediterranean. This sea is much smaller than the Atlantic—I feel safer here—but the distance to our destination is still five days hence.

The intended destination of this ship is the Suez Canal, its 195-kilometer length maintained by dredges. The canal is used exclusively by oil recovery ships now. Some of the crew making the trip with us will rotate out those currently manning the dredges. When we are one day from reaching Port Said, I can feel the excitement of the crew building. To every man aboard, land seems to trump ocean, regardless of how desolate the land might be.

The night before we are scheduled to leave the Marco Polo, huge thunderheads rear ahead. Without warning, the sea becomes an enraged monster in a fit of frothy turmoil. Massive waves batter the ship, making the hull shudder as its screws lift from the water before the ship rolls again into the advancing sea.

The hull pounds against the waves, and the severe list between troughs and ridges drives David and me to the deck where sheets of rain and screaming wind force us against the main superstructure. David grabs the back of my shirt as an inrushing wave sweeps me off my feet and washes me toward the scuppers. He shouts over the roar of the squall as he drags me upright, "Hook your arm over the rail and hold on tight with both hands! I'll find something to lash us down."

In a moment, he returns with a few fathoms of rope, fighting every step like a drunken sailor. He points toward the large mooring winch near the bow as he tugs on my arm. "We'll tie off there."

We make our way along the railing until we reach the bow. The wind attempts to rip his words away as he shouts, "Make your break when the ship dips into the next trough. You'll only have a second, so make it count. When you reach the capstan, hang on!"

The winch is only five feet away but seems like many kilometers. When the hull slams down, and the wheelhouse shudders under the force of the pounding, I step off as David pushes me in the direction of the winch. I fight to maintain my balance and fall onto the capstan's huge steel drum as the bow juts upward into the next oncoming wave. While I hold on with all my strength, David staggers toward me. The ship rolls over the crest of the wave as he begins lashing us to the capstan, his right hand red with blood.

Tsunamis of water rush past, trying to tear us from our steel buttress. The rope and knots hold. I yell over the howling wind as David attempts to bind his hand with his kerchief, "What happened? How bad is it?"

"I got slammed into the bulkhead when I went for the rope. It looks worse than it is. I'll be okay by the time we get through this storm." The battering continues for hours as the gale and waves force the ship northward. I cry like a pathetic fool, but it does no good. I am cold, drenched, and scared to death. Have I left Hope only to die in this raging sea? We expect the weather must improve soon because it simply can't get any worse, but we are wrong. To our horror, in the insipient dawning light, a rogue wave over 100 feet in height approaches at incredible speed from the south. There is little time for tenderness. David takes me in his arms, holds me tight, and whispers in my ear, "I love you, darling. I'm so sorry to have dragged you into this."

The wave hits the ship with the force of many hurricanes, and we hear the gut-wrenching groan of tearing metal as the ship lists hard aport, shudders a final time, and begins its ragged descent toward the bottom. We untie our lashings, hold tight to the railing, and then struggle to enter the nearest unsinkable lifeboat. David secures the small boat's hatch moments before a falling steel crane rips away the support davits. For a moment there is the weightlessness of free-fall, and then we slam against the dark interior of the small craft as it plunges with tremendous force into the angry sea.

We are temporarily righted by the ballast weight of the davits, just long enough for David to belt us both in. In the next moment, the davit ropes tear free, and the small craft rockets upward, breaks the surface, and is thrown northward like a giant Styrofoam bead. Even lashed in with taut straps, the pounding we endure is brutal and merciless.

By mid-morning, the sea begins to settle enough to permit movement within the small, sealed craft. David unleashes his binding and scurries to a small porthole. "I can't be sure, but I believe we're still moving north—the sun is starboard."

"Do you see any other lifeboats out there?"

He shakes his head. "No, just some debris, probably from the ship."

When he returns and sits beside me, I treat the gash in his hand using the gauze and antiseptic from the craft's first aid kit. He strokes the large bruise on my arm with the tip of his finger. "You kept your head back there, Beth. I'm proud of you. We are beat up and bruised but still alive."

I smile back. "I wonder if the worst is behind us...or yet to come."

Despite the choppy seas, we manage to scout the lifeboat for anything that might help our survival. We find emergency rations and water stowed beneath the seats, but our situation is still dire. There are no people in this part of the world and no other lifeboats on the horizon. We have lost our supplies, and rescue is out of the question. All we have in our favor is the knowledge from our survival studies before we boarded the Marco Polo. I squeeze David's hand and wink. "At least we have each other. You can be Adam. I'll be Eve."

As nightfall nears, we believe we see land out the starboard porthole, and we poke our heads out the hatch to hear the sound of breaking waves in the distance. David swallows hard as a grave expression crosses his face. "We're in for another rough ride, Beth. Better buckle up tight."

We don't wait long to experience the truth of his statement. A large roller catches the craft and surfs it toward shore. The wave breaks beneath us as it reaches the shallows, and the lifeboat slams hard into the sand, jarring us senseless. Following waves pound the port side, shoving us farther up on the beach. Then, for the first time in many weeks, I no longer feel the swell. Everything is still. The boat has lodged in the sand. David wastes no time. He grabs the emergency rope from beneath the forward bulkhead, sprints through the hatch, and in moments, secures the small craft to a stout cedar tree growing just inland of the beach.

We have arrived, but where?

Chapter Twelve
Quest for Survival

We don't sleep well that first night on shore. Our need to plan for our continued survival outweighs our need for rest. We search the lifeboat by candlelight, looking for anything we might have missed during our initial survey and mentally inventory everything we find. The boat's supplies will sustain us for a few days but not on a permanent basis.

Around midnight, as David studies the meager pile of supplies we've stacked at the bow of the boat, I slip behind him and wrap my arms around his waist. With my head laid against his back, I whisper, "Tomorrow's another day, love. We should get some rest."

He turns toward me without breaking my hug and then kisses my forehead while brushing my bangs aside with his hand. "We've trained for this. We can do this." He flicks his head toward the supplies. "We have enough to last until we can figure out how to sustain ourselves."

I snuggle into the warmth of his body. "I didn't like the color of the microscope anyway."

At daybreak, we exit the craft to survey the surrounding area. War and mankind ravaged the Eastern Mediterranean flora before BHS, but the native plant life has substantially recovered over the past 183 years. Below the larger cedars and oaks, pines, cypresses, firs, junipers, and carobs are abundant. We don't see any large animals but are aware that bears, lions, and jackals could be lurking within the brush. David shades his eyes as he scans the horizon. "At least it's not totally desolate. Our first priority is finding water. Food is second."

From atop the lifeboat, I sweep the beach with the small field glasses I found in the lifeboat's emergency kit.

"There's something on the beach, but I can't tell what it is. Should we check it out?"

He rolls his eyes and shrugs. "Why not? My schedule is wide open."

David walks the beach a little ahead of me, constantly scanning from the water to the tree line, and his hand never leaves the flare gun he found in the lifeboat's emergency kit. His alert posture makes me nervous. "You seem tense. Is there something I should be aware of?"

He doesn't look back. "Why would I be tense? We are thousands of kilometers from civilization with enough food and water to last only a couple of days. What could possibly go wrong?"

I guess he's not in the mood for talking. As I follow his footsteps, I am taken by how similar this beach is to the ones we left behind near Hope. The warm sun dances across my forehead as memories of better times flood my mind. It would be wonderful to walk hand-in-hand with David along the beaches at home right now.

When we cross a dune encroaching into the ocean, I can more clearly see the object ahead, and my spirit soars. I strain through the binoculars before crying out, "Oh my God, David. It's one of our trunks."

We run toward it, wondering which one it might be, and we are delighted to find not one but all three still strapped together as they were on Marco Polo's deck. We untie them and drag them above the tideline, relieved that our chance of survival has now multiplied 100-fold.

David constructs a crude harness using the ropes that tied the trunks together, and then we begin dragging each one along the beach to the lifeboat. We needed a base camp before going inland, and the lifeboat will be just that. Water is now our most pressing issue. Lingering showers from the storm the night before could provide it, so we set out funnels and plastic collection bags from our survival gear, hoping the storms will come again tonight.

The remainder of the day we secure the lifeboat. The large waves last night deposited the craft far above the tideline. Nevertheless, we dig around the base and let it settle into a horizontal position, held in place by surrounding sand. I am exhausted by the time the sun approaches the western horizon. My hands are calloused from my time in Hope, but those callouses ache from using the lifeboat's small survival shovel. David wipes his brow as he pats the now-stable craft. "This could save our lives in the future. It's important we preserve it as best we can."

I stab the shovel into the sand and shake my head as I drag myself toward the welcoming hatch. "The future? I'm just hoping the bunks are level enough now so I can get a good night's sleep."

When I recline on my bunk, David squats next to me. "You up for a little excitement in our new world tonight?"

I open my eyes and glare with a menacing scowl. "I've had enough excitement, thank you. Go to sleep."

He snickers before slipping into his bunk. "Thought as much, but a guy needs to ask."

I awake refreshed the next morning, thankful to be alive. David thrusts his head in through the hatch when he hears me stirring. He offers a huge smile and tosses in a plastic jug full of water. "The rain gods were good to us last night. The storms that tried to kill us the night before returned to fill our water collection bladders."

Funny, I didn't hear it rain last night. It's amazing how sound a person can sleep when totally exhausted. I smile at David, wipe the sleep from my eyes, and take a sip of the sweet water. We now have all the food and water we need to begin exploring inland, but we have no idea where we are. We will scout the local area today but won't move until we have a clear night. We have a sextant. That and the stars will reveal our location. Perhaps the sky will clear tonight. Then, we'll know exactly where we are and which way to go.

* * * *

I awake before dawn the next day to find David missing. I poke my head through the hatch to be greeted by calm, warm air with bright stars above. "David? Are you out there?"

"Here, love. Above the tideline, shooting the stars."

He's making notes by candlelight. I'm relieved. There'll be comfort in knowing where we are, even if that won't help us get home. In about thirty minutes, David returns to the lifeboat. "We are about ten to twenty kilometers north of Old World Beirut, Lebanon."

That's not what I wanted to hear. The Project Sanitize bombs fell along the borders of Old World Iraq, Iran, and Syria, from the Persian Gulf to the Mediterranean. We are far south of the point where the bombs intersected the coast.

We had originally planned to secure a small boat from the oil recovery workers at the mouth of the Suez and take that boat north until we reached the first blast residue. We would have established a base camp there and then headed east along the blast line on foot. I look down and mutter, "That changes things a lot. In fact, hasn't our mission changed? Even if we could find the source of the shard, what good would that do? We have no way to get back home. Maybe we should just set up a homestead here and make the best of it." I pull the birth control pill bottle from my pocket. "If we do that, I won't need these."

David rubs his chin as if he's actually considering my comments, but I soon know he's not. "I know you want children, Beth. I know that." He removes the shard from its scabbard and holds it up. "I still believe this artifact is far more important than any children we might or might not have. Who can explain this? How can it be three million years old? Come on. How could we sleep at night not knowing the answer to that riddle?"

His comment is like a stab in my heart, and I gasp as my hands fly to my cheeks. Tears well up in my eyes. "It's just a remnant from one of those damn bombs! It can't be more important than our children."

Oh, oh. Now I've done it. I've cast doubt over this entire adventure. David looks away, and his voice trails off into the night as he walks back toward the knoll where he left the sextant. "Maybe it is; maybe it isn't. I'm pretty sure they didn't have atomic bombs three million years ago."

Except for my muted sobs, all is silent. We are near the original Garden of Eden. It could belong to mankind once again—it could belong to us. By the time David returns, I have calmed my emotions. Fighting with him will do no good. Finding the source of the shard has been his dream far longer than having his children has been mine.

David sits beside me for several minutes before speaking. "I used the pointer stars in the big dipper to set the digital clock from our trunk. It's about 4:30 a.m. You need to get more sleep because we are heading south in the morning."

"South? But you said we were north of Old World Beirut."

He pats me on the arm and flicks his head toward my bunk. "Go to sleep now. We are going to Old World Beirut first. It was a huge city with over three million people at one time. Somewhere in its ruins we might find at least one useable boat. That's what cultural anthropologists do."

Oh, I see. He intends to return to our original plan. I guess that makes sense. I'll need my birth control pills after all. I won't argue any more tonight. Tomorrow is another day.

When the sun comes up, we fill our backpacks with sufficient supplies to last two weeks and ensure our weapons are operational. We need weapons for protection against wildlife during our trek. If we're lucky, we'll also harvest fresh meat when we spot game. The walk along the shoreline toward Beirut is pleasant, with temperatures around 22 Celsius and a steady, cool onshore wind. In two hours, the ruins of the ancient city loom in the distance.

As we get closer to the city, olive trees, fig trees, and grapevines are prevalent. We take time to collect several days' supply of figs and grapes. The city itself is overgrown and crumbling but home to thousands of rabbits. With so many cubbyholes and so much vegetation growing on every conceivable surface, the plethora of rabbits here makes sense. The rabbits are also a red flag. They are an open invitation for packs of wild dogs. I walk closer to David, realizing we might be prey, too. He rests his hand on my shoulder for a moment and smiles, trying to offer some form of comfort. I smile back at him, but I'm not sure I mean it. I'm also not sure he's fooled by my plastic optimism.

We move cautiously past the decaying port area where large cargo ships long ago sank to the bottom after becoming victims of disrepair and severe storms. Old World Beirut was once a center for Middle East pleasure boating as well as commerce, with extensive and elaborate marinas and waterfront facilities. We press on to the decaying yacht basin beyond the port. There might be something there that hasn't yet turned to dust.

As we round the bend leading into the yacht basin, a ripe target of opportunity looms—a huge luxury yacht, about 150-meters long. The yacht is grounded parallel to the inner seawall dead ahead. Listing toward the sea, the yacht has been incessantly battered over time, but it might still have an intact pleasure craft aboard.

Adjacent to the seawall, a gaping hole near the bow provides easy access. With great caution, we enter and work our way through interior passageways toward the stern. Sunlight penetrates holes in the hull above. Our hand-powered flashlights prove invaluable where the deck above is solid. About midway through the ship, David dips into a dark, cool room. In moments I hear him exclaim, "Bingo."

A minute later he emerges from the hole he entered, smiling from ear to ear. I smirk as I raise my shoulders and palms. "What? Did you find a urinal in there?"

He laughs. "Not that good. It's a surprise for later."

"Why can't you tell me now?"

"Because that would ruin the surprise."

I sigh and give him an annoyed look, hoping that it'll get him to reveal more. Instead, he just kisses my lips and pulls me forward to walk with him. He's lucky I like the feel of his lips. Otherwise, we'd still be discussing his supposed surprise.

We move on, exhilarated by the possibilities that lie ahead. As we approach the exit to the fantail, a low growl stops us dead in our tracks. David immediately draws his old but lethal .38 caliber Smith and Wesson as I sweep the area with my flashlight. I gasp, and my heart pounds almost out of control when four pairs of bright green eyes reflect back at me.

The low rumble intensifies as we back against the wall. I slowly reach for my .38 as well. Before I can pull my revolver, one pair of eyes leaps toward my throat. A blinding flash of muzzle fire erupts from David's weapon. The entire area illuminates for an instant, and I see several wolves, or dog-hyena mix, in the shadows beyond. We've invaded their den. The bullet from David's gun rips through the attacking dog in mid-air. It howls in anguish before falling lifeless to the deck and sliding to a stop about a meter from my feet. The other dogs are stunned by the sound of the report and back away. They must sense this prey won't be easy.

Like an alpha male, David steps between me and the dogs and shouts, "Git. Go." The dogs retreat a short distance away, cower, and continue growling. They pace and whine with their eyes fixed on us, as if searching for any sign of weakness. "Crank up your light, honey. Hand it to me, and move slowly toward the door. Take the dog carcass with you."

I struggle to pull the dead dog toward the exit, trying not to make any sudden moves. The remaining dogs snarl and glare at the edge of the flashlight beam. The moment I drag the dead animal into the sunlight, David steps out and slams the door as one of the dogs inside throws itself against the opposite side. We hear the thud and then frantic paw scratching amid vicious yips and snarls.

Although almost overcome with fear, I still have the presence of mind to point a shaking finger toward the dead dog. "Why the hell did you want that?"

With the other dogs still attacking the opposite side of the door in a desperate attempt to get at us, he answers in flat monotone, "Protein—waste not, want not."

The lifeboat dangling vertically over the landward side of the yacht will do us no good. It has been battered against the seawall for many years and little remains. However, secured to the seaward side of the deck, an aluminum-hulled catamaran seems unscathed. Fast and light, the vessel must have been a trifle to its original owner. It's a life-saving artifact to us now.

We find a block and tackle with nylon rope in a deck locker and use it to inch the catamaran to the edge of the ship and then lower it into the water below. Time is of the essence. We don't want to spend the night here for fear of the dogs. As fast as I can, I rummage through locker after locker. I find fishing tackle and packaged Kevlar sails before David calls a halt to my treasure hunt and lowers me to the sailboat below.

As soon as David comes aboard, we push off using the aluminum paddles stowed aboard the catamaran and begin paddling toward the outer seawall. From that location we can see the dogs coming for miles. We tie off at the end of the jetty, unpack the sails, and install the mainsail. The sheets are in excellent condition. It's likely this catamaran has never been used.

The sailing lessons David received from Doctor Noble might save us both now. I offer a silent "thank you" to his father as we furl the sail and begin tacking northward, driven by the landward sea breeze. The craft is fast by any measure. In forty-five minutes, our lifeboat base camp comes into view. As directed, I crank all but the top of the mainsail onto the roller-furling collector built into the boom, and we run with the wind toward shore. Once again, the lifeboat will be our sanctuary. We will spend the night there. Tomorrow, we will lash the trunks to the catamaran deck and head north.

As night falls, we build a fire on the beach to barbecue the dog David killed earlier. He also weighs its skin down with rocks in the water behind the catamaran. By morning, the crabs and salt water will have cleaned it enough that we can salt it down and roll it up. It's not much, but if we're still here in winter, it could come in handy.

When we finish dinner, David hands me an aluminum cup containing a dark liquid and winks. "Enjoy. It'll make a woman out of you."

I distort my face into a pout. "I thought you already did that."

He snickers and winks. "Well, maybe, but that's two hundred-year-old rum. You're gonna love it."

"You brought this from the yacht? Is that why you were so delighted? Is this your surprise?"

He grins as he encourages the cup toward my lips. "You've gotta try it. Only the best for my bride."

Still holding the cup, I take a look around. Our situation is not good. I'm eating dog meat for dinner. I need a bath. I might never see home again. "If this is the best you've got for your bride, I'd hate to see the worst."

He winces. "Ouch. I see your point, but you could never find that rum in Hope."

Alcohol and I have never been acquainted, but we seem to like each other that night. David and I laugh through the evening as we both get tipsy. The lovemaking in the lifeboat that night is the most carefree I've ever known. When we finish, the gentle sound of the waves and the warmth of David beside me is nearly hypnotic. Before sleep takes me, I stare through the porthole into the starlit sky in total wonder. *Life is simple in Hope, but perhaps it's more complicated than it needs to be.*

Chapter Thirteen
A Fortune of Little Value

The following morning, I learn about rum's downside. My head throbs and I feel like crap, but David seems delighted when I poke my head out of the lifeboat's hatch. He has built a teepee of green wood over the fire and laid the rest of the dog meat on it to dry and smoke. Our trunks have enough jerky to meet our needs for some time, but it's clear he's already looking to a time when we won't have any at all.

The dog meat, figs, and grapes for breakfast are filling, but I miss eggs. If I ever get back to Hope, that's the first thing I'll do—eat some eggs. As my headache wanes, we move our trunks to the catamaran and then seal the lifeboat. If we're lucky enough to return from this adventure, it'll be a comforting stopover on the way back to the Suez.

After lashing our three trunks to the base of the catamaran mast, we position the mainsail at forty-five degrees to the inrushing sea breeze and move north at a good speed. With each passing hour, I am more thankful for calm seas. The fear of the sea is engrained in me now, and I might never overcome it. On the other hand, David seems quite happy with the serenity of the open water. I don't quite understand it. Considering the death of his father and our own harrowing experience on the Marco Polo, I wonder how he can be so calm. Part of me is thankful for it, the other part perplexed, but his smile is contagious and keeps me going.

We will attempt to make port in the Old World city of Tripoli today—about seventy-six kilometers north of Beirut. Tripoli was both ancient and huge before the BHS extermination. It should provide interesting opportunities for exploration. Perhaps being a cultural anthropologist isn't so bad after all.

Tripoli has a fascinating past. Perhaps, one day in the far future, more will be added to its rich history because of its incredible location. While David tends to our course and the catamaran cuts through the calm blue-green water, I review notes from my study in Hope. I still find it interesting that the son of King Darius, Xerxes, didn't have the same drive to win at war that his father did. Although it is raw speculation, I have come to believe the difference between the two is related to the shard. Xerxes' father succeeded because he had a charge from God, a charge his son was missing.

Early Canaanites established the city of Tripoli, although they were called Phoenicians by the Greeks. Having established trade throughout the Mediterranean, the Greeks became a serious market threat to the Phoenicians, who convinced King Darius to send a military expedition to invade Greece. The Phoenicians promised to provide ships and crews to the Persians in return for autonomy and thus precipitated a protracted fifth century B.C. war against the troublesome Greeks.

When King Darius died, his son attempted to bring the unruly Greeks under control, but his defeat was a disaster for Persian prestige. When some of his captains presented themselves to explain the loss, Xerxes executed them—an act that so alarmed other commanders they deserted. For the next fifteen years, the Phoenicians didn't participate in the war. Then, in 465 B.C., Athens threatened Cyprus. That drew the Phoenicians back into the fray for the next seventy-five years.

At the same time, Egypt successfully rebelled against Persia. That uprising encouraged the Phoenicians and Cyprians to join together in revolt in 366 B.C. Meanwhile, the city-states of Aradus, Sidon, and Tyre united under a common parliament held on neutral ground in Tripolis, the tri-city, and that's how Tripoli got its name.

Decaying Old World cities pass by to our starboard—Zaytun, Magharat, Mar Yusuf, and others. My excitement doesn't rise until we pass Al Mina, round the nearby point, and head into Tripoli harbor. The sun is setting by the time we drop anchor in the lee of the harbor seawall. For fear of animals, we will stay aboard tonight. Tomorrow is soon enough to enter the city. From our position at anchor, looking up at a city that still retains some of its skyline, it is apparent the effects of Project Sanitize didn't reach this far south.

The next morning, we endure another breakfast of dog, figs, and grapes, and then paddle the catamaran to the beach. David secures a line to the bow and then, about five meters down the line, ties on a medium-sized rock. He sets the rock on the tip of one of the hulls, coils the remaining line in his hand, and then shoves the boat away from shore. When the boat is far enough out to protect against marauding animals, he jerks on the line to pull the rock into the water. The rock will tether the boat away from shore and the line between the rock and the shore will enable us to pull the boat in when we return. The precaution is necessary. If animals get to our trunks we'll be in deep trouble.

With the boat secured, we begin the trek toward the city's center, both armed with our .38 caliber pistols. David also carries a 30-30 rifle, just in case.

The city must have been beautiful in its prime, but we aren't here for a sightseeing trip. We are here because the city is a treasure trove of antiquities. If additional shards exist, we might find them here.

Decay is pervasive. Much of the city was built before the advent of modern building standards, and much has already crumbled. A bank building made from solid rock still stands, but its roof and doors disappeared long ago. We step inside with care. We've seen few rabbits here and are less concerned about dogs, but we are still wary.

Most of the bank's interior fixtures have decayed and vanished over time. Only a few marble tables and stainless steel components remain. The vault door is open. The panic caused by the approaching wave of BHS death must have swept through the city with such great speed that only the front door was closed. The interior of the vault is well-preserved, and we marvel at what we find there. Ignoring the safety deposit boxes, we spot a 1-meter cube of gold bars— a fortune of no value. Gold means nothing to us. Our catamaran has little room. The contents of our trunks mean far more to us than the entire stack of gold.

We continue into the city, looking through other substantial buildings, especially museums and trading centers, but our real target is Our Lady of Balamand Monastery. According to Doctor Noble's notes, the site's collection of 450 ancient manuscripts from Lebanon and Syria is largely intact, but that particular note seems odd, almost irrelevant and out of place. We don't know the reason he recorded it, but we intend to find out.

The smell of orange blossoms permeates the air as we ascend the hill toward the monastery. This city was once famous for its fields of oranges, and that crop has apparently gone wild. Everywhere we look there are orange trees. We pick some of the ripe fruit and eat it on the spot—a refreshing change to meals that are becoming repetitive. We'll pick more on our return to the boat and are already looking forward to having scurvy-preventing fresh oranges over the next few days.

As expected, the monastery's wooden doors and window frames rotted away years ago, but some of the lower stone buildings are still more or less intact. Most important, the stone basement of the main monastery hasn't filled with water, so the documents it holds could still be viable. We study artifacts visible within the glass-covered display cases, holding flashlights with one hand and kerchiefs over our mouth and nose with the other. The pervasive stench of rat urine is a warning we must heed. Rat urine is toxic to humans. Ingesting it in any form—even as inhaled dust—can be fatal. I shudder as I mentally review the symptoms of hanta virus.

Thirty minutes is about all we can stand. We are about to give up when I see a small black fragment in the corner of a display case at the far end of the room. "David, you've got to see this. It could be what we're looking for."

David glances at the object and, without hesitation, breaks the glass with the butt of his Smith and Wesson. "We'll inspect it when we can breathe. Let's get out of here."

With our new find in hand, we hurry back to the catamaran, stopping only long enough to pick enough oranges to last a few days. The rat urine odor is still with us when we reach the water, so the first order of business is scrubbing down. We don't want to get aboard until we've cleaned our clothing, shoes, fruit, and weapons. The Kadisha River is too far away, so we take turns on guard duty while the other bathes in the salt water. We can live with the salt film but not the rat urine.

Once aboard, we move far enough from shore to feel secure, wipe our weapons down with rum, and settle in for dinner: dog jerky, figs, and the last of the grapes. We inspect our new treasure while chewing the tough, smoked meat in the fading sunlight. It's a tiny fragment but eerily familiar. It's something that simply can't exist; something more advanced than anything in human history, yet recovered from the archives of an ancient people. It seems impossible, and I hold it in my hand in total wonderment.

Only four golden, cuneiform-like characters are distinct on the new fragment. They are quite similar to those on our shard, the only difference being these are smaller and considerably more delicate. The black substrate appears identical, and we both conclude exactly what Doctor Noble must have—if there are two pieces, there must be more.

I rub the small shard between my thumb and forefinger. It has the same texture as our larger shard. "I wonder if this is the exact same shard that led to the establishment of the Old Persian alphabet." I look down on the piece in awe because of its potential significance in the history of this area and suddenly realize it has impacted my life as well. "Your father must have stopped here on his way back from his first trip to the Kill Zone. That would explain the obtuse note in his journal about Our Lady of Balamand Monastery."

David nods. "Yes. He was probably conflicted about his original find, enough to search for other pieces like it. He probably discovered his shard in such an out-of-the-way place that he believed the site could not have been contaminated by man. In that case, he would have considered the shard quite old. At the same time, he must have harbored considerable uncertainty about it because it appeared modern and machine-made."

I hand the small shard to David. "I think you're right. Your father didn't have the carbon dating report at the time, so he didn't know his shard was three million years old. Still, he could see the shard's technology with his own eyes. He would have been plagued by how an advanced object like that could have ended up where he found it."

David shakes his head as he stares down at the small shard. "I dismissed your comment earlier about the shard being part of a Project Sanitize bomb, but Dad might have come to the same conclusion. The only thing that makes sense is that he could not fathom how it ended up where he found it. If there are more shards where we're going, they won't be easy to find."

I tear off another bite of jerky with my teeth, grind the tough meat until my jaw gets tired, and then wash it down with a gulp of water. David is in rapt fascination staring at the small shard when I interject, "The similarity of the shard's golden characters to Old Persian must have driven your father to stop in Tripoli to see if anything similar might have been found in the past. He probably saw the smaller shard in the monastery's display case, just as we did, and that could have been his justification for having the piece carbon dated immediately after he returned home."

I pause for a moment and then add, "I wonder why he didn't bring both shards home."

Deep in introspection, David seems to talk to the shard rather than to me. "Dad couldn't know he would make it back to Hope. It's a big ocean. Perhaps he wanted to leave some evidence behind in case he didn't."

Handing the shard back to me, he adds, "By itself, the carbon dating report would probably have been questioned. Who knows what might happen to the isotopes of carbon during a thermonuclear reaction? But the carbon dating report, in conjunction with this small piece, proves conclusively the shard Dad found is not some esoteric residual from an advanced rocket. It has been around for a very long time, and that's probably the reason Dad returned a second time—to find the source of both shards."

More than any others, David and I understand his father's drive to know what the shard means. After all, we have put our lives on the line to be here, and if not for the shard, we would be safe at home. It brought Doctor Noble to this destination, and perhaps to his death. Now it has brought us along, too.

After dessert—a welcome splash of rum with a fresh orange chaser—David reaches over to brush the windblown hair from my face. "It'll be hot when we head into the desert, love. We can cut it before we go in if you want."

I swallow hard. My long, blonde hair has been my signature feature since before I developed breasts. "I'll have to think that one over. It'll take years to grow it back."

His hand slides from my hair to my breast. My heart races as feelings of sexual need overtake my body and mind. Why are we wired like this? What logical reason is there for wanting to make love here, now? We hold in our hands perhaps the greatest mystery in the history of mankind, yet I'm driven to hold David far more than to question the origins of that ancient relic. I lean into David's hand, take the fragment from him, place it in a safe location, and then embrace him with the full extent of my body.

Chaffing undergarments were discarded days ago, and he lays me down and inserts himself in one continuous motion. The undulation, the movement of him inside me, drives me to gasp for breath as I move my hips into his, opening my body to him as completely as I can. I want to absorb him, to completely enfold him with the warmth radiating from every pore of my skin. He responds with a deep, short gasp, and my body seems to know its own way, leading to rhythmic pulsations of pure pleasure that flow through us before we collapse in total bliss.

I hold him tight. I want him to stay where he is and not move a muscle. Though we are still, I feel his heartbeat throbbing. I squirm under his weight, wanting him more, needing him more. Without a word, he knows, and he slowly moves out and back in again, gradually intensifying his pace while satisfying a primitive need in me I cannot control.

When it's over, we lie together and pull the rescue blankets we took from the lifeboat over us. I fall fast asleep, content that I've never been more satisfied in my entire life than I am right now. How ironic that I should find such happiness in this terrible situation. We have little prospect of ever going home again and are faced with a struggle to survive at every turn. Yet we are happier and more fulfilled than at any time in our lives. Such knowledge is indeed a fortune of great value.

* * * *

Squawking gulls and eerie barking wake us in the early morning. A yipping pack of hyenas are pacing back and forth ashore, like they are trying to figure out how to get to us. David kisses me on the forehead and winks. "They can swim. We should probably leave before they get desperate enough to try it."

I smile back through sleepy eyes, thinking of the hyenas exactly as they think of us. "Are you sure? How much dog meat do we have left?"

"I'm betting there'll be better things to eat ahead. Get up, sleepyhead. It's time to weigh anchor and hoist the mizzen."

I pull up the anchor while David hefts the sail. We gradually slip out of the Tripoli yacht basin with excited and hungry hyenas running along the shore. They soon tire and begin to lag behind. We have almost 200 kilometers to go before we reach the northern border of Syria, where we should encounter direct blast residue.

We are blessed with fair weather and sail due north, hoping to make 125 kilometers. The sea breeze is fast and constant, and the catamaran skims the water's surface as if gliding on ice.

Sitting against one of our trunks, I look back at my love on the tiller. "On a day like this, I can almost picture a peaceful earlier time, when the Old World was whole. It's so beautiful here."

David smiles back. "It would have been nice. The people back then had leisure time and the resources to enjoy it. Yet they squandered what they had on religious insanity. From our perspective, that whole concept seems crazy, but to them, it must have been vitally important."

I lean forward to shoo a fly off my toe. "It could have been different if the scientists who engineered BHS took an afternoon off now and then just to enjoy the sun on their faces."

David makes a slight course correction and nods in my direction. "If they had, perhaps this wouldn't be just a stolen moment for us but a lifetime of joy instead."

Revulsion of what has been lost temporarily grips me, and a fleeting moment of hatred ripples through my soul.

The compass built into the catamaran is invaluable when we lose sight of land shortly after leaving Tripoli. The shore is only fifteen kilometers to the east, but salt mist shrouds it and blocks it from view. As the land mass to the east juts out further into the sea, we see the ruins of Tartus in the distance. We skirt the shore for another thirty-five kilometers before the Mediterranean shoreline again dips eastward.

We make no stops during this leg of our voyage—our longest day at sea since the Marco Polo sank. Nine hours after leaving Tripoli, we round the point toward the Old World Latakia harbor breakwater—the structure that protected Old World Syria's main seaport.

Founded in the fourth century, after the death of Alexander the Great in 323 BCE, Latakia was named by Seleucus I Nicator in honor of his mother, Laodice. Latakia's major exports were cotton, olives, walnuts, mulberry trees, and wine and, like all coastal settlements in this area, the city passed from ruler to ruler over time. It even got caught up in the mess between Augustus Caesar and Marcus Antonius and, at a later time, the Crusades as well. After its foundation, the people of Latakia experienced almost constant war for control of the city.

Latakia might be the last port we'll encounter that is unaffected by the Project Sanitize zone of destruction, but we won't investigate its ruins. The city is not mentioned in Doctor Noble's notes, and we don't need perishable supplies; we have all the fresh fruit we can reasonably carry with us when we venture into the interior. Besides, the city could be dangerous. The area is geologically unstable and prone to earthquakes. Even from this distance, the city looks like it sustained significant damage from some big ones. The few buildings that still stand could be death traps.

We drop anchor at a protected location near the breakwater and relax for the first time in what seems like forever. We are not driven by schedule but by desire to understand the unknown. Still, we are exhausted. We tie our rescue blankets over the boom as sunshades and lie out in the balmy mid-afternoon air. Despite the residue of destruction all around us, it is pleasant here. I am soon lulled to sleep by the gentle rocking of the catamaran.

As dusk descends, a commotion ashore wakes us. A pack of dogs has cornered a juvenile lion, and there is considerable ruckus in the wild anticipation of a bloody death. The lion appears to be about a year old, and I fear for it. There are too many dogs. The yelping and snarling soon comes to an inevitable end as the lion succumbs. There is a lesson in this. The lion strayed too far from its pride. Packs of dogs are everywhere, and they will probably hunt us mercilessly when we move inland. For that matter, so will the lions. When we go ashore, we'll be just another source of meat.

Refreshed from my nap, I pull out the fishing tackle I took from the yacht where we scored the catamaran, make a jig, and begin fishing off the stern. It doesn't take long. These waters are not overfished like they were when the people of the Old World depleted everything. The fish pulls strongly against the monofilament line, but I soon pull a meter-long Atlantic spotted flounder aboard. I'm so excited I could pee. We won't be having dog meat for dinner tonight.

David is delighted, "Ah, sushi. Well done, Beth."

I'm surprised at his comment. "Sushi? How about flame-broiled flounder?"

He looks toward shore where the dogs are still disemboweling the young lion. "There are a lot of hungry dogs here, and this is their time of night. We'd need to go ashore to make a fire. Is it really worth the risk?"

He has a point. I'm disappointed but can't argue. "I see what you mean. Tomorrow morning, though, promise me we'll stop north of here to cook the leftovers for a proper breakfast."

He nods. "You've got it, love, but I think we'll stop longer than just to eat. We'll catch more fish after breakfast and smoke them ashore before heading inland. It'll be good to have something other than dog jerky and the beef jerky from home."

We remove the hardtack from the sealed food rations left over from the lifeboat and place slices of the raw flounder on it. Hardtack is never appetizing, but it doesn't seem any worse for its age. The flounder makes it almost palatable. We top off dinner with an orange and a few figs before we lie on the deck to look into the star-filled, clear sky.

It is beautiful here—serene and peaceful. With David by my side, I don't feel fear. If this is what the remainder of my life will be like, I welcome it. For a fleeting moment, I question whether I should continue taking the birth control pills. What would it be like to have children of my own? Our family could begin anew here, without impact of any kind. I'd love to have his children now, as many as possible. In twenty years, would anyone care what we did or didn't do here?

Chapter Fourteen
The Hard Way Inland

We anchor just outside Old World Ra's at Tamrah the next day. Rife with expectation, David and I toss our fishing lines into the water. In an hour, we have as many fish as we can possibly deal with. David guides the catamaran to a sandy area ashore where he builds a large fire to keep animals at bay and provide a bed of coals for smoking the fish. It's been quite some time since we've had fresh- cooked food. My mouth salivates. By the time I remove a piece of smoking hot white meat from near the flames, I'm so anxious for barbecued flounder that my stomach is growling. The fish is a delicious meal fit for royalty, if there were any royalty left alive. David laughs at the expression on my face. I ignore him and focus on the food.

We play catch on the beach with a small piece of bark but never stray far from our weapons. Even while sunbathing, one of us must stand watch. We don't expect trouble, but we never know. Caution is better than death. We keep the fire going all day to dry the remainder of the fish. As evening approaches, we put to sea and subsequently anchor in a small cove to the north before settling in for the night. We need the rest. Tomorrow, we'll establish our base camp in preparation for the trip inland.

We wake refreshed at daybreak and then enjoy a breakfast of dried fish and the last of our oranges. The meat is chewy with a strong fish flavor, but it beats dog jerky. Even before we finish, David hoists the sail to begin the final leg of our trip northward. Dark clouds loom overhead as we sail around the protruding point north of Isa Bakli, where I see the first overt effects of Project Sanitize—negative images of long-dead, leafy plants burned into solid rock by the intense light of a nearby nuclear blast. I quickly take a measurement with our portable Geiger-Muller counter. The instrument does not show an elevated level of radiation.

Plant imprints from extreme light exposure don't surprise me, but the lack of elevated radiation readings and blast effects does. Everything looks quite normal ashore. We furl most of the mainsail and move slowly up the shallow river leading to the Old World town of Faqi Hasan. Light rain falls all around us; thunder peals in the distance. In less than two kilometers, we round the bend and spot the remains of the village. Only a few structures made of rock still stand, and those are overgrown with various types of native vines. The remainder of the village turned to dust long ago.

Our catamaran draws very little water, enabling us to come ashore near the largest of the remaining structures. We tie off to a large rock embedded in the shoreline, recheck our weapons, and move slowly toward the structure ahead. Graceful birds scatter for cover as we intrude on their space. We remain alert, not allowing ourselves to be lulled by the rustle of the wind in the trees and the gentle sound of falling rain. We don't expect dogs because there doesn't seem to be much for them to eat, but snakes could be a problem.

The building we've targeted isn't large—perhaps eight meters on a side. It has no windows, and its metal door is rusted through in several places. David walks around the building, poking and prying at the vegetation with a long stick to see what might be lurking beneath. He takes special care to look for snakes as he inspects the vines above and around the doorframe. He's nearly finished when a relative of a domesticated chicken lunges from the vines toward his face, screeching at the top of its lungs. We jerk back as the wild squawking from the enraged bird catches us by surprise. David's flailing arm strikes the first blow, and the stunned chicken flops to the ground. Before it can regroup for a second attack, I nail it with my .38.

David leaps back even farther, more shocked by the report from my revolver than the chicken's blood spatter. "Good grief, Beth. That's like using a cannon on a flea."

I shrug, half-close my eyes, and respond without emotion. "I didn't want it to hurt you. I thought it might get the upper hand."

He shakes his head, snickers, and then picks up the carcass by its feet. "You think there's enough left for dinner?"

While he admires the chicken, I look over the chicken's lair. I thought as much. The vines are laced with poison ivy. I stack up a few flat rocks so I can peer into the chicken's enclave. My eyes widen, and I actually gasp out of pure joy. The nest has eggs. I want to scream David's name so he can partake in this blessing with me, but instead, I keep quiet so I don't attract any more feathered predators. I carefully remove each egg, avoiding the dark green serrated leaves adjacent to the nest. The moment we get a fire going, these guys are going down.

David isn't caught up in my excitement over the eggs. Instead, he continues checking out the building. "This could have been a communications center. There are no windows. Buildings without windows were easier to secure and cool."

I'm aware that David is speaking to me, but all I can think about are eggs. Scrambled. Fried. Over-easy. There are so many possibilities. Without waiting for a response, he kicks in the door and steps back to let the aging dust blow away in the wind. With his rifle at ready, he nods toward me and then toward the door. I set the eggs aside and then peek around the edge of the doorframe with my flashlight leading the way. I don't hear a thing. Nothing is moving inside. With caution, I step through the opening into the darkness ahead. Racks of defunct electronic equipment confirm David's suspicion—the building is an old communications center. The room is dry and cool and, based on the half centimeter of undisturbed dust on the floor, not occupied by large living creatures.

David steps in behind me and begins checking the corners and racks for spiders and other surprises. He soon nods. We appear to be the only living things inside. He sweeps the area with his flashlight before letting the light rest on the ceiling. "Interesting. Reinforced concrete. This building is more like a bunker than a room. They must have had a real problem with people stealing copper wire back in the day."

The building is tailor-made for our needs. We'll have to fortify the door some, but it'll make an ideal base camp, a great place to store our trunks while we travel up the valley to the east. A flash of lightning precedes the rolling boom of thunder that reverberates off the mountains flanking the valley. It's nice to be out of the rain, but David prods me on. "We've got to take care of the boat in case the river floods."

We carry only our pistols as we head for the boat. Heavy rain began a short time ago, but the river is already rising over the rock we used to tether the catamaran. We struggle to free the boat from the rapidly rising flow, being careful to keep hold of its mooring line. The boat alone isn't too heavy, but with our trunks and other salvage aboard, it is all we can do to pull the hull tips onto the muddy bank.

Another lightning strike makes me jump as we hurry to drag the trunks off the boat, one at a time. As the rain intensifies, we must stop unloading to pull the boat higher. The small river continues to rise. Straining at our harnesses, we manage to pull each trunk to the communications building and then return to the boat to pull the last of our vital supplies to safety. David throws smaller items to me, and I move them to higher ground. Before he can pitch the last of our survival gear to me, the riverbank gives way in a gigantic mudslide that sucks the boat into the raging river.

As the catamaran flips sideways, David flails into the churning water. For an instant, I am paralyzed by fear, but his scream jolts me to reality. "Save the boat!"

Another flash of lightning illuminates the churning water, and I see David struggling against the current toward the shore. I follow his instruction without thinking and grab the boat's tie-up line before it's ripped away. The boat bucks in the rushing water, pulling me along the riverbank. I see a stout tree ahead, and I run forward to gain slack in the line. Amid lightning strikes and the roar of thunder, I manage to pass the line twice around the trunk before it snaps taut. I struggle to tie a series of half hitches as the catamaran's pontoons rear against the violent flow of mud and roiling water.

The boat groans, and I hear a loud *pop* before its mast and sail rip from the center member and churn downstream. My heart sinks. All is lost.

Rain pours down in sheets. I strain to make out anything in the turbulent dark water or on the riverbanks as I run downriver. I don't see David. Another lightning strike explodes so close that I can smell the ozone. I continue moving, praying for any sign of life in the churning mud and froth. I see nothing. I move farther downstream, shouting, "David! David!"

Only the roar of raging water answers back.

A half-mile from our shelter, I stop and sink to the ground, panting. Looking across the roaring water, I breathe in shallow gulps as I face the horror of my new reality. He is gone. My darling David is gone. Gut-wrenching agony grips me, and I collapse in a torrent of tears against the nurse log behind me.

Thoughts of my own safety do not enter my mind, but images of David falling backward in slow motion to his death do. Excruciating pain fills my heart. Torrential rain and tears fill my eyes. I struggle to my feet and wander aimlessly toward the riverbank. I don't want to die in this wilderness alone. Shock makes me lightheaded and my stomach sick. I bend over to retch with such force that blood trickles from the side of my mouth.

Nothing matters now. The only choices facing me are to die quick, giving myself to the raging river that took my love, or to die of starvation and loneliness over time. A deep calmness fills my soul as I approach the river's edge. I take a cleansing breath, close my eyes, and step out toward the water. I will not prolong my agony. Life without David is meaningless. My stride lengthens as my resolve steels, but as I reach the riverbank, I lose my footing in the slippery mud and flail backward. A bright flash of light precedes searing pain that shoots from my head to my shoulder before everything grows dark.

* * * *

"Mother, is that you?" I see her in the distance, her blue summer dress fluttering in the wind.

She hears me, turns, and runs toward me with her arms outstretched. "Beth, my baby. You've come home."

She kisses my cheeks and holds me tight as tears stream down her face. My father appears from out of nowhere, touches my face in disbelief, and stammers, "Beth, is it really you?"

We hold each other in a prolonged group embrace. Sobs of joy speak louder than words ever could. I am home. My nightmare is over.

After moments that are far too short, Mother and Dad step back, still holding my hands. Mother brushes hair from over my eyes and then pulls me toward home as Dad trails behind. "You look hungry, dear. We need to rustle up some soup. Is vegetable still your favorite?"

I turn to look back, focusing beyond my father. "B-but...where is David? Why isn't David here?"

They both stop, glance at each other, and then look at me. Dad raises his palms and shoulders. "Is David here?

Did you bring David with you? We've loved your emails and can hardly wait to meet him."

His questions upset me, but I'm not sure why. I've written about David for months. He should be here. A flush of anger rushes through me. I pull away from Mother and look down the empty street with my arms crossed over my chest. "He's here somewhere, Mom. You know how hard men are to keep track of."

She pats my arm. "I know, dear, but they always show up when they are hungry."

I call out in the direction from which we came, "David!" Tilting my head, I listen for a response. Mother and Dad continue to look hopeful.

Mom takes my hand again and pulls me along. "Come, dear. David will find us when he's ready."

Anger rushes through me once again. David should be here. Damn him. Why would he disappear when my parents are so anxious to meet him? I look back over my shoulder. The street is still empty. Mother pulls me into the house, through the living room, and into the kitchen. She pulls up a stool for me to sit on. "You just rest a minute, dear. I'll have some food ready in a moment."

"But Mom, where is David? We can't eat without him."

She smiles. "Of course we can, dear. He'll be along when he's hungry enough."

"No!" I jump from the stool and run toward the front door. The faster I run, the farther away the door seems to be. "David! David!" My calls echo from the walls that are closing in around me. Darkness is setting in, and I suddenly feel as if I am running through a thick, viscous fluid. I can barely move my arms and legs, yet I know I must make it through the door. I know David is on the other side.

Exhausted and out of breath, I fall through the opening and onto the front steps. An invisible force weighs me down. I feel heavy and tired. I reach out as I tumble forward, off the porch and onto the lawn. The moist grass caresses my face, and I push into it with all my strength. I can't get up. I can't move. I cry out with a weak voice, "David...help me."

Where is he? He was here just a moment ago. A feeling of dread sends a chill through my body. Doom encases me like a shroud. I gasp for breath and close my fists on the grass, sensing the unmistakable feel of moist mud squishing between my fingers.

Black spots gradually disappear as I open my eyes. The sun is out, the river is tame, and I hear a familiar voice calling, "Beth, are you out here?"

David. It's David's voice. I try to sit up but can't. My head throbs; it feels split wide open. I grope back with my hand to check my skull, but my arm has a mind of its own. It wanders aimlessly until my hand encounters a large rock embedded in the mud. My fingers probe my mud-caked hair. A lump about nine centimeters across and a centimeter high sends shooting pain down my neck when I touch it. I jerk back by reflex. It is difficult to focus as my hand moves unsteadily before my eyes, but it seems covered with mud and blood. I try to call out but can't verbalize words. Panic sets in. How can I tell him where I am?

My mind races. *My pistol. I still have my pistol.*

I fumble with the holster until I manage to pull it loose and, with great effort, point it skyward. When I pull the trigger, the percussion sends a searing pain through my head that floods my mind with the peace of unconsciousness once again.

Total darkness surrounds me when I come to. There isn't a sound. As my eyes gradually adjust, I make out the interior of the communications building—our base camp.

Our supplies are neatly stowed around me, but David isn't here. My head beats out a rhythm of pain as I sit up. I don't know how long I've been out, but from the feel of my head, many additional hours of recovery still lie ahead. My sunglasses are on the trunk adjacent to my bed of fronds, moss, and leaves—an invitation to go outside if I've ever seen one.

I struggle to the door and peer out with caution. Sunlight hits me like an axe in the forehead and forces me back inside. I'm exhausted. Even groping for my sunglasses takes what little energy I have. I must lie down. I need more rest. I struggle to return to my frond bed and lie down before unconsciousness takes me again.

Darkness fills the room when I reopen my eyes, but now David is by my side. My restless stirring wakes him. "Beth? Are you awake, sweetie?"

Dizziness keeps me down. Even in the extreme darkness of night, the room seems to spin. "I'm here, honey, but I feel...sick." No sooner do the words leave my mouth than I roll to the side and vomit. My body shakes in fits; my head throbs with every violent contraction.

David wraps me with both rescue blankets and holds me close to his body, rocking me gently until the shivers stop. "It's a residual of shock, honey. It will pass soon. What happened out there?"

What an odd question. Surely he knows. "I must have slipped on the mud near the river and hit a rock. Why are you asking that? You must have found me. You had to see for yourself."

He continues holding me until my sick stomach settles. "Just checking. Concussions can cause memory loss and sometimes slurred speech. At least you remember what happened, and your speech is normal. You'll need to take it easy for a while but will probably be okay. Do you hear any ringing in your ears? Are you aware of any amnesia?"

My eyes have adjusted to the low light. I look with love into his eyes and answer with sarcasm, "If I have amnesia, how would I know it?"

He continues to hold me with the side of his face against mine. I feel a tear slip from his cheek onto mine as he whispers, "Ah, Beth. It's good to have you back."

The memory of losing David strikes me hard as he holds me. Images of him being swept away by the current to certain death are still fresh in my mind. The thoughts cause me to gag. I swallow the acrid vomit and pull back as anger sweeps through my mind. He left me alone in this God-forsaken place. I remember the emptiness, the sheer loneliness of being without him…and the reality of choosing the peace of the raging river over becoming a meal for a marauding animal pack. My hand juts to my mouth as my mind clears and the anger wanes. David is here with me—I am alive. *How is that possible?* With my mouth agape, I look into his eyes. "Wouldn't a more appropriate question be what happened to you?"

He pulls me back into a close hug and rocks me like a child. "I got lucky. Just around the bend, I snagged a tree. I held on until an eddy blocked the torrent and allowed me to crawl out. Our catamaran wasn't so fortunate. It's buried under tons of rock and logs at the end of its tether."

"Can we dig it out?"

He kisses my forehead and breathes a sigh of relief as if I've returned from the dead. "I've been trying for three days. It's hopeless. The mud and water fill in any progress I make."

I push back against his hold and gasp. "Three days? I've been out for three days?"

"You've been here part of the time, at least enough to take a little broth and water. You must be feeling better. You haven't said a thing until now."

I suspect he's right, but I've felt better. My head aches. My body stinks. I cup my hand over my mouth and breathe out. My breath smells like a stockyard. "I could use a bath…or some mouthwash and a lot of perfume."

He offers an easy smile and raises his eyebrows. "I can't argue with that, and I've got just the thing when you're strong enough to use it—a shower made from the finest scrap I could find in these ruins."

"That's an incentive to get well quick if I've ever heard one." My stomach growls as I look wistfully into David's eyes. "Right now, though, I could sure use some vittles."

He winks as he releases me and gets up to prepare a light meal. Tears mist my eyes as David leaves the shelter. He loves me and will care for me until I am well. It rips at my heart that I almost threw my time with him away. *Stupid, Beth. Stupid!* I will never tell him of my weakness, of my willingness to die based on supposition alone. That will be a secret I take to my grave. It would hurt David deeply to know I was willing to forfeit our life together over a bad assumption. I resolve on the spot to never again act without reason, to never assume my situation is so hopeless that I would rather commit suicide than struggle to survive.

By the time David returns, I am so happy to be alive that I can hardly wait for him to set the water and broth down so I can hug him like there is no tomorrow. I am alive. David is alive. I will forever be thankful for the slippery mud by the riverbank.

* * * *

Over the next week, David waits on me hand and foot, not allowing me to do a thing but rest. At the end of the week, I'm able to move without an accompanying headache and can even tolerate light. We both believe I've skirted a near catastrophe. We will be far more careful with our footing and safety in the future.

When I finally emerge from the communications center's inner sanctum, David's surprise awaits—an elevated water tank with a section of pipe extending horizontally to an aluminum ewer. A fire is burning beneath the tank, and there are holes punched in the bottom of the ewer to act as a showerhead. I couldn't be more delighted. "Nice. Is the water warm yet?"

David grins. "All it needs is your beautiful little body, dear. Step in. It's all yours."

A second invitation isn't needed. I immediately step onto the shower's base of fronds and moss covered by dog skin, clothes and all. "Show me what you've got, big guy. Maybe I can clean the barf off these clothes as well."

David twists open a valve, and the warm water begins to trickle over my head, causing my wound to sting. I grimace but welcome the cleansing flow. Even more, a clump of soap rests on a rock just outside the reach of the water. It doesn't smell all that great, but I'm able to lather up. "This is wonderful. Where did the soap come from?"

"Hardwood and frond ash, dear, soaked in that tank before I put it up there. The mixture makes reasonable lye to render pig fat. Boil lye with fat and well…you've got the result."

"Pig fat? You killed a pig? You've been eating barbecued pork while I've been drinking broth?"

He smirks. "Sorry, your highness. I thought the shower might ease your disappointment, and it was hard enough to force the broth through your drool."

We remain at our base camp for another week while refreshing our water supply, drying pork, cleaning our clothes, and strengthening the door. By the time we're ready to leave, we both believe I'm strong enough to travel inland and that our supplies will be safe enough stored in the communications bunker. Not knowing what we might encounter ahead, we pack enough preserved food for three weeks. Because water is so heavy, we will only transport a week's worth. We'll need to secure refills along the way. Each of us will also carry three kilograms of salt, which is absolutely essential for preserving any meat we might take along the way.

Part 3: The Kill Zone

Chapter Fifteen
Craters

We begin our trip up the valley to the east looking for blast residue. To maximize the effects of heat for killing the BHS bacteria, bombs detonated above ground. The concept obviously failed because BHS spread across the planet like wildfire anyway. It was all they could do at the time. Even a bad plan was probably better than doing nothing at all.

Dogs and lions are the primary predators in this area, so our security is a significant concern. We continue into the valley, moving with caution and avoiding areas with tall, grassy plants. Several kilometers from our base camp, we note flash burns in the valley that show the outline of plant life on rocks. A little farther in, crumbled greenish glass covers the ground. The heat from the blasts must have been intense enough to melt the surface, and subsequent rapid cooling probably shattered the resulting glass. Although erosion smoothed some of the edges, we know hiking long distances over the shattered glass will destroy the soles of our boots.

Four arduous uphill hours brings us to the top of the first ridge of foothills. Taller mountains loom ahead, but we don't see craters—only lush plant life as far as we can see. Doctor Noble's notes are clear about the presence of craters in the area where he found the shard; therefore, we will continue moving ahead until we find them. Without people to destroy it, the flora in the area recovered well. Whatever plant life was here at the time of Project Sanitize burned to the ground, leaving a fertile ash residue on which the next generation of plants could thrive.

We continue toward the higher mountains, crossing a large steppe for most of the afternoon, and then enter tree-covered slopes as dusk approaches. The distant sound of falling water draws us still higher. We soon reach a rock cliff where a stream tumbles from 100 feet above. A small cave adjacent to the waterfall might be a safe place to spend the night. While I gather wood and then get a fire going, David collects enough small logs and branches to build a barrier at the cave's entrance. As darkness completely closes in, we sit on the cave floor with our backs against the rock wall while eating a small portion of jerky.

David scoots close and affectionately rubs my knee. "We covered a lot of ground today, Beth. You seem to be holding up well."

I nod as I swallow a sip of water. "I feel as strong as I did before my accident, although my pack got pretty heavy by the end of the day."

He leans over and kisses me. "So did mine."

My feet hurt, and my calf muscles are sore, but I refuse to complain about the small stuff. What good would that do? David probably has the same aches as I do. We are in this together and will suffer the same inconveniences, aches, and pains. I glance down at the settler's marks on my wrist. True equality is what I signed up for—it's what the marks mean.

I reach up, place my hands on his cheeks, and bring his lips to mine. Sometimes my love for him just needs a release—like now—and I kiss him softly while gently drawing my tongue over his lower lip. My passion rises, but he gently pushes me back. "Oh, Beth, you are tempting." He exhales while shaking his head. "I wish I had the stamina, but I am dead tired. We have a big day tomorrow. We need to sleep."

I'm a little disappointed but understand. He spoons me when we lie down and sleep quickly takes me.

Grunting sounds wake us; my eyes dart around the cave in the early morning light. David holds his palm up to hush me as he whispers, "Wild boar outside the entrance. Want fresh pork for dinner?"

I nod vigorous approval. I'm already tired of jerky and whisper back, "How about for breakfast?"

He winks before moving toward the entrance with great stealth. In a moment, the report from his 30-30 rifle jars me wide-awake. Breakfast is delicious, but we're a little concerned the smell of cooking meat could draw dogs. We heard howling last night. We assumed that it came from wolves, though we aren't sure if they'd be drawn to man's activities like a domestic dog mix would.

After salting down some of the pig meat, we break camp and continue inland. We have no idea how far we'll need to go but are certain we can make it to our destination if Doctor Noble did. The climb is steeper today, and the sun feels hotter even though the temperature on the mountain is far cooler than near the sea. Day turns to night many times as we continue onward, certain that somewhere ahead lies a monumental mistake—at least one crater from a nuclear detonation that occurred below the surface.

On the fourth day of our journey, we stand on a rocky ridge overlooking a narrow valley below. Evidence of air detonation surrounds us: decaying, burned trees radiating out from a single point of violence and massive, charred rock surfaces. David points west. "One thing about such a wide trail—it's easy to follow even if it is overgrown. Dad's notes indicate he also followed the destruction remnant."

I drop my pack and sit on a nearby flat rock. "I often wonder if we are walking in his footsteps, literally as well as figuratively."

David removes his pack before sitting beside me. "I wish he had included more landmarks." He takes the small book of notes from his backpack and opens to the page describing Doctor Noble's first trek into the mountains. "We need to be looking for a sheer rock spire ahead, something we can see for many miles. Unfortunately, he did not give an estimated distance to it."

In six more days, David hands the field glasses to me as he points east. "That's it. That has to be it."

I squint through the eyepieces…and then I see it—a tall sliver of rock towering in the distance ahead. "You're right. That's has to be the landmark."

We reach the base of the spire about midday the following day and decide to make camp there. We are both exhausted but relieved to be at a location we are certain Doctor Noble recorded. His notes are comforting but also concerning. Mountains completely surround us now. Doctor Noble's notes are sketchy at best, and even though we've been careful to mark our trail and take meticulous notes, it's easy to be overwhelmed with the feeling of being lost.

David constructs a crude lean-to while I build a fire. When we settle in for dinner, I voice my latest concern. "I haven't seen as much wild game at this altitude as I did at lower elevations. We have limited supplies, and your father's notes don't give estimated distances between landmarks. If we're not careful, this trek could deplete all our rations before we reach the end of it."

David stokes the fire and responds to the flames rather than to me. "It's a double-edged sword. On the upside, less wildlife means fewer predators."

He pulls out Doctor Noble's notes once again. "Our next landmark is a high summit that provides an unrestricted view for many kilometers. If we are on the right track, we should be able to see craters from there."

I tend to the pot of tea boiling by the side of the fire and fill my cup before responding. "These mountains go on forever. I'd feel a lot more comfortable if I knew how far we need to travel to reach that summit."

David remains stoic. "If Dad made it, we can make it too."

We break camp early the next day and continue to follow the swath of destruction left by Project Sanitize. I periodically take readings with the Geiger counter. Radiation levels are low. I am not concerned about that, at least not yet.

In two days, we can see the tops of a high range ahead, perhaps the backbone of this entire group of mountains. It is an arduous hike until we breach the summit three days later. We sit on a large rock adjacent to an ebbing patch of snow. I lean back on my palms and lift my face to the sun. "Your dad was right again, David. This overlook provides an unrestricted view for many kilometers. It's beautiful here."

David is as excited as a kid with a new bike as he scans the horizon with the field glasses. He grins wide when he hands the binoculars to me. "This is it, Beth. The source of the shard lies somewhere down there. Look southeast. You can see a massive number of craters, not just a few. Someone in the targeting groups didn't get the memo about only using air detonations."

I whistle low as I scan the horizon. "My God. There are so many. I wish your father's notes indicated which one is most important."

David stands, stretches, and slips his backpack over his shoulders. "Time's a wasting; the craters await."

I am heartened to finally have our objective in sight, but my concern spikes again. "Those things look huge. If we go inside the craters, won't we be confronted with elevated radiation levels?"

David shrugs as he begins making his way down the side of the mountain. "It didn't kill Dad. We'll probably be okay."

I snort. "Probably? Don't you mean radiation didn't kill him during his *first* visit? We have no idea what really happened to your father."

Despite my reservations, we press on toward our goal. Two days later, we stand at the rim of the first crater we saw in the distance. The crater is much larger than it seemed at first—easily 500 meters deep and 1,700 meters across. The center of the crater and the area around the rim is laden with large, square boulders that appear to have rained down at random after the blast.

I look over the edge. The crater is incredibly steep. "This is our reward for two weeks of mountain climbing?"

David ignores me and begins sampling the area with the Geiger counter wand. Almost immediately, he mumbles, "The readings aren't horrible—just slightly above ambient. Nevertheless, we should start taking radiation pills, just in case."

He removes a small plastic bottle from his backpack and fumbles to open it while I look on with concern. "Uh, you haven't mentioned those. What are they?"

"They're for radiation sickness. We'll take them daily as a precaution. They suppress the suicide mechanism in cells damaged by radiation while enabling those cells to recover from radiation-induced damage that prompted activation of the mechanism initially."

I see. If radiation is killing me, I won't know it. He hands me a pill as he swallows one of his own. I study mine. I am suspicious. "Are you expecting trouble?"

"Not really. The pills are just another form of insurance. After all, I don't know what happened to my father." I follow him along the rim of the crater for a few minutes, rubbing my pill between my thumb and fingers. It doesn't feel right.

David is oblivious to my apprehension. Instead of focusing on me, he selects another sample location, takes more measurements, and studies the extent of the crater. "I don't think this crater was an accident, Beth. Based on its size, the bomb must have been in the 100-megaton range. People in the Old World believed a single 100-megaton airburst could cause nuclear winter and pollute Earth for many years. So, the people who produced the bomb that exploded here probably detonated it below ground on purpose. It probably triggered massive earthquakes. No wonder Latakia was so devastated."

I give him my best *tell me more* look, but it doesn't work in his distracted state. I drop the subtleties. "I'm not sure where you got your information. As I recall, the largest Old World Soviet detonation was fifty megatons."

He talks more to the ground than to me as he ambles along, taking more readings. "The largest one verified, yes, but the Soviets claimed they detonated a 100-megaton bomb below ground. Still, the only real data I have is from the Old World Nevada Test Site. 'Sedan' was the code name for a 104-kiloton test to use nukes for excavation. It created a crater 390-meters wide and 100-meters deep. A 100-megaton bomb is a thousand times larger, but the rock here is far denser than the soil in Nevada. It would be impossible to quantify either, so it's just an educated guess."

My stomach growls loud enough for David to hear. I grin as I raise my shoulders and palms. "A girl's gotta eat when a girl's gotta eat."

He closes his logbook, approaches with a big smile, and gives me a tender kiss on the lips. "Why don't we make camp here and take the remainder of the day off? We'll need the rest if we're going to do some serious hill climbing tomorrow."

Now I get it. I finally swallow my pill, but it sticks in my throat, and I have to unglue it with a swig of water. After a mild choking fit, I flick my head toward the gaping hole beside me. "We're going down inside that crater, aren't we? The radiation will be higher in there, won't it?"

He nods. "Probably, but what if that's where my father found the shard? How will we know if we don't look? Isn't that what we came here to do?"

I know he's right but don't relish the thought of climbing down into the crater.

We set about collecting dozens of small to medium-sized angular rocks strewn over the area. Two very large boulders lean together nearby to form a teepee-like enclave, and we use smaller stones to build walls between them. David also cuts fir boughs and stuffs them between gaps in the stones for insulation. Our little enclosure is still drafty, but it does provide some safety and is home for now.

While David disappears over the nearby ridge with his rifle and rope, I collect enough moss and grass for bedding material and then build a good fire. About forty-five minutes later, a rifle report echoes through the surrounding mountains. My mouth waters as I contemplate what he might have killed. By the time he returns, I've gathered berries and greens, sharpened green wood sticks for skewers, and burned enough wood for a glowing bed of coals. He walks up to me with a big smile and holds out a slab of red meat that dangles over both sides of his hand. I didn't expect this—venison back strap. Dinner will be a feast.

Although he hides it well, I know he's as excited as I am about his kill. He pulls out a small plastic liquid transport bag containing some of the rum he found earlier. "We've made it this far, dear. Let's celebrate."

Our meal is a delight—delicious deer meat, dandelion greens, berries, and rum. We laugh like children while playfully bumping each other as we take in the warmth of the fire. Brilliant stars soon fill the night sky, but the fire keeps the chill of night at bay. It's so very beautiful here, almost beyond belief. By the time we make love inside our rock enclosure, I'm absolutely certain I couldn't be happier anywhere in the world.

My joyful elation is short-lived. Even with David snuggling next to me, fears and concerns rush into my mind. The sheer slope of the adjacent crater wall nags at my mind—are we really going to scale that? I am also relatively certain killer radiation lurks at bottom of that damn hole. Wouldn't that be the most logical reason Doctor Noble never returned from his second trip. And sure, David killed a deer today, but what about next week? There is a reason game is scarce here, and I'll bet it has something to do with the radiation. It'll probably kill us too. After fretting a couple of hours, I jab David in the ribs. "I'm worried we could die tomorrow."

He rolls over and yawns. "Go to sleep, Beth. We won't be taking any more risks than we take every day. You survived the Marco Polo. You'll survive tomorrow too."

"The Marco Polo wasn't radioactive."

He sighs. "And that crater won't sink in the ocean. What's your point?"

I drag myself to a sitting position against the rocks warmed by the fire. "We don't even know if your dad went into that crater. We could be taking an unnecessary risk."

"We don't know that he didn't go in that crater, either." He rolls onto his side so he can look directly at me. "You look cute in the flickering light of the fire."

I scowl. "I'm serious, David. It's one thing to talk about the craters in the abstract but quite another to be face-to-face with their reality. Everything about them represents death—from the initial blast to radiation left behind. Nothing good can come from them. I have a bad feeling about going into any of them."

"Oh, please. Don't tell me you're becoming superstitious. The walls are steep, but they're just another climbing surface—like every other obstacle we've faced over the past couple of weeks. We'll take precautions. We'll use our ropes if we need to. We'll be fine."

I cross my arms beneath my breasts. "I'm not happy about this."

He pulls himself up to a sitting position next to me and takes my hand. "Honey, I wouldn't let anything bad happen to you. If you stop to think about it, you'll realize our research is as important to you as it is to me. The only difference is that I've had a few more years to think about it.

We've come a long way in an attempt to find the source of the shard. This could be it. How can we not check it out?"

A tear slips from my eye. "I'm frightened. Not so much for me, but for you. What happens if you get hurt down there?"

He pats my hand. "That's a fair question I can only answer with another question. What happens if either one of us gets hurt anyplace in this part of the world? There is no good answer. We just need to be aware of that and make every effort to proceed with caution."

I sigh. I know he's right. We can't back out now. We've come too far. I slide back down onto my moss and grass bed and pat David's spot beside me. "I'll be really mad at you if you kill yourself tomorrow."

He slips down beside me. "I know. I'll be careful. You too."

I turn my back to him. "Hold me."

He snuggles up and falls to sleep in an instant. I fret about the coming danger for hours.

We rise early. David adds a pile of logs to our fire and then disappears. He later returns with the remainder of the deer, retrieved from high in a distant fir tree. He also has another surprise—eagle eggs. We dig a hole, line it with rocks, put in the deer, cover it with more rocks, and then scrape hot coals and burning logs on top before adding a thin layer of soil. By the time we return in late afternoon, the deer should be cooked to perfection...assuming we return. Suddenly, the thought of roasted deer has a whole new meaning: *make it out of the crater alive, Beth, and that deer is all yours.*

After breakfast, we secure our camp and begin the difficult climb into the adjacent crater. Our footing is solid enough, but we must avoid small ball bearing-like rocks that slip from beneath our feet at the slightest provocation. When we reach the bottom, David begins taking radiation readings. "It's not as bad as I expected," he says with a frown. "I don't understand. The radiation should have washed down from the sides over time, making this the hottest spot in the crater. Water must be running off somewhere."

Leave it to my David to be upset over a lack of radiation. I look around at the crater's high walls, "Uh, how? We're in a rice bowl."

He shrugs. "I don't know, but the readings are much lower than they should be."

The crater appears to have two distinct parts. The upper part could be the result of a huge explosion ejecting a massive amount of material upward and outward, but the lower part, with far steeper sides, seems to have been formed by vertical settling, as if the bottom of the crater dropped straight down.

David explains bunker buster delivery. A hollow blast cavity with fused glass walls normally forms underground, and soil and rock from above sometimes sinks into the cavity when it collapses. As I study the sheer vertical wall at the east side of the crater basin, I still don't get it. "I don't see fused glass here. Wouldn't that mean some of the blast cavity is still intact below?"

He examines the wall with extreme interest. "You would think. Or maybe erosion below caused this area to subside? Runoff might have undermined the substrate."

We begin a systematic search of the crater basin, beginning at the east wall and fanning out toward the west. Just past noon, David calls to me, "Beth, you've got to see this."

I hurry over to his location and see a small hole with considerable erosion leading into it. An eighteen-inch diameter tunnel extends downward at approximately a forty-five degree angle. David points to several rabbit tracks near its entrance. "They seem to go in, but they don't come out. I wonder how long it has been since the last rain."

I smirk. "Maybe Syrian rabbits know how to hop backwards, or maybe it was Alice's white rabbit making a trip to Wonderland?" My grin deepens as I bump his hip and raise my eyebrows. "Maybe a female rabbit seduced it, and it stayed at the tea party?"

He frowns. Not a good time for humor. "Or maybe it's an entrance to the blast cavity, and the rabbits know another way out."

I don't like where this conversation might be headed and immediately move to derail his train of thought. "Not on your life. I get claustrophobic on a mountaintop. There's no way in hell I'd force myself in there. Besides, your father was bigger than me, so we know he didn't go in there."

David chuckles. "Not you, sweetie. I just thought we could lower the Geiger counter wand down as far as possible to see if it picks up higher readings. This could be where the runoff is going."

My cheeks must flush, because prickly heat breaks out across my forehead. "Oh, okay. Just don't get any ideas about tight spaces and me. I don't do that."

Radiation readings rise the moment we begin to lower the wand, and by the time we've pushed it down as far as its tether will permit, the readings reach unsafe levels for humans. David considers the difference in dosage a few feet makes and then suggests, "Must be heavy metals. The same erosion that washed down the radiation has probably deposited a layer of lead around this hole. That would explain why our surface readings are reasonable but these aren't."

We spend the remainder of the day searching the blast cavity but find nothing of interest. The climb out is even more difficult than the climb in. As I huff and puff on a steep incline, David winks at me and then points toward the rim. "Cheer up. There's a delicious venison meal waiting for you just three hundred meters up—and a good night's sleep before we check out the next crater to the west."

David is right about the meal. The venison makes the climb worthwhile—a delicious dinner of tender, succulent meat fit for a queen…or me. In my Cultural History class back in Salvation, I read about slow cooking meat with hot rocks like this, but reading about it doesn't do it justice. David's other point, however, is off the mark. Maybe it's the altitude or my apprehension over climbing down into these hell holes, but for the second night in a row, I don't sleep well.

We rise before the sun. I set out plenty of tea and venison, knowing this could be our last good meal for some time. We only pack enough food and water to last for three days. That minimizes the weight in our packs for the descent and enables us to carry as much climbing gear as we can.

The next crater is only a two-kilometer hike from our lean-to. We walk the distance in silence. David knows I don't want to do this, but I have little choice—he will make the descent with or without me, and I will not allow him to go alone. I'd never forgive myself if something happened to him down there and I was not available to help. As I peer over the edge of the crater in the early morning light, I can see my concerns are justified. This crater is even deeper and steeper than the one we scaled yesterday.

My stomach flips as I mentally scout out the easiest way down. The crater walls are rockier than the crater we entered yesterday. They also have large, layered outcroppings with flat tops, like the whole thing slid down from above to form a huge, inverted wedding cake mold. That should help. David points toward the south wall, "Looks like we could begin our descent there, circling down toward the east from the rim, and then cut back toward the west."

I shake my head. "Yeah. That way, we won't have so far to fall to our deaths."

The climb down is as arduous as it looked from the top, but we are able to reach the bottom with only minor cuts and bruises. This crater is very different from the smaller one we inspected yesterday. The bottom of this one is almost flat with odd, angular rocks protruding upward. David takes radiation measurements the moment we reach the bottom. He shakes his head as he turns the meter so I can see it. "We can't stay long. The radiation is much higher here than we measured yesterday."

He hands the Geiger counter to me. "I'm sure you'll be more comfortable if you can see the readings in real time. I'll go left, and you go right."

As I begin walking the perimeter, I marvel at the smoothness of the dark-colored vertical rock. I pass an escarpment about one-quarter of the way around the crater and am taken by surprise. There is a large, almost square tunnel opening at the intersection of the outcropping rock and the crater wall. I shout out, "David, you've got to see this. There's a tunnel here."

While David trots over, I step inside. The ceiling, walls, and floor are quite smooth, as if everything broke off along horizontal and vertical fault lines and slid straight down. Even more of a surprise, the constant clicking of the Geiger counter decreases and continues to drop as I move farther in. At about fifty feet from the entrance, the clicking stops. I'm thankful for that. The incessant noise from the instrument is unnerving.

David catches up with me about the time the Geiger counter falls silent. He taps the small device with his index finger before looking up at me. "What happened? Did you break it?"

I flip the switch on and off to reset the electronics. The machine remains silent. I stare at the meter, but it is hard to see in the dim light. Just as radiation is reduced inside, so is light. David removes two hand-crank flashlights from his backpack, and we take several minutes to turn the handles to top off the batteries. It's not just the speaker. The meter reads zero as well. I shrug. "It was working before you came over. Maybe it's you."

David swings his flashlight beam from the machine and points the light into the darkness of the tunnel. "We'll try to fix the Geiger counter later. Let's leave our climbing gear here and see if there is anything in here worth exploring."

That's not what I wanted to hear. I hate close spaces. On the upside, walking deeper into the tunnel is easy because there are only a few rock chips scattered around on the floor. About three hundred meters in, we encounter a barrier—a vertical cliff where the floor falls away. We shine our lights over the edge with both beams focused in the same spot but can't penetrate the inky blackness below. I drop a small rock over the side and tilt my head to listen. It bounces on a solid surface out of flashlight range with almost no delay, so the next level down must be just out of sight.

David shines his flashlight on me. "If you're game—" He gasps. "Whoa. What's this?"

He walks past me without so much as a glance, staring straight ahead, and I am stunned as I turn to follow him. "Oh, my God." Scratched on the wall before me are three familiar initials: "PGN," Doctor Peter Gene Noble.

David touches the surface of the rock, tracing the initials with his fingers. "This might be it, Beth. He was here and must have gone on to the next level. He left his initials so others could follow him. We need to get our ropes."

He turns to look back at me, but his right hand remains fixed on the initials scratched on the wall. His eyes are wide, his mouth agape. I believe there is a slight tremor in his arm, and it looks as if his face is flushed. I cannot imagine what it must be like to be confronted with such an incredible clue after an entire lifetime of study and speculation. The look on his face says it all—this is the reason we left our home and sacrificed our safety.

I look over the edge again and swallow hard. I don't like not being able to see the bottom. "Your father's body—

his bones—could still be down there. Are you sure you want ours to join them?"

David sighs. "Don't be silly. If his remains are down there, then who removed his ropes?"

* * * *

We are greeted with another surprise as we return to the mouth of the cave. The Geiger counter seems to resurrect itself. The closer we get to the entrance, the more radiation it registers. David taps the meter once again, but the needle remains constant. "We need to watch this thing on our way back in. Maybe it's telling the truth. Maybe it's not broken."

After retrieving our packs and ropes, I find the walk back into the squarish cave much harder than the first time I came in. I can't shake the feeling that the cave walls are getting closer and closer together. It could be my imagination, or perhaps this cave feels like a giant vice because David expects me to repel down a sheer cliff into a pitch-black abyss.

I take each step with trepidation, suppressing periodic light tremors by telling myself over and over what a good thing it is that Doctor Noble's rope is missing. Nevertheless, nagging doubt plagues me. What if the rope rotted? What if his knots above were poorly tied? What if radioactive rats chewed through the rope's upper end?

Crap. The only thing we really know is that Doctor Noble never returned from his second trip. I don't know if he died at sea or made it this far the second time around…and died here. By the time we reach the precipice, my palms are wet with sweat. I turn to David to make one last plea, "Do we *really* have to do this?"

My flashlight illuminates his easy smile as he pulls a couple of pitons from his pack. "One of us does. I can leave you with the rifle if you think that's best."

Crap again. He's called me out. He knows I won't stay in this damn tunnel alone, and I'm sure as hell not sitting in the high-radiation waiting room outside the adit while he starves to death down there by himself. I sigh. When he doesn't respond, I snort louder. I know I've got to climb down, but I want him to know I'm not happy about it. Nothing I've done in the past has prepared me for this. It's not a fear of climbing that troubles me. It's the darkness and the closeness of the walls. *You're climbing inside your coffin, Beth. Once the lid is sealed, you'll be down there forever.*

My emotional self wants to run. My saner self wants to be with David. If he dies, I want to be with him when it happens. At least then I'd know for certain. I remember the sickening feeling of not knowing his fate when he was swept away by the river. I never want to be in that position again. Not knowing if the love of my life is dead might be worse than knowing. At least I can act with certainty if I know. One thing is very clear to me: if David dies, I'll likely die as well. We are in this together, and our fates are woven together as one. As much as I hate to do it, I will follow him over the edge.

David's climbing pick strikes against a piton, jarring me from deep thought. It's a foreign sound here like it is anywhere in nature—metal against metal, a human derivative that reflects both how far we've come and how far we've fallen. He throws the rope over the side after attaching it to the pitons, and I strain to hear the muffled sound of rope against rock at the bottom of the cliff. The moment we hear the rope hit the surface below, David nods in my direction. "You ready?"

The real answer is *hell no,* but I swallow hard and mutter, "Sure, why not? What do we have to lose but our lives?"

He pats me on the butt before slipping over the side and into the darkness. "That's my girl. I'll meet you at the bottom. Try to get your beautiful tail down there in one piece."

My heart sinks as I watch the top of David's head disappear into the darkness. I can't make out details below. All I see is the faint glow of his flashlight, and all I hear is an occasional grunt. A chill runs through me. I look around the pitch black darkness behind me. It would be easy for some blood-thirsty swamp creature to attack me here. I couldn't see it coming or hear its moist feet on the smooth rock floor. In a split second, it would be on me, tearing at my flesh. I shiver and then laugh out loud. *You need to stop watching those Old World horror movies, Beth.* What a stupid thought. I'd have to be in Salvation to watch something like that, and the likelihood of ever seeing home again is pretty much zero.

I shine my light over the edge again. "Are you all right down there?"

It seems forever before I hear him call back to me, imitating the voice of Bob Barker who we've seen on internet downloads of the Old World television show, *The Price Is Right*. "Come on down!"

I slide over the edge and rappel down, not knowing exactly where the next ledge might be. Rappelling in the mountains near Salvation never made me nervous, but I could always see what was below me. This time, all I can see is a faint glow from David's flashlight. One thing is for certain. We won't be doing much of this. We each carry thirty meters of line, and one is now spent.

David greets me at the bottom with a hug, a kiss, and a compliment. "I knew you could do it."

We crank up the charge on our flashlights and cautiously move down a tunnel that seems to get smaller with each step. It's not my imagination this time. The tunnel is getting smaller, and we are soon forced to move forward while stooped over. About fifty meters farther in, the floor comes to an abrupt end, but this time the next ledge is only a meter down. We ease ourselves onto the level below and continue forward, finding dozens more one-meter to two-meter step-like ledges as we follow the path less traveled to God knows where.

An hour in, the constricted cave begins to get larger. It feels good to walk upright again, probably like early man felt when he finally stopped dragging his knuckles. The cave continues to expand until it opens to a huge underground room with vertical sides and sheer rock columns. Our flashlights aren't strong enough to reach the ceiling, but I'm certain it's up there somewhere.

Unlike other caves I've been in near Salvation, this one is dry. There are no stalagmites or stalactites—just sheer dark rock everywhere we look, as if this room fell straight down when the bombs exploded. David walks to a nearby wall and runs his hand along a shiny, golden streak on the surface of the stone. "Amazing, isn't it? Old World people died for this stuff, but it has no value now."

I look with mild interest at the long vein of gold running along the vertical surface of the wall as it reflects light back at me. Too heavy for weapons and too soft for tools, it's beautiful but useless. I walk down its length, admiring its golden glow, and stop abruptly when I find "PGN" scratched near the end of the vein. This would have been the most expensive directional sign ever created in the Old World. I snicker as I call out to David, "He went this-a-way."

I'm beginning to understand Doctor Noble's confusion. If he found the shard down here somewhere, then how did it get here? These caves are new, fragmented out of sheer rock by the force of explosions above. No delivery vehicle, no matter how tough, could have penetrated the rock to this level. It just isn't possible.

We continue in silence, but I'm sure David's thinking the same thing: how could a three-million-year-old shard get down here? How could something that old and that advanced exist at all?

The wall containing the golden pointer comes to an abrupt end where the floor falls away to new depths beyond the reach of our lights. I step back from the edge, suppressing a shiver that starts at my toes, works its way to the top of my head, and sets loose butterflies in my stomach along the way. It's a long way down. My apprehension doesn't settle until I move farther from the edge. We follow the ledge toward the next wall that must exist ahead and are surprised to find another ledge jutting back toward the cave where we entered. This ledge doesn't disappear into total darkness below. In some places, we can see the next level down, and from that level, passageways continue into the distance—dozens of them.

Looking at what appears to be the vertical ledge with the least depth, David asks, "What do you think, Beth? How do we pick a path to go down?"

I'm not anxious to go down into *any* of that blackness. Hell, I can't even see where I am now. "I think we should get a permission slip from your father. After all, why would he leave two notes behind and not one ahead?"

David nods. "Good point. There could be another message…or at least a pointer."

We begin sweeping the area near the closest ledge with our flashlights but find nothing. We also walk the adjacent edge until we reach another solid wall and then follow that until it reaches the cave where we entered. If there are marks from Doctor Noble, we've missed them. With much greater focus, and moving with great care, we retrace our steps, convinced there must be another sign somewhere. On our third pass along the far ledge, David pauses to shine his light on the floor about two meters from the edge and mutters, "Interesting."

I scurry over but see only rock. Brushing away a light stone powder, he points at several small holes, "Pitons. He's been here."

We peer over the edge in front of the tiny holes. We can't see the next ledge down, but dropping a small rock confirms its reachable using our last rope. David shrugs as he looks in my direction. "We've come this far. Might as well see where all of this takes us."

I raise my shoulders and palms. "I'm game if you are."

After driving in pitons where Doctor Noble had, we affix our rope and descend the wall. The floor below is exactly like the floor above, but the way ahead is a narrow passage. We move forward with great caution. It's as black as carbon, and we don't want to fall over some unseen edge into oblivion. Even worse, the ceiling steps down, and we must crouch low to accommodate it. This time, the walk isn't short. We cover at least three kilometers before we catch our first whiff of water. As we continue forward, the walls become slimy with condensation, and the floor is slippery with some type of clear, fluorescent algae.

The passage narrows yet again, both in height and width. Even so, I feel less insecure than I had earlier because it's easy to see where we're going in the glowing algae. Still, the tight quarters aren't ideal, and I try to keep my claustrophobia at bay with humor. "Don't get any ideas back there." I would wiggle my ass at him if I had room to do anything other than move forward.

He huffs back, "No chance. I can barely breathe." The narrow passage is much tighter for him.

A little farther on, we must crawl forward, pushing our packs in front of us. My knees throb. I'm soaked to the bone and covered with clear slime by the time the passage gives way to an amazing large room. We both stand and stare in awe at the surrounding spectacle. David turns his flashlight off. "The walls are covered with living material. Whatever it is gives off enough light that we can see in the dim glow without flashlights."

I turn my light off as well. Some of the slimy creatures scintillate, and others give off a constant glow. The greens and purples are beautiful beyond measure.

We can't see it, but we hear water falling somewhere nearby. Wherever it is, there's a lot of it. The roar doesn't shake the rock, but my body feels its thunder. Covered in glowing green slime with specks of red, David's face looks clown-like. I can't help but snicker. He just points back at me with a florescent finger. "If I look anything like you do right now, I understand."

We embrace each other for a moment, and I kiss his gooey lips. When I pull back, I coo, "I don't know where we're going from here, dear, but I'd rather be here with you than anywhere on the planet—not! How long do we have to stay down here?"

He kisses me back and then flashes a smug smile. "Turn around, love. We're closer than you think."

I turn slowly, expecting the unexpected, but not this. On the wall in front of me are large, dark letters formed by scraping the slime off the surface, "Shard found here" and, below the letters, a dark arrow points toward the floor.

Based on the other clues left by Doctor Noble, I'm surprised this one is so obvious. "I don't get it. Why aren't the letters filled in by slime? Your father had to write that message a long time ago."

David shrugs. "I can't imagine. Maybe the oils in human skin are poison to the living creatures that glow in the dark, like they are to stalactites and stalagmites. That aside, if this is where my father found the shard, as the message indicates, a more important question is how did the shard get here in the first place?" He looks in the direction of the noise from the falling water. "I bet the river left it behind, and that should be a warning to us as well. If water can rise to the level of that wall in this confined space, we might be at risk from a storm above."

Despite our experience with the catamaran, I ignore his warning. "If the river left it here, then we'd have to follow the river upstream to know where the shard came from."

"That's probably what my father intended to do. After he got the carbon dating report, he must have been burning to know its source, especially after seeing the smaller piece in Tripoli on his way home."

That makes sense because curiosity always bites me like a rabid pit bull. "I can understand that. Do you think he ever found where the shard came from?"

"He might have. His missing ropes don't tell us much. He might have taken the ropes with him on the way out the second time he was here, and died with the secret somewhere at the bottom of the ocean...or not. Equally probable, he might not have made it back here a second time. Without more evidence, we'll never know for sure."

I take a moment to turn in a complete circle, admiring the beauty of the phosphorescence around me. Now that my eyes have adjusted to the dim glow, more colors seem to rise from the surface. In addition to the greens and purples I saw earlier, light yellow, hues of red, and many shades of blue glow iridescent. I look toward David and speak loud enough to be heard over the roar of the nearby river. "What now? Do we follow the river upstream or go back for more supplies?"

He takes my hand and faces me. "We have food and water for three days. That's enough to support travel upriver for one day, and still give us two days to get out of the cave complex. At least we'd have an idea of what to expect along the water, if we have to come back."

I give him a playful hug. "We'll smell pretty bad by the time we get out of here."

He grins and bumps my hip with his. "We don't have to wait for that. You smell wretched now."

The river is only 200 meters away, flowing without ripples within a nearly square channel sunk into the surrounding stone. Broken, fragile bodies of clear phosphorescent creatures illuminate the edges of the channel like a living flame. The water flows over a sheer cliff about fifty meters downstream, causing the roar we've been hearing, but the water in the river channel slips by without a sound. The river's channel must be quite smooth, like the floor of this cavern.

At first, the walk along the edge of the river is slippery, but easy and serene. We pass several smaller tributaries that enter on the opposite side of the channel, but only two add appreciable water to the main flow. The peaceful nature of the river changes when we hear rapids ahead. We approach with caution as the cave narrows, forcing us near to the river's edge where glowing, frothy water cascades down toward us. Light-emitting creatures streak by in the swift current. The rushing water looks both dangerous and beautiful. There is little climbing space adjacent to the flow. We cling to the slippery, narrow ledge between the river's savage water and the cave's vertical wall as we inch forward.

We soon decide the risk is too great. Going forward could mean certain death. Disappointed, we retrace our steps along the narrow ledge to a safer downstream location where the ledge alongside the river is about a meter wide. David surveys the top edge of the cave with his flashlight and motions me to fall back. I don't complain. The wider the ledge, the more comfortable I feel. Although I've spent my entire life walking narrow mountain shelves in the area surrounding Salvation, all those experiences took place above ground and in daylight. Down here, everything is different. They bury people in the dark, below ground.

Chapter Sixteen
The Pit

David continues to study the rock above the edge of the river's channel until he spots what he's looking for. "There, Beth—a crawl space."

Crawl space? Shit, that's the last thing I want to hear. I see it, but I don't like it.

He paces back and forth, alternately looking up at the small, square hole and then stopping to rub his chin. He stops pacing beneath the opening and stares up at it for a very long time. My heart sinks when he glances in my direction. "Give me a boost, dear. I need to check this out." He drops his pack, removes his bedroll strap, and ties it to his ankle. "If that's what I think it might be, the strap might help you get up there, too."

This is insane. There's no way I'd ever enter that little death trap no matter where it might lead. David throws his hands to the side with his palms up. "Come on, Beth. I need a little help here."

I huff my displeasure with a snort. "I'd ask if your will is signed, but you don't have a damn thing to leave to me."

He puts his closed fists on his hips. "Your resistance is noted; it is also futile. We are going to do this if it kills us."

"And it might—it killed your father."

David sighs and pulls me close for a hug. He kisses the top of my head. "Look, we've talked about this. I need to do this. You—especially you—should understand. Look around you, Beth. How did the shard get here? You've see it with your own eyes. That thing did not come from anything that impacted above. We're too deep. It just isn't possible."

Even though I can see in my mind the look on David's face when we found Doctor Noble's initials scrawled in the cave wall above, I whimper. "I know it's important, but I still don't want you to go."

He wipes away my forming tears as he shakes his head. "I have to, Beth. I need to know...*we* need to know."

I wipe my nose on my sleeve and look at him with moon eyes. "Make damn sure that strap is tied tight, so I can pull you back out when you get stuck—and don't go in so far that I can't reach the strap."

He nods as I amble over and glare at him. I exhale a loud sigh and then stoop over so he can step up on my shoulders. When he has a sufficient grip on the edge of the opening to lift most of his weight, I stand with all my strength as he pulls himself up and in. It doesn't take long before the strap tethered to his ankle slithers into the hole and disappears.

I hear fewer and fewer shuffling noises as he moves forward until I hear nothing but the roar of the nearby rapids. I wait. Time grinds to a standstill. I become more nervous by the second. I don't know what to do. Fits of anger shake my body between bouts of deep concern. *He's done it again. He's left me here alone.* He could be trapped somewhere in there, and I have no way to get him out. *For that matter, it will be difficult to get myself out.*

It suddenly occurs to me that we made no contingency plans—not one. How long do I wait before I assume he isn't coming back? When do I try to reach our base camp on my own? Even if I can make it back to our base camp, is it possible for a lone woman to walk hundreds of kilometers back to the mouth of the Suez Canal to find help? There is no question in my mind that I will try to save myself if David doesn't return. I promised myself I'd never take the easy way out again, and I intend to keep that promise. I might be eaten by a bear, but I'll go down fighting.

Alone, surrounded only by the soft glow of light-emitting organisms, my mind spins out of control. I begin to cry. It's not just my current situation that weighs me down, but pent up fear and anger over an out-of-control life that has been getting worse since we left Hope. I'm tired, afraid, and now, perhaps abandoned. I jerk off my backpack and throw it against the wall below the small entry hole. *Damn him, anyway. Why did we have to come to this hellhole? Is anything worth this—even the shard?*

My anger turns to gut-rending sobs. Unstoppable tears flow beyond reason. I curl up below the opening that took my David away and cry myself to sleep.

* * * *

"Wake up, sweetie. You're pretty enough without more beauty rest."

I have no idea how long I slept, but it seems only minutes before David shakes my shoulder. I wonder if this is some sort of dream, something similar to the dream I had about being home with my parents. I try to stretch, but my ribs ache from sobbing. The pain reminds me that this is real. That's good, I guess, but the throbbing is becoming an annoyance. "David? How did you get out of that hole without stepping on me?"

He slips on his backpack and then kisses my forehead. "There's another way. You don't have to use the hole. Come on. I'll show you."

I don my pack, and he practically pulls me along the river. I can tell he's excited, but he has no idea I'm still mad as hell. My initial relief for him being alive gradually brews into anger, and then overflows. I stop walking and glare at him. "Hold on, hot dog. We need to get a few things straight between us. How could you leave me alone without any plan? How could you desert me like that?"

I shine my flashlight on his face to increase the intensity of my interrogation, and his face pales at my sharp words. I know he can't see my face through the glare, but my anger is evident enough. Good. His shoulders stoop, and his eyes stare down at the cavern floor. "I didn't think of it like that. This whole complex is a maze. Once I got into it, there was little choice but to go forward. Honey, I'm sorry if I worried you, but there wasn't much I could do. I either had to go forward or back, and I just kept going forward."

My tears begin again as I scold him like a child. "Damn you! Don't you *ever* leave me again, even if it means going back. Do you understand? Even if it means we go back!" My voice is loud enough to crack as I yell at him, my fists clenched at my sides.

He pulls me close and caresses me, stroking my hair and kissing the top of my head. Sobs come from deep inside me, from places I didn't know existed. My whole body shakes. He tries to comfort me, but my tears continue despite his reassurances. "I love you, Beth. More than anything in this world, I love you. If it comes to that again, then we'll act together or not at all. If that means going back, then we will go back together."

He lets me cry out my frustration and anger, and when I am able to take normal breaths again, I am amazed by my own behavior. I don't understand what's going on inside me. I want to hurt him and love him at the same time. Then, it hits me. *My God, I'm acting hormonal. Could I be pregnant?* I pat the pills in my pocket. No, I'm just angry, and I have every right to be.

When I'm certain I am in control of the waves of emotion crashing over me, I break his hold and glare into his eyes. "Never again. *Never.*"

He nods. "I understand, honey. I'm sorry. It won't happen again. Can I show you something wonderful now?"

Curiosity is my weak spot, and David knows it. He's acting like a schoolboy about to steal his first kiss, and it's infectious. *Damn it! Why is it so hard to stay mad at him?* I can't imagine what he's found. After I nod my willingness to follow, he pulls me along at a trot. About a kilometer downstream, he takes a hard left into a narrow slit in the rock. We begin a gradual, upward climb. We're both breathing hard, and through his panting, I hear him say, "This path goes to the headwater."

A headwater? Underground? My excitement spikes to match his, and I begin pushing him to accelerate the climb.

It's a three-hour haul through corridor after corridor, following darkened arrows David dredged out of the living slime that covers the walls. It isn't long before our heightened pace slows to normal, long before we reach our destination. When we finally emerge at the end of the maze, the sight takes my breath away.

A large, green-glowing lake fills the panorama before us—a stunning spectacle. In my wildest dreams, I could not have imagined the existence of something like this. "How can it glow like that? It's like a giant nightlight."

"Maybe it's the collection pond for the craters above, and the harvested radiation stimulates the florescent creatures that live in it. Beautiful, isn't it?"

"It definitely gives a whole new meaning to the expression 'Nuke 'em 'til they glow,' but it's beauty could belie its danger. I pull the Geiger counter from my backpack and scan the edge of the water with the wand. The indicator needle immediately jumps into the red zone. "This water isn't safe. We can't stay here long."

"Then, come away from the edge."

I back away until the meter needle drops below the red arc on the gauge. "Have you given any thought to how this might help us find the source of the shard?"

He digs in his pack for a piece of pork jerky and offers some to me. "I have. If this is the main drainage pond for the craters, and the shard was found where Dad left the note on the rock, then it had to come from one of the tributaries we saw on our hike up to this lake. A torrential rain above would have flooded the tributary basin."

"Do we have enough time to check any of those out? We'd have to walk around the lake until we find an outflow and then follow that tributary down its channel to the main riverbed."

David continues to chew his jerky until his mouth clears. "We might be able to scout the largest outflow we can find, but we'd need to ration our food and water. Even then, we could be damn hungry and thirsty by the time we get back to the surface. We can't drink the water here. If it contains dissolved plutonium, it will poison us. For that matter, just being here for an extended time could be a problem."

We eat our jerky snack in silence, each contemplating the risks facing us, until I offer, "We've come a long way, and we could be sitting on the most significant discovery ever made by man. I say we go for it." I've never been a "damn the torpedoes" kind of girl, but I am, after all, a cultural anthropologist. What anthropologist worth her salt would walk away from this?

David nods and exhales the deep breath he took when I started talking. I suspect he's relieved I've made such a choice. After the debacle back at the river, he will be darn careful about taking the lead on such things in the future. "Okay, then. If you're up for it, we'll give it a try. Can you chew and walk at the same time?"

I nod, dust myself off as I get up, and then follow him along the shoreline. The ground slopes gently into the water and glows green with the bodies of small organisms. Rocky spire structures jut upward around the lake's oval circumference, and a few large stalagmites hang from the cave ceiling. The dome over the lake glows blue, red, and yellow from the slimy creatures growing on it. We make it most of the way around the perimeter in about two hours and find three tributaries in the process. Two are dry, making our decision easy. At the outflow, the tributary carries little water. Nevertheless, we don't wade in it. Instead, we follow the narrow ledge that abuts its channel. Like the main outflow, the tributary and its adjoining ledge soon begin to step down, but we are surprised when it veers right and heads away from the main flow.

In another hour, we trace the gentle flow to a small waterfall about one meter in height. To our amazement, another lake extends in the distance downstream. This one is as bright as the first but even larger. I sigh and shake my head as I look toward David. "What now?"

He strokes his chin as he surveys the extent of the lake. "It appears this tributary doesn't know our schedule. We don't have enough food and water to investigate the entire lakeshore. About all we can do is cross the tributary and follow the shoreline until we find another to lead us downstream."

Without taking my eyes off the huge, glowing lake, I mumble, "We could retrace our steps. Go back for more supplies."

"We could, but the main channel is probably closer if we continue downstream. Besides, we don't know any more about the source of the shard now than we did several hours ago."

I take a deep breath and, in that moment, realize we've taken part of our survival for granted. "Which way does the air flow in here?"

David holds up his small butane lighter and flicks the flint. The flame flickers in random directions in the open air. "Kind of hard to tell, but on average, it seems to follow the water."

I study the flame too. To me it's inconclusive. The air could be going straight up. I sigh, shrug, and raise my palms. "Okay, we'll follow the water, but in another few hours, we won't have any alternatives."

As much as we hate to, we wade across the tributary. Our boots are waterproof, and the water is shallow; nevertheless, the soles of our boots now glow as bright as the water itself. We skirt the shore of the lake until we find an outflow point and then follow the gentle flow of water downstream. The thin path adjacent to the new tributary channel becomes quite irregular, jutting one way and then another. We continue to follow it until it abruptly ends where the water disappears under the rock ahead.

A dead end.

David shakes his head as he leans against the cavern wall. "We passed a square cleft in the rock about four hundred meters back on the left. Let's see if that'll take us around the obstruction. If not, we'll try to return to the surface by the path we know."

The cleft is just wide enough for David's shoulders, and we begin our trek through the maze beyond. The small, narrow corridor has many turns, right and left. It rises and falls but continues to head in the general direction we believe we want to go. About forty-five minutes later, we come to a near vertical drop about fifty meters above the floor of a vast, glowing cavern. Looking down, we can see the tributary emerge from beneath the rock below, flow slowly through the cavern, and then disappear over the edge at the far side.

David peers over the edge, carefully looking down toward the cavern floor. "The wall telescopes as it descends. It's not a single, sheer piece. I think we can scale it if we keep ourselves plastered to its surface."

I look down as well. It won't be a cakewalk. Some of the small ledges are two to three meters apart in the vertical and only a few centimeters wide. "Assuming we get down, we won't be able to come back up. Even if we make it down without killing ourselves, there are no assurances that tributary goes where we think it does. We might never get back out."

David doesn't answer. He seems distracted, so I prod him with a sarcastic remark, "Hey, what could be more important than going back or going down?"

He points across the cavern. "That."

I strain through the dim glow, wishing I had brought the field glasses. What I see doesn't make any sense at all, at least not here. Everything we've seen so far consists mostly of vertical and horizontal surfaces derived from rocks falling straight down or breaking along linear fault lines. Yet across this chasm there appears to be a large, angular structure sloped at forty-five to sixty degrees. The structure is different from anything we've seen so far. I glance at David, trying to disguise the fear in my eyes. "Is knowing what that is…worth dying for?"

He strokes his chin again and answers in a measured tone, "It could be, if it's what we came here to find. On the other hand, if we find the source of the shard and can't get out of this underground complex, what's the point of taking the risk? The way I see it, either the tributary leads to the main channel, or it doesn't. If it doesn't, we might never find this place from any downstream location. If it does, there's a good chance we can get to the main channel from down there—a bet we already made when we followed this tributary in the first place."

I consider his words, remove my backpack, and then take a moment to wrap the Geiger counter and my flashlight in my blanket before binding everything tight inside with the pack straps. The packaging effort gives me time to think. *Are those sloped rocks really worth the risk?* I sigh as I stand, and then nonchalantly kick my backpack over the side. "Oops."

He removes his pack and does the same. "Guess we're committed. I'll go first because I'm taller. I'll help ease you down to the next level where I can."

It's a tricky descent by any standard. I'm thankful we're far enough from the tributary that very little slime grows on these rocks. David slides to the first level about two meters down and moves a little to the left. "Okay, honey. Just stay glued to the rock."

I slip over the ledge, holding onto it until I've stretched out as far as I can. David reaches up to press my pelvis into the rock as I let go. The rock is smooth, but I still lose a little skin on my palm. We take each level with care and deliberation until we reach the bottom. We both have cuts and bruises, but we're safe for now. We pick up our packs and begin walking toward the unusual structures ahead.

The closer we get, the odder the slanted structures look. As we stare at them from just across the tributary, David mutters, "This makes no sense. They look man-made."

I glance at him with an excited smile. "Maybe they are. Someone had to make the machine that made the shard."

We've been reluctant to discuss that possibility because it seemed so impossible. Yet we are now approaching something that could be even more improbable—the remnant of a civilization more advanced than ours, but three million years old.

We wade across the tributary hand in hand, in total awe of what lies ahead. About fifteen meters beyond the opposite side of the stream, a sharp pop suddenly echoes through the cavern. David's eyes grow wide as he shoots a quick glance at me. His free arm darts out to his side as the rock gives way beneath him.

There is no time to react. The square patch of rock on which he stands slides straight down and comes to a stop with a huge thud about six meters below. He is weightless for only a moment before his falling weight slams me to the surface. Black spots fill my vision. I gasp for breath but manage to hold on.

He gropes upward with his other hand, trying desperately to reach the edge above. Before I can recover my wind, his weight begins to pull me toward the edge. He sees what's happening and screams, "Let go, Beth. Let go!"

My mind is fuzzy, but I know one thing for certain: I can't let go.

We're in this together. I vowed never to be separated again, and I cling to him as to life itself. As hard as I try to hold on, though, I just can't overcome his weight. In moments, we both tumble into the pit below.

I see the fall in slow motion, especially when David's head strikes the bottom hard. Saliva ejects from his mouth as blood spurts from his head. His body quivers, and his arms jerk spastic-like before he stops moving. I land on my side, my head cushioned by his body. When I catch my breath, I drag myself close to him. My tears begin to flow as I cradle his head in my arms. Soon, the silence surrounding me is punctuated by my deep sobs and muted words, "No. No. No. David, come back to me. Don't leave me here alone."

Part 4: Reunion

Chapter Seventeen
The Process of Dying

It is amazing how quickly the lessons of survival training kick in when you need them. I force my personal fears aside and inspect David as objectively as I can. Other than from the wound on his head, I don't see any protruding bones or other bleeding. I lift his eyelid to see a blood-red eye. I put my ear to his chest. His breathing is shallow, and his heartbeat is faster than normal. His color seems ashen. Trembling shakes his body from time to time. He is cold to the touch, and his brow is moist with perspiration. I know these symptoms. He's in shock. I lift his feet and slide his backpack under them, wrap the two of us with our survival blankets, and then hold him close. In about an hour, his shivering gets worse.

I feel helpless. The edges of the gaping rock opening above might as well be a kilometer away. I can't reach them and have no materials for building anything to help get out. I'm not sure what do. I won't leave David alone under any circumstance, and I don't have the strength to pull him out even if I could get myself out. There's no help up there anyway, so I continue to hold him. The love of my life could be passing from this life, and all I can offer is body heat. At least we're together; at least he's alive for now.

In another four hours, his shaking settles. I don't know if he's getting better or worse, but this is my opportunity to nurse his wound. I lift his head, slip his backpack under it, and roll him on his side. After removing the first aid kit from my backpack, I clean his wound with antiseptic wipes and then suture the wound closed as best I can. With every stitch, I am thankful for survival training.

It feels good to stand and flex my body after I've closed David's wound. When the blood flow returns to my legs, I walk the perimeter of the trap we've fallen into. The walls are vertical. The stone is smooth, as if carved by a master stonecutter. The rock floor fell straight down without leaving any telescoping ridges. Our situation seems hopeless. I curl up next to David and cry myself to sleep.

* * * *

I wake from fitful sleep some time later when David stirs. My body aches and my pulse races. Our situation is just as dire as when we fell into this hole, but at least David is still alive. I roll over to face him and place my hand on his warm, dry forehead. Listening to his strong and regular heartbeat gives me hope. After pulling the crank flashlight from my backpack, I look him over in detail. I don't see evidence of swelling or discoloration around his joints, so I assume nothing is broken. The stitches on the back of his head are crusty with dried blood, and one of his eyes is black and swollen. He opens the other and whispers, "Water."

I nurse small sips into his mouth until he waves me off. Afterward, I tear off small bites of jerky with my teeth and slip them into his mouth. His good eye darts around our prison while he chews. He soon moves his head slowly back and forth. "Looks like we're in a hell of a fix this time."

I kiss his forehead. "Yes, dear. Things have been better. How are you feeling?"

"Like I've been run over by a garbage truck, but I don't think anything is broken. How about you?"

"Sore ribs—sore everything—but don't worry about me. We just need to get you functioning as best we can."

He strokes my face with his fingertips and smiles through the hardened blood on his lower lip. "I'll be fine. I took a hell of a hit, but my pain is easing. I'll be good as new in no time." He tries to stand but can't. He leans on the wall for stability and then lowers himself into a sitting position against the rock. "Looks like I've still got a little dizziness to overcome."

I kneel next to him and stroke his hair with one hand and his cheek with the other. A tear slips from my eye. "I thought I'd lost you."

He turns, braces himself with one palm on the wall, and gags. His body quivers as he mutters, "Sorry. It isn't personal."

I pat his back. "Nausea is a shock residual. Just take it easy."

He slides his free hand to the back of his head. "I have the mother of all headaches and feel like I've grown a cantaloupe back there."

I gently move his hand away from the stitches. "Leave those stitches alone, or I'll have to put a cone on you. I had to sew you up while you were unconscious."

He gives my hand a light squeeze. "I guess that way I get to feel all the pain now."

I squeeze back. "I'm sorry, dear. Sewing isn't my strong suit. Can I get anything for you? More water? Food? Sex?"

He tries to laugh but grimaces instead. "I'll take a rain check on the sex but could sure use a dump. Looks like we've landed in the toilet this time. This isn't going to be pretty. Got any leaves?"

I shrug. "Fresh out. We were supposed to be out of here by now."

He inches up the wall and balances himself against the rock as he makes his way to the far corner. I hand him a single square of gauze from our first aid kit. "This'll have to do. Knock yourself out." I immediately bite my tongue. "I didn't mean that literally."

It was bad enough in this hole before his potty break. Now we'll have to gag on the smell of our own waste. Can things get any worse?

David finishes his business and then makes his way to the corner most distant from his pile. We wrap ourselves in blankets and snuggle together for warmth. In short order he falls fast asleep. That gives me time to take inventory of our supplies. As I look at our meager rations, I wish I had packed more. Even while exploring the cave above, we had begun to conserve what we had because we thought we might not get back to our base camp before our supplies ran out. Now it's worse. I know David won't be eating much for at least a day, but he will need water. I resolve to save most of my portions for him. If we have any hope of getting out of this mess, it will take both of us. He needs to be well.

David seems much better when he wakes. His grogginess has passed, and he is alert. He sits up and reaches back to feel his stiches. "My head still hurts, but the swelling has gone down. I guess you'll have to put up with me a little longer."

I kneel in front of him and kiss his forehead. "That works for me. How's your strength?"

He flexes his arms and reaches over to pat his bicep. "Want to arm wrestle?"

I snicker and kiss him again. As we eat a little jerky and take a few sips of water, I can almost see the wheels turning in his mind. After some time of alternately staring at the backpacks and then at the wall, he says, "The packs might be our only way out, Beth, but we'll need to take them apart. If we can separate the aluminum back supports and then tie them together, we might be able to make a bundle that's strong enough to support our weight."

"How's a bundle of aluminum rods going to help us get out of here?"

He points to where the rocks above come together at right angles. "We could cut the backpack fabric into strips to make a rope, tie the rope to the center of the bundle and then throw the bundle over the rocks where the walls intersect. If we're careful, we might be able to pull the bundle across the open area between the two sides. If the bundle will support our weight, it might be possible to climb up the rope."

I drag the nearest backpack to my side to study it. The aluminum horizontal supports are bolted to the vertical rods, so I use our hunting knife to unscrew them. When I've freed all four vertical rods, I bind them into a bundle using the shoelaces from my boots. My excitement rises. With luck, we might get out of this hole.

We decide the packs are too important to dissect, so I remove the shoulder straps and connect them end-to-end, knot our blankets together with David's pants, and tie everything to the center of the bundle of aluminum rods. We now face the daunting task of throwing the bundle and rope six meters up and over the pit's upper edge.

David's first few attempts are miserable failures. I step in before he gets too frustrated. "Let it go for now. Give yourself another day to recover. Then we'll try again."

He reluctantly agrees, but his concern is valid. "We only have a little food and water, Beth. The longer we stay here, the weaker we'll get. We can't wait too long or we'll never get it done."

I untie the blankets from the rope, take his hand, and then pull him gently to the floor beside me. "Only one more day. Then we'll give it everything we've got."

He smiles. "All right, dear, but we can't hold back tomorrow."

Although it is impossible to tell night and day in the cave, we wake quite rested some time later. After a little water and jerky, I re-tie the blankets to our pitiful rope. This time we work together, with me throwing the escape rope at exactly the same time he throws our bundle of rods. We score in only three attempts—the ends of the bundle rest on adjacent walls and the rope dangles down the corner where the two sides meet. David then hefts me on his shoulders. "Okay, babe. Don't make any sudden moves. Make sure those rods can hold your weight. Climb as smoothly as you can."

I grab the leg of the pants and incrementally add more and more of my weight, wondering the whole time why I just didn't let go when David fell into this damn hole, but then, who would've kept him warm and taken care of his wounds? He could've died down here without me being next to him. I shake off my nagging hindsight with a single thought: the past is irrelevant. All that matters now is climbing out of this pit. So I pull myself upward until my feet leave David's shoulders.

When I reach a point about two meters from the top, I feel the bundle shift. The movement is almost imperceptible but enough to make me freeze in place. I hold my breath as I look up. The left side of the bundle has shifted a few centimeters toward the opening. My heart sinks; my stomach feels queasy. I look down at David and grimace. He can only offer encouragement. "Move slow and easy, honey. Slow and easy."

Twice more, I reach up, grasping the rope above my head. Squeezing the rope tight between my feet, I push up with my legs and pull down with my arms…slowly and methodically. Only one meter to go. I take a deep, slow breath as I prepare to reach upward once again. The aluminum bundle shifts again, and I hear it scrape against the rock's sharp edge as it pivots toward the pit. My heartbeat pounds in my ear drums, but I can't worry about my impending fall. David will do his best to catch me. I stretch my arm out and pull down with constant, steady force as my body moves up another half meter. One more upward reach and I'll be able to grasp the edge. I stretch my arm out slowly, but the bundle shifts once again. In an instant, the entire apparatus begins to slide toward the abyss.

The nauseating grip of weightlessness seizes me as I begin to fall backward. In that moment of terror, watching the bundle fall toward my face as it screeches against the sharp edge of the pit, something grasps my wrist from above. I gasp as the rods tumble past me and look up in abject fear.

An older man looks down and asks, "Can I be of assistance, young lady?"

Dangling from his arm, all I can blurt is, "Doctor Noble?" He pulls me up and over the edge and offers the same unmistakable smile I've seen on David's face so many times in the past. "Please, call me Peter."

Although completely out of character for me—especially with all of the questions swarming in my mind—I am struck silent. He looks over the edge to see his son below. "David, is that you? You really should put some pants on, my boy."

I watch in silent wonder as David's father lowers a rope and pulls our gear and his son from the pit. David is as stunned as I am. After putting his pants on, he asks the burning question that's on both our minds. "How is it possible you're here, Dad? Everyone thought you were dead."

David's voice cracks when he asks. It's clear his emotions are running wild. From almost being killed in this terrible place to standing face-to-face with his assumed-dead father, I wonder how David can manage to stand, let alone ask questions.

Doctor Noble gestures toward the pit. "If you mean 'here,' you were making considerable racket with that contraption as I was coming to work. Clanking metal in a place like this is as out of place as a clown at a funeral. I simply had to see what was going on. In truth, the thought of a visitor intrigued me. I've never had one. A more appropriate question is, 'What are *you* doing here?'"

David continues to stare at Doctor Noble as if looking at a ghost while I relate the story of our journey and how we followed the earlier trip notes in an attempt to find the source of the shard. When the shock of seeing his father wears off, David hands the smaller shard to his father. "This was our final clue."

Doctor Noble rubs the smaller piece between his thumb and forefinger, feeling its shape in the cavern's dim light glow. "Yep, it was my final clue, too. Good sleuthing, Son." He then shifts his focus back toward me, "And why do you have this relic?"

I swallow hard. Perhaps we have violated some sacred archeological tenet by smashing the ancient cabinet from which we stole it. "The monastery in Tripoli won't survive over time. We thought it best to save that piece while we could."

His spontaneous laughter echoes through the cavern, magnifying its comical effect. When he settles down, he offers, "Oh my, I needed that. I didn't mean the shard, dear. I know why you'd have that. What I meant is why would a pretty young thing like you be here with my son?"

"Oh, that." I quickly introduce myself and then explain the story of my internship, computer mate assignment, and our courtship. The older man nods with great interest, barely able to take his eyes off me. "I see. Arrangements for the sake of good DNA alone don't always work out, but it appears the computer made a good selection this time. It's my pleasure to welcome you into the family, Beth."

It's clear that he's talking from experience. David hasn't discussed his mother with me and has never mentioned how she and his father got along. Their relationship could've been turbulent. "Is that the reason you didn't return from your second trip—a good DNA match but a bad emotional one? You must've known everyone would think you were dead."

"Ah, you get right to the meat of things, don't you? Okay, yes, in part, but also to avoid the politics of the day...and to try to understand the shards. I suppose it was inevitable people would think me dead, but I just couldn't leave here until I knew everything there was to learn. I also wanted to wait until the bastards controlling our lot from

Salvation were replaced." He sweeps his hand toward the structures ahead. "Whatever lies in the past isn't relevant. I've some marvelous things to show you in the here and now."

Doctor Noble coils his rescue rope as he steps in front of David. "It's good to see you, Son, but you and your computer bride must not stay here. If you do, I'll never be a grandfather. The radiation is bad, particularly near the water."

David shakes his head in disagreement. "Of all people, you must know we can't leave. We need to know what you know. We've risked everything seeking the same answers you came here to find. We're not leaving without them."

Doctor Noble gives David a very quick hug and then shakes his head as he steps back. "I don't agree, but I do understand. Something like this can change a man—" He glances at me. "Or a woman." He continues when he looks back at his son, "Under the circumstances, I'm a little sorry I trained you so well. But you're here now, so come. Let me open your eyes to something marvelous."

David glances at me, and I wave my forefinger back and forth at him. I know he has a thousand questions, but they can wait until we get out of here. Doctor Noble said he would never be a grandfather if we stay in this cavern too long. For me, it has already been too long. I hold my finger to my lips and gesture for David to follow me as I fall in behind Doctor Noble. There will be time enough for questions and answers when we reach the light of day.

We follow David's father through many twists and turns, gradually rising to the level of the slanted stones we'd seen from the other side of the cavern. As we near the front of the structure, I see rock columns at an angle, apparently pushed to the side when a very large building skewed sideways and collapsed onto itself. The base of each column is huge—about six meters in diameter. If unbroken, the columns would be thirty meters high. From side to side, the extent of all the felled columns taken together is at least two hundred meters.

I'm in awe. "What is it, Doctor Noble?"

"Remember what I said before, dear. Call me Peter." He smiles and winks before continuing. "Near as I can tell, it might be something like a time capsule—a collection of artifacts from beyond our understanding of human existence. It might be from a time before humans walked the earth, something older than the shard I found when I first came here."

Agape, I stutter, "Ma...made...by humans?"

He flicks his head toward the structure as he chuckles. "That building was not made by aliens, my dear, if that's what you mean. It had to be crafted by human hands, or something very similar to human hands."

We squeeze between gigantic rock sections as we move toward the center of the structure. The green glow from the cavern fades into darkness. David and I pause to retrieve our flashlights, but Peter knows the way in the dark by heart. "Come along, children. Our past awaits our future."

We zigzag through a maze of fallen rock until we enter a large area barely two meters high. Massive, rectangular rocks dominate the area, each about fifteen meters on the smaller side, with a one-meter walkway between them. The rock ceiling above collapsed onto the gigantic rocks when the building fell, but the spaces between the rocks still enable us to navigate the area.

Doctor Noble stops and turns toward us. "These rocks were placed where they are on purpose. They are designed to withstand the collapse of the mountain from above, in case that ever happened. Obviously, it did— probably with the execution of Project Sanitize."

He continues guiding us forward until we reach a vertical wall made from a single stone. Peter motions toward the wall and says with considerable pride, "This is the center of the complex and the source of the shards."

We step closer. With our lights fixed on the wall, David mutters, "Holy shit."

I'm equally amazed. Embedded in the wall are hundreds of irregular shards, some large and some small, and all apparently constructed of the same material as the one Doctor Noble found. I glance at David's father. "It's amazing. Do you know anything about it?"

He shrugs. "I know there are three more walls just like it but with different embedded shards. The four stone walls form a square at the exact center of this building. I also know there are many entrances to this building, but no matter where you enter or which pathway you take once you do, you will end up here. Going back out is quite a different matter. You must be very careful which path you take."

I'm surprised. "Why would anyone go to all the trouble to build this structure and then make it difficult or dangerous to study it? Are there booby traps?"

"I haven't found any, but the maze is quite interesting. I believe it's something like an entrance fee—it requires you to be smart enough to get out, or you shouldn't be here in the first place."

David walks the length of the twenty-meter-long wall, scanning it with his flashlight. "The shape of the missing shard on this wall doesn't match either of the ones we brought with us. Have you found the source of the ones we have?"

"The larger shard is from the wall opposite this one, David, and the smaller one is from the wall to your left. Two others are missing as well, but all the rest are intact."

We begin walking the square perimeter of the gigantic stones. David stops to study the impressions from which our two shards came. After his preliminary survey, he joins his father, who pulls up a small rock to sit on. "I don't get it, Dad. This structure is at a higher elevation than the river, and the shards that remain are solidly embedded in the rock. The river probably doesn't come up this high, so how did your piece get where you found it? For that matter, how did the smaller piece get out of this mountain in the first place?"

In the dim glow of David's flashlight, the older man seems tired as he looks up. "Indeed how—or why? Perhaps we should have some dinner first. You must be famished."

David squats down to his father's level. "Are you okay, Dad? You don't look so good."

Peter nods. "I'll be fine, but you don't look so good either. At least I can see out of both eyes. I just don't have the spunk I once had." He stands with apparent difficulty and quips, "Come on. Let me take you both to my hotel."

We follow the tributary toward the main river channel and then walk along the main branch. It exits into the sunshine through a cave-like opening on the east side of the mountain. From its exit point, the river flows onto a narrow shelf before plummeting about 100 meters into a large lake below. Peter escorts us to the edge of the shelf where we look out over the lake at the base of the falls. "I call it Crater Lake, but you'd never want to swim in it. I think the water continues to flow east southeast until it merges with and poisons the Euphrates."

The view is incredible, with water-filled crater after water-filled crater stepping down before us, each receiving effluent from the one above. I look back to where the glowing water flows from the mountain, somewhat peeved we didn't know that cave was here before entering the maze complex from above. I don't know why we always do things the hard way the first time, but at least I understand why we didn't run into any of Doctor Noble's ropes on the way in. Doctor Noble notices I'm deep in thought and touches my arm to get my attention. "Come on, Beth. We don't have far to go."

I see him now for the first time in full sunlight. He doesn't look healthy. His skin is pale, and there are open sores on the back of his hands and neck. "What happened, Doctor Noble? What are the sores?"

"Please, Beth. Call me Peter. But to answer your question, it's the radiation. The degeneration takes time, but it gets to you after a while. It's the reason you and David must leave here as soon as possible. I won't survive this, and in that sense, the assumption of my death back home isn't far off. In fact, soon it will be the truth."

David joins us as I cover my mouth with my hand and blurt, "Oh no. Can't we do something?"

"Death isn't a sad thing, Beth, but a necessary thing—a process we're all going through. It's just a matter of when. And yes, you can do something, something very important. You can protect what I've found here. Take all my notes with you. Make David's mother proud."

His words carry a heavy shot of understanding. He loves his wife, yet he stayed here knowing he would die. He knew he'd never see her again but kept trying to resurrect a better world for those who are yet to be born. He's not a renegade at all. He's just like our forefathers, giving everything he has for the benefit of the community of humanity. I hug him, kiss him on the cheek, and whisper, "It's good to meet the real you, Peter."

David stares down at his empty hands, trying to cover the mist forming in his eyes. I reach over to take his hand. "Your dad is right. We need to take his notes far away from this place."

He looks off into the distance and mutters, "I know, but it seems wrong. He leaves us, he finds us to save us, and then he leaves us again."

Doctor Noble puts his hand on David's shoulder. "I'm sorry. I'm sorry I didn't come home. I know I let you and your mother down, but now, you know the reason." He flicks his head toward the maw of the cave. "That building in there is important. I don't know all its secrets, but I can feel it in my heart—it will change the world if we can just understand it. I just couldn't let it go."

David turns and then hugs his father. "We never thought ill of you. Mom and I knew the shard could not be explained, that it drove you. There were times she wished a mistress had taken you away. She said she could compete with a mistress, but she knew she couldn't compete with the shard. Part of her didn't want to. That's the reason she encouraged me to follow in your footsteps. That's the reason I'm here now."

Doctor Noble steps back and holds David by the shoulders at arm's length as he looks into David's eyes. "When you get home...tell your mother I never stopped loving her. Tell her for me."

This time tears form as David nods. "She knows, but I'll tell her again for you."

We follow Doctor Noble along the barren ridge for a few hundred meters until we reach the mouth of a shallow cave. It's like a funeral procession. No one utters a word. Stacked rocks and logs form a protective barrier across the entrance. Peter stops us before we go inside, ducks in alone, and soon reemerges with a plastic bag full of water. "You need to wash off your boots before coming in. Radiation makes the algae in that cave glow, and your boots looked pretty hot in the dark."

At the edge of the shelf overlooking the lakes below, we do what he asked, using a bristly native plant to scrub the edges and soles of our shoes. When they're cleaned sufficiently to prevent tracking high-dose radiation into his shelter, he ushers us through a small entrance covered with animal skin and says, "Welcome to my digs. What's mine is yours."

A bed of coals still smolders within the confines of a square pile of rocks used both for cooking and heating. Peter adds two small logs that soon burst into flames. Above the fire is the equivalent of a rock chimney that carries most of the smoke to the outside. "We'll have to fetch a little more wood before nightfall, but animals won't be a problem. They rarely come here because the water kills them. Feel free to help yourself to what I have. It's collected from rain, not the river."

My glance at the aluminum cooking pot filled with greenish liquid sitting near the fire is not missed by Doctor Noble. "It's leftover breakfast, Beth, and also dinner. Stew made from native Syrian legumes that grow plentifully now that they're not over-harvested. Mix in a few dandelion leaves and natural herbs, and you have a tasty, protein-rich meal."

It looks gross, but I'm starving. "Are they good cold?"

Doctor Noble gestures toward the pot. "Please, help yourself. To a hungry person, everything tastes good."

David and I pull out our mess kits and fill our aluminum dishes. Doctor Noble notices my eyes fall on a stack of flat rocks near the shelter's entrance. "I use them to block the cave's entrance at night. Feel free to use them. They make good chairs."

We stack several near the larger rock Doctor Noble uses for a table, sit down, and immediately begin stuffing ourselves. The stew is delicious—or I'm just hungry, I'm not quite sure—and we remain focused on Doctor Noble as he retrieves a small pile of journals and hands them to me. "Protect them, Beth. Without them, my life has little meaning, present company excluded."

I stop eating long enough to place his journals in the side pocket of my backpack as David asks, "Can you debrief us now...on everything you know?"

Peter serves a small portion of beans for himself, adds more to our mess kit plates, and then sits down to face us. "Yes, I can. First, the reason I believe the structure is a time capsule is simple. It's built like a vault and designed to withstand the ravages of time—even the collapse of the mountain above it. I've found no additional evidence of the culture that created it; therefore, I believe whoever tucked it away in such a secure location meant for it to be found by future generations, just as similar vaults were prepared by some Old World organizations. Project Sanitize probably revealed in seconds what the movement of the African and Eurasian Plates took millions of years to conceal."

We stop eating as our hunger takes a backseat to the impact of his words. "Second, I don't believe the shards we possess were originally embedded in the vault's rock wall. The embossing that would receive each piece has sharp edges in the original stone. The pieces we have were not chipped or pried out. Besides, all the other shard-like pieces are still held solid in the rock, as if they were placed there yesterday. Furthermore, there are only four missing pieces—one on each wall."

David's eyebrows dip, and he scratches his temple as he stares at his father. "If they didn't fall out of the wall, then what are they?"

Doctor Noble clasps his hands together. "I don't believe the missing pieces are an accident of time but a deliberate sign of design. I'm quite certain of that because each missing piece has a fixed, linear relationship to the others."

David's perplexed look deepens. "I don't get your meaning."

"If all the missing pieces were located on one wall instead of four, but in the identical relative locations they occupy on individual walls, then there would be one missing piece on each end, with the other two evenly spaced between them. I've measured the relationship many times. That the four missing shards would cause a single, composite side to be exactly trisected cannot be questioned."

Now, I'm perplexed. "If the shards were never embedded in the original walls, then where were they kept, and why would anyone separate them?"

"The *where* might be easier than the *why*, Beth, but both are challenging questions. I haven't located the source of the shards, but I believe it must be upstream from where I found the larger one. I've searched for years but haven't found any location that would allow two pieces to be washed downstream and the other two not to be, especially if I assume they are secured like the ones that still remain on the vault walls."

He stops to eat a spoonful of his dinner and nods to us. David and I take the hint and continue to eat, but not as feverishly as we had before. "As to *why*, I can only speculate. Perhaps the shards have religious significance, but it's hard to imagine that a culture advanced enough to produce them would attribute anything to a god."

While biting my index fingernail I ask, "If you had all four missing pieces, would it make any difference? Is there a message written on the walls that requires all four pieces be present for a complete decode?"

Peter shakes his head. "If there is a message, I haven't made any progress deciphering it. In fact, I'm pretty sure the symbols on the shards aren't a language at all. Over time, I've sketched every fragment embedded in the walls, all documented in my journals, but no two shards are the same. Even in languages with unique symbols for objects and concepts, there are occasional repeat symbols."

David finishes his beans and looks into the empty pot for more. "We need to go shopping when we finish this talk." He then looks back to his father. "We've considered that too. In fact, we've speculated the shards might be layered circuit boards—perhaps very complex circuitry."

The older man smiles, "Oh, I see. Great minds think alike. I've been too timid to write that down. It seemed so...far-fetched."

An improbable idea strikes me, and I stop chewing to blurt it out. "If they're complex circuits, they could be electronic keys."

David and Peter glance at each other and then look back at me. I feel like a schoolgirl about to be chided for lack of self-control. "Sorry, sorry. It was just a thought."

David's good eye sparkles. "Sorry? Hell, they could be exactly that. What would happen if we put the shards in their indents in the wall? Would it hurt to try?"

Peter remains stoic. "That would probably be a waste of time. Even if we put the two we have in the wall, we're still missing the other two. If they're some type of electronic combination, we'd only have half of it."

He's right. We'd need the other pieces to try anything like that. David strokes his chin and then suggests, "There are three of us now. We could cover a lot of ground down there working together. We could scour the cavern upstream from where you found your shard, especially the area around the lower lake."

Peter's brow furrows, and his eyebrows dip. "I know everything about those caverns, but I've never seen any lakes. Where are they? How did you get to them?"

David verbally retraces our route, going backward from the pit we fell into to the vertical wall that's part of the main cavern, past the lower lake and on to the upper lake. His father listens with rapt attention but interrupts before David's story reaches the massive crater above. "The narrow slit in the rock jutting away from the main river flow, the one that took you to the upper lake? That's new. I've been up that river channel a hundred times, but I've never seen such an opening. The small tremor last week must've created a new pathway."

I'll be damned. The rock that tried to entomb us isn't the only one that has shifted lately.

We spend the rest of the evening accomplishing the mundane tasks of survival: gathering wood and food, and rebuilding our backpacks. David would like to go back into the cave now, but Peter discourages it. "You two should never go in that cave again. You've probably already received a harmful dose of radiation. You could end up like me if you spend a lot of time in there."

David shakes his head. "Sorry, Dad, but we are part of this now. There is no guarantee any of us will ever get back to civilization, and we didn't come all this way just to be presented with more questions than answers." He looks over at me. I nod. He winks and then continues. "Beth and I knew the risks when we came here. Nothing has changed."

Peter glares at his son. "You're a lot like me when I was younger, so arguing with you probably won't do any good. Besides, I'm exhausted."

I pat him on the arm. "Why don't you get some rest while David and I hike back to our base camp to get the rest of our supplies?"

Peter nods. "There's a trail around the south side of the mountain that will take you to the upper craters. The trail is a lot easier than going back through the caves."

While Peter sleeps, David and I make the long hike to our base camp, collect our food and remaining equipment, and return to Peter's shelter. By the time we return, we're exhausted too.

* * * *

We wake the following morning to the smell of simmering beans, having set the cooking pot near the fire before we went to sleep. Tender chunks of roast deer retrieved from the fire pit at our base camp float amongst the greens. I look forward to stew loaded with real meat—a treat to be savored.

For the first time in weeks, breakfast isn't hurried. We relax as David and his father catch up on many lost years. Peter is especially interested to hear about the political landscape in Salvation, but neither David nor I can enlighten him in detail. He just huffs. "Those old farts couldn't cover their asses fast enough whenever I was around. When I taught in Salvation, they didn't like my theories on the Old World, especially the link between hatred and terrorism. There wasn't room for preaching normal human behavior in their computer-controlled world. I think that's the reason they were so happy when I left the country the first time."

David's head jerks back. "Ah, Mom said she was one of your students, and that you got in trouble for getting her pregnant with me instead of having children with your assigned mate. She said that's the reason she was banned to Hope to join you."

Peter waves his hand in front of his face, as if swatting at a fly. "My assigned mate was so ugly the doctor slapped her mother when she was born. You would have been ugly too." He glances over at me while he continues to talk to David. "You might have been smarter if I'd done what they ordered, but Beth would probably have run from you screaming."

David chuckles. "So, you left the first time to save me from a life of ugly? Mom said you left without the state's consent just to spite them—to show them you could not be ordered around. Politicians don't like it when people act on their own. Then, when you returned with the shard and enough conflicting information to whet their appetite, they were kind of stuck with you. When they sent you back to Hope, she said they expected you to dig into that artifact until you could explain it. You didn't do that. You left again. You left them hungry."

"Don't be so naïve. I helped set up Hope long before I headed overseas the first time, and those bastards knew I could be of use again. They also knew I could never understand something that shouldn't exist. No one can explain the unexplainable. They couldn't order me back to the Kill Zone because the area is so damn dangerous. Nevertheless, they knew I'd run off again. *That's* the real reason they sent me back to Hope. Never underestimate a politician. They have their own reasons for everything."

David raises his eyebrows as he leans back on his rock. "So, you believe they knew you'd return here, even though it wasn't good for you?"

Peter's hands jut out to the sides. "Of course they did. That way, they could put an end to speculation that would never go anywhere except into endless conspiracy theories…and get rid of me at the same time. No Peter Nobel, no teaching about hatred. They never liked the fact that I questioned everything—even their authority."

I lean forward with a grin. "Don't be too hard on them. After all, they did continue to fund David's research. They also selected a really good mate for him."

Peter's eyes sparkle as he pats me on the arm. "That they did, Beth. That they did." He turns his attention back to David. "And how is your mother? I still miss her. I never missed civilization as we know it, but I always missed you and your mother."

David looks down at his feet. "Mom returned to Salvation after you were declared dead. She knew I was following your research, and she decided she had paid her dues. She moved back to Salvation to join up with her originally assigned mate. She's still there with my half-brother and half-sister. She told me once that she still loved you but didn't want to spend the rest of her life alone."

The news doesn't overtly impact Peter, but I sense sadness in his eyes. He just looks down and nods. "She was always the pretty one, and Hope didn't set well with her. A life of adventure isn't for everyone, and neither is living alone. You should never blame her for anything that happened in the past. It was all my doing."

David leans forward. "Mom and I accepted life as it is long ago. Neither of us have recriminations or regrets, but you might. If you're right about the radiation—that it's killing you—do you want me to give her a final message from you?"

Peter strokes his chin as he looks into the far corner of the shelter. "You can tell her I never stopped loving her. You can also tell her I am very proud of our son." When he looks back, his eyes are misting. He quickly clears his throat. "Mankind's greatest unsolved mystery waits. Curious minds want to know. Is anyone here besides me anxious to explore the caverns?"

As for me, I'd like to forget the whole thing and get as far away from that God-forsaken hole as possible...but I can't. Like David and Peter, I *need* to know everything that can be discovered in the caves. I follow the men inside the cavern, trudge along the river upstream to the point where Peter found his shard, and then hike beyond to the recent separation in the rock—the trailhead for the path to the lakes.

To my surprise, the hike in isn't as scary this time—partly because we've brought additional food and water, and partly because Peter is with us. No one knows more about these caves than he does. If we get in trouble, we'll have an expert to help us get out.

The upper glowing lake is as beautiful and dangerous as it was the last time we were here. The Geiger counter still registers a high level of radiation—enough to kill a human with prolonged exposure. I hate this. Every second we spend in these caves will shorten the time I have with David...and vice versa.

Peter sweeps the shoreline using our field glasses, looking for anything that might be man-made. "Nothing looks out of place, and the cavern walls are very close to the shore. I agree with you, David. We should look at the lower lake. If the shards came from somewhere up here, they would collect downstream anyway. Let's follow the opposite side of the tributary this time, so we won't have to cross it later."

I am relieved. The Geiger counter readings decrease the moment we begin our descent, following the tributary to the larger lake below. When we reach the shoreline, Peter again scans the cavern walls. "I can't believe this was here all this time, and I didn't have a clue. If lakes can be hidden right in front of me, I wonder if there's more to this civilization than what I've found so far."

He audibly gasps as he abruptly stops scanning. After fidgeting with the fine focus on the binoculars while staring at the far side of the lake, he mutters, "Interesting." He points across the lake as he hands the glasses to David. "What do you think? Is it worth a closer look?"

The little girl inside me is jumping up and down. *Let me see. Let me see.* Still, I manage to wait patiently for my turn with the glasses. Time drags until David hands them to me, and I stare into the distance a moment before I gasp too. "My God. That could be it."

We begin walking as one, picking up our pace as we move forward. We soon arrive at four massive square stones, each set at one corner of an even larger square. Each stone is easily thirty meters on a side, and the space between them is about one meter—just enough to walk between any two adjacent rocks. We move forward until we see that each large rock is notched near the center where all four rocks come together, forming something that would look like a huge, square donut divided into quarters if it could be viewed from above. A fifth large rock sits at the very center of the square donut hole.

We approach the fifth rock in awe. Like the vault in the collapsed building below, this structure has been built to withstand enormous vertical pressure. The outer rocks are designed and situated to protect the center rock, with enough strength to hold up the mountain if it collapsed straight down. The center rock is different than anything we've seen so far. It captures our immediate attention.

The center rock is jet black, carved like a squat obelisk—a truncated tetrahedron. It has a surface sheen unlike any of the others. We approach in awe and touch its shiny, smooth surface with the same reverence ancient man might have exhibited if he had touched a grand piano. To our surprise, the surface doesn't feel like rock at all. It's more like some type of plastic, or maybe carbon fiber. Even more surprising, we sense warmth coming from it and a periodic, low frequency vibration that passes through the surface.

Peter shakes his head. "I don't know what to say. I've never seen anything like this."

The Geiger counter is going crazy with clicking noise, so I glance down at the meter. My mouth drops as I begin to back away. "We'd better get away from this thing fast. It's extremely dangerous."

David also backs away, following my lead, but Peter walks around the obelisk with reckless abandon. "What the hell. I'm a dead man walking anyway."

David and I continue backing away. The Geiger counter readings drop when we position ourselves behind one of the huge external stones, and David shouts to his father, "Get away from that thing. It will kill you for sure."

He glances at the Geiger counter meter again; the reading is low where we are. He pats the massive corner of the huge rock we've retreated behind. "In addition to protecting the thing inside, these rocks must be radiation shields."

Peter soon emerges, grinning from ear to ear. He holds up both hands touchdown-style with a shard in each one. "They were embedded on the opposite face of the obelisk from where we entered. The obelisk has four cut-outs in a vertical column, with the smallest on top and the largest at the bottom. I haven't the slightest idea what they are, but at least we have all four now."

We don't have time to relish his findings. We've got to get out of these caverns as quickly as we can. With every passing hour, we receive as much radiation as might be expected outside in a lifetime. We don't stop on the way out, but Peter must. He falls behind while urging us on, stopping twice to rest and puke. I'm sure I see blood, and lots of it. That last dose of radiation was severe and must have hurt him a great deal. Like a man who has been standing on the edge of a cliff for some time and has now been shoved off, he seems to be spiraling down in a hurry. I fear for him but know he's right. We can't wait for him. We need to get out now.

Gasping for breath, we wait for Peter outside the entrance to the cave. It's hard to believe something so beautiful can also be so toxic. About twenty minutes later, he stumbles out. He looks horrible. Despite his claim that he just needs rest, we know better. His face is no longer pale but ashen, and his body shudders with dry heaves between bouts of coughing up blood.

Back at his home base, he makes notes in his final journal and hands it to me. "I don't know how much time I have left. Make sure you and David—and these notes—get back to civilization."

I take the journal but don't like it. There's something final in that gesture. He wouldn't give it up unless he was sure he wouldn't need it again. I set the journal aside and give him a prolonged hug. There is finality in that as well. I can't hold back my tears. "I'll miss you. I wish I had more time to get to know you. I wish you could meet your grandchildren."

He lies back on his bed and takes my hand. David scoots up next to the bed alongside me. He gives my hand a gentle squeeze as he looks me in the eyes. "Time and children are the most precious commodities on Earth. I hope you have lots of both." He glances over to David and then back to me. "Make him leave here. Even though we have all four shards now, make him go. Promise…me—"

I am relieved he falls off to sleep before he can finish his request. I would hate to promise something I might not be able to fulfill.

David and I eat a little more stew before preparing the shelter for the night. Peter wakes now and then, but he can't hold anything down. We sit by his side while he slips into a coma-like sleep. Tears roll down David's cheeks. We both know Peter will never wake again. When he takes his last breath, we hold each other and cry for the passing of a great man.

Chapter Eighteen
The Key

The next morning, we carry Doctor Noble's body to the edge of the river. The obelisk might have dealt the final blow, but prolonged exposure to this radioactive river was mostly responsible for his death. We surrender his body to it now, silently holding hands as the gentle flow moves his body downstream and over the edge to the lake below. There is no soil for burial here, and wood is far too precious to use for burning a body, so we return Peter to nature the best way we can. There is little else we can do. I'm sure he would be pleased.

I open Peter's journal to his last entry and read it aloud. "Of all the discoveries I have made during my life, the rediscovery of my son and meeting Beth are by far the most significant." Standing together on the rock outcropping above the stepped lakes below, we hold each other and weep openly. Despite my sorrow over Peter's passing, I am blessed to have known him, even if only for a short time.

My tears come and go for the remainder of the day. David and I cry together at times. At other times he just holds me. Our grief comes in waves. I'm depressed and saddened that Peter is gone but relieved his misery is over. By early evening, I'm ready to talk with David about his father. "He wanted us to get out of here, knowing his fate will be ours if we stay too long. You know that's true, sweetie. We need to consider abandoning this craziness."

David kneels by my side. "I know, and we will. All I ask is one chance to put the shards into the vault stones. We have all of them now. It wouldn't take long to try it."

"And what do you expect? Magic? Whatever that thing is, it has been there since before the Old World knew how to measure time, before the Old World existed at all. It wouldn't hurt to leave it there a little longer, or maybe indefinitely."

He strokes my face with his hand, probably to soften me up. "True, but then we'd never know what the shards might do, would we?"

I have to admit I am curious. David knows it. I also know Peter didn't die from the obelisk exposure alone. He worked in the cavern long before we arrived and accumulated doses of radiation over all that time. On the other hand, he had never been to either of the radioactive lakes, and we've been there twice—not to mention the black obelisk hot spot. I've no idea how much damage we've already done to our bodies. "Your father wanted us to leave here. He knew this place was killing him. He also knew it would kill us if we stayed longer."

David wipes his hand across the back of his head and then down across the back of his neck before looking up at me. "My father also gave his life in an attempt to find out what the shards mean. We could be on the verge of finding out. If we go in one more time, we could make his sacrifice count for something."

I am not comfortable with this. I cross my arms over my chest and glare at David. "Look, if we go back, at least promise me it will be the last time. We can put the shards in their place, but if nothing happens, we have to leave and never come back. Agreed?"

David nods, "Of course. I understand. I promise."

We take our revolvers, flashlights, the shards, my journal, the Geiger counter, and a small amount of food and water—just enough for the trip in and back out again. We have no idea what to expect, but we know we can't linger there. The caverns will kill us just as they killed Peter.

I don't need to document the contents or appearance of the cave and vault. Peter's journals already do that. Besides, this incursion is about speed, not documentation. We approach the vault as fast as we can and squat down at the first embossed shard location. David pushes the matching shard into its receptacle with his thumb, and we move to the next location, doing the same. When all four have been inserted, we stand back, waiting to see what will happen.

Nothing does.

I glance over at my disappointed mate. "I guess that's it. Pry out the shards. At least we can take them with us."

We make one more pass around the vault to remove the shards and begin our trek out. David is quiet. His face is set in a hard, discouraged frown as he looks at the shards in his hand. Even though I'm eager to leave this place, I hate to see him like this. I wish I could say something to lift his spirits, anything to get the sullen look off his face. Suddenly, our earlier conversation with Peter plays in my mind. "Your father mentioned a combination. Do you think it might matter what order the shards are inserted?"

David stops dead in his tracks. "Maybe, and I can think of a couple of possibilities that would make sense. We could try entering them from left to right, as they would appear if lined up on a single stone, or from right to left."

"Peter also said they were ordered on the obelisk with the smallest on top and the largest on the bottom. That could signify a combination too."

Returning to the vault, we immediately notice the smallest shard would be on the right side of a linear depiction of the shard impressions and the largest would be on the left. We insert the largest first. The next to the largest is on the opposite side of the vault. We insert it, and move to the third largest, and then to the smallest. Breathing in short gasps, we stand back.

Nothing happens.

David throws up his hands. "Only one thing to do. Try the smallest first."

We repeat the process in reverse order and immediately hear a deep rumble, like a small earthquake. We briefly glance at each other. I shrug and timidly suggest, "Do we run now?"

We hold our ground, trying to determine if the rumble is getting worse, but it stops in less than a minute. Nothing has changed. I raise my palms and lift my shoulders. "It could have been a coincidence."

David shakes his head. "I don't buy it. Let's see if anything changed on any other side."

As we turn the first corner, we know something dramatic has happened because bright light now streams from the vault's far wall. We hurry along the darkened, adjacent side toward the light and are stunned silent when we round the final corner. The solid stone that covered this side of the vault five minutes ago has lowered into the floor, revealing a brilliantly lit interior.

When we step across the threshold into the vault, the Geiger counter falls quiet, and its indicator needle drops to zero. Except for David's heavy breathing, everything is quiet as death. Even the roar of the nearby river is so muted we can no longer tell it's there.

"I don't know, David. If this vault is a time capsule, as Peter speculated, they sure didn't put much in it."

There are only three containers inside. Two are long and horizontal. They look a lot like coffins. One is smaller and vertical—a podium-like structure located near the head of the room and centered between the two coffin-like containers that flank it. I can't tell where the light is coming from. It seems to come from every direction at once, as if every surface in the room is emitting light.

David is caught up in silent awe. I find that disturbing because it likely means he will want to stay longer. We have made a huge discovery. I need to talk about it. "David? Are you there?"

His eyes are more wide open than usual, perhaps a little glazed over as well, and his mouth is still open, like he's star struck. "Don't you see, Beth? Lighting requires power. Where does it come from? After millions of years, how is this possible?"

"Maybe the obelisk is a fusion generator? Such things are fictional, but if they were real, wouldn't they last forever? Wouldn't that have been a global surprise, if the Project Sanitize bombs had breached such a thing?" I throw my hands in the air and shout, "*Whump.* Goodbye, world."

He ignores my attempt at humor and moves to the closest of the larger boxes. "There could be people inside, and if there's power here, maybe they aren't dead. Maybe they are suspended. We know nothing of this technology. Anything is possible."

"If that's even a remote possibility, then we dare not open them. Without our manmade genetic modifications, the BHS would kill them in eighteen hours."

David runs his hand over the surface of the first coffin-like box, feeling the texture of the raised symbols that cover its surface. "True, but I'd give my right testicle to know what's really in here."

I point to the Geiger counter, mumbling aloud as I step up to feel the coffin-like boxes as well. "Maybe you already have."

He grins. "Thanks. I needed that. The symbols look a lot like Old Persian but with enough difference to be their own language. Given enough time, I'll bet we could decipher it. Is there any indication of radiation in here?"

Of course, he already knows the answer. The Geiger counter is silent. He just wants me to acknowledge it. "Thinking of moving in?"

He gently takes both my shoulders and looks me in the eyes. "Do we really have a choice? Besides, my appointment calendar is wide open. How's yours?"

I look around the room. The walls and floor are smooth and shiny—like polished, white plastic. The place is immaculate. "Well, this room is certainly cleaner than anywhere else I've stayed for the past few months. As long as the radiation in here stays at zero, I suppose it's no worse than anywhere else."

"That's odd, isn't it?" He takes the Geiger counter wand and runs it around our feet, but there's no reading at all. "I don't understand this. We just came in from the cavern, an area with significant radiation, but the machine isn't picking up anything. How's that possible?"

The alarm on my face must be obvious. "Do you think there's something here that interferes with the Geiger counter? Is it possible we're being radiated even though it says we're not?"

He continues to move the wand around our legs and torsos. "I don't know, but you'd think there would be some indication, unless something in this room neutralizes radiation. Do we have any dosimeters?"

I nod affirmatively. "We have a couple of the self-indicating type, still in the original lead foil. I didn't see the point of using them earlier because I knew we were being exposed to huge doses then. In fact, I really didn't want to know how bad it was."

"Let's bring them with us tomorrow. They aren't dependent on anything electrical. If they show this room to be clean, then it is clean, and we both can believe it."

Frankly, even though I didn't want to know before, I'll feel better when I know for sure. For now, we move to the podium-like enclosure and marvel at the raised symbols over its surface. As are the coffin-like boxes flanking it, the dais is completely covered with symbols, except for a small twenty- by thirty-centimeter window near its top that faces away from the horizontal boxes. We shine our flashlights through the window and see an iridescent, transparent, rectangular object about the same size as the window but oriented in the vertical.

I'm fascinated with the way the lights reflect off its surface, like oil on water. "It has a beautiful patina. I wonder what it is."

A broad smile covers David's face. "It could be the mother lode. If my dad was right about this vault, I'd bet it's something like an Old World Kindle book reader."

Before we leave for the day, I make copious notes in my journal to document the appearance of the vault's interior and our first impressions of what the artifacts might be. Of course, everything is just speculation, but we believe the obelisk we saw yesterday might be a power generator and that Peter was right about the vault being some type of time capsule.

The more I write, the more convinced I am that the horizontal boxes could contain a man and a woman, perhaps suspended, and that the podium-like box is a library of all that was known at the time the vault was sealed. That would be a perfect way to pass knowledge to future generations or to preserve one's own civilization.

During the hike back to our base camp, we discuss many theories as to why the vault was built and what might have happened to the people who built it. David is troubled that the horizontal boxes might contain suspended people because if they do, then the vault might not have been intended as a gift to people of the future but rather an attempt to preserve a race gone extinct. If the latter is true, then waking the people in the boxes could be a disaster—like waking a T-Rex in the middle of Old World New York.

For starters, they might not like sharing the world with us, and they are far more advanced than we are. We also don't know why they chose such a remote location for the vault. Did they hide the vault as a last ditch effort to prevent extinction? Did they destroy themselves like the people of the Old World did? And if they did, would they kill us if we didn't subscribe exactly to some extreme ideology, whatever it might be? Beyond such sociological unknowns, we believe they couldn't possibly tolerate BHS. Waking them would be a death sentence, even if they liked us.

Speculation aside, our task ahead is clear. We'll move into the vault if radiation isn't a problem and then work to understand the language written on the boxes. If David is correct, the key to the language is located somewhere in the symbols. The remaining symbols are probably instructions, perhaps revealing how to use the library—if that's what it is—or maybe details on what to do with the horizontal boxes.

As we approach our base camp, a fleeting thought of Mrs. Hathaway back in Salvation enters my mind, and I can't help but giggle. She would never have guessed that the girl who filled her car with toilet paper would be the woman who helped make the greatest discovery in the history of mankind. I'm delighted her low expectations for me will be greatly exceeded.

Even in Peter's primitive shelter, after his father's death, David is upbeat and playful. I suspect he has had years to mourn his father's passing, having thought him dead until a few days ago. Instead of mourning, we celebrate the accomplishments of Peter's life. With what we found today, the mystery of the shard has been magnified a thousand fold, and we speculate with rampant enthusiasm about what the days ahead could hold. A new beginning for mankind? A new power source more powerful than anything ever conceived? Our imaginations run wild.

We are too excited to sleep. David playfully tickles me as we lie down on our bed of dried moss near the crackling fire in the cooking pit. He kisses my bare skin from my navel to my chin, rubbing his body over mine as he moves slowly up my torso. The feel of his skin on mine sends exquisite chills through my soul. I pull his face from my chin to my lips, and he slips inside me as he moves up to place his mouth on mine. An explosion of pleasure follows as I discover that heightened excitement also ratchets up sexual enjoyment—a natural high atop a natural high.

Chapter Nineteen
Revelation

Despite little sleep, we rise refreshed early in the morning, anxious for what lies ahead. I can't help but believe a library of knowledge exists within the vault. It's far more fun to speculate about such a thing than not, and my mind fills with possibilities. What mysteries will the library reveal? Will it shed light on our own civilization's chances of survival?

After a hearty breakfast of stew and jerky, we load our packs with all the food and water we can carry, plus Peter's journals and the dosimeters, and set out for the cavern. We are optimistic about remaining in the vault until we learn the new language but aren't sure if we can pull it off. A great deal depends on how often we need to leave the vault's protective interior. Gathering food, collecting water, and taking bathroom breaks will require us to leave the vault now and then. During those times, we'll be forced to enter the radioactive cavern. We'll need to monitor the dosage each of us receives over time to limit damage to our tissues.

We put our supplies in one corner of the vault and immediately tear open one of the dosimeter packages. They are fast-acting strips, and in five to ten minutes, we'll know the truth. If they remain white, we'll be okay. If they turn dark blue, we'll need to leave.

Time passes slowly. I reassure myself by turning on the Geiger counter. The battery still shows some charge, but the machine remains silent. In fifteen minutes, the dosimeter strip is still stark white. Both the dosimeter and the Geiger counter indicate it's safe to be here, but neither of us understands why that should be the case.

I arrange our food and water supply in one corner while David carries in several rocks and stacks them to create rough chairs and a table. In short order, we're ready to go to work. David first measures the radiation emitted by the rocks he brought inside from the cavern. To our surprise, no radiation registers. This place is a puzzle within a puzzle. We don't understand any of it.

We begin by making a detailed survey of the symbols on all three boxes, looking for anything that might be distinct from everything else. Something here is probably a key— the Rosetta Stone for this new language. Whoever built this vault expected it would be found at some future time, and whoever that was would have wanted its finder to know how to read all the messages they left behind. My task is to sketch every surface symbol, noting the location and appearance of each character. At times like these, I wish I had my computer and a digital camera.

Despite its time-consuming nature, my mundane task leads to our first breakthrough the following day. With great excitement, I document identical symbols in similar locations on each of the larger boxes and realize they must be numbers. If the symbols represent instructions, then they are probably numbered because equivalent characters on each box precede each group of symbols. The numbers are also set off by a special symbol from the characters that follow, giving us our first clue to punctuation. I am both ecstatic and quite pleased with myself.

The learning process is slow for the first two days, but on day three, David calls me to the podium. "You've got to see this, honey. There are two identical characters near the top on either side of this thing. They are set apart from the other symbols as well as raised and moveable. Shall we?"

My anticipation spikes. "If you think they might open something, then go for it."

Standing at the podium like he's about to give a speech, he pushes the two characters inward. An image of an apple flashes on the wall directly in front of us. We're speechless as we stare at it.

Our confusion mounts as sound floods the room, "Uondo…ooo-on-doe."

Moments pass, but nothing further happens until I utter, "Apple?" A new image flashes on the screen, this time of a beautiful lake. We wait and soon hear, "Azona…aye-zone-a."

We stare at each other. The wall waits until I respond, "Lake?"

Image after image appears on the wall, with the machine pronouncing a word, and me responding, until the apple appears again. We glance at each other. A sly smile crosses my lips, and I respond before the machine does, "Uondo." The lake picture immediately reappears. We don't remember what it was called when we saw the lake the first time, so we wait until the machine responds with, "Azona…aye-zone-a."

Hot damn! We're back in basic training, learning to read. We could not be more delighted—they have left a primer. The sequence of images continues until we are able to parrot back each of the names provided. After that, the first image reappears, this time with a blank line above the image and a long line of symbols below it.

We study the display on the wall, trying to figure out what to do, until one character at a time lights up on the long string of symbols, and as each symbol illuminates, it also appears on the blank line above the image. When the word above is complete, the machine illuminates each character and sounds it out. Then it pronounces the entire word. I see, now. The long string of symbols must be the alphabet. The machine is teaching us to speak its language and to read it so we can understand the instructions on the boxes. We are blown away.

When the image of the lake appears, I walk to the wall and touch each of the characters that make up the word for lake. This is amazing. In just a few days, we'll know the sounds of their letters and how to put them together into meaningful words.

With each sequence of images, the game gets harder. After we have mimicked the spelling of the simple images many times, the images appear yet again. This time, the machine says, "Lake."

It waits. I'm stunned. Whatever the machine is, it is learning our language as well as teaching its own.

On the fifth day, I become concerned. We've been wearing our dosimeters since we moved into the vault, and mine is turning light blue. David thinks it's because I pee too much, but I think it's our situation in general. Anytime we leave the vault, we are exposed. That same day, we discover the roast deer we brought with us when we moved in isn't decaying as we expect. It should smell like rotten meat by now, but it still seems as fresh as the day we brought it in. We don't understand.

David doesn't have much to go on, but in an unthinkable act of faith, he pees inside the vault near the open door. I glare at the man I love as his urine splatters on the floor. "What the hell are you doing? Seriously, now we're going to smell your piss all day." Before I finish berating him, I watch in amazement as the floor absorbs the liquid, leaving no mark, residue, or smell.

I stare in shock as David zips his pants up with a triumphant look. "In this hotel, you really can take advantage of the chambermaid. Next time you take a dump, do it inside. The vault seems to neutralize both harmful radiation and bacteria. It also seems to clean itself, and we should let it. Anything we can do to cut down on our exposure to the cavern, we should."

How glamorous. Now, I can poop on the floor while David sits at the other end of the room watching me. It's both disgusting and amazing at the same time.

We also find we can drink water from the river if it's allowed to sit overnight on the vault's floor. Just as the rocks we use for chairs were cleansed of radiation, so too is the river water. Once we understand how the vault works, we minimize our hunting and water retrieval trips by bringing in as much as we can whenever we leave the room. It's better than staying outside and gives us protection from the bleak situation that left David's father dead. We are optimistic; we have hope.

* * * *

After six months, my dosimeter has turned deep-blue. We don't have severe radiation poisoning like Doctor Noble did, and we haven't returned to the obelisk, but minimizing exposure isn't the same as no exposure at all. Part of me wonders if we could've saved Peter's life if we had learned about this enclosure sooner. I believe David has pondered the same thing, but I won't bring it up. He doesn't need a reminder of his father's passing, and there's no guarantee this room will spare our lives. After all, my dosimeter is dark blue.

As we've accumulated radiation exposure, we've also become quite familiar with the language. We have decoded the writing on all the boxes, thanks to the considerable help given to us from the teaching machine. It was learning our language while we learned its language, and over time, it began to offer suggestions in broken English concerning the meaning of the instructions.

I snicker when I think back at the machine's first crude attempts at communication. While we were in the process of discovering the coffin-like boxes must contain some type of liquid, the machine offered: "While solution is not toxic, it will not make child edible." It also stated, quite emphatically, "The bubble liquid has not poison, but do not for eat," and, "Smell from this fresh product when open will go after explosion in air." "Be aware of invisibility," and, "Flash the box after open it," were also gems I had to record in my journal. David would often respond back in kind with smartass comments like, "Do not hold the wrong end of the chainsaw," and, "In case of monkeys are in the forest, you cannot find them." We took only one of the terse vocal translations as an ominous sign, "Only a few of the dead were buried carelessly in a discarded storage pit. They were probably dead not normally." I recorded that comment verbatim in my journal. We are still trying to figure out what it means.

David was right about most of the text being instructions, and we are finally able to follow them to open the podium-like box. When the exterior clear panel slides down, I reach inside to retrieve the iridescent vertical piece we now know is the entry point to all knowledge the people who built this vault amassed over time.

My shaky touch brings the device to life, and it displays an organized index. We select a reading called "Extinction of the Endohl," a name appearing on every box in the room—the name we believe they called themselves.

We understand the language in general but are too inexperienced to be fast readers. Still, by late afternoon, we have a fair concept of what happened to them. The Endohl were much like those in the Old World—warlike and opinionated, a bad combination. As near as we can tell, the only major difference between the Endohl and our predecessors was their advanced technology. In the end, one group created a weapon that destroyed everyone, but much more slowly than BHS killed the Old World.

In their case, it appears the Armageddon weapon of choice was influenza, released into an unsuspecting population without any natural immunity. Pointing to the information on the screen while struggling with the translation, I mutter, "Crap, I guess we have them to thank for the common cold."

David just grins. "Or for our immunity to it. Until BHS, influenza killed more people in the Old World than any other disease—hundreds of millions."

His grin quickly morphs into an expression of dismay, and he sighs as he continues reading. When he shakes his head, he summarizes with, "Ashes to ashes, dust to dust. They only built one vault, the one we're in now, but they suspected influenza's creators built another in an unknown location. When they sealed themselves inside this vault, they thought only a few of their people would survive in the outside world. In a very real sense, the people of the Old World owed their existence to the extinction of the Endohl. Their influenza extinction was an evolutionary horizon, a point in history where one species dies off and another arises. Their near extinction begot the people of the Old World—people with influenza tolerance. We are an evolutionary horizon too—the aftermath horizon, the people with BHS immunity who are now expanding into the New World."

I believe his interpretation is correct. "That would also explain a lot of Old World biblical history—the reason Adam and Eve's children found mates. Not everyone died. Some of the Endohl were naturally more resistant than others. It could also explain the long lifetimes attributed to some of the original survivors in the Biblical book of Genesis. The original survivors probably had access to Endohl serums to extend life but not the knowledge to create it. When the supplies were exhausted, the life spans reverted to those we now experience. It's even possible that long ago, at the very beginning of what became the Old World civilization, fanciful tales about the fountain of youth might have been true."

David studies the reader's index once again and then selects a new category: "Dispersion of the Endohl." In a moment, he mumbles, "You could be right, sweetie, about the Old World Biblical stories. The Endohl might have attempted to save themselves in more ways than this tomb."

When he turns the reader toward me, goose bumps rise over my arms. The image of a large, saucer-shaped ship being loaded with animals is clear enough, even without studying the words. "So, when the plague swept the earth, some of them left with a living cargo. If they had the technology to escape into space, does that mean Noah's ark was real?"

David reads down several pages before glancing up. "Maybe so, and that could mean we might see them again someday. If they left, they would have the capability to come back in the future. Based on the coffins here, they might have had the technology to suspend living tissue for a very long time."

I shake my head from side to side as I glance at the nearest coffin. "If they ever come back, BHS would certainly be a big disappointment for them. Kind of ironic, isn't it? The same ability of mind that allowed mankind to eradicate itself twice before us is what enabled humans to evolve into our civilization. Unlike our predecessors, however, we don't exist because of a fluke of natural selection, but by the intentional design of man. We are the first people genetically engineered to survive in a world toxic to all humans who came before us. How many times, David? How many times do you think that has happened?"

He shrugs. "Hard to say. Not much carries forward. After enough time, everything reverts to dust. We can't rule out that the periodic extinction of humankind might be just another evolutionary strategy, repeating the process over and over until nature gets it right."

I gesture toward the horizontal box in front of me. "So, if we wake them, they'd be throwbacks from two horizons back—completely unable to survive in the outside world?"

"That's probably true. They'd be prisoners in this vault until they died. This room might keep influenza and BHS at bay, but they could never leave its protection. Would you want to wake up to such a fate, a life sentence in a room without windows?"

I'm not sure David's conclusion is the right one. In fact, I might choose life, no matter how limited, over eternal sleep. Our ancestors in Cheyenne Mountain faced a similar choice, and they chose to live entombed. These people could simply be the eternal equivalent of our ancestors. At a minimum, if people from our horizon were ever to wake these two, they would have to struggle through the same genetic engineering process we did. The two in the coffins could never leave this vault, but under the right circumstances, their children or grandchildren might.

One thing's for sure. I can't imagine waking them until our civilization knows everything they knew, and I answer David's question with a question of my own, "Maybe we can't wake them, at least not now, but can we take their reader with us?"

He continues reading and responds without looking up, "We could try, but I don't know how far we can take it outside the vault before it quits working, if at all. We also don't know how to charge it, assuming it needs charging."

A revelation in my mind answers my own question as tears well in my eyes. "Sorry, David. I guess my question was silly. There's more to it than that. We really can't take it, even if it works outside the vault. We don't know if we'll ever encounter another living person, someone to pass it to. What good would it do to take it if we were just to lose it forever, along with our lives?"

David nods agreement and then ambles over to hold me. He whispers as he strokes my hair, "Of course you're right. It would be a travesty to take it under the circumstances. The best we can do, if it will work outside this vault, is read what we can at my dad's camp, make notes, and return it before we try to head back to our camp on the coast. At least the reader would be safe in this vault if we die along the way. Maybe we can leave clues about what we've found here as we make our way out, in case we never get back home."

I look at his dosimeter. It's as deep blue as mine. "Whatever we do, we can't be coming back and forth through the cavern. When we leave here today, I'm not coming back. We may already be damaged beyond repair. I don't want any more exposure than I already have."

I take the reader to the open side of the vault and step across the threshold into the cavern. We should've guessed—it immediately goes dark. The device isn't charged at all but derives its energy from the same mysterious field that kills bacteria and absorbs radiation inside the vault. "It doesn't work outside. I guess that limits our options."

As I step back inside, David takes the reader and then embraces me again. "We have one more day of food and water, sweetie. If you have any burning questions you want answered, now is the time to ask them. The day after tomorrow, we will leave here and try to make our way back home."

The word "home" fills me with hope. I smile at him and exhale a long, slow breath. I am relieved he agrees. We need to go, or we'll die here. "How will we lock the door on the way out?"

He kisses me on the forehead. "We'll pry the last shard of the combination sequence out of the wall. That should close the door and, since there'd only be one choice, that'll make it pretty easy to open in the future. We can leave the key under a pile of rocks next to its indent. Even if we don't make it home, some future generation could find it again. By that time, the radiation might be low enough to permit a detailed evaluation of the knowledge base in here. Who knows? Maybe we aren't supposed to know what they knew. After all, their knowledge killed them."

I shake my head in disagreement. "No, David. It wasn't their knowledge that killed them but the application of their knowledge in combination with flaws in their innate character. Meanness and the need to be right at all cost—

that's the part that needed to be evolved out. Their horizon didn't get the message. Maybe ours won't either."

Faced with the ability to research almost anything we might want to know, we aren't sure what's most important to ask or where to start. We scan for information on fusion power but are hampered by our poor understanding of their technical language and our own lack of subject matter expertise. The same is true of space travel. As much as we'd like to take the secrets of fusion power and how to lift massive numbers of animals into space back with us, that won't be possible. It could take years to understand the enormous amount of information available on those topics alone, perhaps forever.

After much discussion, we decide the best we can do is to bring the Endohl language back with us in as much detail as we can. We are, after all, linguists and anthropologists. If we ever again reach civilization, at least we can give returning teams a head start on what they'll encounter here. If properly trained scientists are sent to this vault, we can ensure they're prepared to begin their research.

We spend one final, bittersweet night in the vault. It has been our sanctuary as well as the location of the most exciting and rewarding discovery of all time. It has also been the location of many warm and tender moments with David. He quips as he makes love to me one final time, "Enjoy this while you can, sweetie, because we'll only have rocks to sleep on in the foreseeable future."

He's right, and I whisper back as I hug him tight, "My enjoyment has nothing to do with the floor we sleep on."

In an odd way, I'm saddened to leave the vault. It has been our protective home for over six months, but staying here would mean the end of our lives. When we exit for the final time, we remove the largest shard from its wall and verify that the massive door closes. David then places a stack of rocks atop the shard, immediately beneath the shard's impression in the huge stone door.

Only time will tell if the vault's door will ever be opened again.

Chapter Twenty
The Spa

We spend the night at Peter's base camp and organize our backpacks for the long trip to the coast. During the morning and afternoon, I read through Peter's journals while David hunts fresh meat for our journey. Although there aren't many animals in this area, I never underestimate his hunting skills. In several hours, he returns with a prize. Proudly displaying his animal while flashing a wide smile, he proclaims, "Porcupine, the other white meat."

As it turns out, porcupine is a lot like pork when mixed with native beans and spices. When we sit down to eat, I can tell David is itching to head out. His humor mimics an Old World mountain man as he digs into his stew with his elbows flailing out to the sides. "I wuz born hungry, and I ain't never filled up yit…but I'm workin' on it, and this critter's gonna help."

I smile back without comment.

After dinner, I lead him to the edge of the shelf where we look out over the expanse of the crater lakes below. "Beautiful, isn't it? Will you miss it?"

He chuckles. "I'm not sure, actually. This area holds the discovery of a lifetime, but it's slowly killing us in the same way it killed my father." Before I can comment, he plasters a plastic smile on his face, trying to shove his feelings away. "Besides, it's cold up here, and you're too boney to provide much heat."

I talk into the distance, not looking directly at him, "I could be getting fatter soon."

He's a fast study. He stammers out, "A-are you pregnant?"

I cock my head and shoot a sly glance out of the corners of my eyes. "I don't know. I ran out of pills a week ago, and my period is late. Anything could happen."

He turns me toward him, kisses me on the forehead, and holds me close. "That's not all bad. We're leaving the danger zone tomorrow, so radiation won't be an issue. I don't have any idea what the future holds, but there are only two options over the next nine months: we will get home, or we won't. If we get home, you will have our baby there. If we can't get back, then we can start a family on the coast. Either way, a baby shouldn't be a problem. Seems to me that if you want a baby, you should have one, and if that choice has already been made, then so be it."

Alone in the wilderness, it's easy to feel like the Old World Eve with David as my Adam. There's nothing to stop us from settling anywhere we choose and forging a life for ourselves, wherever that might be. As it was in the Old World biblical story, by the time our children are old enough, mates for them will probably have migrated to wherever we put down roots. I reach out to take his hand and squeeze it, knowing that settling here or anywhere in the wild is not my goal, nor will it ever be. "I desperately want our baby, dear, but I want to raise him in Salvation."

His eyebrows rise, "Him? We're supposed to have three daughters, and only one son. If you're going to be that picky, you'll have to wait until we get home."

Once again, the word *home* sounds so comforting that it gives me pause. I snuggle hard into his side, making my point more strongly than I could with words alone. "We'll see what happens on the way. Either on the coast or in Salvation, when our son comes to us, we'll call him Peter."

David's eyes mist, but he suppresses his tears. "That would be fitting. Dad brought us here, and he saved us here."

I look up at David with all the love I feel, caress his face in my hands, and give him a short, soft kiss. "And he might just take us home as well."

David moves me back to arm's length, studying my face as his eyebrows dip. "Might take us home? What aren't you telling me?"

I rub my cheek along his strong arm, loving him as the sun disappears below the horizon. He can't possibly know how strong I feel about going home. "It's all in Peter's journals, love: the details of his voyage across the ocean, the hardships, and the glories. Ever wonder what happened to the Dorothy Elizabeth when he reached the Syrian shore?"

David tilts his head to the side as his eyes narrow. "I thought he was dead until a few months ago. I've never thought about his sailboat."

My eyes must sparkle in the deepening twilight. I love being the bearer of good news. "He beached it, David. He put it in dry dock on a sandy beach just north of the river where we came in. If we had gone a few kilometers farther north, we would have seen it."

His head jerks up, and his eyes widen. "That makes sense. The weather can be so foul offshore that a moored craft wouldn't stand a chance over time. Dry docking the Dorothy Elizabeth would keep her safe from the weather, but getting her there would've been a rigging nightmare, even for a skilled sailor. There must be a fairly deep stream inlet where he put in. The Dorothy Elizabeth's fin keel and spade rudder are designed for shallow water sailing, but she still needs about three meters to skirt the bottom."

I can almost see the wheels turning in David's head. I bet he's trying to imagine how his father might have dry docked the sailboat, so I suggest, "Or maybe he waited for a rainstorm at high tide."

"Could be. Is that in his journal too?"

I poke him in his ribs but don't give him a direct answer. "Hey, girls can figure things out too."

As we take our first steps toward home, we say farewell to Peter's shelter and dedicate our return trip to him. Carrying his discovery to the rest of civilization is our responsibility now. In time, others will revere him as we do, assuming we get back home to tell his story. We steel our resolve. No matter how difficult the way ahead might be, we must overcome every obstacle. We must live to tell the world about his marvelous discovery and brave sacrifice.

Our boots are wearing thin, and winter is setting in, so we will follow the route detailed in Peter's journals on the way back to the coast. On his return home, he kept to the lowlands rather than going over the mountains like we did many months ago. It will take longer to reach the sea, but the trek out should be far safer and much easier.

We follow the narrow rock shelf south until it intersects the mountainside and then begin a gentle, spiraling descent toward the southwest. David wants to cover about twenty kilometers a day, but the topography will determine what we can accomplish. Exhausted by the time we set up camp on our first night, we eat only a little jerky with water before sleep takes us both.

We spend a peaceful night in our small tent but wake in the morning to a new danger—snow. These mountains receive considerable precipitation in winter. If we aren't careful, we could get stranded in the high country and starve to death. We break camp with new urgency, munching jerky as we travel. It's not just the cold. Peter's notes were made in the spring and summer, and we fear we could miss landmarks buried under a blanket of whiteout.

About midday, David urgently signals me to crouch down. A wolf pack has brought down a deer just ahead. He doesn't want to surprise them or, worse, allow them to surprise us. There are only three alternatives: stay on guard and wait them out, confront them, or try to hike around them. Before we make a decision, the lead dog senses our presence and issues the alert. They stop eating in unison and stare menacingly in our direction.

Without making any fast moves, David removes his rifle from his leather backpack scabbard and stands ready for the unexpected. For a moment, there's a standoff, but in the next instant, the largest wolf lunges toward us at blinding speed. David's reflexes are far faster than the wolf, and the bullet rips through its flesh in midair. The animal plummets to the ground, burying its nose deep in the snow before momentum swings its hindquarters forward and up over its head. The other wolves continue to stare. Guttural growls penetrate the frigid air as the pack waits for their leader to stir. This time, David doesn't wait for them to act, and another shot drops the second largest animal straight into the snow. Six remain. They begin to back away as we stand erect without showing fear and walk toward them.

Either they will attack, or they won't, but at least we'll see them coming. Within seconds, another round blows a huge chunk of flesh off the third largest wolf's neck, and it wails a blood-curdling screech as it thrashes in the snow before bleeding out. The others back farther away, far more timid now, and then turn to run as we come closer.

We've been in the mountains for nearly seven months and have used about half our ammunition during that time. Three shots to dispel the wolves might have been excessive, but we now have enough frozen venison and wolf meat for the remainder of the trip home.

After taking all the meat we can carry and covering it lightly with our remaining salt, we try to put as much distance between the wolves and ourselves as possible. In all likelihood, they will stay near what's left of their kill and the other dead wolves, at least until that food source is gone. On the other hand, we are carrying meat as well as being food ourselves. They could very well come after us.

Peter's notes indicate we should pass a large, vertical outcropping rock soon. After that, we're supposed to descend in a gentle, southern curve into a distant valley and follow the valley due west. Unfortunately, we haven't seen the jutting rock. The sun is moving rapidly toward the southwest, and freezing weather will set in soon. The six inches of snow on the ground are but a gentle reminder of what can happen if we're hit with a major winter storm. So, we push on as hard as we can, hoping we haven't missed the landmark.

We camp against a sheer rock cliff that evening after gathering enough wood to keep a large fire going for the night. The cliff faces south, and the wind is calm. Barring marauding animals, we should be comfortable and safe for the night. The deer steak sizzles as I place it on the hot, flat rock by the fire. David puts his arms around my waist and hugs me from behind. "I love the aroma of grilling deer steaks." He pushes the rock nearer the edge of the flames with his boot.

I pat the back of his hand and move my head back to rub against his face. "If we weren't so damn exposed out here, and so concerned about the potential for worsening weather, this would be a pleasant campout."

I tend the fire while he wipes down the rifle. He cranks a shell into the chamber and sets the rifle beside him as we settle down to eat with our backs against the rock. The deer meat is delicious, but every snap of the fire and howl of wind through the trees brings us to full alert. When we finish dinner, we clean our mess kits with snow. David kisses me and then flicks his head toward the boughs he has arranged by the fire. "You take the first shift, honey. I'll stand guard."

He doesn't have to ask twice. It will be my turn to stand guard soon enough. He wakes me early in the morning, hands me the rifle, and then lies down. Neither of us gets enough sleep. We are reluctant to get moving in the morning but know we must. Winter is setting in. We eat the meat leftover from dinner, pack our gear, and then head out as soon as possible.

By midday, I'm getting worried. I pull out Peter's journal and check it for what must be the hundredth time, and then look toward David. "We should have seen it by now."

He nods and looks down at his compass but doesn't stop walking. "One would think, but we are going in the right direction. I don't know how we could have missed it. All the other landmarks are correct. You just need a little faith."

"People of faith die of exposure all the time in the mountains around Salvation."

"I'm still an atheist, thank God. Just keep walking."

His attempt at humor doesn't belay my concern. If we've somehow missed the landmark because of snow cover, we could be walking in the wrong direction. In about two kilometers, just before I can get myself worked into a tizzy, David points in the distance and hands the field glasses to me. "Dad's still watching over us, love."

I see the rock. Thank God, but the way ahead isn't easy. We are at lower elevation now. It's warmer here, but our forward progress is greatly hindered by fallen trees and brush. Although we trust our compass, David periodically climbs a tall fir tree to ensure we are heading true toward our target destination.

It is dusk by the time we reach Peter's first major landmark, putting us almost a day behind Peter's schedule. We convince ourselves the time of year is slowing us down, not our general physical condition in comparison to his. We're delighted Peter's old shelter is still in place when we arrive at the rock, and after gathering firewood for the night, we opt to share the shelter with the hibernating lizards and spiders rather than to set up our tent.

Morning brings more snow—another six inches. Peter's notes indicate a steep descent faces us today. We look forward to warmer ground below, but not to the difficult trek ahead. We break camp soon after breakfast and head into the wind, now blowing a good thirty kilometers per hour with the temperature hovering near zero Celsius. I fall flat on my face in the snow when I trip on a hidden limb under the frozen surface. "Damn!"

My cry catches David's attention, and he turns in my direction. "We don't really have time to play in the snow." He walks back and helps me pick myself up. "Are you okay?"

I whimper, "No. I am not okay. I'm cold. My feet are frozen. My fingers ache. I feel like shit."

He kisses my forehead. "Okay. For a minute there, I thought there might be something wrong. Let's move on."

My core temperature plummets in the freezing wind chill. My teeth are chattering, but I continue on. David trudges through the snow ahead, and I shout to him over the screaming wind, "It's a damn good thing we didn't try to leave the mountains the same way we came in. The temperature is probably twenty degrees colder in the high country."

We reach the steep slope mentioned in Peter's notes by noon. It's wicked. Not exactly a rappelling surface, but close. We tie ourselves together, with David taking up the rear, bracing for the worst as I work myself slowly to the next stable object below. After I tie off, the leapfrog process begins. We are almost down when David slips on an ice patch and tumbles out of control toward the bottom. There is little I can do except cinch up the line and wait for the inevitable hard pull as he reaches the end of his rope.

I hear him yelp as the line snaps tight, but I can't rush to his aid. He's still conscious and orients himself along the slope with his feet braced against a small outcropping rock. I move down cautiously, trying to avoid the ice patches that cost him his footing. His breathing is normal by the time I reach him. "You didn't need to take the express. We are almost at the bottom."

He begins to laugh but grabs his side and grimaces. He wheezes out a response through quick hitches in his breath. "Shit…I might have a rib problem."

It took us two weeks to reach the craters in good weather. We are only three days into the trip back, taking the long route, and the snow is already piling up. A broken rib could be serious. "We're almost down, honey. Can you make it the rest of the way?"

He sits up with a low groan. "I think so. Let's re-tie the rope under my armpits, and you can ease me down from here. Sorry to be such a wimp, love."

We assess his injury when we reach the bottom, concluding he might have a cracked rib. That type of injury does not heal quickly, so he'll need to take it easy for a few weeks. We shift weight from his pack to mine, enough for him to tolerate the pain, and press on.

It's a slow walk through the snow-filled valley toward the west. The wind drops to a gentle breeze, the weather holds, and David is able to keep moving, though not as fast as before. The clear sky, in combination with snow cover, means the temperature will plunge tonight. As night approaches, our major concern is finding a protected location to pitch our tent. David points to a clump of trees ahead. "We'll camp there, even though we'll be exposed from all sides."

Luck is with us. The snow isn't as deep in the protected confine of the trees, and there's plenty of wood to build a fire. I snap the flexible tent rods together, set up the tent, and ease David inside before staking the corners. He can't help much. The trees will provide good shelter from the wind but not much from animals. As a precaution, I tie a rope barrier around our shelter and hang our canteen parts from it. Some alarm will be better than no alarm, but we both sleep with cocked pistols near our headrests that night.

Morning brings bitter cold. We pack our gear as fast as we can and head west down the valley. The air is still, and the sun's warmth is welcome as we continue hiking into afternoon. I take the lead to plow a path in the snow and try to moderate my pace, but I worry David is moving slower than yesterday. I stop often to rest and allow him to catch up. He lies down in the snow, clutching his side and breathing in shallow breaths when I stop for another break. His cough is getting worse—a bad sign. I sit next to him. "You need to breathe deep now and then, even if it hurts. We don't want fluid to collect in your lungs."

He nods, takes a deep breath, and moans. We have many more hours of sunlight, and the night will be bitter cold. We need to move on, but we can't risk hurting him more. "Should I set up the tent here, honey, or do you feel up to going on?"

He grimaces when he coughs. "I'll be fine. I just need a minute. We need to get to a lower altitude before we get caught in a storm."

I know he is in great pain; I also know he is right. I squat next to him on his good side. "Pull yourself up using me as a prop. I'll try to stand up for both of us."

He yelps on the way to a standing position, and then reassures me he's fine. He then points in the direction we were heading before the break and shoos me on with several flicks of his wrist.

My poor David. I'd give anything to be able to share his pain.

* * * *

Moderate but cold weather prevails during the remaining five-day hike as we travel through a series of valleys south of the steppes we crossed on the way in. David's pain has eased some by the time we approach the final range that separates us from the coast. Peter's notes indicate we should follow the northern route around the mountain that towers ahead, even though the pass to the south looks less dangerous. We are torn, and the sky is threatening. I glance at David. "Looks like we've reached one of those 'road less traveled' moments. Do we take the high road or the low road? Do you have a preference?"

He rubs his chin as he studies the sky. "Something's coming in. We don't want to be caught out in the open."

We brush the snow off a large, flat rock and sit side by side. David shakes his head as he flips through the pages of Peter's journal. "The notes are a bit cryptic, but Dad indicates there is something called 'The Spa' on the northern route."

I was afraid of that. "He also made the trip when the weather was better. That pass looks like a hard climb. It could be a mistake."

David points toward the south. "That direction looks wide open. There'd be no shelter from the wind screaming up the valley. It looks easier, but it could be a mistake."

We sit in silence until he stands. "We've dedicated this trip to him. I vote we cast our lot with Dad."

I stand beside David, dust off my butt, and shrug. "Damned if you do, damned if you don't. It's a tossup. Let's get moving; Peter has never steered us wrong."

The cloudy sky lowers as the sun arcs toward the southwest. The wind picks up; blowing snow clouds our vision. I sense a severe winter storm will be on us soon; the way ahead is becoming a howling wilderness. The climb is not easy, and ice forming on rock surfaces makes it more treacherous with each upward step. Heavy snowfall hampers our progress before dusk approaches. If we don't find a protective campsite soon, we'll be forced to camp in the open on sheer rock—something we are loath to do.

We spot a rocky ridge a short distance above that might offer a flat area large enough for our tent and lean into the screaming wind to make it there before sunset. It is frigid, and the temperature is dropping faster than the sun. David chuckles as we approach the crest of the ridge and then shakes his finger in my direction. "Good grief, Beth. Can't you wait until you're downwind?"

I give him a playful, disgusted look. "I didn't fart, but if it wasn't you, what is that wretched smell?" As my head clears the edge of the ridge, all I can say is, "Oh, my God, honey. You won't believe this."

A dense cloud layer blankets the area immediately below the ridge, and the air is heavy with the stink of rotten eggs. David peers over the ridge as well. "It's hydrogen sulfide. The gas is heavier than air and, in high concentrations, very poisonous, flammable, and explosive."

"What does high concentration mean? Do we need to worry?"

David winks. "I don't think so. With all the wind and open area here, I suspect the concentration is low enough to not be a threat. You'll just have to adjust to the stench."

I sigh. "That's what we thought when we took Geiger counter readings at the first crater too, and that didn't work out so well."

We walk with caution into the layer of mist that shrouds a large, natural rock depression. It is difficult to see in the dense fog and fading light. The air temperature increases enough to melt the frozen slime hanging below our noses as we move further into the mist. We grope forward until we hear sounds completely out of place in these freezing mountains—bubbles.

"It's got to be geothermal, Beth, but that doesn't make sense. These mountains don't have any documented activity of that type."

"Maybe not in the past, but things have changed. They're on the boundary between the African and Eurasian Plates and took the brunt of the largest release of mankind's fury in the history of the world. The caverns we left behind aren't on anyone's map, either."

The scurry of hoofs spikes our concern as the rocky basin levels out. Through the fog ahead, we can make out a small pool of steaming water with bubbles rising in it. "It must be Peter's spa. Your father must have come this way in the summer. No one in their right mind would take this pass in winter."

David rubs his hands together, basking his near frozen skin in the heat rising from the pool. "We're here—

that could be a testament to our state of mind. We might be crazy for being here, but this looks like a great place to ride out the storm."

I pitch the tent and weigh the corners down with rocks while David watches for animals and holds the flashlight. It's a relief to be out of the freezing cold wind and to remove our backpacks. Melting snow in our canteens has provided plenty of water during our journey, but our food supply is low. I suspect the animals that come here for the warmth will soon provide meat, even if there's no wood to cook it.

The wind howls above us, but the small depression filled with clouds is calm. Peter is still watching over us. I walk to the edge of the steaming pool and dip my finger in. It is warm, about thirty degrees Celsius. I make a quick check for radiation and, finding none, grin at David. "You're on watch."

David retorts with a lascivious lilt, "I'll be watching, all right. It'll be good to see my real woman again."

I strip and enter slow enough to adjust to the hot water. The heat feels heavenly, and I'm almost able to forget about the cold wilderness we've been living in. I've complained about living in the wild many times, but if outdoor living comes with a warm "spa" like this one, then I could be convinced to stay.

Darkness closes in, but I don't want to leave the water, not when months of grime, sweat, and body odor buildup continue to ooze from my skin and float effortlessly into the soothing, hot water surrounding me. David soon approaches, lays his rifle down, places his clothing and flashlight within reach, and slips in next to me. Being filth-free is the greatest luxury any explorer can experience.

Almost.

David moves slowly in front of me and presses his body against mine. I wrap him in my arms and kiss his face and forehead as he begins to make love to me. His undulating body stirs the water around me in a rhythmic pulsing that cleanses my soul. He is gentle, and I am swept away in euphoric splendor when his body quivers and I hear him whisper, "I love you. I love you. I love you." At that moment, I am awash in joy, basking in the unadulterated, raw pleasure of just being alive.

When we finish, we sit together on a jutting rock below the water's surface. David strokes my leg and raises his eyebrows as he grins at me. "That could be the one. If you weren't pregnant before, you might be now."

I playfully splash water on him and giggle. "That was a notch above so-so—good enough to tell me your ribs must be better—but I doubt you created anything that wasn't there before. I'm already two weeks late, and we both know it."

He hangs his head like a scolded child. "So-so? You're setting your standards pretty high these days. Good grief. Give a woman a hot bath in the middle of the wilderness, and she expects maid service to come with it."

I reach over, cup his face in my hands, and draw his lips to mine. "You are my entire world, my love. I can ask no more than what you give me every day."

He hugs me while rubbing his whiskers against my hair. "I love you. With all my heart and soul, I love you."

For me, the time with David in the hot water is the highlight of this trip. Not because of the lovemaking or the exchange of commitment to each other, but because we talk for almost an hour. For months, we have been so concerned with survival that talking about anything else is a luxury we have dearly missed. The spa gives us time to talk together about things beyond our day-to-day existence; it gives us time to dream. David reaffirms how much he is looking forward to our children, something I've been increasingly excited about since I missed my last period, and I tell him how wonderful it feels to be going home—to Hope or to wherever circumstances take us. So much has changed over the past year. There was a time I could not conceive of using the words "home" and "Hope" in the same sentence, but now there's no place I'd rather be.

When my skin has wrinkled enough to make dried prunes look smooth, I pat myself off with my dirty clothes before putting on the only change of clothing I have left. David does the same, and we wash our dirty laundry on the rocks at the edge of the pool before turning in. No animals appeared while we frolicked in the pool. We should be safe for the night.

The storm continues to rage when we wake to animal sounds in the morning. David peeks out through the tent flap with his rifle at the ready and gives me a "thumbs up." In another instant, the rifle's report echoes through the mountains. Animals scatter, and a lone mountain goat drops to the ground. We scout the immediate area before attending to our kill and are delighted to find extremely hot vents of water trickling from surrounding rocks down into the pool. David looks at me with a sly grin. "Are you thinking what I'm thinking?"

I stretch suggestively to get the kinks out of my back, intentionally jutting my breasts as far forward as possible. "You had sex last night. Why don't we just use the hot water to cook the goat?"

He laughs out loud and then turns his attention to the animal. While he sections the goat, I position our small cooking pot so the hottest water vent I can find flows into it and then add thinly sliced meat and beans. The beans have never been fully dried, and the stew is ready in thirty minutes. We're both ravenous and glut ourselves. If we could find firewood here, this would be an ideal place to spend the remainder of winter.

The storm breaks in two days. We strap the cooked goat we've frozen under rocks outside the spa area to the outside of our backpacks and continue following Peter's route. In four hours, we breach the summit. The Mediterranean extends as far as our eyes can see into the distance. Temperatures are well below freezing but warm up with every hundred meters we descend. By late afternoon, two days later, we step onto a windswept, sandy beach.

We're not home, or even close to our base camp, but I feel much safer here. There is comfort in the eternal roar of the surf and the sounds of the birds that hover aloft—far more so than the screaming wind through the mountain's trees. *Thank you, Peter, for bringing us safely through that nightmare.*

We believe we are seventy to one hundred kilometers south of our base camp, but without a sextant and a clear night, that is only a guess. We hike north for a few hours on full alert, knowing the goat on our backpacks has thawed, and that dog packs rule the coast. The meat could be an irresistible call to the dogs, so we stop long before sunset to build a large fire near a huge, fallen tree. We'll roast and dry the meat before pressing forward. We extend the fire in a semi-circle around us that night, with the large tree covering our rear.

It's always something—weather, dogs, or dangerous treks. Survival isn't easy, but at least I don't have to face it alone. David must feel the same way because he holds me tight as we drift off to sleep.

On the third day of our trek up the beach, we find the river leading to our base camp, but our shelter is on the opposite side. Trudging upriver, we pass the tips of our catamaran jutting out of the sand and rock across the muddy flow. We continue on until the communications bunker comes into sight. The river is about twenty meters across at this point and running fast with frigid water.

I pace back and forth as I stare across the river. "Now what?"

David picks up a small stone and throws it across. "Now, we need to follow that stone, but I have no idea how. Seems to me there are only two choices. We can go back to the delta and try to ford the river there, but we'd probably lose some gear and risk hypothermia in the process. Or we can continue upstream until we find a dry way across. What's your pleasure?"

I point upriver. "I hate being wet and cold."

We are so close to our shelter, yet so far. We hike along the river the remainder of the day but don't find a suitable crossing spot. We make camp beneath a rock outcropping that evening, disappointed. We didn't follow the river on our way up the valley but believe its headwaters must originate in the steppes ahead—*way* ahead. Nevertheless, we're committed now and will stay the course.

About midday on the second day of our trip up river, the channel narrows at a deep gorge where the rushing water follows a sharp bend in the rock. Large trees grow on our side of the bend, and we set about cutting one down. The task is labor intensive beyond belief. A hatchet was never intended for this kind of job. We take turn after turn for hours on end, chopping out small chips, before the giant tree finally succumbs and careens across the ravine. The tree seems stable enough, but large limbs block a clear passage. Time after time, we tie off to a nearby tree and make the perilous trip out on the trunk over the raging river to trim a path sufficient to pass through. It is late in the day before enough branches are cleared that I am able to step off on the other side.

David ties one backpack at a time to the rope, and I pull them across as he keeps the line taut. Finally, I tie the rope off on my side, and he makes his way across. The river has cost us three days by the time we return to our base camp. I am filthy and tired as I wait for water to heat up in our makeshift shower. Being able to wash the top layers of dirt out of my hair will be a luxury. No matter how humble, it's good to be home.

Part 5: Home Is Where the Heart Is

Chapter Twenty-One
The Dorothy Elizabeth

Clean but exhausted, we sleep better in our bunker-like shelter that first night than we have for months. The precautions we took before leaving worked well. Animals did not get to our supplies, and everything is intact—just as we left it. It's amazing how little it takes to make us happy here. The security of knowing there's enough food to last through winter, in combination with plentiful firewood and rainwater, brings total peace of mind.

Life is much simpler here than in Hope, and we remain at camp for over two months, as if on vacation. Time has become more of an estimate than an exact science. Things like birthdays don't matter. We survive one day at a time, celebrating each day we aren't hurt or threatened by death. We relish our showers, naps, and daily lovemaking. When we're not walking on the beach or exploring the ruins of Faqi Hasan, we refine the notes we took back at the caverns. David's rib has healed over time. He is as normal as he can be. Life is good. I could live here forever without a care in the world.

Only one thing nags at me now. It has been over two months since I ran out of birth control pills, yet I'm not pregnant. As we sit on the log we've placed before our campfire, I take David's hand. "I know it isn't for lack of trying, love, but I have no indication of being pregnant except for my missing monthly cycle. You would think, by now, I might be showing a little or at least have some morning sickness."

David stirs the ashes with a long stick. "Your breasts aren't getting larger, either."

I put my finger on his side and push in gently. "You would notice that, wouldn't you?" I add a little pressure. "Is that the rib you broke?"

David pulls to the side. "Easy now. I was just agreeing with you. I don't know what to say. I know you want children; so do I. We have no idea what condition Dad's boat might be in, so we might never get home. As I see it, this would be as good a place to start a family as any. We have everything we need here to live well."

I scoot closer to him and nuzzle into his shoulder. "I wanted to be pregnant now so I can work through the summer, helping gather food and wood for next winter. Then, with fewer chores in winter, I'd have more time to care for the baby after he's born."

He pats my upper leg and winks. "There isn't much we can do except keep trying. You can count on me to do my part."

I know David is trying to make me feel better by making a light-hearted comment, but a feeling of quiet dread drifts into my soul. I stare at the coals and say nothing, but turmoil roils within me. All my life, I have considered having children as one of life's givens, something I've taken for granted that would just happen when the time is right. Now, for the first time, I am confronted with a new reality. Maybe something's wrong; maybe children won't be part of my future after all. The thought sickens me.

David notices my silence and lifts my chin with his finger. "Honey, are those tears?"

I shake my head. "No, just a whiff of smoke in my eyes."

Winter passes. I do not get pregnant. I do not understand. When the crocus and phlox finally begin to poke through a light dusting of snow, we decide it's time to hike to the Dorothy Elizabeth for an overnight stay. The weather is warming, and David wants to get a good assessment of what needs to be done to free her from dry dock and prepare her for use, if that's possible. The hike isn't comfortable. The area might be warming to a new season, but salt spray driven from the top of moderate rollers still slaps at my face with near-freezing tiny droplets.

As always when the weather is foul, our objective is much farther away than we believed when we started out. The rain intensifies as a few kilometers turns into five, and then to ten. By the time we round the final bend and see the boat in the distance, we are drenched, miserably cold, and ready to get inside anything with a potential for being dry.

Heavy drizzle has turned into a blowing downpour by the time we board the sailboat, which itself is at least a third embedded in a sandy grave. The boat's fore and aft hatches are sealed with heavy tarps tied in place with nylon rope, and we struggle with binding knots for what seems like an eternity before David abruptly says, "Screw this," and cuts them with his hunting knife.

The cabin is damp and cold, but it is fully intact. It even has a small wood/oil burning stove. I remove the canvas covering on its exterior stainless stovepipe while David collects firewood for the night. We have food and water to last for several days, so we'll let the storm pass before doing a detailed hull inspection.

David soon returns with a bundle of wet wood and moss. Although difficult to kindle, we eventually encourage it to burn using the rancid tallow from a recent kill we brought with us. The moldy smell of the cabin gradually dissipates as the stove warms the interior. We shiver and shake, rubbing our hands over the small metal box while waiting for our body temperature to reach normal. I've only been away from our shelter for a day, and I already miss it.

Once heat fills the inside of the cabin, the boat is quite pleasant. We begin by taking an inventory of everything Peter left behind—a plethora of supplies and contingency gear. It is clear Peter expected to return home someday because he stowed away everything he needed for an extended trip across the ocean. Like our shelter ten clicks away, there's comfort here. As darkness falls, we remove the sails from the forward bunks and fall fast asleep.

A chilly, clear day greets us the following morning. After a breakfast of canned fish from Peter's food store, we carefully inspect the epoxy-coated aluminum hull. The material is almost indestructible. The hull is sound. At first blush, the effort to free the boat—which is landlocked in a sand-filled depression about thirty feet from a nearby small river—will be monumental.

David strokes his chin while studying the situation from fifteen meters back. "I can't imagine how he did this. It'd take a man at least a year to dig a channel to reach the stream."

I snuggle in next to him and put my arm around his waist, pulling him close. I can't let him believe this problem is too big to tackle. I want to go home. "There are two of us, dear. We could do it twice as fast."

He shakes his head. "No. Digging it out isn't the answer. We're missing something. Dad would never have set himself up for such a difficult task in order to leave. He knew something we don't. Are you sure there's nothing in his journals about this?"

I've read Peter's journals so many times that I've almost memorized them. "Absolutely certain. You've read them too. There's nothing about how he put the boat here in the first place, let alone about getting it out again."

After a few moments of silence, David shakes his head. "No. Dad documented everything. If it's not in the journals he gave us, then there's another one somewhere else, probably on this boat."

That makes sense. We went through the boat in fair detail last night but might have missed something. At least now we know we're looking for some type of book or log, and we both come to the same conclusion at the same time. "The chart locker."

The plasticized charts are neatly rolled in the long, wooden drawer specifically designed for storing them. We expect to find notes written in grease pencil on one of the charts—something to explain how Peter put the boat in dry dock in the first place. To our dismay, every chart is pristine. There are no marks of any kind. David just sighs. "Dad was always meticulous about his charts. I should not have expected he would leave notes on them."

I rummage through the long drawer again, hoping I missed something the first time. I reach in as far as my arm will allow and feel a raised edge. Scratching with my fingertips, I work the object until I can slide it forward. This could be it—a small, blue notebook labeled "Maintenance Log." With adrenaline pulsing through my veins, I begin leafing through the pages, reading what I find aloud to David. "According to this, there's a loose cleat on the port stern."

David looks up from the chart showing the cove where the boat is beached. "Anything else? Anything useful?"

"Not yet, only that Peter ripped the primary jib on his way over from Hope. The one we moved off the bunk last night was the spare." I fall silent as I flip the pages. My excitement wanes as I near the back of the book…and then I stop cold. I look up at David. "Does that map show the confluence of two small streams or rivers near here?"

He traces the coast with his finger. "The one next to us seems to split upstream on this chart, but that could be a mistake because there's only one small river out there."

"Or it could be correct, and that could tell us how he did it. His final entry says, 'Dammed the river, and let her settle.' If there were two rivers when your father arrived, and he dammed one, his sailboat could be sitting in the old tributary channel."

David smiles from ear to ear. "You could be on to something. That's more like my father. Destroy the dam to refloat the boat. Rechanneling the water would be a lot less work than digging the boat out."

My heart races. My excitement spikes. I want to jump up and down like a little girl. I want to go home. "Could be, dear, and if I interpret the sketch on this last page right, then the dam is only a few kilometers inland."

When the fire in the wood stove dies out, we begin the hike upriver. True to Peter's sketch, about three kilometers upstream the river widens and becomes shallow above a split falls where a large rock separates the flow into two channels. A large, fallen tree with piles of rock stacked along its length blocks flow on the north side of the rock and diverts the water into the southern channel.

David takes my hand and hugs me. "This is perfect. When we're ready, we can put the sails on the boat and prepare it for ocean travel while it's on solid ground. Then, we can gradually open this channel, a little at a time, and the water flow should wash the sand away from the hull. Dad planned this well. He's still looking out for us."

I'm so excited I could pee. I jump up on him with my legs wrapped around his hips, squeal, and then smother his face with kisses. When I finally drop to the ground, I take a deep breath and let out a slow sigh of relief. "That's just to let you know how happy I am about the possibility of going home." Then, as I cast a lascivious leer at him, I add, "Just imagine what it will be like if you *actually* get me back."

Over the next month, we prepare to refloat the Dorothy Elizabeth. We load her with food and water, and lay in a considerable stock of rose hips. Loaded with vitamin C, the hips will keep scurvy at bay before the oranges to the south ripen. We also bring in some of the inner pine bark we dried during winter—a solid source of vitamin C that is less susceptible to spoilage than rose hips. It takes far more than just filling our stomachs to survive. A wide variety of berries, grasses, weeds, and bark is also necessary to keep us fit over the long haul.

The final item we bring aboard is one of our trunks with Peter's journals wrapped in a tarp inside. The trunk also contains the last of our jerky, unused ammunition, and the like. We leave nothing that might be needed for survival in the days and months ahead.

When we are ready, we begin removing the upriver obstruction to the river's natural flow, and water again cascades toward the Dorothy Elizabeth. It is fitting that the boat that might take us to Salvation was brought here by David's father and that it carries the name of both David's mother and David's wife. I'm not superstitious, but it feels right, like it was meant to be in the grand scheme of things.

We follow the water downstream as it fills the long, dry streambed until it surrounds and caresses our waiting sailboat. Where the dry channel merges with the existing river, we use paddles from our pontoon boat to help wash away the sand that has accumulated over time from the dunes at the edge of the sea. Every few days, we return to the dam to increase the flow of water until we restore the full stream flow. Wooden bracings Peter put in place as the water level dropped wash away as the water now rises, and soon the craft floats free above the natural rocky bottom of the streambed. Our moment of truth is at hand.

My heart is both saddened and overjoyed as we leave the mouth of the river and head south along the coast. Our shelter in Faqi Hasan has been our refuge, our salvation. We shared great love and closeness there. I will never forget the beauty of simply being alive with the man I love, of needing nothing more than the fundamentals of life. David notices my tears as our former home disappears in the distance and leaves the helm long enough to comfort me. He holds me until my tears stop, and then adds playfully, "Suez is waiting."

We walk to the stern hand in hand, and I sit beside him as he retakes the wheel. Looking back over the wake, I take a deep breath. "It's hard to believe I'm sad about leaving here. I guess, even with all of the bad things that happened, there were enough good things to bring tears to my eyes."

He nods and smiles. "It's just a shelter, my love. Our real home is in our hearts."

We will not attempt an Atlantic crossing, as Peter did. David is not comfortable with his open water skills and believes we should secure passage on one of the oil recovery ships that visit the area every six months or so, or at least they did when we came over. We don't know if the loss of the Marco Polo has changed that. If the loss of that ship has put an end to oil recovery ships coming to Suez, then we will revisit our decision. Only if we can find no other way will we consider sailing across that vast ocean.

Chapter Twenty-Two
The Cooks

Our trip south toward the Suez Canal is slow and unexciting. We are thankful for that. Excitement can be a bad thing at sea, as demonstrated when we first came to this part of the world. We skirt the shore and, when bad weather threatens, anchor in protected coves until it passes. We enjoy catching fish along the way and only go ashore when our firewood supply is low. In about two weeks, the approximate halfway point of our journey to the canal, David spots the Old World city of Beirut off our port bow. He points to the city's silhouette on the horizon. "We should stop there to do a little shopping."

I shake my head. "You want more rum, don't you? No way in hell. The rum was good but not good enough to risk being eaten by dogs. It's one thing to risk being shredded to obtain lifesaving transportation, quite another for something as frivolous as liquor. If you want rum, you can make molasses when we get home and distill your own."

He shrugs but doesn't alter course as he grumbles, "Aging it for two hundred years could be a problem."

The air temperature continues to increase as we sail farther south. Spring gives way to summer. If we're lucky, we'll catch the returning early summer oil recovery ship and not have to endure a season of blistering heat in Old World Egypt. More fair weather means the return of predominantly onshore sea breezes during the day and longer, faster tacks with the sheets close-hauled. Our progress toward the canal increases in direct proportion to the temperature and, in another week, we see Port Said dead ahead.

A workman gawks as the Dorothy Elizabeth glides alongside the pier. We ease up to the small craft service float on the pier's port side and tie off. The onlooker continues to stare, as if he's unable to move—as if he's never before seen a sailboat or a woman. They must not get many visitors here, especially like me. David grins as he finishes lashing the sail to the boom. "You've made his day, sweetie, but you should probably stay out of your bikini."

We've been at sea for many weeks with only an occasional foray to shore for essentials. Being on the dock feels foreign because I still feel the boat rocking even though I know nothing is moving. I guess it will take a little while for my inner ear to adjust to the normalcy of solid ground.

Although few ships dock here, the place reeks of crude oil and dead fish. We walk the 400-meter length of the pier, up the gangway, and then onto a concrete walkway that leads to a rusting door inscribed with the word "Office" in large red, grimy letters.

The door groans as we push it open, catching the attention of the lone attendant inside. The man is thin and pale—an odd look in an area where the sun blisters everything. His mouth drops and his eyes widen as he stares at us. He is hesitant but stands without taking his eyes off us and then ambles toward the counter. With one eyebrow raised and a suspicious look, his throat seems to rumble with a threatening voice, "And who might you be? You don't look like oil people."

We introduce ourselves and ask to speak with the person in charge. The man wipes sweat from his forehead before answering, leaving a small smudge from the carbon paper sticking out of the wad of papers in his hand. "I guess that'd be me, since the real boss is back in Salvation. I'm Logan, the office manager, communications specialist, and general gofer. HF communication here sucks, periodic at best, but when I can contact the boss, I'll pass a message to him if you've got one." He glares at us individually, and then adds, "Why are you here?"

David identifies Mister Avery as our benefactor, the head of the Federation Energy Agency, and briefly summarizes the reasons we are authorized to be here. It's a carefully concocted story. "Several years ago, the Federation uncovered evidence for the possible existence of extensive Old World Syrian strategic oil reserves, similar to those maintained by the United States. As volunteer cultural anthropologists with enough sailing experience and training to scout the area and uncover the truth, we were sent to investigate. We are a small team because the area is still considered quite dangerous. Based on our investigation, the Federation was correct about the area being dangerous but not about the existence of reserves. We found nothing to substantiate the original evidence and now believe it was nothing more than Old World planted propaganda to make the West believe the East was more prepared for war than it actually was."

As David continues to embellish his story, I am a bit surprised that he can tell so many lies with total sincerity, and Logan seems to buy the entire load. I remain silent. David has obviously practiced this story in his mind, and anything I might add would just muddy the water. Lies are, after all, quite hard to keep track of.

Before David can launch into the events that have transpired since our arrival, Logan interrupts, "You were on the Marco Polo when she went down?"

He stares at us in silence as his mouth falls open once again. David nods and then begins relating the tale of the rogue wave that rolled the ship over in terrifying detail. By the time he pauses, Logan's eyes are full of mist. He chokes out, "I had a brother on that ship. Never saw him again. You two were damn lucky to get off. No one else did. If you got relatives back home, they probably think you're dead." He takes a deep breath to recover from his passing grief and then adds, "But you ain't so lucky today. The early summer ship sailed a week ago. Got a good break in the weather, and she was full of crude, so she made a run for it. They've cleared Tangier by now."

My heart sinks. Our only chance of going home anytime soon just vanished, and my family probably *does* think I'm dead. Mother must be heartbroken. David notices my forming tears, takes my hand, and then strokes the back of it. "It's okay, honey. This is just a temporary delay. I'm sure Logan can get word of our survival to our relatives."

I know he's right. If we've come this far, we *will* get home. I beseech the man with my eyes. "When does the next ship leave for the colonies?"

Logan takes time to look at the schedule in his hand, but I know he already knows what it says. How could he forget the departure date when there are only one or two ships a year? I believe he's stalling for time, thinking about how to respond because he knows we won't like what he has to say. He soon looks David in the eyes. "There'll be another ship in six months."

I gasp, and my hand juts to my mouth. Logan notices and casts his eyes on the floor, apparently not wanting to watch my distress. He shakes his head in a way that gives me the distinct feeling more bad news is coming our way. He soon lifts his eyes toward David while rubbing the back of his neck. "We're damn shorthanded around here. The ship that just left dropped off some replacements the company was able to scavenge up, but it's hard to replace all the expertise that went down with the Marco Polo." His hand moves from the back of his neck to his chin, where he slowly strokes his stubble. "I can get you on the next ship, but I'll expect you to pull your weight around here until then."

David looks at me and then back at Logan. "Can you excuse us a moment? We'll be right back."

We step outside, and David begins talking in a soft voice. "It seems to me we've got two choices. We can work here for six months and hope the next ship arrives when it's scheduled, or take a chance crossing the Atlantic in the Dorothy Elizabeth. I'm afraid if we wait for the ship without pitching in, scheduling us on the next ship could be a problem."

I frown. "But our return passage was assured by the higher-ups in Salvation. This guy can't keep us off the ship."

David shakes his head. "Yes and no. We have assured passage on a ship, but you can be certain the man in there will determine which one. I suspect he's right about being shorthanded. Because the crew of the Marco Polo was lost, he probably needs all the help he can get. I also suspect if we help him, he'll help us. If we don't help him, well…who knows which ship we might or might not be assigned to, if any?"

I sigh as deep disappointment washes over me. "I don't want to cross the Atlantic in the Dorothy Elizabeth if we can avoid it. The water can be violent, and the boat is too damn small."

David nods. "I agree. Let's see what we can negotiate for quarters and supplies."

I catch David by the arm as he turns to go back inside. "Hold on a minute, honey. Why did you make up that story in there? Why didn't you just tell the truth?"

He stops and faces me. "Oh, you mean why not just tell them we came here to rewrite the entire history of the world, even before that man gets to know us? You and I, and everyone who has ever come in contact with the shard, have had trouble accepting what it might represent. I think it's best if we don't complicate that man's world view with what we found. If there's to be an announcement about what we've really been up to, I think the people who sent us here will want to make it. Don't you?"

After giving David's response a minute to sink in, I believe he might be right. "Okay. I understand. I just want to be on the same page."

Logan is leaning on the counter when we return. If they're so darn shorthanded around here, then why doesn't he have more to do? It's probably best that David talks to him. I might say all the wrong things...or punch him out of frustration.

David smiles as he approaches the man. "What about quarters, food, and showers for the two of us? And what do you think we can contribute? We aren't trained for oil recovery."

Logan smiles back, showing at least two missing back teeth, which I suspect was a result of poor dental hygiene. I divert my eyes as he responds. "All good questions. Follow me."

He ducks through an opening under the counter and leads us outside, across an expansive, weedy yard, and into a poorly-painted, large yellow building. When he opens his arms wide, he remarks, "This'd be it. Home away from home." He swings one of his arms across his chest, dramatic like, and points toward a dirty door. "Your office would be over there."

We follow his gesture into an adjoining room—the kitchen. I glance at Logan. He's still grinning. "How many men eat here? What supplies do you have? Where would we sleep? Where's the shower?"

He clasps his hands together like a greedy old man about to count his money. "Being you're the only woman within, say, seven or eight thousand kilometers, you two can have the room above—the cook's quarters—but don't expect much. Everyone here should be a gentleman, but I'd lock the door when you're alone just the same."

I don't really like that last bit of information, but it's not like I have a choice about being here.

"When we're all here, we are a crew of fifteen. The men are out tending the dredges now, but they'll be back come sundown, and they'll be hungry. I try to prepare what I can, but they haven't been too receptive. They just call it shit no matter what I fix. I hope you have better luck with them than I have. Don't be surprised if none of them appreciates a thing you do. Breakfast is from 6:00 to 7:00

a.m. Lunch boxes must be ready to go by 6:30. Dinner is from 8:00 to 9:00 p.m."

I assume he's finished listing off our tasks, but to my dismay, there's much more—a never-ending flow of work. "When the dishes are cleaned, you'll tend the small farm out back, including feeding, milking, and butchering the chickens, cows, and rabbits, as the case may be. You'll plant and tend the crops, recycle animal and vegetable waste into the compost pit, pick worms off the plants, and water what needs to be watered. If you're not working all the time, you're not doing the job right.

"Flour, salt, spices, and dry goods are in the pantry to the left of the sinks. I'll issue each of you two agency coveralls and basic supplies—the same as everyone else."

I expected Logan to take a breath somewhere during his discourse, but he doesn't. He's trying to be casual, but it's clear he needs us as much as we need him. I think he's been doing everything himself. That has to be tiring. David stares into Logan's eyes, a look that conveys as much meaning as his words. "And if we do this, you'll guarantee we'll be on the next ship back home?"

Logan's response leaves no doubt he's desperate. "If you do this, I'll not only get you on the ship, but I will personally carry your luggage up the gangplank."

David takes Logan's hand and gives it a firm shake. Logan then does something quite unexpected. He extends his hand to me. "And you, young lady, are you on board with this as well?"

At least he's not taking me for granted. I take his hand and shake it, summarizing our deal, "Private quarters for David and me, fresh clothes, reasonable shower times, and meals until the ship arrives. Then we go home."

Logan nods. "Done. You've got six hours before the men arrive for dinner. I'll tend the farm today to give you time to get settled, but dinner is on you, and everything is your duty from tomorrow morning on."

When Logan leaves, we hurry upstairs to inspect our new quarters. David rushes to my side when he hears me squeal. As quick as he reacts, he must think I've found a poisonous asp or some horrid similar thing. That's not it at all. I am dancing with excitement as he scurries into the room. "Score! Logan gave us the honeymoon suite."

Considering what we've been living in for months, our quarters are a dream come true. There are three rooms. One is a separate area with a toilet and a shower/bath. The other two are a bedroom with a double bed and a sitting room/office. Elated with our digs, we scout the kitchen and supply pantry below. There is an abundance of food, as well as an electric refrigerator, freezer, and washing machine. In Hope, such things are extreme luxuries.

Logan soon returns with soap and shampoo, dark blue coveralls, underclothing, socks, and boots. Except for the soap and shampoo, everything comes in only three sizes—small, medium, and large. They'll be ill-fitting, but they're new. He smiles as he hands the neatly folded stack to me. "Sorry, Lady. We don't stock bras and panties here. You get what the men get."

I couldn't be more pleased, and I give him a light hug out of excitement. "You have no idea what these things mean to me."

A puzzled look crosses his face. "You guys are easy to please. That's unusual because everyone hates being here. You've been in the wilderness a long time, haven't you?"

We thank him again and rush him out. We are anxious to shower, shave, and dress in our new duds. There's a mirror on the back of the bathroom door—another luxury. After I shower, I take the time to study myself for the first time in almost a year. I've aged, and not in a good way. I am gaunt and pale. Although I look bad—almost sickly—I feel like a princess in my new, clean clothes. Overalls have never looked so good. I nudge David with my elbow. "Time to pay the piper. What's for dinner, big guy?"

He laughs. "I don't know. Do you remember how to cook?" He becomes more serious before I can send a barb his way. "We have a little time before we need to start dinner today, so I think we should go fishing. I didn't see anything like fresh fish below. If we want to ride this gravy train, we should try to please the passengers."

We take our boat out far enough to get away from the oil stench, drop anchor, and quickly bring in a large variety of Mediterranean fish. After mooring against the small boat float, we rush to the kitchen where David fillets the fish, being careful to save all remains for the garden. I prepare batter to fry them. There are advantages to working at an energy source, and power to heat water and oil to cook with is one of them.

As David dips the fish in batter, I roll out dough for pie crust. I brush the hair from my forehead as I glance at him. "I want this to be really good, like all the meals I wanted but didn't get over the past year."

David nods. "It's more than that. If we make Logan look good, you can be sure our stay here will be a hell of a lot easier."

I know he's right. I add canned cherry pie filling to the pies, cover them with the rolled-out crust, and pop them in the oven. "It won't be long before the aroma alone will drive the men crazy."

David reaches over and dabs the tip of my nose with a light dusting of flour. "You make the salad, and I'll fry the fish."

The men arrive almost exactly at 8:00 p.m. They are stunned when David serves batter-fried fresh fish with a side of peas, garden salad, and fresh baked bread. Logan seems delighted to be able to eat with the men instead of serving them. From the kitchen, David and I peek out around the doorframe as the men chow down. David flicks his head toward Logan and whispers, "Based on the smug look on his face, I'll bet he's waiting for the carping to begin, the grumbling about the food that he's become accustomed to."

I am pleased when the only comments the men make are: "Isn't our waiter new?" "Where'd he come from?" "Will Logan be sunbathing all day now?" "Must be tough to push paper instead of steel."

Logan answers with a reserved grin. "He and the cook floated in on the tide—on that little sail boat moored at the float. And yes, if I can manage it, I'll spend the rest of my tour taking it easy on the sun deck while you oafs are working dredges in the blistering hot sun."

When David brings out the cherry pie for dessert, I hear many "Ooohs" and "Ahhhs" drift into the kitchen from the dining room. Dishes clatter as the pieces are passed out, and one man says, "What's the best thing to put into a pie?" After a moment of silence, he adds, "My teeth." There are a few snickers, but mostly all I hear is the scraping of tableware against the plates.

When the meal is over, the men call for the cook. David steps out of the kitchen with me in tow. I tuck one hand behind my back and one at my stomach, and I make a silly encore bow.

Except for a few gasps around the room, the men fall silent. It's awkward. They are shocked to see a woman in this place. I flash them a big smile and bow once again, sweeping my arms from my chest outward like a ballerina as I dip down. When I rise up, I offer, "Good evening, gentlemen. My name is Beth." I extend my hand and arm toward David and add, "This is my helper, David. I hope our menu choices and service met your fine dining expectations this evening."

That must put them all at ease because they applaud and cheer as a sly grin spreads across Logan's face.

Chapter Twenty-Three
Home

We wake at an obscene hour the next morning and grope our way to the kitchen. No one should have to get up this early, but there is a lot to do. While David kneads the bread dough that will become sandwiches for lunches, I mix up a sweet cinnamon paste to fill the breakfast pastry and make several cakes for lunches. I suspect the men haven't had any gooey treats for some time, and I believe they will love them.

After baking, we head to the barn and garden. David collects eggs while I pick fresh tomatoes, peppers, and spinach for the omelet we have in mind. The bread is cooled by the time we return from the farm, so we slice it and begin making sandwiches. We have to work fast. Even with an early start, there is much to accomplish in order to provide two full meals for fifteen hungry men and ourselves.

As David cuts the canned turkey and Spam-like pressed pork into thin slices for lunch meat, he shakes his head. "Surely we can do better than this." He grimaces as he moves his head aside. "The meat smells like preservatives. I hope it doesn't kill them."

I'm too busy whipping eggs to look up. "Just add a lot of mayonnaise. They'll never notice."

By the time the men arrive, we have laid out a smorgasbord of food: tea, reconstituted orange juice, toast, sweet rolls, canned fruit, grits, spinach omelets, and biscuits and gravy. I smile ear-to-ear when I hear the first man in line remark, "Oh, my God. I think I've died and gone to heaven." The other men react in similar ways.

Logan sidles up after the men take their lunches and leave for work. "That's going to be a hell of an act to follow. I hope you aren't getting their expectations up too high."

David puts his arm around my waist and pulls me close as he responds, "Not a chance. We'll do almost anything for a ride home."

Logan nods and then adds, "If Beth doesn't mind cleaning up, I'd like to show you around the area today."

David looks him in the eye and speaks without hesitation. "How about you wait just a bit? Let Beth and I clean up this mess together, and then you can take us both around to see the area. We always back each other up."

Logan smiles and nods. "That works. I'll be back in an hour. I assume you have a rifle aboard your boat. Bring it."

I am delighted David did not allow us to be separated. He gave that message to Logan in a way that could not be misunderstood. We are a team in every respect. We always have been, and we always will be. I'm also delighted about touring the area outside the compound. Why else would Logan ask us to bring weapons?

An hour later, Logan escorts us to a small garage-like outbuilding. A beautifully restored Old World four-passenger four-wheeler sits inside. I can hardly believe my eyes as I stroke its smooth finish in awe and mutter, "Wow. How did you get such a thing?"

Logan just laughs. "Oil recovery teams get what they want, and the guy I replaced wanted that."

We head out after Logan fills the fuel tank. He drives due south and then turns east. David and I take note of things Logan apparently doesn't consider important—things like native plants and fruit trees. I poke the back of David's neck with my finger as we pass a fig tree. "We need to stop here on our way back."

David reaches behind the seat and pats my leg. "You bet. And the next time we come this way, let's be prepared to take some cuttings."

We have lived in Hope and in the wilderness far too long to take natural opportunities for granted. There are many plants and trees here that can be exploited to make our jobs more interesting and the food we prepare tastier.

We soon reach the top of a gentle rise in the land and look out over a grazing herd of gazelles. David's eyes widen. "Whoa. Dinner on the hoof."

Logan hands his rifle to me and nods toward the animals. "Gazelle would make a delicious meal."

David and I slip to the front of the vehicle, take aim, and drop four animals before they stampede out of range. As we pick them up and toss them in the bed, Logan quips, "You kill 'em, you clean 'em." Now I understand the reason he handed the rifle to me.

To my surprise, Logan joins us in the kitchen the next morning. He drifts in, pours a cup of tea, and begins to chat by thanking us for the incredible gazelle stew we served the night before. I soon coerced him into helping make the bread and pastry. He seems to enjoy the instruction.

Logan's morning visits become a regular occurrence over time. At first, I thought he was just another oil man, but he turned out to be much more than that. Well-educated and interested in almost every topic, he enjoys picking David's mind and seems to relish being part of our little kitchen world. It's clear he likes our company, especially the scientific discussions with David, and we appreciate the considerable help he offers. Despite his disgusting teeth, we become great friends over time. I believe he is a very lonely man, but I never broach that topic. I've always believed it best if something like that be brought up by the individual involved, or not be brought up at all.

Time passes faster than an Egyptian jack rabbit. In many ways, being here is like being in Hope, but with more chores and a large family to care for. We tend the compost pits and the huge garden with great care, harvesting seed, starting new plants, and keeping those that produce fruit and vegetables healthy.

Logan gives us full use of the four-wheeler, and that enables us to scout the surrounding area for local wild fruit trees. In addition to providing fresh fruit for meals, David transplants some to start an orchard adjacent to the garden. The trees won't bear fruit until after our departure, but when they mature, the apples, olives, pomegranates, mulberries, pears, peaches, almonds, and cherries will be our legacy—something for the men to remember us by.

The farm animals also come to know us. We collect eggs from the chickens and milk the cows daily. We slaughter older animals for meat and continue to fish at least once a week. We manage to serve pork, beef, chicken, and rabbit often enough to keep our meals non-repetitive. Sometimes, David and I hunt local game, bringing in an occasional gazelle and even one crocodile, although that meat tastes a lot like chicken.

The men are rough-cut, but we become quite close to them as time goes by. They have tremendous respect for David's education, his practical application of knowledge, and his willingness to work as hard as they do. They are quite appreciative of the meals we prepare and heap lavish praise on me for the delicious food. They often bring Egyptian lotus, chrysanthemums, red poppies, irises, and other flowers for table decorations. I have never felt threatened by them, as I thought I might at first. Most are David's age or older, and all treat me with love and respect. I think they all have sisters or children at home, and that's the way they treat me—like a little sister or a daughter. Maybe there are advantages to being as young as I am.

After our kitchen duties become routine, Logan designates David as the camp medic. That makes sense because David has more medical knowledge and survival training than any of the others at this site. That assignment helps us become part of the working family here as well. After David sets a few broken bones and stitches up some nasty cuts, the men almost revere him.

After three weeks, Logan notifies us he has confirmed the message he sent through headquarters to my parents has been received. I am relived they now know I am alive. I can only imagine the suffering they went through thinking me dead. Logan also moves the high frequency radios to the kitchen, where we can monitor them most of the time. The responsibilities transferred to us enable Logan's dockhand to man a dredge, the job he came here to do, and allows Logan time to supervise work in the field. David and I are now in charge of this compound when no one else is around.

About three months after our arrival, David urgently wakes me in the middle of the night. "Sweetie, get up. Come on, quick. You need to come with me."

I am groggy and awkward as I descend the stairs. He drags me along in a rush until he stops at the radio rack. He picks up the microphone. "Hello? Peterson? Are you there? Over."

The radio crackles a little, and then a distant, teary voice responds, "Beth? Beth, dear. It's Mom and Dad, dear. Over."

I almost pee my pants. David has a huge smile on his face as he hands the microphone to me, kisses me softly on the forehead, and says, "Happy Anniversary, darling."

At first, I don't know what to say, but then the words and tears begin to flow. "Mom. Dad. I've missed you so much. Wherever we've been, I've never stopped thinking of you. I'm so very sorry to have caused you so much anguish—there was just no way to let you know I was alive. Over."

I hear Mom bawling in the background. Dad answers, "You had a really nice funeral. I'm glad you missed it. Over."

Dad always knows what to say to soften any situation. He even got me through my hormone years with little conflict. "Hi, Dad. Everything here is great. I guess you've already got to say hello to David. Over."

"Yes, dear," Mom chimes in. "What a wonderful man. I can hardly believe he was able to arrange this call for us. Over."

"This is my anniversary present, Mom. It's the best one I've ever had. Over."

Dad remarks, "And the only one, I'm guessing. Over."

The conversation with my parents lasts almost a half hour before the signal fades away. I am trembling with excitement when I hand the microphone back to David. "How did you coordinate that? How did you get the agency to allow my parents into their Salvation headquarters?"

David gives me a prolonged hug and whispers in my ear, "I love you...and the men love having us here—especially you. They've passed the word back home. I think the agency will try almost anything to keep us here."

I push back. "That's not going to happen."

"I understand, honey, but they don't. So, I didn't discourage their thinking. Besides, I wanted to be sure someone verified for your parents that we survived the Marco Polo. I thought you would be the perfect messenger to offer definitive proof. To paraphrase Mark Twain, 'Rumors of your death have been greatly exaggerated.'"

I snuggle in close, looking up with moon eyes while playfully batting my eyelashes. "Is this really our anniversary, or did you just make that up?"

"Best two years of my life, and I wouldn't want it any other way."

I stroke the bottom of his chin with my index finger while giving him my sexiest smile, although I don't feel too sexy in this small T-shirt and men's boxer shorts. "Then you better come back upstairs. Your anniversary present is getting cold down here. Over."

* * * *

Farming and cooking are hard manual labor, but I enjoy working alongside David. As the months pass, my ashen skin color blossoms into a fine Egyptian tan. I relish each day. Even though I'd leave here in an instant if I could go home, I am as happy here as anywhere I've ever been. Perhaps it doesn't matter where I am or what I have as long as David and I are together.

In what seems like weeks but is actually six months since our arrival, the blast from the incoming oil recovery ship's horn pierces the air. The ship's arrival isn't unexpected. We've been receiving daily ship-to-shore messages over the past week. Still, the sound is a sad one. It means we must say goodbye to the family we have come to love here. It surprises me how attached I've grown to this place, but no matter how hard it is to leave, I can't get the static-filled sound of my parents' voice out of my head. Soon, I will be able to see them in front of me, hear them call my name, and feel them embrace me. It's been far too long.

From the walkway just outside the office, David slips his arm around my waist as we watch the huge ship position itself against the pier while men scurry to secure it with gigantic ropes. The sweet perfume of excited glee fills the air. All hands are anxious to welcome their replacements, receive mail from home, and offload materials to restock supply shelves. I'm happy for them yet sad at the same time. I've grown to love my life here as well as the men. I will miss everything about being here.

We don't notice Logan's silent approach and are startled when he says, "You can train your replacements tomorrow and then relax for the rest of the week. I'll let you know when she's ready for you to board."

I turn toward him and give him a big smile and a hug. "You're coming with us aren't you?"

"If I had someone like you waiting for me, I would leave, but I don't." He looks at me with such sincerity that it almost breaks my heart. "I appreciate everything you've done, as do the men. You've made this a second home for them while they worked out their time. Having you here was a joy for all of us."

David steps forward and slaps Logan on the back. "We appreciate you taking in a couple of strays. We're sorry to go but simply can't stay. Since you're staying, perhaps you could use a sailboat and some fishing gear? Starting the day after tomorrow, we'll have time to give you a few sailing lessons."

Logan smiles and then whispers, "I'd like that."

I see tears form in his eyes that match my own.

* * * *

We leave Port Said a week later, with Logan waving goodbye off our starboard side from the deck of the Dorothy Elizabeth, which he has renamed, "Beth." I know we'll never see him again. Silent tears stream down my face as he fades into the distance. I won't forget him, and I throw him a kiss for the very last time. Leaving him is like leaving family, but it's necessary to reunite with my own.

With luck, we will skirt the end of the hurricane season and reach the colonies before winter storms become prevalent. In the time of satellites, sea travel was easier. Without them, mariners must rely on reading the clouds and winds aloft, almost like they did three centuries ago.

* * * *

We are thankful our captain has the experience needed to bring the ship safely across the ocean, and in less than three weeks, land looms in the distance. Our hearts literally leap for joy. We hold each other tight at the bow, with the warmth of home breaking through the chill of the November wind.

Captain Murray personally sees us off as we prepare to step into the tender boat for the short trip to the Hope pier. He hands David an envelope before giving him a departing handshake. "These are your return papers, if you choose to use them. The agency says you two are welcome back anytime. If you're up for a vacation, it'll be my pleasure to take you back."

No one greets us when we disembark the tender boat. The pier is empty. I'm not all that surprised. Everyone is busy with his or her own business, and few people, if any, would even know we've returned. Unlike our departure, we have only one suitcase now. It's as if we've been out of town for an overnight stay. It is strange how perspective changes things. I once considered Hope almost too primitive to comprehend, but now, it seems like a bustling metropolis. I am amazed at all the activity around us as we walk hand-in-hand toward our cottage. The air is cool and sweet, punctuated only by an occasional whiff of diesel from the clothes we wear. There is much I'll miss about our recent experiences, but the stench of diesel isn't one of them.

David opens the door to our home, carries me over the threshold like a new bride, and kisses me with great passion before setting me down. "Welcome home, love."

I pat his face, kiss him back, and then break away without warning and run for the bathroom, shouting back, "Right back at ya, but I've got first dibs on the shower."

After cleaning up, we spend the evening at our computers. We've missed this—the wonderful technology and associated instant communication. I feel like a caveman from our ancient past, like the one who just discovered the wheel. The euphoric feelings pass as we try to get through the thousands of emails waiting for response. I'm touched and saddened that my mom never gave up hope. She continued to write even after being notified of my death. She refused to accept that she had lost another daughter, and her pain is evident in her words. I bawl like a baby while reading her messages.

"Beth, darling, my mind knows you are gone, but my heart just won't let me accept your death. Your father and I try to cry the pain away, just as we did with your sister, but that has never worked, and it isn't working now. We take solace knowing you are at rest with David, the love of your life. We regret deeply that you had to leave us to find him but are eternally grateful you found each other. To know you experienced such great love before you died is our only consolation."

They are all similar, and all are far too emotional to answer.

I settle down some when I read the email Mom wrote after the call David arranged for our anniversary. Her veil of depression is lifted, like she came back to life after my resurrection. I can deal with that email. I respond, "We're safe in Hope. We're home, but I'm too tired to write more. I love you."

We are exhausted that first night and fall asleep after eating only a bowl of home-canned cherries.

* * * *

Sharp pounding on our front door wakes us early the following morning. David nudges me back from the brink of narcolepsy. "We've got company, sweetie. Better put some clothes on."

I dress with zero enthusiasm. I need more sleep and can't stop yawning. Company is the last thing I want to see this morning. A short man is talking with David when I enter the living room, but he doesn't break eye contact with David when I walk in. I should have stayed in bed. It's as if I'm not even here. Wearing a dark suit and blue tie, his dress is quite out of place for Hope. No one from this area has clothes like that. I amble to the kitchen, ignoring him as well, and make myself a cup of tea.

David turns to me as I reenter the room. "Guess we don't need to unpack, honey. We're leaving for Salvation this morning."

I am so stunned I spill some of my tea. "Home? We're going home?"

He nods. "Apparently as soon as we're packed. There's a bus waiting outside. By the way, this is Mister

Nigle. He's with the Federation Energy Agency. They supported Father's research for years and support ours now. As you know, I reached them by high frequency radio while we were in Port Said. They've been following our whereabouts since then. They're anxious to protect Peter's journals and ours, and they can hardly wait to hear our conclusions."

It all feels like a dream. I swivel to my computer and send a short email to my mother, begin disconnecting cables, and glance up at David. "I can be ready in thirty minutes if you can."

Chapter Twenty-Four
Salvation

The trip between Hope and Salvation takes far less time when the bus doesn't stop every few miles. This time, relief drivers are pre-positioned at every stop, and a toilet and food on the bus ensure there are no delays. We are on the fast track. Someone important must want to see us. We didn't bring much with us—two changes of clothes, our computers, and all our journals. We don't own fancy clothes for formal meetings anyway. Perhaps that won't matter at all.

In three days, the bus pulls under the entrance overhang at the Federation Energy Agency headquarters in Salvation. The driver ducks outside without saying a word, and a few moments later a young man with red hair and a small goatee boards the bus. He hurries toward David with an expressionless face and an outstretched hand. "Doctor James, I presume."

David shakes his hand and then turns the man toward me. "And this is my mate and co-investigator, Beth James."

The man dips a bit at the waist and extends his hand. "My pleasure entirely, Mrs. James."

That we are married is a fact established by the Salvation main computer, but the title catches me off guard. I've never been called Mrs. James by anyone other than David. The man's handshake is limp, like he's afraid to hurt me. That seems rather odd because my hands are as rough as a scouring pad. People from the frontier consider rough hands a badge of honor. That might not be the case here. I grin and retort, "Work and survival are facts of life where we come from, sir. I won't break. And you are?"

He introduces himself as the personal assistant to the head of the agency. We exchange pleasantries while our bags are removed from the bus. Then, with our computers in hand, we follow him to a large, empty briefing room. He bows again before leaving and adds on the way out, "Lunch will be served momentarily. President Arnold will be joining you as well."

Color drains from David's face. President Arnold is the leader of the Federation of Colonies, not the head of the energy agency. "I'm not sure I'm ready for this, Beth. They must understand what a big deal this is."

I smile. I could not be prouder. "You had plenty of time to prepare your presentation on the ship, love. You just didn't know the audience. Now you do. You are about to reveal the most important discovery in the history of mankind. I can see why President Arnold might want to hear about it directly from you. You'll be great."

We don't wait long. David has just enough time to connect his computer to the agency briefing equipment before the door swings open and lunch service is set down for twelve people. The plates are real china—this won't be a soup and sandwich affair. Waiters with white coats and gloves stand near each chair as a fastidious, middle-aged woman inspects each place setting and each waiter, and then places scripted name cards above each plate.

Before exiting the room, she nods in our direction. "You two are quite the buzz around here. I'm delighted you made it back safe and sound. I wish I could stay for your presentation, but attendance is restricted as you might imagine. Your place settings are by your computer. Enjoy your meal, and good luck with your presentation."

Moments later, President Arnold enters with an entourage of nine others, including Mister Avery, our benefactor and the head of the Federation Energy Agency. The President is a slight man about my height with short gray hair. He pushes hexagonal wire-framed glasses up on the bridge of his nose as he scans the room. When he spots David, he walks directly over and offers his hand. "Doctor James, it's my sincere pleasure to meet you. Welcome home." Before David can respond, the President turns to face me with a huge smile. "And Beth. I can't tell you how much I look forward to hearing what you two have to say."

I didn't expect a receiving line, but the other dignitaries follow suit, each introducing themselves before sitting down for lunch. When everyone is seated and the food served, David flashes his first presentation slide on the screen at the end of the room. The President waves him off. "Not yet, Doctor James. I'd like to talk with you and your lovely wife over lunch first." I am surprised by his interruption. These are busy people. I expected this would be a working lunch and that David and I would eat cold leftovers later.

Although I wouldn't have guessed it, lunch *is* pleasant and delicious. I've never tasted food so good and may never again. It beats dog jerky all to hell. During each course, the group asks question after question concerning our journey and discovery. They marvel in rapt attention as we relate our harrowing tale. By the time I finish my dessert, everyone is anxious as children to hear David's presentation.

David begins by explaining his father's role in the discovery and how Doctor Noble acquired the first shard. He then chronicles our journey, telling of the sinking of the Marco Polo and showing maps of the region. He moves his spellbound audience through the dog attacks, finding the second shard, the establishment of our base camp, and our trek into the mountains. He then presents sketches of the area and details our entry into the underground labyrinth, the discovery of radioactive rivers and lakes, and our narrow escape from death in the pit with the aid of his father.

By the time he relates the story of his father's death and explains the contents of the vault and Peter's suspicions concerning the underground power source, the room is quiet enough to hear a pin fall on the carpet. David also tells of our journey from our base camp to the Suez Canal and of our stint as cooks in the oil recovery camp. He then completes his presentation with something not heard on Earth for over three million years—a closing statement in the language of Adam and Eve's ancestors.

President Arnold has mist in his eyes by the time David sits down. All he can say is, "My God. Where do we go from here?"

David responds in a bold voice, even though the President's question is rhetorical. "Forgive me, sir, if I am too forward, but there is something you could do that would mean a great deal to Beth and me. My father ruffled many feathers throughout the Salvation hierarchy, enough to cause his lineage to be administratively erased. We now know he did what he did for the benefit of all of us, even giving his life to contribute what he found. If possible, sir, we would like his good name restored and our names changed to Noble as well."

The President scans the room. Each person nods in agreement. He then turns his attention back to David. "That's not too forward at all. From what you've told us, it's fitting. No one knew the real truth. It will be my pleasure to honor your request."

Discussions continue for the remainder of the day, but the group does not decide on any particular firm course of action. I'm not surprised. I suspect it will be years before the next expedition is sent to the Project Sanitize craters and the labyrinth beneath them. Whenever that happens, David and I will make sure the exploration team is prepared for the dangers that lurk there. While David delivered his presentation, the agency copied every page of Peter's, David's, and my journals—notes that could become the most widely read documents in history. I am relieved when the copies are complete and our journals returned to us. The burden of keeping that information safe for eternity has now been passed on to someone other than me.

Before the meeting concludes, the female administrator we met earlier schedules David and me for complete physicals the following day. We are also offered the finest accommodations in Salvation. We decline, opting instead for transportation to my parents' home.

* * * *

My mother's mouth drops, and she seems somewhat paralyzed when she opens the door to find me standing in front of her. In moments, she comes back to life, breaks into tears, and then hugs me as if afraid to let go. Dad hears the commotion and joins our long, wet group hug. In time, they also notice David. I am proud to introduce him as my husband.

Dad doesn't take David's hand. He hugs him instead and, while embracing him, chokes out, "Thank you. Thank you for bring Beth back to us. We thought we had lost her."

Mom takes my hand and drags me toward the living room with Dad and David in tow. "You kids must be hungry after such a long journey. Can I get you anything to eat or drink?"

David chuckles. "Got any two hundred-year-old rum?"

Mom looks confused, so I make an equally odd request. "We haven't had any dog jerky or roasted grasshoppers for several weeks. You wouldn't have any of those would you?"

"Ah…ah…we don't have those things, dear, but I might have some canned newts."

We all break out laughing. "We're fine, Mom. They fed us more for lunch than we normally eat in a week. Please, sit down. Let us tell you of our incredible adventure."

This time, I do the talking, relating our tale up to the point where we sought out the Our Lady of Balamand Monastery in Old World Tripoli. That's when David clears his throat and interrupts. "We found a massive pile of gold in a bank vault there, but the real treasure was the oranges. The fresh fruit was far more valuable to us than the gold."

I see. The second shard will be a secret only known by the president's council and us. I nod understanding toward David, and then continue with my story. At the point where Peter saves us, David jumps in again. "In our wildest imagination, we would not have guessed that following my father's notes would lead us to him rather than to the source of the shard."

It is soon clear David intends to finish the story, and he does. He tells them his father searched the mountains for years without finding anything except radiation poisoning, and how Peter warned us to leave the area before he died. Mom never met Peter, but she wipes away tears as David relates how we floated Peter's body over the edge of the waterfall before we began our trip back to the coast.

I am relieved David took the lead on this part of the story. He is older. He's had more time to perfect lying. He knows I am terrible at that and is right to assume I would have trouble lying to my parents. This is for the best. We can correct the story later if we are ever authorized to do so. Through it all, David never once mentions the Endohl, the reader, or the power source that still produces energy after 3,000,000 years.

When we finish our story, Dad asks, "But what about the shard your father found? That's the reason you two went overseas, wasn't it? Did you ever find out anything about it?"

David shakes his head. "After scouting the area and talking it over with my father, we all agreed the shard was a fragment from a Project Sanitize missile. We also believe the carbon dating indicated the wrong date because of the massive release of radiation when the bombs went off."

When David finishes, Mom goes to the kitchen and returns with some plates and a chocolate cake. I stuff bite after bite into my mouth, and between exclamations of how good it is, I manage to ask, "Enough about us. Tell us what's been happening here. Are my cousins as rowdy as ever?"

Dad leans back in his chair and snickers. "Tommy cried like a little girl at your funeral."

Mom lightly slaps him on the knee. "That's not fair. So did you."

I will have a good time with that information later. Tommy always teased me. He always said he didn't like me because I was too skinny.

We chat for hours that night, but Mom doesn't call our relatives to let them know I've returned. She and Dad want time alone with David and me. As I did a few years ago, they fall in love with him. Who wouldn't? This day is unlike any in my entire life, with every important person in the world at my side. Not just the President of the Federation, but my family and, most importantly, my husband.

David and I sleep late the next morning and enjoy blissful lovemaking on the soft bed in my old room before slipping into a clean, hot shower. Both are incredible luxuries. I feel pampered and spoiled. I'm thankful to be alive. We are home. There's no rush to do anything. I look around the room as I finish combing out my hair. Nothing has changed. They kept it exactly as it was when I left Salvation. They did the same thing with my sister's room after she died.

It is a good thing we allocated plenty of time to get to our medical appointments, because when we descend the stairs from my old room for breakfast, all my relatives from the Salvation area jump from hiding and shout, "Surprise!" I didn't see this coming. I frown at my father. He shrugs. "It's the first resurrection party we've ever had—the first that Salvation has had. Consider it a post-wake gathering."

Tommy slips up and hugs me. "You're scrawnier than ever."

I shoot back. "You cried at my funeral."

Aunt Mary embraces David. "Oh my, such a handsome man. My sister has told me lots of good things about you."

David flushes. "Maybe that's because we just met yesterday."

I hope with all my heart that my darling husband isn't overwhelmed by all these people. Aunts and cousins kiss him, uncles hug him, and everyone laughs and celebrates our return from the dead.

The party is still going strong when we leave at quarter past noon for our physicals. Many doctors are waiting to inspect us when we arrive at the hospital. They must have been told to pull out all the stops because we're subjected to significant blood loss and many tests I didn't know existed. Doctor after doctor examines us in a blur of white lab coats, medical instruments, and questions. Hours later, we are allowed to redress, and we sit together in a cold conference room while a team of doctors in the adjacent room confer over the results.

An older man with a white mustache and tan sports coat enters first. Several younger men in glaring white lab coats and with stethoscopes hanging from their necks trail behind him. They all sit across the table from us, avoiding eye contact as if we aren't in the room. The older man soon clears his throat and begins. "I'm Doctor Mathis, the lead physician on your case. Other than your father, David, you and your wife are the first to return from the Project Sanitize blast zone. No one had the opportunity to give Doctor Noble a physical when he returned because, as you know, he was quite uncooperative. He disappeared before we could dispatch one of our own to evaluate him. If we had been allowed to examine him, we might not be sitting here with you now."

My heart sinks. His introduction stinks. It has an air of impending doom about it. The radiation must have left a mark. The older doctor must see the flash of concern cross my face and attempts to moderate his tone. "Under the circumstances, you are both relatively healthy...but there are issues. Your tests results show considerable tissue degradation due to radiation, even though your radiation pills helped you avoid the nasty symptoms of radiation poisoning."

I lean forward on my elbows. "What do you mean by considerable tissue degradation?"

Doctor Mathis shifts back in his chair and places one hand over his mouth and chin. "There isn't any way to put this gently, Mrs. James, so forgive me if my bluntness offends you. You both sustained a great deal of damage to your internal soft membranes, similar to internal burning."

My blank expression should speak volumes, but the doctor doesn't pick up on it. I tilt my head and narrow my eyes as I stare him down. "I'm still not getting your point, Doctor Mathis. What's wrong with us?"

The younger intern to his left leans forward. "I'm Doctor Ruben, your gynecologist. What Doctor Mathis is trying to tell you is that your fallopian tubes have been cauterized. There is also massive scarring across the entire surface of your uterus and ovaries. With the technology we have now, you will be unable to produce children."

David jerks upright as tears well up in my eyes. He reaches over to take my hand, but before he can ask additional questions, Doctor Ruben turns toward him. "Doctor James, forgive me if I am too direct, but you are similarly affected. Your sperm are no longer viable. Prolonged exposure to radioactive material has permanently damaged you. We cannot provide a prognosis as to your life expectancy, or that of your wife, but we will scan you monthly for lung cancer—the tissue most likely to sustain damage when radioactive particles are inhaled. That's about all we can do."

My face pales as my tears fall onto the table. I feel like I've been hit hard in the stomach with a large hammer. I gasp for air and flag David toward a nearby trash container, unable to speak as the queasiness of shock overtakes me. David barely has time to fetch the container before I vomit.

When the retching has run its course, David pulls me close. His tears join mine. We are a mess.

I try to hold back the flood of emotion that fills my heart but can't help myself. I want David's children more than anything in the world. That will never happen now. All I can find the strength to do is bury my face on his neck before breaking down completely. The doctors know the impact of the information they've provided and exit the room, leaving us alone. They can tell us what's wrong, but they cannot ease our pain or share our grief.

Unable to stop my sobbing, I am lost in my own little world where babies don't exist. I am angry and hurt. It's so unfair. The vault where we stayed absorbed radiation but did nothing to reverse the damage caused by the radiation we were exposed to outside its walls. I was concerned the entire time because our dosimeters continued to darken, and now my worst fear has materialized. I thought I was pregnant before we left for the coast. I would have been happy to raise my children anywhere, even in that God-forsaken place. I'm home now, but my children never will be. I wish I had never gone to that awful place. I am barren.

David tries to comfort me, but it's difficult when his tears match my own. My mind wanders through a minefield of depression and self-blame, and try as I might, I can't stem the flow of tears or the gut-wrenching sobs that tear at my soul.

I don't know how long we cry together, locked in a tight embrace. It seems like forever. In time, rational thought creeps into my emotional outpouring, and I realize, for David's sake, I need to get hold of myself. I need to be stronger. I am devastated by the news of our sterility because I wanted his children so badly. In my heart, I know he wanted them as much as I did. Even worse, he's probably beating himself up with guilt because he took me to that terrible place. He provided the birth control pills and then failed to protect me as he promised, so his grief must be multiplied many times over my own—not just for the children we'll never bring to life, but also for me.

When I regain enough control to speak, I break our mutual hold, take his face in my hands, and look with great love into his reddened eyes. After kissing him first on the forehead and then on the lips, I offer what little strength I can. "We'll get through this, honey. We've survived trials before, and we'll survive this." I take his hand with both of mine, place it over my heart, and press it hard to my chest. "Even knowing what I know now, I would go again. I would walk by your side every step of the way. I would never let you go alone. With or without children, I will always be here for you. I will always love you."

Tears stream down his face. He gives me a soft kiss on the lips before looking toward the floor and slowly shaking his head. His voice trembles. "I-I'm so sorry. I never meant to hurt you. I'd rather die than put you through this."

I raise his chin with my finger and manage a faint smile. "Don't you dare. Don't say another word like that. Life without you wouldn't be worth living at all."

We hold each other again, breathing deep while allowing our love for each other to moderate our grief. The physicians must have been standing just outside because they soon respond to the lull in our outpouring of grief by reentering the room. They sit at the table, and David takes my hand as I brace myself for more bad news.

Doctor Mathis seems far more contrite this time, apparently moved by our reaction to his earlier bad news. "I'm sorry for being so abrupt. Sometimes, there's no easy way when the news is so awful."

David nods and takes a deep breath. "We understand. We needed to know. What more can you tell us?"

Doctor Mathis opens each of our file folders to a red sticky note protruding from the top of a page. "Well, according to these records, you both contributed to the Life Bank before being assigned to Hope."

His words jar me upright. He's right. Sperm and egg harvesting is *required* before anyone can take a frontier assignment. Because there are so few people, the genetic engineering teams don't take chances when an individual's life might be at risk. That's the reason they harvested my eggs and David's sperm too. All might not be lost after all. My spirit soars. I want to shout for joy.

This time, Doctor Mathis senses my internal reaction and moves to constrain my budding excitement. "Please, Beth. Don't rush ahead. While both your eggs and David's sperm are on file, there are very few surrogate volunteers. Even though we have the ability to fertilize your natural children *in vitro*, we no longer have the power to direct anyone to carry them as we once did. Laws regarding such things were changed a decade ago. All we can do is place you on the list of people awaiting surrogates and hope for volunteers."

David glances at me. I nod agreement to the thoughts I know he's thinking. He then turns back to the doctor. "Our condition is directly related to Federation business. Won't that count in positioning us high on the list?"

The doctor looks down at our medical records and begins speaking without looking up. "All business is Federation business. That won't get you far, even with President Arnold's input. You and Beth have a beneficial genetic outcome rating of A+. That will move you up on the list more than any Federation activity that caused your condition."

I know he's right. We can't say or do anything. We are bumping up against precedent. The genetic molding of our society must trump political input, regardless of the level of attempted influence.

The remainder of our out briefing is mundane. More tests are scheduled over the next few weeks, we are placed on the surrogate waiting list, and the doctors thank us for our contribution to the community. Of course, they have no idea what information we've brought back, but they do know it must be important because President Arnold's staff directed our testing be done. That can't hurt. We hold out hope that, because of the President's involvement, we will be placed higher on the surrogate waiting list, even though no one would ever admit it.

The shock of initial grief lessens as we travel without speaking to my parent's house. Nevertheless, I am thankful my relatives have left by the time we arrive home. My mother waits at the door as David and I walk hand in hand up the stoop. The little girl in me breaks free when we reach the top step, and I drop David's hand as I rush into her arms. Before she can say a word, I burst out crying again, even though I've already cried far too much for one day. She holds me until I gain control, not knowing what the problem is. "There, there, dear. Whatever it is, we can work it out."

Mom coaxes David with her eyes, imploring him to tell her what's wrong. His eyes mist, and his voice falters. "W-we have medical issues, Mrs. Gooding. The kind no one can do anything about. We were exposed to considerable radiation while we were overseas, and we've just learned...we are not able to have children."

Hearing David say we can't have children and seeing the tears form in his eyes rips open my wound. My bawling gets even worse, and both he and my mother try to comfort me.

We move to the living room and sit together on the couch while they explain the situation to my father. Dad is quiet and appears quite disheartened. Following my sister's death, he looked forward to grandchildren from me. When David finishes the explanation, the room is silent except for an occasional sniffle. It feels like a wake, like when we mourned my sister's death.

In our developing world people are rare—surrogates rarer still. We explain that we've been put on the surrogate waiting list, that the list is long, and that politics apparently can't move us up on it. The only case my father is aware of involved a sterile female who agreed to carry two *in vitro* babies as long as she could keep the one she chose following birth. His input is interesting but not very helpful. None of us has any idea how the surrogate list really works, or how long it might take before we rise to the top.

David squeezes my hand. "It might take a little time, but we'll find a surrogate. I'm sure, with what we've brought back to the community, they'll make it happen."

My parents give him a curious look, and I squeeze his hand much harder to get his attention. I shake my head, telegraphing as clear as I can, "Stop, don't say any more." We are never to discuss what we brought back to the community. We were Old World explorers, nothing more. That's our story, and we must stick to it. I try to change the topic, but my mother interrupts. She didn't notice David's slip up and doesn't pursue it.

Instead, she begins talking to me while exchanging knowing looks with Dad. Now that I have David, I understand. Married people can communicate through glances in a silent language learned over the years. "Beth, dear, a surrogate might not be that hard to find after all."

She stands and walks to my father's side, taking his hand while looking with deep love into his eyes. "We could do that for you."

Dad nods back to my mother and smiles as his eyes moisten. It takes a second or two for Mother's statement to sink in, but when it does, David and I stare at each other in utter amazement, and then back at them. "You would do that for us?"

She holds my father's hand with both of hers, "Of course, dear. We've considered petitioning for another child since we lost your sister, but we'd be happy to settle for grandchildren."

I didn't think I could cry anymore today, but my mother's kindness and my father's warm smile prove me wrong.

* * * *

The next few weeks are a blur of activity for us all. Most important, my mother passes all the physicals required for surrogates and is successfully impregnated with an embryo created from my egg and David's sperm. Even more uplifting, Mom is already talking about our next baby. I am amazed how the relationship between us has changed. When I left Salvation, she was my parent. Now she is more like the sister I lost and my very best friend.

David and I stay with my parents for several months while the Federation Energy Agency prepares a new facility and home for us. They cover all our expenses and even put my parents on salary while Mom carries our children. It is clear they believe our discoveries will pave the way to mankind's future. They must also understand that all forms of energy known today—even artificial fuel—is the past. Because my parents are now employees of the Agency, they are briefed on the findings Peter, David, and I made. Mom is stunned silent. Dad just says, "I always knew you had it in you, Beth. I always knew." As we all are, they are sworn to secrecy.

I'm not entirely certain why our discovery is so hush-hush. We are a very small community of people with common objectives—nothing like the Old World where nations pitted themselves against other nations. David assures me the only reason has to do with raising expectations. The politicians don't want to make promises they can't keep. As I understand it, that's another huge difference between our society and the Old World.

I am sorry David's mother might never know the truth, but we do visit her often. I get to meet his half-brother and half-sister, as does he. They are wonderful people and much closer to my age than David. I am certain we will become great friends over time. David tells them of the incredibly brave things Peter did and how he saved us. He also relates his father's last request to his mother. Dorothy breaks down in tears as she hugs her son. Her new husband is a gentleman. He understands and gently pats her on the back as she works through her grief.

Five months after construction began Mom and Dad attend the ribbon-cutting at the Nobel Institute, our new research facility. Instead of being part of the university, the facility is separate as a security measure. David and I will teach the ancient language of the Endohl as part of the curriculum. We won't have all the advantages of the computer intelligence that helped us learn it, so what took us over six months to learn, living with it every minute of every day, will take far longer here. We have our notes and our memories but nothing more.

Before the Federation Energy Agency officially opened the doors to the new facility, they screened the first batch of ten students. As I begin teaching them, I can hardly believe my own intermediate training now consists of training others. I grin as I step up to the podium, hold up a picture of an apple, and say, "Uondo…ooo-on-doe."

The ten men and women selected are special volunteers. Just as we did, they understand their assignment could be a one-way ticket, perhaps for all of them. All have completed advanced training, and all are older than I am. Like the astronauts of the Old World, these people are the brightest and most dedicated the Federation has to offer. It is my privilege to teach them. When their language training is over, they will enter the Kill Zone wearing leaded suits and carbon-filtered breathing gear, fully prepared for the deadly radiation they'll encounter. They'll also be armed with the language skills needed to understand the mysteries that lie ahead. A flood of new knowledge will be revealed to our world through them.

I wish we could go with the science team, if nothing else to pay our respects to Doctor Noble. I would love to look out over the expansive crater lakes from the ledge high above—to where his body rests—and thank him once again. That has been forbidden at the highest levels. We will never be allowed to return. We are considered too important to risk further radiation exposure. In fact, we may never be allowed to leave Salvation, and that doesn't trouble me at all. We will teach; others will do.

Our home is finished about the same time as our classroom facility. As we did while we served as cooks, we have tried to make ourselves part of the team at my parents' house. We do chores, cook, and help with repairs. Nevertheless, I suspect they are happy to get their lives back when we move out. I pat Mom on the tummy as David carries our luggage to the waiting vehicle. "You take care of our little one, Mom. I'll never be able to thank you enough for what you are doing."

She kisses me on the cheek and gives me a light hug. "I was taking care of little ones before you were born. I know this one will bring as much joy to your father and me as you have."

I'm not sure why, but she has a way of making me feel like a little girl sometimes.

Our new home is incredibly fancy by Hope standards. The paved sidewalk leads to 1,500 square feet of pure luxury. We have two full bathrooms, four bedrooms, and an office—more than enough for us and the two children Mom will carry for us. I'm so excited I could pee.

Three months later, during an advanced language class, Mister Avery steps into our classroom and declares, "Time for recess, ladies and gentlemen. David, you and Beth need to get to the hospital. It's time."

Everyone knows what's happening. It's like I'm having the baby myself. Our students cheer as we dart out of the room. An hour later, my mother delivers a beautiful, healthy baby boy. Our baby. The nurse hands him to me while David and my father each hold one of Mother's hands. The nurse's eyes twinkle as she asks, "Now that you have your little miracle, Mrs. Noble, what will you call your son?"

There's no question in my mind, and I answer with brimming pride, "Why, Peter Gene Noble, of course. And we hope he grows up to be exactly like his grandfather."

* * * *

Our son is almost a year old by the time our students know and understand the Endohl language and culture as well as we do. Six of our students will soon travel to Old World Syria, and four will remain behind with David and me. The Federation Energy Agency has been busy over the past year. They have established a high frequency radio relay site in Hope and a base station community at the site of Old World Faqi Hasan. Our six graduates will carry a radio into the mountains that will link through the local base station to Hope and then on to Salvation. Even if the exploration accomplished by Peter, David, and me leads to nothing more in the long run, it has become the impetus for opening that part of the world to humanity once again.

Remaining in Salvation, David and I, along with our other four graduates, will decode the information sent back by the other six and pass it on to specialists in various disciplines. We will be part of the team that decides whether to open the coffin-like boxes back in the caves, and we will have considerable help. Our campus will grow with specialists and experts as the on-site team discovers and passes on new information to us. A chill runs up my spine. We are at the precipice of the greatest infusion of knowledge in recorded human history.

After our first class graduates, I stand on the bus station platform once again with my mother and father. It's much better now because David and Peter, Junior are with me. Where I once felt alone, I now feel full of joy and hope as six of our graduates line up to board the bus.

My baby nuzzles into my bosom as I glance over at my mother. She is beginning to show our daughter now. I feel so much love, I could burst out singing, but a part of me is sad as well. Will I ever see these men and women again? Will some die in their effort to bring knowledge back to our society? They seem excited to leave, but their parents and relatives are far less enthusiastic. I see tears amongst the group. I can only imagine the pain Mother must have felt as my bus pulled away so very long ago. The graduates boarding the bus today are a lot like E12-A and E12-B once were. They are stepping into a brave new world that none of us can yet imagine.

Peter Junior coos as I look down to stroke his angelic face. My hands are smooth. The only remnants of colony life I now carry are my memories and the settler's marks on my wrist and ankle. Life could not be better than it is at this moment, but the marks are stark reminders that everything can change in an instant. The six we are sending off today also bear settler's marks. I believe they will wear them proudly, just as I have. I also believe they will change everything, just as I have. As the last graduate boards the bus, I can't help but wonder what this world will be like on little Peter's Day of Positing.

The End

Other Solstice Books by James L. Hatch

___*The Substitute*___ -- A hilarious romp through the final days of Miss Havana's life, her trials in purgatory, and her tormented afterlife with Lucifer. Witty and spicy, it leaves readers in tears of laughter.

Blurb: Miss Havana's public persona was far from the truth. In her capacity as substitute teacher, the small community where she lived knew her as the breathtakingly beautiful young woman who demanded every student learn. However, in her private life, she raced through the lives of powerful men, leaving a wake of destruction and a deep desire for revenge. Little did she realize her conflicted life would end in a chaotic death at an early age, and to eternal conflict with the devil. Their child is evil personified, and the backstabbing and deceit between the King and Queen of Darkness drips with hilarity as Lucifer struggles to become the antichrist and Miss Havana works to subvert him. A surprise encounter with God at the end leaves the reader stunned and gasping for more.

___*Oh, Heavens, Miss Havana!*___ – Advice columnist by day and assassin by night, Miss Havana's spirit considers herself the Angel of Death. She administers painful and fatal judgment until being brought to task by God.

Blurb: Having performed a single selfless act, Miss Havana finds herself on probation in heaven. After many missteps, she discovers she still retains the powers she had as The Queen of Darkness and realizes she's on probation to keep her from joining forces with her daughter, The Princess of Darkness. The Brazilian, a large black man with a dreadlocks beard who waxes regularly, is her "guide," but she ignores his advice until he's taken off her case. Guideless and in a foreign environment, she consorts with evil spirits from her former realm, especially Waldo, a shadow creature so named because he's so hard to find. She acquires a copy of "The Angels Guide to Earth," comes to believe she is the Angel of Death, and returns to the surface as an advice columnist by day and assassin by night. She wreaks havoc before God intervenes for a final showdown, which might not be as final as most surface dwellers would hope.

**The Training Bra** – Miss Havana is reincarnated into the body of an 11-year-old girl. Her daughter, Lilith, and hubby, Lucifer, attempt to steer the little girl onto hell's wide and wicked path while plotting against and usurping each other.

Blurb: An outrageous comedy that will leave the reader with aching sides. Starting as an innocent young girl, Miss Havana slowly creeps toward the evil side of life before being murdered at age eighteen. In death, she reconnects with her daughter, Lilith, the supreme ruler of hell. She is tested severely and then given an assignment that will lead to the enslavement of mankind. Driven by ambition, Miss Havana plots the overthrow of Lilith while expanding her knowledge of her former kingdom, especially relative to her interactions with three of the four horsemen of the apocalypse. She conspires with her ex-mate, Lucifer, to overthrow Lilith while appearing to following orders. Miss

Havana regains her throne, only to be double-crossed by the conniving Lucifer, who introduces her to spiritual death the hard way. Instead of unending death; however, God intervenes for most unusual reasons.

__The Trophy Wife__ – Miss Havana struggles to become the person God wants her to be while Lucifer subjects her to pain and misery at every turn.

Blurb: Lucifer's rage simmers until he kills Miss Havana out of revenge, but God intervenes to save her. God places her spirit in a dying six-year-old child, who becomes a flawed but beautiful high school teacher. In attempt to destroy his ex-mate, Lucifer sends the Princess of Darkness, Lilith, to haunt Lily, one of Miss Havana's students. Through the body of Lily, Lilith rains comical torment on Miss Havana. Natural enemies, Lilith and Miss Havana ratchet up the level of destructiveness as they discover more of their underworld power … until murder becomes the preferred option. Despite dips into horror and tragedy, the novel is a hilarious romp through heaven and hell. God continues to help Miss Havana, frustrating Lucifer and Lilith enough to char the pages. Miss Havana's journey toward happiness is fraught with peril, but she finds inner faith and strength along the way.

__Ordinary People; Extraordinary Lives__ – A vivid, first person description of the Pacific War, the fall of Bataan, the Death March, Japanese captivity, and recovery after WW II.

Blurb: Otto Whittington joined the Army and subsequently endured the surrender of Bataan and the Bataan Death March. During Otto's 3.5 years as a Japanese POW, he was a slave conscript for building roads in the Philippines. Few POWs survived that duty. Later, after a harrowing trip from the Philippines to Japan on a "Death Ship," Otto was a slave in the Japanese steel mills. Otto survived two near beheadings, beriberi, malnutrition, malaria, and torture— and twice the steel mills where he labored were targeted for nuclear destruction. Otto could hear the B-29 circling overhead; only the weather spared him. While Otto struggled through severe torture and sickness, his brother, Harold, joined the Navy and searched for Otto throughout the Pacific theater whenever his supply ship put into port. After the second bomb was dropped on Nagasaki, Otto escaped the POW camp and made his way to a small POW collection point outside Manila. His exit from Japan was also remarkable because the aircraft just ahead of his exploded about 100 feet off the end of the runway. Harold subsequently located his brother in Manila, although, after years of torture, Otto did not recognize him. Harold and Otto returned to the USA after the war. Otto became an attorney and Harold became a professor of sociology at Temple Junior College. The incredible lives of these men, fraught with daunting labor, terror, and pain, serves as a poignant example of why they, and others like them, are called "The Greatest Generation."

Reviews for *Aftermath Horizon*

<u>5.0 out of 5 stars</u> Love and deep meaning in the story

      This is an incredible novel with a profound message. About 200 years after biological warfare devastates mankind, population rebuilding and exploration lead to a discovery almost beyond imagination. There are no zombies; however, you'll find excitement, love, and deep meaning in the story.

<u>5.0 out of 5 stars</u> A sci-fi adventure mixed with coming of age romance
      Aftermath Horizon is a book that transcends to all ages. I would call this book a close match something like Twilight. If you never gave Twilight a chance either you should have. Books like this aren't chained to any specific genre. It's not just sci-fi, it's not just romance, it's all of the above. The way the author makes such a strong connection with his characters allows the reader to make that connection as well. You don't have to be a young teenaged girl to be able to connect with the main character Beth as she carves her path in life after a massive biological war that makes the Earth uninhabitable. You don't have to like sci-fi thrillers to become enveloped in this story that crosses through several generations. You will be hooked from the first chapter guaranteed.

<u>*5.0 out of 5 stars*</u> A swashbuckling adventure book.
July 13, 2016
Format: Paperback
What a privilege to read this book!! It was one of the best, adventurous books I have read in a long time. I didn't want to put it down, I wanted to see what was going to happen at each turn. I can't wait to read it again!! Wonderfully written!!

<u>*4.0 out of 5 stars*</u> Action story or SciFi
After the human race is almost wiped out by a terrorist biological attack, some doughty survivors make the slow comeback. Every twist and turn makes you think, and say, "Yeah! It might be like

that."

Each step is plausible, exciting, or novel and makes you want to see what happens next. You admire the main characters' brains and nerve, and wish them well, and yet, this is also a "Love story". There's something to suit the tastes of every reader. I liked the story.

www.ingramcontent.com/pod-product-compliance
Lightning Source LLC
Chambersburg PA
CBHW060943030726
47503CB00003B/708